WHERE THE ARROW FALLS

TRACY DALEY

NIGHT NOOK
PUBLISHING

WHERE THE ARROW FALLS

TRACY DALEY

For my all my children, who are now adults leaving the house to live their own adventures.

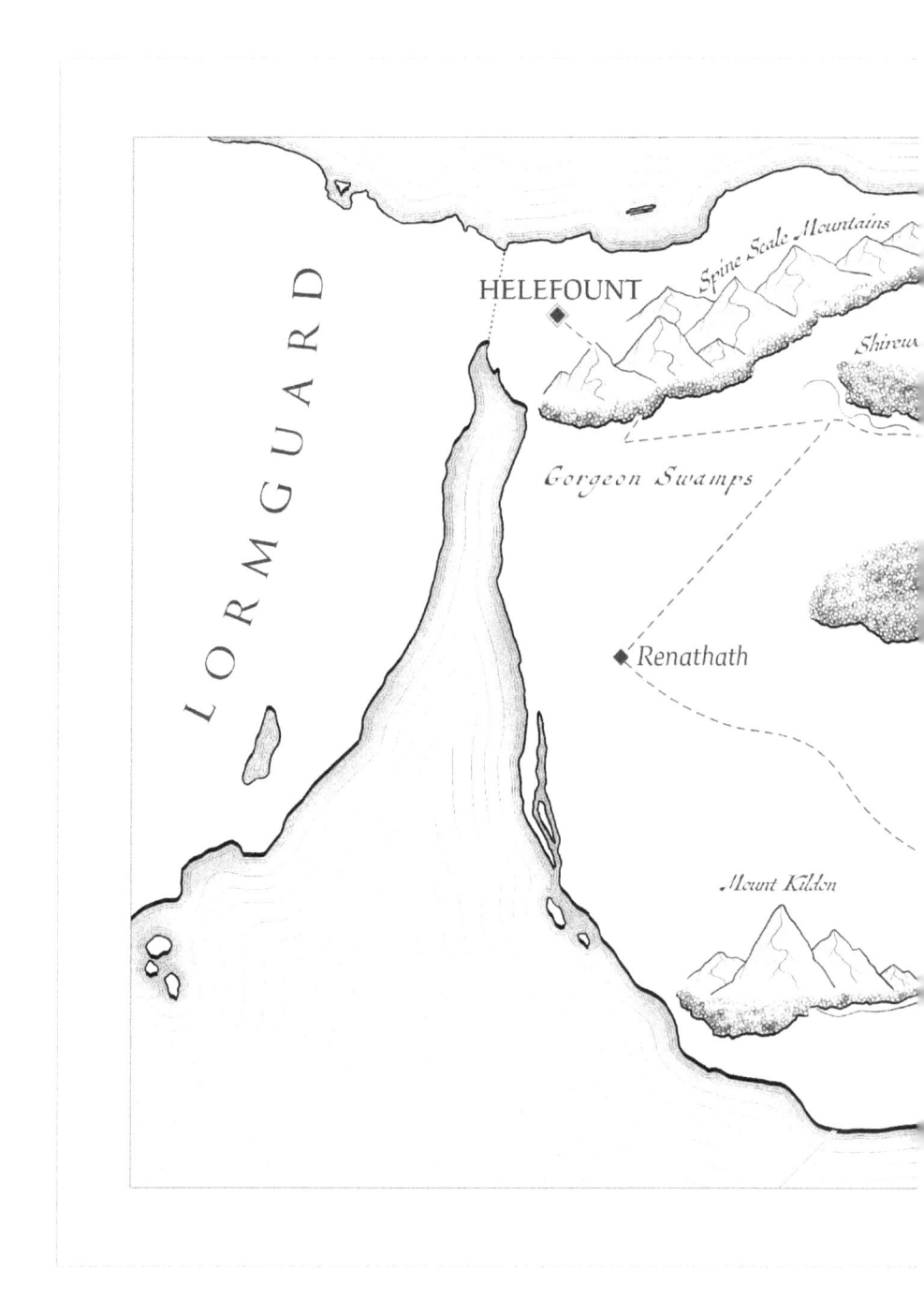

CHAPTER 1

HIDING in the branches of a solitary bangi tree on the edge of a caravan protected by soldiers was almost enough to make me regret some of my life choices.

Life choice I didn't regret: Robbing a caravan of the exorbitant taxes they had collected from the local farmers. My father had taught me long ago that the scales of justice would never be balanced, but that I should never stop trying to make things better. Never turn away from someone with less.

Life choice I was regretting: Letting my brother, Jaimeson, talk me into another one of his plans. There had to be a better way to rob a caravan, but I'd never been a strategist.

My feet tingled from balancing in a crouched position on a thin branch since dark had swallowed the field. The third watch of the night was about to make their rounds.

I shifted without shaking a leaf and focused on the sounds of the camp. A single fire cracked and spat a spark into the air. A flag flapped in the light breeze. At least one soldier had a snoring problem. Sounds expected of a sleeping camp.

Stars speckled the sky bright enough to expose white tents spread across the blackness like ghosts.

The soldiers had trampled the field where generations had worked to tame the edges of the Swamps of Gorgeon. The crops reduced to worthless compost in a matter of hours. The disrespect for the farmer's property irritated me like a sliver under my fingernail.

Righting the wrongs of others with wrongs of your own is like shooting with a crooked arrow. You'll never hit your intended target. Mother's voice made me feel guilty sometimes. I could push the guilt away when I reminded myself that her attempt to right wrongs had left her with a dagger in her belly.

Jaimeson believed he was shifting the winds of a world gone wrong by taking back the taxes that were bleeding the country dry. I was angry, like a wildcat in its cage, wanting to take the balance of power from the people who had destroyed my family. I wasn't naive enough to believe I could ever create an equal system. The only satisfaction I felt was having the power to make one side of the scale was a few bags of dinarah lighter when I felt so helpless the rest of the time.

We returned the money to the farmers and villagers who needed to pay more taxes to keep out of debtors' prison. I wanted to pay for Father's freedom from what we stole, but his tax debt had never been declared. I had no idea how much dinarah would free my father. And I could never free him with the stolen coin. He would never forgive me for taking another man's livelihood in exchange for his freedom.

I robbed with Jaimeson, not because it brought me a solution to saving Father, but because in the cloaked darkness of night, I could become someone else. I followed Jaimeson's plans because it gave me a purpose, even though I could see this plan going wrong as quickly as a street swindler swapping a card.

Footsteps interrupted the silence. The slight clinking of metal and shifting of cloth heralded the soldiers on watch. I tensed, flexing my fingers around the nearest branch. Time for regrets was over. I closed my eyes and pushed down the urge to run that washed over me in a wave. It was an emotion I constantly battled. But the Hooded Robber wasn't about to give in to fear.

The third watch sentries came into view below me, passing each other with a nod. This was my cue. I jumped down between the sentries, swinging the branch I'd cut earlier, catching the first soldier with an upward hit to his jaw. He crumpled to the ground.

I had my bow off my shoulder and the arrow nocked before the second soldier had his sword out of his scabbard. I held the bow taught, but didn't release. Not only would shooting him ruin the plan, but I would never kill a person with the bow my father had made me; his last gift to me before the Grand Councilor's men dragged him away to debtor's prison.

My feet crunched on the spoiled habala husks as I moved toward the soldier, using my height for intimidation. I had turned sixteen before the harvest season and was already tall enough to look most men in the eye. If the soldier had known I was a girl, he probably would have considered trying to catch me with his sword before I released the arrow. Fortunately, I wore a long dark robe, half of my face covered with a black mask, my eyes shadowed by my hood. My favorite outfit.

In these clothes, I was no longer Arianna, the gift-less healer's apprentice. I was the Hooded Robber. That was all the soldier needed to know.

It worked like a charm. Instead of trying to stop me, the sentry sounded the alarm like Jaimeson had predicted. He would gloat about this for the next three days. The sentry used his gifting of sound to shout at the volume of a roaring river. Within three heartbeats, the camp came alive like a disturbed ant hill. Soldiers jumped from their tents half-dressed, lighting torches and yelling instructions. The fire in the center of camp flared with flame as a heat giver pushed his spark into it.

I used the blinding flash to slip away from the sentry. At the same moment, Jaimeson released the wildcat. The frightened animal screamed as it darted into the camp. The wildcat only wanted to escape into the swamps in peace, but the camp and the fire and the soldiers were all in its way. It would run in circles, causing confusion while I did all the hard work.

I ran across the field to the adjoining road. The bumpy ground slowed me down only for a moment. I'd spent most of my life training with Mother at night. I moved by the light of the moon and the stars as well as I did with the sun at full zenith. I reached the road, my heavy breath echoing inside my mask. I quieted my breathing and listened. In ten heartbeats the sound of a creaking axle, clopping horses' hooves, and the crack of a whip cut through the darkness.

Thinking a string of curses, I stepped onto the road into the path of the oncoming wagon. Jaimeson was always right no matter how many things could go wrong. He could predict the reactions of men with incredible accuracy.

I lit the tip of my arrow wrapped in an oil-soaked cloth and lifted my bow high, aiming to the right of the driver.

"Stop the wagon," I commanded. I couldn't amplify my voice like someone with the gifting of sound, but no one had ever accused me of having weak lungs.

"Whoa," called the driver. His form was silhouetted against the starry backdrop as he desperately pulled on the reins. "Don't shoot! Don't shoot me! I'm not a soldier. Please don't shoot."

I moved so my flaming arrow exposed the man and the sturdy buckboard wagon. A dozen sacks labeled "Tax Collection" littered the inside. The driver's face was lined with age and fear. He wore a simple tunic and trousers. No weapon. The soldiers assigned to follow the wagon had been waylaid by the wildcat. No trick of the cards for Jaimeson's plan. Yet.

"Get down and keep your hands high so I can see them," I said, frustrated I was facing a commoner instead of a soldier. "Why did they send you with the tax wagon?"

"I was a professional chariot driver in my prime. The Grand Councilor hired me to get the wagon to safety in case. . . of. . . well. . . you."

Dread spiked up my spine, making me straighten and aim the arrow at the driver again. "The Grand Councilor himself?" I had to focus to keep my voice deep and unidentifiable.

"You make him look bad. He doesn't like that." The smile on the driver's face could have been that of a proud father. Sorrow rose in my throat as I thought of my own father. I covered my arrow with a scrap of wet leather, dousing the flame with a hiss. The smell of smoke filled my nose. I returned the arrow to the quiver.

He kept talking. "My wife died of an infection last spring because we were denied access to the Sanatorium. My oldest son was almost taxed out of his land and home until he got an anonymous. . . donation." The driver leaned toward me, eyes lit by a passion from the inside. "You will get no resistance from me." He stepped away from the wagon, motioning me forward.

I shook my head, about to explain that Jaimeson and I never took it all, only whatever we could carry and still run several hours to make our escape. No more. That's why I thought we wouldn't have come under the direct notice of the Grand Councilor. We were insignificant thieves.

Bushes rustled behind us, the sound traveling fast toward us. I expected Jaimeson, but what jumped out of the bushes and onto the road was a fear crazed wildcat. Our wildcat.

"Look out!" The driver turned, his body coming between me and the cat. The cat pounced.

The driver fell, pinning me against the wagon as the cat attached to his back with a guttural yowl. The man screamed and reared back. The cat slashed with a fury born of sheer panic. The man and cat hit the ground. I knocked an arrow on the string and pulled back. The tangle of fur, claws, and human flesh was a moving, pulsing target. I released.

As close as I was, the arrow pierced the wildcat all the way through its heart. It dropped instantly. I felt the loss of life like the weight of a mill stone on my chest.

"I'm so sorry," I whispered to the animal, wishing I could stroke the silky black fur in a final farewell. But more noises were coming from the field.

Jaimeson burst out onto the road, not even looking around before grabbing two bags from the back of the wagon. He was almost to the other side of the road, a step away from entering the Swamps of Gorgeon before he realized I wasn't behind him.

"Come on," he said. "It worked perfectly. They'll be after us in a moment, but they'll follow the wagon. Slap those horses' rumps and let's go."

I turned to follow him, the urge to run overwhelming me, making it impossible to think. Wait. Something was wrong. There was a reason I couldn't run. The driver. Where was the driver? He was face down in the middle of the road, blood pooling around him.

"We have to help him," I said, not even able to whisper. "The cat died because of me. We can't let this man die because of me, too."

"One casualty isn't worth sacrificing the greater good." Jaimeson checked up the road and opened his mouth like he was about to argue more. Then his shoulders fell with the weight of the bags in his hands. "Fine. We'll improvise." He said it like he'd accepted a challenge.

He threw his bags back into the wagon, taking a moment to rub the puckered scar on his neck like it pained him. I had given him that scar one year ago. We lifted the driver's body and laid it as carefully as we could over the lumpy sacks of coins. I sat in the back with the injured man, trying to use the scraps of his clothes to stop the bleeding. Jaimeson took the reins.

The horses moved with the slightest click of his tongue, but instead of moving forward, they backed up, pushing the wagon almost into the ditch. I jerked with the movement as the horses pulled the wagon forward again, turning back in the direction it had just come.

"What are you doing?"

"See if there's a blanket or tarp you can use to cover up." Jaimeson used the same tone of voice he had when we were kids building a fort out of mother's fine quilts, with the confidence that he could always get out of trouble.

Grumbling, I shifted the bags of coin around. Under the driver's bench, I found a canvas tarp, probably used to cover supplies when it rained. I flung it over the driver and the bags, quickly climbing beneath the tarp as the thundering of a dozen horses came up the road.

"Ho!" Jaimeson's voice hailed the very soldiers we were running from. "Can you help me?"

"Out of the way." The wagon jostled as the horses sped by on either side. Surely, they would recognize their own wagon, even if it was dark.

"You, boy." One of the soldiers must have stopped. "Did you see a wagon going this way?"

"Yes, sir," Jaimeson said in a youthful tone, with the drawl of a back-country peasant. He sounded fourteen instead of his eighteen years. "Drove past not a hare's breath ago. Comin' at me like a tornado across the Cracked Plains. Almost ran me into the ditch. Wind so strong it blew out my lamp. Do you have the gifting of heat? I could sure use the light. It's dark out tonight. Don't want to be run off the road by crazy drivers no more."

Only Jaimeson could face down a soldier, sitting on the Grand Councilor's wagon and convince a heat-gifted soldier to light the lamp. As aggravating as he was sometimes, he was the only person I'd ever rob caravans with.

The wounded driver beside me groaned. I tensed at the noise and covered the driver's mouth. I waited for a sword to slice through the covering and stab me in the back. Instead, the wagon rumbled forward, the hoofbeats disappearing as the soldier rode off, chasing a ghost. Jaimeson had slipped under the nose of the king's soldiers once again.

I sensed the wounded driver's spark weakening. All joy at the close escape seeped out of me like the blood soaking the canvas bags. There was nothing I could do to help the man who had used his body as a shield to save me from the wildcat. I had not been blessed like everyone else. I could not give. Only take.

I put pressure on one of the man's many wounds and wished, for the millionth time, that Kadasha had granted me a gifting.

CHAPTER 2

SAVING lives was not my gifting. I didn't have a gifting at all. That didn't stop Orblee from pushing the kettle at me as Jaimeson and I laid the dying man out on the table.

"I need snow," Orblee said, making eye contact with me for a moment before turning back to the victim of our wildcat attack. His shirt was shredded in a crisscross pattern where the cat's claws had dug deep into muscle, exposing small specks of bone. Blood dried in spots, fusing fabric to flesh. He would not live without Orblee's gifting of life.

"The wagon is in the barn on the Havisham's land," Jaimeson told Orblee. The Havisham's farm had been abandoned two seasons ago, when they could no longer pay the taxes. It sat there, unused, uncared for, while people starved.

Orblee was the only other person in the world who knew what we did at night. She had taken us in after she'd caught me returning a bag of coin to a farmer's child.

She and Jaimeson presented me with the Hooded Robber's cloak less than a week later. She'd seen a usefulness for me when no one else did. She always seemed to know who needed the money and when.

"The snow will keep the wounds cool and help with the pain after I've cleaned them." Orblee nodded in acknowledgement to Jaimeson's comment about the location of the wagon. He glanced sideways at me and then approached the door.

"I'm scheduled at the Sanctuary this morning. It's the butcher's son's gifting ceremony." He avoided my eyes as he left.

Orblee had been training me as a healer for the last year, despite my lack of a gifting. She kept me busy when the rest of Tuleves would have turned me out, pulling me into her work like she could sense the desire in me to run, an instinct I'd been fighting for the last year. Sometimes the urge was so loud in my head it drowned out all other thought. I wasn't a coward, though. I didn't understand why I had to fight myself every day. I hadn't run yet, but my heart always skipped a beat, and my soul yearned to leave the room each time someone called on Orblee for help.

In the robes of the Hooded Robber, I could forget who I really was and be exactly who I wanted to be.

I stepped outside the healer's hut, squinting as the bright daylight burned black spots into my vision each time I blinked. A group of children ran through the street chasing a blown-up pig's bladder as they kicked it back and forth. Laughter floated through the air, carried on a breeze that failed to realize death was hovering just inside the door behind me. Orblee would be able to keep him alive for a while, but she wouldn't have enough spark to heal the wounds completely. The driver would need the snow for relief.

The heavy air of late summer held heat down like a blanket that needed to be thrown off. Despite the heat, the busy streets and playful chattering hinted at the approaching holidays. Three things happened at the beginning of fall: harvest, gifting ceremonies, and tax collection. The taxing cast all other joys into shadow.

I angled my path toward the river that flowed along the edge of the village, separating Kadasha's Sanctuary from the other buildings. Kadasha was one of the seven immortals of Helefount. Kadasha was the most generous. Over a thousand years ago she had granted each citizen under her protection the power—a gift—to share their spark in different ways that served the community. A gifting gave a citizen purpose, a role in society. I had attended four ceremonies with no sign of a gifting. Jameson said it happened from time to time, but I had never met another person who had been denied a gifting.

I hurried toward the bridge connecting the two banks of the river. It was just wide enough for people to walk single file. I paused as a family approached the opposite side of the bridge. I stepped back, jaw clenched, head bowed. It would do no good to show my impatience, even if a man's life depended on it.

I waited on the far end of the bridge as six children followed their parents across from the Sanctuary like a family of waterfowl waddling in a line.

The parents passed me without comment. The oldest child lifted his gaze to mine as he stepped off the bridge. He wore the red and silver robes of the gifting ceremony. Even though I was taller than his father and four years older than his age of twelve, he smirked at me with a superior grin. I often wished that I was a small, short girl that could hide behind a pole. Most of the village girls were wisps of things that held an amazing amount of strength and sometimes cruelty inside. I couldn't hide. Both my height and my girth were comparable to the village warriors, making it impossible to avoid the condemning gazes as each year passed without Kadasha's blessing. Even this twelve-year-old knew that his status would be greater than mine now that he'd been gifted the ability to share his spark.

I crossed over the bridge. North of the Sanctuary was a deep spot near the bank of the river perfect for filling the kettle. The Sanctuary's shadow fell over the water, the tall tower keeping an eye over the entire village of Prontwick. I shivered as I stepped out of the sun, not because of a chill—the temperature was still above sweltering—but because I felt someone watching. Perhaps it was Kadasha looking down on me with disappointment. She had had sanctuaries built hundreds of years ago, in every town, in every village, in every place Tulevians could possibly settle, so that her protection and her gifts could be accessed by all, no matter how poor or isolated a community.

The Sanctuary was built of granite, smoothed shiny, stacked and carved identical to the home of the immortals in Helefount, the city of Deity. Each stone block was larger than the healer's hut. The only other things in the country of Tuleves made of granite were the castle in

Tuleves City and the ruins of the Oracles. The Sanctuary shot out of the ground like a stone thumb, dwarfing the trees and hills around it. Dawn, my best friend before everything changed, and I had always talked about visiting the city together. She wanted to see the markets and swarming crowds. I wanted to ask Kadasha why she had abandoned me.

There were other reasons. Helefount was a haven, a place of knowledge and invention where anyone could become anything they wanted. If we could find out how much taxes father owed and pay off his debt, we could all go. Jameson, Father, and I finding respite in the beautiful city. I wanted Dawn to come with us, too, but I hadn't seen her since the night we lost everything.

My mother. My home. My best friend. And the boy I loved. All gone. Jaimeson and I had been forced to run with nothing but the clothes on our back and the bow my father had given me. I hadn't even had a chance to say goodbye to Marion. We'd been seeing each other in secret for months. That day I'd promised to introduce him to my family. Instead, I had run away.

I quickened my pace up the path to escape the memory. I reached the edge of the river and bent over. The water slipped into the kettle as I pushed it below the surface, creating a circular waterfall over the lip.

When I arrived back at the healer's hut, Orblee stood over the small corner stove, mixing some herbs. A person with the gifting of life could heal another person by sharing their spark, but it came at a cost. Orblee closed gashes in an instant, her eyes closed, her hand on a person's forehead or arm. The more serious the wound, the more spark was required. Kadasha's blessings required sacrifice. One couldn't give energy without losing some. The ability to give of oneself taught selflessness and generosity. The gifting of life required life-spark to heal. It sucked away a person's strength and youth if they gifted too much, too often.

The wounded driver's deepest wounds had been healed, the blood vessels sealed off. Orblee's fingers shook as she tried to crush herbs. I hung the kettle over the fire to let the water boil and turned to take the bowl and muddler from her. She handed them to me and sunk into the rocking chair in the corner.

"Press the herbs into the deepest wounds and then bandage them," she said, sounding short of breath. She'd given too much spark. Her face was pale and the wrinkles on her forehead and around her eyes were deep and shadowed. I followed her instructions, flinching when the man groaned or twitched. "Now, make the snow and cover his back."

I had not been given the ability to give the spark within me. I could only take the energy from around me. I could steal the spark that surrounded everything without consequence. I was an abomination, but Orblee had found a use for me, both as the Hooded Robber and a healer's assistant. Removing heat spark from materials helped with healing in the hot summer months.

Calming myself, I let Mother's voice echo through my head. *Everyone has different gifts, but not everyone develops the skills to use them.* She would want me to help with whatever I could do. I put my hands into the steam above the boiling water in the kettle and pulled.

Heat pricked at my skin. I sucked it into that dark place inside me where a spark should have been. There was an emptiness that could never be filled. The steam cooled, forming flakes of frozen water around my hands. I continued to pull the heat from the steam until I had a handful of snow. I then placed the frozen mass into the wounds on the man's back. His sigh of relief pricked at the corner of my eye.

I worked until I had made enough snow to cover the wounds with a thick layer. Water dripped and puddled all around the table, but the man's breath relaxed and eased. He would live, thanks to Orblee.

Orblee slept sitting in the rocking chair, her soft snores echoing through the hut. The dying embers popped in the fire and water dripped on the floor. I felt no exhaustion from my work and the emptiness inside was still black and hollow. No matter how much I took, I could not be filled.

A warning bell cut through the walls of the healer's hut. I stepped outside and followed the sound to the main square. The streets had turned into a chaos of people running different directions, mothers grabbing the hands of children, sellers covering their wares in the market, shop owners slamming doors. The street that had been lively and buzzing with activity only moments before became silent, desolate in a matter of moments. Living in a village close to the crossroads between Lormguard, Deusterra, and Tuleves City meant taking extra caution when strangers approached.

The town crier trotted down the main street on a grey donkey, through the market, and right past me as he yelled the news. "Bounty hunter coming down the north road."

My fingers itched for my bow and arrows. Bounty hunters were heartless men who traveled Tuleves searching for the less fortunate, those who had crossed the Grand Councilor, or who owed enough taxes to be of interest. They had no heart or mercy in them. Each life they destroyed equaled no more than a good day's pay.

Dust rose from the northern end of the village. The sound of hooves striking the hard dirt reached me. I couldn't move. A part of me wanted to run, but a deeper part knew I could fight, that I had the skills to save whatever poor soul had their name on the wanted poster.

Or it could be me.

Hands grabbed me and pulled me behind the nearest shop just as the bounty hunter came into view.

"Arianna." Jaimeson pushed me up against the wall. Slivers poked me through my shirt, my hair catching on the uneven slats of the shop. "What are you doing? What's wrong with you?"

He could push a smile onto my face the way a heat giver could rouse a bonfire from a candle flame, but there was no laughter in him now.

"I can't," I said, gasping. My mind was dizzy from the effort of fighting the urge to run. "I couldn't move. I'm. . . I'm sorry."

Jaimeson let go and stepped back. "And I thought you were trying to face down a rotten bounty hunter. You're always trying to be a hero at the wrong times."

I shook my head, unable to look at the white scar that ran up his neck from his collar bone to his ear. He was talking about the night I'd given him a scar trying to be a hero. I dropped my gaze to my feet. Both the boots and the trousers I wore were borrowed from Jaimeson. No dresses from Tuleves City came in my size and the seamstresses in the village charged extra for enough fabric to make a dress for me. I preferred trousers anyway.

The sound of shattering glass pulled our attention back to the street. Jaimeson peeked around the corner of the shop. He jerked back as if he'd been burned.

"What?" I asked, trying to look. "What is it?"

His face was grim. "It's a bounty hunter."

I already knew that, but the way he said it made me feel like we were sinking into the ground. "Is he here for me? Do you think they found out about. . ."

"No," he interrupted. "No one knows about you."

As if in response to Jaimeson's claim, the bounty hunter's voice echoed around the square. "I'm here for Horace Youlman. He's here in your tavern. I can smell him. Send him out. No one else has to get hurt."

Smell him. My breath froze in my lungs. There was only one bounty hunter who used scent to sniff out his prize. Some called it his gifting, but there was no gifting of scent. Of the seven giftings: life, strength, speed, reasoning, heat, sound, and time, nothing allowed someone to track by smell.

Ignoring Jaimeson's motion for me to stay back, I peered around the corner. The tavern was only three buildings north of us. The bounty hunter paced back and forth in front of it. He wore leather leggings, boots, and layers of fur, even in the late summer heat. His hair was shaggy and graying, his face leathered, but his eyes were as sharp as an eagle's. His neck was long and skinny. A tattoo of a creeping vine was etched into the skin above his collar, the leaves and stem nearly reaching all the way around his throat like a noose.

I knew him. I'd seen him the night my life was destroyed. The man who had killed my mother.

Iranus the Tracker.

CHAPTER 3

I SEARCHED my belt for a knife. No weapon. I'd left everything hidden with the wagon. Jaimeson was already in his priest robes for serving in Kadasha's Sanctuary. No weapons on him either. I cursed. I never imagined my chance to face the man who killed Mother would involve me being weaponless. Still, I wouldn't waste the moment.

The tavern was owned by the mayor of Prontwick and often served as both an ale house and law offices. I avoided the place like a hunter stayed downwind of prey. The mayor came out to stand in front of Iranus, arms crossed.

Stepping out from the alley took every ounce of effort I could give. My body shook from fighting the urge to run. I didn't want to run. I wanted to fight. I took a breath to yell at Iranus, but Jaimeson put a hand on my shoulder.

"Wait." It was a calm command. "Now's not the time. You'll get another chance, but we need to plan it out. Do it right. Running blindly into the dark only proves someone a fool."

He cheated with that last sentence, using one of Mother's many lines of wisdom. She had imparted sayings like some mothers sprinkle children with kisses. And he wasn't wrong. The wisdom of his words seeped into my chest and slowed my racing heart. Another time. We could make a plan.

A few other men came out from the tavern. Curious onlookers began to peek from shop doors and windows. We were not the only faces on the street.

"What is the man's crime?" asked the mayor. "We can get a group together to help you hunt him down."

Iranus the Tracker pulled a dagger from inside one of his fur coverings and flipped it end over end into the air. He caught it by the blade. "I'm not asking for your help, only your cooperation. Send out Horace Youlman and I will leave your town in peace."

The mayor widened his stance and lifted his chin. It was a brave act. "In this town, a man has a right to a fair trial."

Iranus flicked the dagger again and the blade caught the light, flashing as it fell back to his hand. With a motion too swift to follow, he threw the dagger over the shoulder of the mayor, driving it into one of the posters on the announcement board that hung outside the tavern.

The mayor reached up and touched his bloody ear where the blade had nicked his skin. His fingers shook as he pulled them away and turned to look at the still vibrating dagger.

"Horace Youlman is wanted for the collection and trading of fake relics from the ruins of the Oracles. He cheats people into thinking that the items can influence the gifting of time."

The mayor stepped back, his eyes widening. The other men who had come out of the tavern looked at each other, unsure. Using the gifting of time was punishable by death, outlawed by Kadasha herself since the Oracles betrayed her. This was a bounty from the immortal goddess, not the Grand Councilor.

The dagger's handle stuck out from a piece of parchment that was white and thin, far finer than any parchment found in Tuleves. The other announcements flapped pathetically on the board, crude and yellow in comparison.

Iranus stiffened and sniffed. He looked in our direction, his nostrils flaring as he tested the air. My heart dropped to my feet. I heard a scuffling, scraping sound behind us, down the alley between the two shops. Another man, wearing a colorful shirt and pants with a frilly seam crept past the alley. Horace Youlman had snuck out the back of the tavern to try and get away. I almost felt sorry for him. He must not be aware of Iranus the Tracker's reputation.

The air shifted and I pushed Jaimeson away from me as another dagger passed between us. I hadn't seen Iranus reach for the blade or flick his wrist to throw it. I was trained to see things that moved fast, almost imperceptibly. Still, I could barely keep my eyes on the dagger as it sped past Jaimeson's nose. The point of the dagger impaled Horace Youlman's palm and sunk into the wall at the end of the alley, pinning his hand to the wood.

It was an impossible shot.

Jaimeson grabbed my arm and pulled me across the street, next to other observers who had crept slowly out into the light, watching, petrified and fascinated at the same time.

"Let's go," he said.

"No." I tried to turn and watch as Iranus crossed over the spot where I had been standing. Nearly one year. I had been waiting almost an entire year to find the man who had killed my mother. I couldn't just walk away.

"Now's not the time." Before Jaimeson could pull me out of the market square, the village warning bells rang again. Twice in the space of a half glass. Seven chimes sounded in a row, the signal announcing soldiers from Tuleves City. As much as he wanted me out of the square, even he knew we would draw attention leaving now.

The effect on the market was opposite as the previous bell. Doors opened. Children were brushed free of dirt, hushed, and ushered outside, and lined up with their families along the edges of the square. Seven bells meant to show respect even if you didn't feel it.

All I could do was watch with anger boiling in me like a pot of water over a fire as Iranus dragged Horace Youlman out of the alley, threw him on his stomach, and tied his hands behind his back with the swift efficiency of a master hog-tier.

We were resigned to leave our personal rebellion to the shadows of the night. In daylight, I was Arianna, the healer's assistant with no gifting. Jaimeson was a priest of Kadasha with the gifting of reason. One of us was above reproach in the village. The other was below notice. It kept us safe. It allowed us to make things better, one small bag of coins at a time.

If we ended up on a wanted poster for the likes of Iranus the Tracker, that would put an end to our exploits. I swallowed the anger and passively watched with the rest of the villagers.

The soldiers entered the square with swirling dust, sweaty horses, and a silent crowd. All the riders, a dozen in all, wore the uniform of Tulevesian soldiers. Dark blue fabric lined with the silver and red of Kadasha. Silver buttons. Red medals of honor. The captain, a woman aged from the sun and thick as an oak in the legs and arms, raised a hand. The company stopped a horsehair shy of Iranus and his captive. He made no move to get out of the way. He stared up at the captain with one hand on his hip, as if waiting an explanation for the interruption of his work.

This captain was a female Havish warrior. Many Havish came to Tuleves City as children from the isles to train as warriors and accept positions in the army. All I knew about them was their reputation for their fighting prowess and their superstitious rituals that no amount of training could cure.

The captain gave Iranus a tight nod.

"I'm Captain Tevya of the First Rank," she said. "I have authority to pay your bounty. Are you transporting this man back to Tuleves City?"

"No," Iranus said with a voice that sounded gravely from lack of use. "This bounty comes from the City of Helefount. He's a traitor to Kadasha and I will collect my due reward from the goddess."

"The Grand Councilor has requested you specifically. I'm afraid your trip to Helefount will have to wait. We are on a mission to take a message to the goddess and will deliver your prize." Her voice brooked no argument.

With a flick of her finger, two soldiers dismounted and faced Iranus the Tracker. He looked like a cornered wolf. I could almost visualize him biting the jugular of the nearest soldier's neck.

Even the children in the crowd stared with open mouths, waiting. Iranus accepted the bag of coin and released the arm of his captive. The entire town seemed to sag with relief.

The captain straightened on her horse, her gaze sweeping the crowd with no sign of emotion. I tried not to flinch as she looked in my direction, but I didn't need to worry. She was bored, distracted. I recognized the hunger to be moving, hunting. This captain had other places to be. Something had brought her to this tiny village when she had another mission calling her away.

A soldier moved his horse forward as Captain Tevya pulled a worn and creased parchment from the pouch on her saddle. She handed the parchment to the soldier with no decorations on his uniform. A herald.

"An Official Decree." The herald had the gifting of sound and a small child at the front of the crowd covered her ears at the volume of his voice. "The Grand Councilor declares war against all citizens of Tuleves who act against the Crown. Theft of property or taxes of the Grand Councilor will be met with immediate imprisonment. The Grand Councilor has placed a thousand dinarah reward for the capture of the criminal known as the Hooded Robber. Both mercenary and citizen are encouraged to give us any information that will lead to the capture of this criminal."

My heart throbbed in my ears above the sound of the herald's voice. The crowd seemed a thousand miles away like I stood on the very top of the Spine Scale Mountains where the air was too thin to breathe.

A thousand dinarah reward had just been placed on my head.

CHAPTER 4

Run! The impulse shot through me with so much power that I had to grip Jaimeson's priest's robes to keep from fleeing. A thousand dinarah reward was ten times the amount of coin we had stolen the entire year.

Iranus the Tracker reached up to accept the bounty parchment for the Hooded Robber. There was no escape now. The desire to run won out and I turned, grabbing Jaimeson by the shirt and pulling him with me.

"What are you doing?" he asked.

"We have to get as far from here as we can." I pulled Jaimeson like I could drag him to safety. "We can run over the mountains, we can hide across the border, or we can disappear into the city of Helefount."

"Stop," he said, his voice calm.

I stopped, frustration a maelstrom inside me. I had a plan to escape to Helefount. I had researched the most beautiful city known to humankind, found maps, marked our journey, but it had always been for the three of us. Running now would mean leaving Father behind.

"Calm down," he said, whispering into my ear. "They've been trying to catch the Hooded Robber for over eight months. And what do they have to show for it? Nothing. There are only three people in the world who know."

"But Iranus?"

"He hunts by smell," Jaimeson said. "He can't get your smell from parchment."

I took a deep breath and pushed the desire to run as deep into the darkness inside me as I could. He was right. Only he, myself, and Orblee knew our secret.

A few of the villagers turned to give us dirty looks, but when they saw Jaimeson in the priest's robes, their glares turned into smiles. When they saw me, their smiles twisted into grimaces of disappointment.

If they knew a thousand dinarah reward was inches from their fingertips they'd show more love.

"Not this." Captain Tevya's voice snapped over our heads. I turned to see her pull the parchment away from Iranus' reach.

"This is the job, no?" Iranus asked. "I will catch the Hooded Robber for you."

"No," Captain Tevya said. "The citizens will bring in the Hooded Robber. We'll discuss your contract in private."

She replaced the scroll into her saddle bag and pulled out another, handing it to the herald.

"The second decree."

A murmur of interest wove through the crowd like a breeze moving branches in the forest. There had only been two official decrees since my birth. First, the decree of the Desolation the Oracles after their betrayal of Kadasha. That was over fifteen years ago. I couldn't remember the moment it was announced. The second decree was related to the moment King Tyndall, ruler of Tuleves, had gone missing during his crusade to regain the favor of Kadasha. That decree declared that the King's Council would act as peacekeepers and rulers until King Tyndall returned. That announcement I remembered clearly. Six years ago, Father had been asked to join the council and refused. Our family's status had fallen far since that time. But now, two decrees in one day. There must have been some unrest in the council.

Captain Tevya spurred her horse forward two steps, her gaze chilling. The crowd fell silent. I searched for the insulted Iranus but couldn't find him. The wind held its breath with the people in the market. Even the children and animals were quiet. The smell of bodies crammed together after a hot summer day's work rose to take the place of any noise.

I was dizzy with the heat and the pressure of fighting off the urge to run. I took comfort in Jaimeson's presence anchoring me to my place. I clung to his side like a frightened child. He pushed me off and rubbed the puckered skin of his scar that curled up around his jaw, barely extending onto his cheek. His priest robes covered most of his neck, but a reminder of that night always showed along his sharp jawline.

The herald took an exaggerated breath before continuing. "Grand Councilor Levante and the King's Council joyfully announce the birthday celebration and official coronation of Prince Garreth taking place the evening of Oplana, one week from today."

I wanted to scoff. The King's Council would never willingly hand over the rule to the Prince of Tuleves? The prince had been the bane of the council since his father had disappeared six years ago. He had crossed every council member and broke laws for fun. He was as spoiled as a cat in a milk bucket.

"In honor of this occasion, and for strengthening the future of the prince's reign, taxes for the next four years. . . will double." The herald stumbled over the last words, losing his focus on his gifting so his voice wasn't intensified. It didn't matter. Everyone heard.

Despite the captain's icy glare, several voices rose in protest. Hands flew up in the air, some in open panic, others in fists.

"We can barely pay them now!"

"We'll starve!"

"Kadasha save us!"

"In association with this glorious day," the herald continued, louder than before, though his words now held a slight tremor, "there will be an archery tournament celebrated as The Tournament of the People. Any may enter and the winner will have the choice of their prize."

"Probably not enough to even cover their taxes," Jaimeson murmured behind me. Without thinking, I sucked the words from the air, worried Iranus the Tracker's hearing might be as good as his renowned sense of smell. I elbowed my brother in the stomach as a warning.

"The man declared as the greatest archer in the land will have a choice of two prizes. First, they may choose to raise their status to that of lord in the country of Tuleves. . ." Even in their fear, the villagers let out a collective intake of breath. There was no way to become a lord except to be born of a royal line. No one had ever been offered the status as a prize.

"Or the victor can choose to pardon the debts and crimes of one prisoner from the dungeons of Tuleves. This is in celebration of new beginnings."

This time the gasp came from my lips. I turned to Jaimeson, unable to help it. "Father." I was so choked with excitement I could barely get the words out. "We could pardon Father."

Jaimeson raised one eyebrow, but his attention stayed on the herald. How could he not be ecstatic at this moment? We could save our father. Between the two of us there were no greater bowmen in a thousand leagues. Mother had trained us both with skills that had been lost since before the Desolation of the Oracles. We could win the Tournament of the People.

The herald paused as if waiting for a reaction, perhaps applause, but the crowd remained stunned in silence. I searched again for the wool cap of Iranus the Tracker. I found him in the shade of the tavern's porch, watching Captain Tevya with a glint in his eye, his arms crossed.

When I turned back, Jaimeson was gone. Curse my brother and his constant planning.

CHAPTER 5

I CROUCHED in the dark behind the Sanctuary, a battle raging inside me. Jaimeson had insisted meeting after the village curfew. He wouldn't tell me where he had gone. The tracker and soldiers had left immediately following the decrees and the village had returned to a hesitant normalcy. Fear of Iranus prevented any immediate discussion of the decrees, even the news of the Tournament of the People.

Before Captain Tevya had ridden out of town, she'd crossed the bridge and staked a reward poster for the Hooded Robber onto the door of the Sanctuary. I got a close look at the image. A drawing of a hooded figure, a common mask covering the generic features. They had no idea who had been robbing their caravans.

I twisted my fingers around the grip of my bow as I waited. Father was the greatest bow maker on the continent, and he'd made this bow for me to my measurements and pull strength two years ago. It was getting a little small, but it was Father's craftsmanship sealed with his love. I imagined myself winning the tournament, calling out his name. He would be free, and we could all go to Helefount together. I could plead with Kadasha for a gifting in person.

A shadow moved in the corner of my vision. I pressed tightly against the wall before I realized it was Jaimeson. The excitement in his eyes danced as bright as the stars over our heads.

"What's going on?" I asked.

"There's a caravan to rob."

"Not with soldiers and Iranus the Tracker so close to the village. And not right after they announced the bounty. Did you hear that the Grand Councilor has declared war against me? We should wait for the next caravan."

Jaimeson was shaking his head before I'd finished talking. "Don't you see? This is perfect. Everyone would expect the Hooded Robber to lay low for a while." He shifted and pulled the cloak and mask of the Hooded Robber from behind him. I reached out and touched the fabric, a thrill running through me. In this cloak, I was someone else. I could leave behind the weak, despised healer's assistant and become a force of reckoning.

"Besides," he said. "The soldiers were talking about a gift, something special. I want to find out what it is."

"What good will that do us?" I put the mask on my face and pulled on my hood. The movements muffled my argument.

He wasn't listening. "I found out something else."

"You got the soldiers to talk to you before they left?"

"The two holding Horace Youlman were hot and bored. It was only a matter of asking the right questions."

"What questions did you ask?"

"The important ones. The caravan is camped only a half glass from here."

"You've already scouted it out?" I asked. Of course he had.

"Aaaaand. . ." Jaimeson drew out the word, a sign I wouldn't like what he had to say next. "I have a plan."

That was to be expected. He'd come up with dozens of different plans for robbing caravans, from acting like poor farmers standing next to a wagon with a broken axle to sending caravan horses on a wild stampede through the camp. He always knew exactly how to distract or inspire fear to allow me to move in and take out the soldiers guarding the tax wagon. I crossed my arms and waited.

"They've had a death. The funeral pyre is built and ready for you.

It's the perfect place to hide. The soldiers are Havish which means we can play on their superstitions. The best part is I've already been asked to give the death rites. I offered my services before sunset, and they accepted."

"You want me to hide on a pile of wood next to a dead body that's about to be burned?"

Jaimeson was already moving into the forest behind the Sanctuary. I finished tying the string that held the hood in place while running after him. "Not about to be burned." He paused long enough to smile at me over his shoulder. "It will be burning."

The battle inside me flared to a raging point, then died down as I realized what he was asking. Jaimeson wanted me to use my curse to pull heat into me. He'd always been so disappointed that I didn't have a gifting, but now, for the first time, he's found my lack of gifting useful. I wanted to swallow my protests, but one last fear wriggled its way out of the growing hope of making Jaimeson proud.

"I might be seen," I said. "There's a price on my head; in case you forgot."

"No one will know who you are," he said. "Have I ever steered you wrong?"

I didn't bring up the time a bull had chased us into the field, catching the bag of money on its horn. We had run for half a mile before we realized we were leaving a trail of coins. Or the time we'd hidden inside a stagecoach, only to find out the driver had been wounded by an arrow and died during the night. We'd had to jump from the coach when we realized the horses were spooked and running out of control.

But that wasn't what he was asking. We'd worked together on every robbery, giving what we stole to those who were about to be taken to debtor's prison, or who couldn't afford the help of a healer, or whose food supply had run out. It'd been the two of us since Father had been taken and Dawn, who was almost a sister, had run away. Jaimeson wasn't asking if he'd never made a mistake. He was asking if I trusted him, and the truth was, I did. I always would.

I took a deep breath. "Okay, but promise me we will cut and run if anything goes wrong."

"Promise," Jaimeson said. "I wouldn't want anything to happen to the Hooded Robber."

CHAPTER 6

THE CARAVAN HAD SET up camp in the only dry flat land between Shirewood and the Swamps of Gorgeon. Everyone avoided the Swamps, a mess of sinking sand pits and komdor infested ponds, but the bangi trees that lined the edges of the swamp gave us cover and we skirted along the road that led toward the lands of Lormguard. The bangi trees had squat trunks with bark that smelled of mint and thick leafless branches that twisted out like broken fingers. Orblee had taught me to use the bark in healing drinks. I brushed my fingers along the trunks as we moved, hoping the minty smelling sap might protect me from any sickness the dead body might be carrying.

We stopped when we smelled the smoke and saw the glimmer of light from the cook fires. Jaimeson gave me some final instructions, and we went our separate ways. He walked with open confidence toward the caravan's camp. I stole silently across the field beyond the tents and cook fires to the funeral pyre.

The Havish believed if a person's body was left to rot instead of burned to the dust from which it was formed, there was a possibility of a rising—the dead reanimating and spreading a curse.

I climbed up to the road, staying low to the ground and keeping my bow high on my back so it didn't drag through the dirt. Once I made sure the road was clear of soldiers or travelers, I crossed into the long, grassy field where the funeral pyre had been built. It wasn't quite swamp, but the mud still squished beneath my feet. Thick brown tufts fluttered at the end of each tall stalk. If there had been wind this would be easy, but the grass stood at attention.

I moved carefully and paused often to make sure no sentries were on patrol and the soldiers in the camp had their backs to me. Moving grass would catch anyone's eye. Cold water seeped into my boots, and my pants grew heavier as the cloth soaked up the moisture.

The soldiers had built the pyre in the center of the field, high enough to ensure the spirit could take wing and far enough from the dryer edges to prevent the fire from spreading. I slipped around to the opposite side of camp, the pyre of wood blocking the view of me from both the soldiers and the road. The thick branches were stacked criss-cross from bottom to top. Smaller branches were woven through the gaps to ensure a hot flame. It was the perfect hiding place. The pyre was three times my height so I would be above the soldiers, but not too high for me to jump down without injuring myself.

I tested each hand and foot hold before putting my full weight on it. This pyre was built haphazardly, quickly, with only enough stability to support the body on top. There was a ramp on the far side that the soldiers had used to carry the corpse to the top, but it was in full view of the camp. No going that way.

The laughter of the soldiers carried across the top of the grass, Jaimeson telling the same old jokes that I had never found very funny. I wondered if he had to share his gifting of reason to help the soldiers find the joke in his stories or if I really had no sense of humor like he always accused.

I was only a few feet from the top of the pyre. The higher I got, the less secure the branches became. My foothold shifted and I froze. If the entire pyre came tumbling down, it would ruin our surprise entrance.

I found a hold where the branches supported my weight and curled my fingers around a stick at the top of the pyre. I peeked over the edge where the dead soldier was nestled in an indent in the wood. I pulled my bow and quiver in front of me so they wouldn't snag and then slipped over the edge of the pyre and down into the bowl where the corpse lay.

I grimaced, careful to keep my weight balanced so as not to disturb the haphazardly placed sticks. The soldier's body was cool but didn't smell of death yet. A lingering smell of sick hung about his face, and I covered my mouth and nose. It was difficult to shift his body while keeping my head below the top of the pyre.

The man was an older soldier with silver hair and an enlarged nose. Despite the smell, I checked his face carefully for spots that indicated he had died of the pox. His skin was cratered and scarred from a life in the army, but there were no signs of the pox. I almost felt disappointed. That, at least, would have given me a solid excuse to abandon this ridiculous plan and leave Jaimeson stuttering excuses to get himself out of the mess he'd created.

In the end, with zero success of getting the body to shift, I lay with my back to the old soldier, hugging my bow and quiver to my chest, ignoring the sharp pokes from uneven branches sticking in my side from the poorly constructed pyre.

Now came the hard part.

Waiting.

Mother had trained me to wait patiently for the prey. It was a skill, something I had excelled at even as a child. Since that night, waiting plagued me with memories. The crackling of fire. My own screams. My mother's eyes widening in surprise as Iranus pulled her to the ground. I closed my eyes and tried to breathe. I reached for happier memories, something to replace the panic and pain. His face took their place.

Marion. The boy who had come into my life and stolen my heart. I breathed easier as I pictured his easy smile. His kindness when we found a bird with a broken wing. I had wanted to put it out of its misery, but he had said it was a break that could heal. The bird could have a full life if we gave it a chance. He was the optimist to my pessimism. I found his hope more filling than all the spark in the world. We had never had a chance to meet each other's families. He never talked of his. We would meet in the fields while Father worked on his bows, Mother slept from the night's hunt, Dawn worked on her writing lessons, and Jaimeson attended the local town meetings. Marion had filled my loneliness.

And I didn't even say goodbye.

My sweet memories turned sour, and my stomach flipped. I pulled my hood close around my face as the night flies began to inspect the corpse. The soldiers had cleared a wide area of marsh grass away from the front of the pyre all the way to the caravan tents so that they could hold a vigil. Even though the ground had been cleared only a few hours before, it had already dried and hardened. Without the presence of the grass, the moisture had been sucked into the air like a puddle in the heat of the summer sun.

The sound of approaching footsteps pulled me out of my uncomfortable doze. A stick was settled firmly between my lower ribs, and I desperately wanted to shift to take the pressure off, but any movement would be noticed.

"Your contract is confidential." Captain Tevya's voice rose in the dark.

"I understand," said a second voice, grating like rocks being rubbed together, vocal cords tight and unfamiliar with use. A chill ran down my spine. We weren't robbing a tax caravan. We were robbing the soldiers who had brought the declarations.

"The Grand Councilor has laid a bounty on the head of the prince. He's requested you, personally. Make sure to find him and return him before his birthday celebration." Captain Tevya spoke evenly, without inflection. She might not see the irony that the proud and fearsome Iranus the Tracker was refused a thousand dinarah contract to find the Hooded Robber and instead, ordered to babysit the spoiled prince.

Humorous as it was, dread spread through me like a chill freezing the top of a pond. Iranus the Tracker stood at the base of the tower not fifteen handspans away. The air caught in my throat, and I nearly choked as I tried to take shallow, silent breaths.

There was a harsh bark of laughter. "The Prince of Tuleves has run off again? You'd think he was a disgruntled slave rather than the next in line for the throne. Is he alone?"

"No." Captain Tevya did not sound amused. "He has one other with him. The son of the Grand Councilor. Two spoiled royals should be no match for a man with your reputation."

Iranus the Tracker was the most feared and successful bounty hunter in all seven lands. He claimed no allegiances, answered to no laws, obeyed only the call of the highest bidder. My memories of that night one year ago were blurry, incomplete, but the image of his knife sticking out from my mother's stomach was as clear in my mind as if it was a framed painting.

My fingers tightened around the grip on my bow. How quickly could I stand, pull an arrow and have it notched, aimed at the heart of my mother's killer? I would make an exception with my father's bow if it meant vengeance for Mother. If I were on solid ground or even the steady movement of a tree branch, I would have the arrow released before he could draw a second breath. But the unsteady stack of wood could shift and throw me off balance, making me miss my shot or have the entire pile collapse beneath me.

"Will you stay for the ceremony?" Captain Tevya asked Iranus.

"The prince's scent is weak." The sniff was loud and deliberate, long, as if Iranus could pull in air from across the ocean. "It gets weaker as time passes." Rumors claimed that once Iranus had his bounty's scent, he could track them across the entire continent. No hiding place or disguise would work at that point. "And I have little time to waste. I intend to return to my real purpose."

"You still hunt those with the gifting of time? I thought there were none left."

"Perhaps there are none left, but they often hide and use their gifts for healing. Those with the gifting of life can share their spark to close wounds. Those with the gifting of time can simply speed up the body's natural healing process. If there are any left, they will be pretending to be healers. The Grand Councilor keeps the most powerful healers close, not to have protection for the royals, but to watch for those who might become an Oracle."

"That explains why the people protect their healers. Most villages have weak healers who can barely ward off a cough, but I have heard a rumor of a powerful healer that refuses to go to the Sanatorium. No one will tell where she is. The people revere her. Protect her. Maybe after you get the prince home, you can find this healer for me."

"Would you turn her over to the Grand Councilor?" Iranus spoke more quietly, sounding even more dangerous than before.

"That would be my duty." Captain Tevya swallowed. "But my

youngest sister has a lump. The Havish soldiers aren't allowed access to the Sanatorium. If I could find a healer that could help. . ."

"Do not confess such things to me." The tightness in Iranus's voice relaxed, as if knowing Captain Tevya's secret gave him power over her.

They couldn't be talking about Orblee. She was an average healer and didn't hide her skill. Perhaps we were far enough away from Tuleves City that Orblee wasn't worth dragging to the Sanatorium. There must be another healer who had been noticed by the Grand Councilor.

I heard the huff of horses and the clop of hooves as one horse moved away. I readied to climb out of the pyre and find Jaimeson. We needed to get as far from this place as we could. I thought Iranus would have left the camp before we got here, but he had stayed and was too close for us to think about pulling off a robbery.

That's when I heard the clink of steel on rock. The captain was starting the fire.

CHAPTER 7

A LOW CHANTING CARRIED on the wind, deep and barely discernible. Smoke trickled into my nose smelling of cooked sap. Crackling teased my ears as the fire caught the kindling at the very bottom of the pyre. Every instinct in me told me to jump, run, get away, but I stayed. It was too late. I couldn't leave without warning Jaimeson, and even if I tried to climb down, the soldiers would be on me before I could reach the ground.

Curse Jaimeson and his plan.

The chanting in the ancient language of Labdor grew closer, beautiful, mesmerizing low strains of honor for the deceased. The rise and fall of the soldier's voices held me down while the fire climbed higher.

I never imagined it would be so difficult to wait for a growing fire to reach up with its hissing tongues of flame to bite me. The chanting stopped and Jaimeson's words floated on the air, teasing me as much as the flames. He was so close, but I could not call out or warn him or yell curses down upon him for getting me into this.

Heat tickled my back. Smoke rose to fill my hood. I pulled the fabric tighter over my head, waiting until the hood of my cloak was hot and nearly burning. Jaimeson's words were winding down, almost to the end of the ceremony. It was time.

I pulled in the energy around me, sucking heat from the licking flames, from the wood itself.

With careful balance, I shifted my weight using two thick branches that still held some semblance of support. I only had a short time before the weakened foundation would cave in on itself, swallowing the dead soldier and me with it if I wasn't off the pyre.

I stood slowly, in full sight of everyone.

Jaimeson stopped talking when the soldiers pointed. Some dropped to the ground.

The flames continued to lick up around me on all sides, but directly beneath me the energy I had absorbed left the branches cold enough to frost over, the heat creating steam that rose around me. I lifted my arms to my side, as if I was as light as the steam. Then I jumped.

I had not bothered changing clothes with the dead soldier. Jaimeson had assured me that their superstitions would consider my black hood a symbol of death. My cloak flowed out behind me as I fell and landed in a crouch.

I checked my hood, making sure my mask was still in place. I kept my head down, glancing to the side so I could see Jaimeson through the shadow of my hood. He was the only person who had not fallen to the earth.

"Save us, Priest," yelled one of the soldiers.

"What madness is this?" Jaimeson cried, his words directed at the sky. This was the part where we put all arguments aside. During a robbery, we worked together, playing off each other's movements with perfect accuracy. It was like our minds became one.

"The dead will rise," said a shaking voice not far to my right. It was another of the captains. "The curse will fall."

Havish lore taught of a curse that plagued their ancestors when the gifting was misused. They did not worship Kadasha but followed the faith of their motherland. Their immortal god was called Helloran. And from what I could tell, he was vindictive. Instead of blessing his followers for obedience, he would curse them when they stepped out of line.

"Help us!" The call came again from many voices this time.

Jaimeson threw back his colored hood, exposing his face, the light from the fire dancing on his skin. He looked powerful, even to me. I stepped forward. Soldiers trained for war whimpered.

Another step.

Jaimeson threw up his arms. I shielded my face like his motion had burned me and stumbled back toward the fire. It was raging now, an inferno. I absorbed the energy that reached me to keep my cloak from catching fire. My entire body was engulfed in steam as heat battled the cold.

I pushed forward, slowly, like the motion took great effort. I leaned into the invisible force. My brother's timing was perfect. He moved back with me like we were caught in a battle of wills.

"He's strong," Jaimeson said, voice strained.

"What can we do?" the captain to my right asked.

"There must be a reason," he said, his feet appearing to slide backward as I approached slowly. His feet left skid marks in the dirt. I had watched him practice this motion, but it still impressed me. "Have you misused your giftings? Have you failed to show respect for your blessings?"

"We follow all of Helloran's rules," the captain shouted. "We are all devout."

Another step. Jaimeson let out a growl of frustration. "I can't hold it much longer. There must be something. A forbidden item? A foraged prize that has displeased the immortals? An item that touches the gifting of time?"

Someone to my left stood, shaking. The uniform of another captain reflected in the firelight.

"It's the blood jewels," she cried.

"Hush," Captain Tevya said. "Do not mention those."

Jaimeson and I paused, only for an instant; no one watching would have noticed. I pushed forward again to cover our mistake. I had never heard of blood jewels, nor did I know their worth. It wasn't taxes we could return. It wasn't something that could be sold on the market. We had no need of the prize, but I saw the gleam in my brother's eyes that went deeper than the reflected firelight.

I raised my arms and sucked in more heat from the fire. The steam increased, creating a drip on the end of my nose. Jaimeson let out a yell and dropped to one knee.

"That definitely made it angry," he said. "Are you sure there is nothing else?"

"No, nothing."

"It's the jewels, then." He grunted, pushing back to his feet. "They must be destroyed or sent away from the camp."

I took a breath and stepped forward, hands out.

Jaimeson retreated. "There's no reasoning that can hold this thing back. We must appease it."

I wanted to scowl at my brother. He should have asked for a payment, a price to be rid of me. Blood jewels, whatever they were, would do us no good.

"We have them," cried the standing captain. She reached into her tunic and pulled a pouch from an inner pocket. "If we give them to you, can you rid us of it?"

Two other captains stood, their shadows long behind them as the fire grew higher. Smoke surrounded me, choking me and filling my nose with the smell of fire. The heat seeped into me as I slowed the amount of energy I absorbed. The emptiness within me had not filled, but a strange pain was growing near my heart.

"Not the jewels," said Captain Tevya. "We have sworn an oath to deliver them or our lives are forfeit."

"Is that a greater price to pay than releasing a curse on the land?" The captains were arguing among themselves now.

The two closest to Jaimeson had their pouches in hand. The other two, closest to me, had a hand over their chest as if protecting their own hearts. They moved back as I turned my hooded gaze on them, their fingers shaking over their military decorations.

Jaimeson lifted a hand, not toward me, but toward the two captains near me. Their hands moved, their faces lined with horror. As one, they reached into their tunics and pulled out pouches that matched those of their sister captains.

"Stop!" It was a new voice, one that rose from the back of the crowd. Iranus the Tracker led his pack horse through the prostrate soldiers. I thought he had left.

We were out of time. Iranus was no Havish. With no religion or superstitions at all, he would see through our act in a moment.

I made our sign, two fingers curled next to my elbow, to cut and run. We would get no ransom or reward for saving this caravan from the curse of the rising dead.

"Help us." The pleas continued.

Jaimeson turned and saw Iranus.

"There is only one way." His voice was loud, almost like someone who had the gifting of sound. It was like the words carried directly into my mind. "Everything must burn."

Jaimeson reacted before I could think. He accepted the bags from the two captains who held them out in offering. Then he moved close enough to rip the bags of jewels from the unwilling grips of the other two captains.

He sprinted toward me, tackling me straight into the burning pyre.

CHAPTER 8

THE HEAT CONSUMED US, fire raging inside and out. In an instant, I was taken back to a year ago, my brother's arms wrapped around me, my arm pressed up against his neck, pushing him away, fighting him as the flames licked up the walls of our house, the smoke blinding me.

This was a different fire, a different time.

I sucked in like I could use the heat to burn the memories from my mind. The pull was automatic, fueled by surprise and desperation. I pulled the energy in, protecting us from the heat and the flames. We hit the ground, wood cracking and creaking in the pyre above us. The bags of jewels were sandwiched between my body and Jaimeson's. The pain in my chest flared up as if I was being consumed from the inside. There was a flash of white that exploded out of me, extinguishing the flaming pyre, a plume of ash and dust shooting out in all directions.

"What was that?" Jaimeson asked.

I opened my mouth, not to answer him, but to ask some angry questions of my own. The creaking and shifting of the wood over our heads told us the pyre was coming down. Jaimeson pulled on my cloak, jerking us both out the opposite side of the pyre just as the top caved in. The second wave of ash covered our escape, rising into the air behind us, engulfing us as we found our feet and ran.

"That was the Hooded Robber." Iranus's voice carried over the sounds of coughing and groaning. "Not some spirit rising from the afterlife. Get up. Get up!"

Yelling followed. I was not worried about the movement of grass or the mud squishing beneath our feet. We ran parallel to the camp. They would expect us to head directly away from them; any fleeing prey would take a straight line from the predator. We had to do something different.

Iranus the Tracker was on our trail.

We ran clumsily. The ash and smoke still choked the air and blocked us from view. I couldn't see where to place my feet and stumbled over thick tufts of grass or mounds of dirt. My lungs burned and my throat was raw from breathing in the smoky air. I barely noticed the shadow as it loomed up in front of us. I bumped Jaimeson out of the way before we both barreled into a huge tree trunk.

We'd reached the edges of the marsh where the grasslands succumbed to the foliage of Shirewood. This was our territory, where we took shelter after each caravan was relieved of the council's overburdening taxes. We had several escape routes timed to perfection.

There was no running through Shirewood. The undergrowth was dense and full of barbed branches, reaching vines, and moss-covered trunks. We had to move carefully to leave no trace of our passage.

The lightening sky chased away the night, inviting life to wake and stir. One look at Jaimeson revealed how we both must look. His whole body was covered with ash, the edges of his cloak singed and colors barely visible.

The air was clearing, though still thick and full of shadows. I glanced behind and couldn't make out any movement. The soldiers hadn't recovered enough to give chase, but that didn't mean we had a lot of time.

"We have to split up and do cross-the-fox," I said. Cross-the-fox was a maneuver we had planned for a situation like this. Actually, I had never imagined a situation quite like this. The plan was for one to create a path one direction, cross each other while the other led them a second direction, and then double back and meet up at a chosen location.

Jaimeson nodded. He stumbled and leaned against a tree trunk for support.

"Are you all right?" I asked. "What's wrong?" I checked his body with my hands, thinking of the stagecoach driver with an arrow in his back, but I could find no injury.

"I'm fine," he said, trying to move again. He slumped back against the tree. "Give me a minute."

"We don't have a minute," I said, pulling on him. "The soldiers will not wait for you to recover."

"Soldiers?" He looked up at me, confusion fogging his eyes.

I stepped back, shocked. "You used your gifting?" The gifting of reason allowed a person to increase someone's courage, inspire them with wisdom, and help them to see the right course. Using too much of the spark to gift reasoning resulted in confusion and forgetfulness. "To get the blood jewels? I didn't know you could force reasoning on someone."

Jaimeson's eyes cleared a little. He took a deep breath. "We were out of time. I had no choice." He handed me the small bags. Their weight tugged my hands toward the ground. "I'll lead the soldiers away first. You need to hide these where only you can find them. If I hide them, I won't remember where they are." He smiled like this was a game.

I wanted to yell at him, but my mind was whirling. Kadasha's gifting was to use for good and helping others. Was that what we had just done? I stared at the four bags, holding them by the strings as they dangled from my fingers. Blood jewels bound for Helefount, guarded by four captains who'd sworn to protect them with their lives.

Shouting reached me from across the field through the still settling ash. The noise broke me from my stupor. Mother's voice echoed in my head. *Never hesitate during a hunt. It could cost your life.*

Jaimeson had already followed Mother's advice and disappeared through the underbrush. I could easily follow his trail since that was the point, but I had my part to play. I tucked the blood jewels into the pocket of my cloak, checked to make sure my bow was undamaged, and then climbed into the branches of the nearest tree. The trees in Shire-wood had thick branches that intertwined with neighboring trees like snakes in a den. I could travel faster through Shirewood in the air than I could fighting through the brush on the forest floor.

After a quarter of a glass, I checked my location carefully, finding specific landmarks so I could find the place again. I located a hollow in a large trunk high in the canopy and tucked all four bags of jewels into the hole. No one would find them here. I moved quickly ahead, knowing that if Jaimeson had followed our plan, we would be crossing paths soon. I would take the ground, and he would climb up into the branches.

But he didn't come. I continued to move through the branches in a systematic search around the place where we should have crossed paths. No trail. No sound. No Jaimeson.

Panic blinded my judgment. I wouldn't know what to do without him. He was the last member of my family. My best friend since Dawn had abandoned us. I would not leave him.

I moved back through the twisting branches, climbing around and under and over and through back toward the place where we had entered Shirewood. I was moving toward the soldiers who hunted us.

I saw the twinkling of lantern lights through the leaves and changed direction. The noises came from a clearing, but still far from the field where the soldiers camped. That gave me hope. If only a few soldiers had Jaimeson, I could separate them in the forest, confuse them, and lose them while I rescued my brother.

"Where are they?" Captain Tevya's words echoed through the forest like a feral scream. "What did you do with them?"

I lay on my belly and crawled forward until I could see through the branches. Jaimeson knelt between two soldiers, both with a grip on his arms. One held a handful of Jaimeson's hair, pulling his head back at a painful angle. Captain Tevya paced back and forth in front of him. She whirled with a sudden ferocity and backhanded him across the face. The slap sounded like a whip cracking through the forest. I flinched.

Jaimeson's head snapped to the side and when he turned back to face the captain, blood dripped from his nose.

"I don't know," he said, hesitant. "I don't know. I had them. I had them right here. Let me go and I'll show you." He struggled against the two soldiers, but they held him tight. "Check my pockets. They were right here. They couldn't have fallen out." His distress seemed so real, I almost believed him. He had a look of pure horror at the mention of the jewels falling from his pocket. It was possible he was still confused from using his gifting of reason.

The captain kicked Jaimeson in the stomach. He let out a retching sound, but the soldiers wouldn't even let him curl forward into the pain.

Gasping, he fought to catch his breath. I scanned the forest below me. The sunrise approached, glowing along the horizon. The forest remained in shadow, but I could make out no other movements than the captain and the two soldiers. Three would be no problem. And I wouldn't have to use the bow and arrows my father had made to take a human life.

The next blow from the captain caught Jaimeson on his temple and he crumpled to the ground, unconscious. That wasn't good. I'd have to revive him. There was no way to carry him through Shirewood.

I pushed carefully to my feet, balancing on the branch that was as thick as my thigh, dry from the summer heat. I pulled my bow from over my shoulder and nocked an arrow without swaying.

Don't hesitate.

I released my arrow. Then another and another. Three in a row within a heartbeat. One pierced the captain's calf. The second went through the foot of the soldier holding Jaimeson. The third arrow went through the palm of the soldier who'd had enough time to step back, hands raised.

Before I could jump down, a figure stepped into the clearing, materializing from the trees like he was made of shadows. Somehow, I had missed his presence. Iranus the Tracker had been watching the whole time, and I hadn't prepared an arrow for his heart.

I reached for my quiver, but Iranus's movements were just as quick. A blade appeared in his hand, ready to throw. It was not aimed at me. The blade was aimed at Jaimeson's exposed throat. His eyes pierced through the branches directly to where I hid.

Iranus raised one eyebrow as if that was all he needed to do to interrogate me.

He spoke to the captain. "Follow the clumsy one's trail back to camp and search for the jewels. Take care of your injured."

"There are others," Captain Tevya said through clenched teeth as she gripped the arrow impaled through her calf. "At least two bowmen in the trees."

"I smell only one."

"I've never seen someone shoot so fast," the captain said.

"I have things under control."

The captain dropped her head in a sharp salute and the two other soldiers, one limping, the other cradling his hand, followed her back into the forest.

Iranus flicked his hand that held no dagger. An invitation. I jumped down from the branches, keeping my hand raised to the arrows in my quiver.

We stared, neither of us blinking. A muscle twitched below his thumb like it was aching for an excuse to release the blade. My fingers hovered over the shaft of an arrow with the same pulsing desire. Iranus sniffed, his nostrils flaring. Curse the ruins. He had my scent now. The only way to escape would be to kill him. The only way to kill him would be to watch Jaimeson die.

CHAPTER 9

"YOU ARE NO GIVER." There was no question in his words, no crack for an escape. My stomach felt as if I'd been kicked like Jaimeson. I blinked, hiding my pain.

"I can smell you," Iranus said, his words wrapping around me like a forced caress. "You smell of darkness and destruction. All who come close to you will get sucked in. That is your curse."

"No," I said. A whisper again, but it wasn't to cover my voice. I couldn't suck in enough air.

"You will absorb everything good into that black pit inside you until there is no light left. You can already feel it, can't you? The destruction starts here and winds up and around until it hangs you." He pointed to his chest, the spot just above his heart. The place where I could still feel the echo of the searing pain I'd experienced while absorbing the heat of the funeral fire. His fingers moved up to trace the vine tattoo around his neck.

"I don't know what you're talking about," I said. "I fight to bring good to those who've been granted too little in this world."

"Altruistic thievery." Iranus said the last word with a snort of derision. "Fine. I will leave you to rot in your twisted morals. I wouldn't want to rob these people of collecting on your reward. I'll take him in to balance the scales. Justice cannot go unfed." He spoke as if justice were a wild beast that would break free of its bonds if it got too hungry.

He was offering to let me walk while he took Jaimeson in to face the consequences meant for the Hooded Robber. We stood for a moment, the sun rising high enough to send slanted rays through the leaves. Settling dust created visible lines of light dancing around the clearing, tricking the eye so that I couldn't be sure if Iranus moved slightly or if it was only a shadow. My fingers tightened on my arrow. Iranus lifted his dagger. We were in a stand-off with death as the only solution.

"I'll take his place," I said. "You could collect the reward for me." I hadn't known until that moment that I would take his place. The coward in me, always running, fighting the love I had for my brother. But facing the choice, I buried the coward.

Iranus's eyes shifted for an instant to my brother and then back to me. "You would give your life for him? Perhaps a lover or a brother. But still, what good would it do? One of you would be dead, the other broken and alone."

"He's my brother. You're right, leaving one of us alone is too cruel. You don't have to take us in. You already said, this isn't your bounty. You have another prize to chase." My arm was beginning to shake from holding it over my head, crooked and ready to pull. Jaimeson groaned and I ached to run to his side.

"I will not walk away without one of you to show for my efforts. I'm giving you the chance to run. If you want to live, I would take the offer."

"I will show you where the blood jewels are. I would trade them for our freedom." If the captain wanted them bad enough, surely, they would be enticing to Iranus.

Jaimeson moaned but managed to lift himself to his knees. Blood dripped from his nose, and he held his side like a rib was broken. "Don't trade the jewels. He won't keep his end of the bargain. Let him take me in while you escape. It's the only way."

Iranus threw the dagger, another appearing in his fingers almost instantly. The dagger flew, but the spin was wrong, and I knew before it struck Jaimeson's head that it wasn't a death blow. He slumped to the ground. Iranus had knocked him unconscious. My fingers pulled an arrow free, but the tracker was by Jaimeson's side, his second knife to his throat.

"You can watch him die today or watch me take him. The jewels are best left where they are."

It took all my effort, but I dropped my hand, leaving my arrows in the quiver, relaxing my bow to my side. Iranus flipped the dagger and caught it by the handle, no longer threatening my brother. The muscles in his face didn't relax.

"Don't you have a date with the prince?" The sarcasm came from desperation. Anything to hold on to my brother for another moment.

A muscle in his jaw flexed, bulging beneath his stubble of black hair on his cheeks. "That is my charge, but I travel fast. I will get the prince home soon enough. If I were you, I would be so far away your smell won't tempt me when the people fail to bring you in." He let out a low whistle with his bottom lip bit between his teeth.

A horse trotted into the clearing and stepped between Iranus and me. The pack horse was a tough breed, with thick hair and hide to protect it from the stinging vines and nettles of the forest. It seemed to have no trouble moving through the dense undergrowth. Iranus threw Jaimeson over the horse's haunches without a grunt. It should have taken three men to lift my brother like that.

I had a shot. The tracker couldn't throw his dagger while he climbed up in the saddle, but I hesitated. Then he was on the horse, dagger back against Jaimeson's throat. "There is no where you can hide. This is your only chance to escape. Once I return the prince, I will come for you. Run as far as you can and pray it is far enough."

Exhaustion swept over me. My knees buckled. I fell more than sat, using a large root protruding from the ground to rest on. Why had I hesitated? Why hadn't I killed Iranus the Tracker when I had the chance?

Watching my brother disappear on the back of Iranus's horse, I knew my hesitation had cost someone their life. I just didn't know whose.

CHAPTER 10

I CLIMBED INTO THE TREES, making my way back to the place where I had hidden the blood jewels. The pain in my chest was only a dull throbbing, but my heart felt as if it was being squeezed in a wine press.

Iranus the Tracker had to find a way to get Jaimeson back to Tuleves City, to the dungeons that had held my father for the last year. I didn't know how he would do that while needing to find the prince. He could leave Jaimeson in the charge of the captains. They had been on a mission to Helefount, but I held their prize.

I wanted to enter the Tournament of the People to save my father, but what if Jaimeson and my father were both standing there, waiting for my decision? I didn't know if I could choose to save one over the other. My father would tell me to choose Jaimeson. The decision would split my heart in half.

None if it mattered now that Iranus the Tracker had my scent. He'd given me the chance to run but cursed me to do it alone.

I pulled the blood jewels from the hollow in the tree and dumped the contents of one bag into my palm. Red diamond-shaped stones rolled around on my skin, reflecting the small amount of light in the trees with an unnatural sparkle, casting glimmering red light on the leaves around me. These I would have traded for Jaimeson's life, but

Iranus hadn't seemed interested in the blood jewels, only taking my brother and convincing me to run.

I wished Dawn were beside me. She had always had a clear head and was confident in her decisions. I didn't know what to do. I had just sold my brother, my security, my identity for a handful of red rocks.

I squeezed the blood jewels, closing my fist as the stones ground against each other in a high-pitched protest.

I could run.

The thought, the thump of excitement in my chest at the prospect, made tears fall down my cheeks. I was still a coward. I couldn't push the urge to run and hide out of my mind, not even when Jaimeson's life depended on it.

I let my mind wander, imagining myself hiking the pass over the Spine Ridge Mountains alone. A small pack on my back, the cold wind biting my cheeks, the silence suffocating me as the thin air scraped through my lungs.

I changed the image. My father stood beside me as we crested the summit, placing his hand on my shoulder as we looked down at the dazzling city of Helefount, Marion and Jaimeson and Dawn all on the journey with me.

Stories said the city glowed brighter than the sun. At night, it sparkled like the stars in the sky, dancing with power that did not drain the spark. An eternal glory of energy and light where the people were happy and full, where food was plentiful, and illness was rare.

In my mind, Jaimeson walked with his arm draped over Dawn's shoulders. They smiled at each other and then at me, our journey nearly complete, the safety of the city at our fingertips. My entire family, everyone I loved, together.

Not all. It was too late for Mother. We had not even had time to mourn her as a family. I didn't even know what had happened to her body. And I'd never had a chance to explain or say goodbye to Marion. Jaimeson and I had hidden through the night and when the sun rose on the smoking ruins of our house, we had run. Father had been taken by the soldiers. Dawn, who I considered a sister, was gone with only a single written message.

Do not follow.

Those words had been as hard to resist as the urge to run was now. She had been my best friend since we were both only a year old. She had been brought to my father's land when we were babies, and my mother had raised us together.

We ran to the pond often, hiding from Jaimeson in the tall grasses at the edge of the water. We would lie on our backs, looking up at the sky through the waving stalks. She would take my hand and talk of the future. She dreamed of being a healer since she had been given the gifting of life and a spark strength of at least three people.

When we were twelve, she asked what I dreamed of.

"I want to help people," I said. "The way you do. I want to give of myself. But until Kadasha sees fit to grant me a gifting, I will work hard to be like Mother, one of the most renowned huntresses in all Tuleves." With my hands on my hips, I stood up straight despite my habit to hunch so I wasn't always taller than people around me.

"Your path will end in glory." Her head tilted to one side, studying me. "But you will travel through darkness much deeper than any night." Dawn's eyes were a deep golden brown and she always had a poetic saying.

I laughed. "There is no glory unless I can gain Kadasha's favor."

"You have much to give," she said. She didn't smile at my teasing but had almost looked sorrowful.

That was when Jaimeson found us. Laughing, he ran straight into the reeds and shoved me into the water. I was quick enough to grab his cloak and pull him in with me as we wrestled. I was already nearly as tall as him and getting stronger. He didn't want to lose a wrestling match with his younger sister, especially in front of Dawn. He pushed my head under the water and held me down too long. The sound of Dawn's voice came garbled through the water, my lungs burned, and time slowed as I tried to find purchase for my feet and push up for air.

I remembered the fear, the panic, as the water pressed in. He let me up, but the terror rose out of the water with me, a swirling, black emptiness that had always been inside me but was now a roaring storm. I yelled, splashing water at Jaimeson with all my strength, slamming my fists against the water to create a spray that would sting him.

As the water shot out of the pond from the force of my hit, I pulled in energy from around me for the first time. The water froze. A sharp spear of ice hurtled toward my brother and impaled his chest. I wouldn't have been able to move if it hadn't been for Dawn. She caught my brother as he fell into the water and dragged him to the shore. She called my name, reached through the frozen fog that held me, and commanded me to come help her.

The memory seared into me as I squeezed the jewels tighter. Dawn healed Jaimeson as the ice melted out of his chest, her hands on his face, her skin growing paler, her dark hair turning gray.

When Jaimeson opened his eyes, he shuffled back from me, frightened. "What was that?"

I looked down at my shaking hands. "Maybe that was my gifting?" I was a fool, half-drowned and out of my mind with guilt. It was wishful thinking, but I had wanted it to be true so badly.

He shook his head. "That was no gifting. That was an abomination. Never do that again. Ever."

He ran off before I could promise. I would have run after him, but Dawn collapsed, her life spark drained temporarily. She hunched over like an old woman as I wrapped my arms around her.

"Thank you for saving him," I said.

But Dawn's eyes were locked on where Jaimeson had disappeared into the rushes. "He'll bring you a lot of pain."

"All brothers do."

The blood jewels dug into my palm as the memory faded. The sharp pain in my chest returned. I let out a single strangled cry of sorrow of all I had lost. The boy I loved. My mother. The girl I considered a sister. I could not, would not, lose Jaimeson, too. I would save my father and my brother. The pain flared with so much intensity it blurred my vision. I gripped the branch of the tree, the bark digging into my skin. I screamed again, pushing all my anger and frustration in my soul out into the night air.

The pain lessened like I had forced it out with the noise.

When I opened my eyes, I gasped. The entire forest, as far as I could see, was covered in a thin layer of white frost. The leaves closest to me were encased in ice. A small bird sitting on her eggs in a nest on the branch beside me lay motionless, frozen to death.

Iranus's words echoed in the chill around me as I stared at the dead bird. *You will absorb everything good into that black pit inside you until there is no light left.*

CHAPTER 11

ORBLEE WALKED into the room I shared with Jaimeson as I shoved my few belongings into a canvas bag.

"What are you doing?" she asked. "You didn't come for work this morning. Are you all right?"

I was sure my appearance answered her last question. Her eyes took in the clothes I'd tossed on the bed, the empty dresser drawer hanging open.

"What happened last night?" she asked.

I turned my back to her, clutching the straps of the canvas bag. I couldn't form the words to explain why I had to leave. I had to run before I hurt anyone else. My weakness had destroyed my family one by one.

A pressure on my arm made me turn. The skin around her eyes wrinkled in concern, her forehead creased. I wanted to reach out and smooth the lines of worry from her face. While she looked like an old woman, she couldn't have been more than a decade older than me. Ten years of healing had aged her fifty.

"Thank you," I said. I didn't know if I would ever have a chance to thank her again. "For everything you've done for me."

Orblee narrowed her eyes. "That's no answer."

"He's taken Jaimeson," I said.

"Who?"

"Iranus the Tracker."

Orblee covered her mouth with the back of her hand, brows rising and disappearing into the wrinkles on her forehead. "Why?"

"Because of me." I lifted the bag onto my shoulder. Bare necessities. One pair of underclothes and an extra shirt, the Hooded Robber cloak, a hunting knife, flint and steel, and buried at the bottom, the bags of blood jewels. "I have to leave before I bring destruction to you, too."

"The world won't come to an end if you take a minute to explain things to me." She pushed me toward the bed, motioning for me to sit. She was as weak as a leaf about to be blown from a tree in the fall, but I couldn't resist her. The need to talk things out with someone was as strong as the urge to run. Orblee was right. It would make no difference if I ran now or when the sun dipped a little lower in the sky.

I told her about the bonfire charade and the chase through the woods, skipping over the detail of the blood jewels. I explained how Jaimeson didn't show up at the meeting point and I had searched for him. My jaw clenched with anger as I described the captain's treatment of him.

"Iranus the Tracker was there, and I didn't even see him. Didn't stop him before it was too late. I don't understand why he took Jaimeson instead of me. I offered him the trade."

Orblee leaned back, looking up at the ceiling. "It's possible he didn't want to take his chances against an Arjodite."

"An Arjodite?" The bed we sat on felt like it tipped sideways. Orblee acted as if she'd said nothing of significance.

"It has not been so long." She waved a hand in front of her face like she could wipe away the lost years. "You were only a baby then, but I remember visiting the Oracles to get my gifting. The Arjodites were warriors, women who towered over me as a child, fierce in their dedication to protect those who had the gifting of time."

"I'm not an Arjodite." I gripped the blanket beneath me. "I would have to have come from an Arjodite line. My father was a landowner. My mother. . ."

"A huntress without a home." Orblee twisted her fingers together. For the first time, she seemed uncomfortable with the conversation.

"You never knew my mother." The words snapped with more cruelty than I intended. She didn't flinch.

"I do not heal using the gifting of life." She swallowed like a great secret was caught in her throat. "When you first brought the wounded woman to me, when you first came to the village, I touched your hand. I saw a moment from the past and a moment in the future. I knew that you were descended from an Arjodite and that one day, you would protect an Oracle just like your mother had before the massacre. But your story will not end as your mother's did."

Orblee was placing her life in my hands. Using the gifting of time was forbidden and yet she admitted it to tell me a piece of who I was. Her aging was not from giving away health. She'd been giving away time.

"My mother?" She was a hunter, a tracker, skilled with the bow and the ways of the land. But an Arjodite? The image of Iranus's dagger hilt sticking out of my mother's stomach flashed through my mind. "Is that why he killed her?"

"Iranus the Tracker has hunted the Oracles relentlessly, but I have never heard of him killing one. In fact, it is his golden goose, the treasure always beyond his reach. He has never collected on the reward for bringing in an Oracle, despite his renown for bringing in criminals with rewards on their heads. If he killed your mother, there was another reason behind it. Iranus brings his quarry in alive."

None of this made sense because what Orblee said was true. He always brought his quarry in alive to collect on the reward. He was money hungry. I'd watched him kill my mother, but take my brother alive, dangling from the back of his horse. Even Horace Youlman had been brought in alive, a knife through his hand instead of his heart.

"What else did he say?" Orblee asked.

I turned my head away as Iranus's words echoed through my mind. *No light left.*

"He said he would come for me once he finishes his contract for the Grand Council. I can't stay here and put you in danger." I blinked, a single tear escaping as I pushed the rest back. Orblee held my gaze, her face full of concern. No judgment. No fear or revulsion. She could not see the darkness inside me that threatened to extinguish all light.

"What will you do?"

She asked the one question I didn't want to answer. Inside I knew. I could no longer fight it.

"What can I do?" I said, standing so that anger could push back all other emotions. "I have no gifting, no family name, no brother to help me. I have nothing to give. The more I fight what's inside me, the more people I'll hurt."

She didn't flinch at my tirade. "Do not measure your ability to give by your weakness."

I didn't know what that meant, but I did have a true answer for her, one that would prove exactly who I was.

"I'm going to run."

CHAPTER 12

ORBLEE DIDN'T ARGUE or beg me to stay. A part of me wished that she had, that she would tell me I was needed here, that I had a chance at helping my brother or finding another solution. But all she said was to get a good night's rest before I traveled.

She did give me a final hug goodbye. The first and last hug she had ever given me. Orblee wasn't known for affection, being strict and hard with high expectations and swift consequences. She was my only ally. And she didn't even wait to see if I would fulfill her last request.

My exhaustion was far beyond anything I could describe, and after staring at the door Orblee had shut on her way out, I agreed to rest one night and leave before first light.

As I took off my shirt in preparation for bed, a smudge of dirt just over my heart caught my attention. After exploding a burning pyre and running through the Shirewood Forest, I wouldn't be surprised to find dirt everywhere. Orblee had left me a bucket of fresh water on top of everything else she'd done for me. I wished I had found a better way to show her my gratitude.

Lacking the gifting of fire, I could not warm the water in my room. I could always make it colder, but that did me little good when it came to cleansing. I used a sponge to clean myself and spent an extra moment scrubbing at the spot above my heart. It wouldn't come off.

I tucked my head to try and get a better look, wishing for the silver-lined mirror that used to hang in Mother's room. As I looked closer, I barely swallowed the scream that jumped into my throat. There on my chest, where the sharp pain had been, was the small tattoo of a vine with a single leaf. I covered the stain with my hand and took a few deep breaths.

Iranus the tracker had a vine tattoo that snaked around his neck. Mine was too small to be sure, but the way the small vine grew two leaves that seemed to be reaching upward reminded me of his. I was no giver. I would absorb all light around me. His words had sounded like an insult, but I was beginning to wonder if it was possible he understood.

I could not accept that my mother's killer might be the only other person I'd ever met who was giftless like me. It couldn't be true. He could catch a person's smell, magnify it across leagues. He wasn't like me. More importantly, I wasn't like him.

I did not know what it meant. It couldn't be the same as the man I hated so much. If it didn't hurt, what could one small marking mean? Nothing. Unless perhaps, it was the mark of a coward about to run from her home and her family.

To protect them. I had to believe that it was the best choice for all of us.

I put on fresh trousers and a loose linen shirt, ready to travel as soon as my eyes opened in the morning.

———

I STOOD on a grassy field cut shorter than after the harvesters finished with the scythe, an unnatural green compared to the dry stalks of habala. Across the field were rows of targets, piles of hay wrapped with colored circles. I gripped the bow in my hand and the weight of my quiver pulled down on my shoulder. A pulsing roar echoed in my ears, coming from the stands filled with spectators behind me.

The Tournament of the People. I had made it to the competition. I stepped up to the archer's line and lifted my bow. The noise increased a hundredfold as the onlookers rose to their feet, cheering for me. I looked down and realized I wore the robes of the Hooded Robber. I was their hero.

I pulled a quiver from my shaft and turned toward the targets. The bullseyes quivered like a heat mirage in the desert sun. I blinked. They were no longer bales of hay, but people tied to long stakes, wood bundles stacked at their feet. The arrow on my bow burst into flame. I tried to pull the heat into me, but the flame only grew bigger.

The crowd fell into a mesmerizing chant. "Kill them. Kill them."

I sighted down my arrow and saw the faces of three people, knowing even as I recognized them, that my fingers were releasing the string.

The arrow flew and divided into three separate arrows, perfectly aimed at their hearts. I could only watch in horror as my arrows flew toward my father, Jaimeson, and Dawn.

I yelled, diving forward too late. Marion stepped between the burning people, shaking his head and pointing at me, condemning me.

I sat up with a gasp, my forehead drenched with sweat. I didn't know what time it was, but I could wait no longer. That dream would haunt my steps all day. The sounds still echoed in my mind. Even the smell of burnt flesh seemed to hover in the air. There would be no returning to sleep. I had to escape the room and the memories of that dream.

Once outside the healer's hut, I headed for the main road. I didn't take the shortcut through the woods but followed the path along the edge of the Spine Scale Mountains. Disappointment filled me as the road turned away from the mountains. If there was a pass straight up and over, I could reach Helefount in two days, but there was none, only jagged cliffs and unforgiving canyons.

At the intersection of Prontwick and the Northern Highway, I paused and looked south. The highway was empty until it curved around the southern edge of the swamp, a white line against the dark foliage on either side. The breeze picked up and whipped around me, leaves attacking me like a group of insects. A warning to listen to the urging inside.

I felt as if my soul was being ripped in two.

Run.

Save them.

Run.

Help them.

The words warred in my brain like two jackals for their territory. The sulfur of the Swamps of Gorgeon wafted through the air, and I took shallow breaths against the stink. In order to get to Helefount, I would have to walk three days northeast around the swamps, then turn west and cross the pass through the Ariantum mountain range.

Tuleves City was a day-and-a-half walk directly south, but Faengsel Forest and the Cracked Plains were unforgiving landscapes for travelers. The Northern Highway stretched two days southwest to skirt around the dangers. North or south, neither was a journey I wanted to take on my own.

The weight of a thousand bags of sand pulled me into the ground. The journey I had so long dreamed of, hoped for, planned for, was now only a cowardly retreat to hide from the dangers I could not hope to overcome. To face Iranus the Tracker again made my very core tremble. I didn't want to go to Helefount without my family, but the pull to escape and run the other way, stole my breath, crushed my chest, clouded my mind.

I stood frozen at the crossroads, one boot pointed south, the other slanted north. I didn't move. I couldn't move. The forces within me pulled equally in opposite directions.

A clinking sound pulled me back to the present. A strong breeze carried the smell of fresh horse manure and human sweat. I scrambled off the road, hiding behind a bangi tree as the sounds of voices and the crack of a whip grew louder.

There was no creak of wagon wheels or the shifting of leather I'd come to associate with caravans. Only a faint clinking, scraping, and the clop of two, maybe three horses. Confused, I allowed myself a peek through the branches of the tree I hid behind. A line of two dozen hunched and tired people walked chained together, wrist to feet, feet to wrist. The chains provided the clinking sounds. Bloodied bare feet made the scraping sound as skin dragged against the cobblestones.

I had never seen a caravan like this in all the times Jaimeson and I had been robbing caravans. Of course, I only went out at night, after he had scouted and come up with a plan. He would have told me of these human trains of sorrow.

The men on horses were bearded and rough, their clothes resembling the thick leather of hunters. These were not soldiers. From their pale skin and high foreheads, they did not even appear to be Tulevesian.

A child chained in the middle tripped. The woman behind him helped him stand before the line of people walked over the top of him. A whip cracked and the woman fell beside the boy. The man on the horse lifted his whip again.

"Get back in line," he yelled, spitting on the woman. She covered the boy with her own body. "Get up." The whip flew again and struck the woman across the face, breaking skin and leaving a weeping wound on her cheekbone.

Rage roared up inside me. I pulled my hooded cloak from my bag and tied the mask to my face. As the Hooded Robber, the urge to run faded. I felt free. I stepped out from behind the tree. The movement pulled the attention of the man with the whip.

The people in the chain tried to continue moving, some with eyes glazed over like they were no longer aware of their surroundings, others flinching from the whip and pushing forward to get away. The woman and boy were connected, dragged by their chains as the line moved. Neither had been able to get to their feet.

The man with the whip spat with an air of dismissal as he turned his attention back to the woman. He lifted his whip again.

"Stop," I yelled.

All movement ceased. I felt powerful for an instant, to be heard, obeyed. It was a new sensation.

The moment passed as the man lowered his whip and urged his horse forward, the hooves of the horse barely missing the boy and woman on the ground. As soon as the horse was out of the way, the woman lifted the boy back onto his feet and into line. Tears streaked both their dirty faces. There were two other slave drivers, one at the front of the line and one at the back. Both came forward. No one in chains dared move.

Three men. Three horses with small packs. No wagons. What did they feed these people? What did they drink?

"What do we have here?" the first man asked, a black substance rolling around on his bottom teeth and dribbling down his beard.

Before I could answer, the small boy's voice rang out.

"Mum, it's the Hooded Robber. He's come to save us." The hope warring with desperation cut right to my heart. I was the Hooded Robber, but I couldn't save anyone, not even my own family.

The men got down off their horses, standing in a semi-circle around me. The one on my left pulled a piece of paper from his breast pocket. A second piece of paper fluttered to the ground. He held the wanted poster for the Hooded Robber. The man looked back and forth between the drawing and my masked face. He flushed red with excitement when he concluded it was a match.

My bow would do no good. Three against one this close meant I could use their own weapons against each other.

"I don't want to hurt you," I said. "But human slavery is illegal, and I will not let you continue in these conditions."

"Slaves?" The first man moved his hand to the hilt of his sword and drew it from the scabbard. "These aren't slaves. These are indentured servants, sent to work off their debt in the city of Helefount. Couldn't pay their taxes, so they owe the government a service, don't they?"

Tax debtors. They were sending tax debtors to Helefount like animals.

I quickly scanned the faces for my father, but no one was familiar.

"They don't owe their government a service," I said, tossing my bow and quiver behind me so they wouldn't get damaged. "The government owes them. A lot, from the looks of it. Let them go. All of them."

Apparently, I'd picked up a few lines from Jaimeson's political rants.

"We'd love to," said one of the men, stepping closer to me. I shifted slightly, rolling onto the balls of my feet. It would help if they all drew their swords. "We really would, but that's our paycheck, see? We're hired to deliver the indentured and then we pay our taxes like they should've. Of course, if we get a reward for you, we don't have to pay taxes on that." He pulled his sword out. Two of the three.

"No taxes on collecting a bounty?" I rolled my shoulders. "That doesn't seem right. Not when these people worked hard all their lives and you make dinarah by taking advantage of their suffering."

The other man went for his weapon. Three swords raised and pointed at me. Now to turn them against each other. Jaimeson was the best at that.

"Who gets the reward?" I asked. "Even split?"

"I do," said the first man. "I saw you. I stopped you."

"We get a share," said the second man, turning his sword toward his companion.

"It should be an even split." The third man was smart enough to keep his sword on me.

The first man didn't even waver. "This one is all mine."

He stepped toward me. The second man tried to intercept. I moved forward, making the third man move in at the same time. I twisted into the third man's reach, grabbing his sword hand and shoving it forward into the second man's gut.

I ducked and rolled, kicking the leader in his tender spot as I moved between his legs. I pushed him forward from behind. He lost his balance and tumbled onto the other two men who were still connected by the sword. I jumped on the leader's back and he took a swing at me, connecting with the temple of the other man, knocking him unconscious. By the time the leader had found his feet, I had an arrow aimed at his eye.

"I won't shoot a man in the back," I said calmly. "If you turn and run now, you'll live to pay taxes another day."

He paused a moment, breathing hard, then he looked at his two companions on the ground. He turned and jumped on his horse. I cursed as he grabbed the reins of the other horses and took them with him south along the highway. I could have used a good horse.

"What did I tell you?" said the boy. "He's the Hooded Robber all right."

I allowed myself a small smile behind my mask as I found the keys on the belt of the man with the sword sticking through him.

I took the keys to the front of the line and unlocked the padlock on an older man who might have been the same age as my father. He took my hands.

"Thank you," he said.

"Why is the council sending you with hired men instead of soldiers?" I asked.

"We had soldier escorts up until Renathath. Then these men took over. That's all we know."

The chain was only locked in a few places as it dangled through the hoop of the shackles. Once the last person was free of their chains, I turned away, realizing I had yet to make my decision.

"There's a village less than an hour walk in that direction." I pointed them toward Prontwick. "The healer will help you."

"What about you?" A young girl I hadn't noticed before pulled her father closer. Her long dark hair reminded me of Dawn. "Will you come with us?"

"He can't come with us." It was the boy. His mother held his hand with a grip as firm as the shackles. "He has to go save everybody else."

"But there's a price on his head," said the girl. "He won't get far."

"Come with us." The woman, man, boy, and girl were all part of the same family. Some terrible fate had led them here together in chains. And they had invited me to join them, become a part of a family again.

I tried to imagine a life of freedom while my father rotted in debtor's prison. The image wouldn't come. Instead, I saw my father in a similar line, shoulders sagging as he was marched to Helefount to work off debts he'd been wrongly accused of.

"How long ago were you arrested?" I asked.

The mother answered. "They gave us a year to come up with the difference we supposedly owed. A year in the prisons. Only someone else could come and pay for our freedom. No one else has extra. No one could help us."

One year. My father had been taken almost one year ago. I imagined my father sharing this fate, walking with chains around his wrists and ankles, starving, being whipped. The image made me take a step back. Something crunched beneath my feet. I bent over and picked up the second paper the first man had dropped.

It was for the Tournament of the People. I read the prize printed at the bottom of the flyer. If I won, I could have one prisoner pardoned.

The girl stepped forward. "Will you come with us?"

"Thanks, but your brother's right. There's at least one more person I can help." I could ask for Father's pardon when I won the tournament. I would find another way to free my brother. All I had to do was find him. He already probably had a plan in place. I might not be able save them all, but one person was worth risking everything for and running wouldn't save anyone. Not even myself.

The girl nodded as her mother and father walked toward Prontwick.

I turned south, pushing the nagging dread into the back of my mind. I'd had enough practice ignoring the impulse to run that it almost felt as natural as swallowing a bitter tonic with a hope that the result would be worth the nasty aftertaste. I had to try. I couldn't leave Father to this fate. I couldn't abandon Jaimeson to Iranus the Tracker.

Someone needed to help my broken family. I just wished it could be someone other than me.

Directions were not a problem. I had studied maps with tutors when I was young, learning the layout and history of Tuleves. Both of my parents had a deep love and loyalty to our country. Jaimeson had always been the one to complain about the problems with the council's rule, with the strain of taxes on the people. He was given the gifting of reasoning because his ability to recognize right from wrong was unmatched by anyone else I had met. That was how Kadasha worked. She saw a strength in the person who brought themselves forth for the gifting. She would bestow a gifting based on a person's inherent talents and abilities.

Some people had said that Kadasha had refused to give me a gifting because I lacked the natural talent or Kadasha saw my limited potential and refused to waste a gifting on me. Those same cruel people taught their children that when I grew up, I would be a criminal because Kadasha had seen it.

Jaimeson called it a self-fulfilling prophecy. He said that without the gifting of Kadasha, I was reduced both in status and opportunity. What else could I become? I had set out to prove them wrong, developing skills with Mother, studying subjects with Dawn to increase my knowledge and understanding. I had failed to change Jaimeson's so called self-fulfilling prophecy. I had turned to a life of crime. I had a large reward on my head for exactly that.

Which meant I could not travel the roads as the Hooded Robber. If I met soldiers I would be arrested. Or meet a villager that couldn't resist the reward on my head. Nor could I travel the roads as a lone woman. Even with my size, it wasn't a safe prospect. That would mean staying off the roads.

I studied the skyline and debated the mode of travel. The white top of Mount Kildon interrupted the horizon like the sharp tip of a dagger. Tuleves City was east of Mount Kildon, sitting atop the plateau near the Azure Bay. The highway traveled west for over fifty leagues to Renathath before turning back toward the capital. It would be far shorter to travel to Tuleves City as the bird flew, but that meant traveling through Faengsel Forest. Many claimed that Faengsel Forest was home to beasts of legend—wildcats as large as a wagon, snakes as thick as a man's body and longer than a habala field.

Marion had loved the stories. He spoke of beasts of legend with reverence and a quiet passion. He'd brought me books with pictures, imitated the animal sounds and movements until I was rolling with laughter.

It didn't help that the punishment for trespassing in Faengsel Forest was death. King Tyndall had claimed ownership of the forest. As if anyone could own land as wild as that.

I debated only a moment more. It would take four days to travel on foot along the highway to Tuleves City. That would put me at the city gates only a day before the Tournament of the People if I had no delays. But if I cut straight across, I could make it in a day and a half. Besides, I already had a reward on my head. Why not add a capital punishment as well?

Jaimeson would have laughed with me. He knew how to find levity when a situation was dire. He'd gotten me through the last year when darkness and despair had threatened to consume me. Even though I had left a scar on his neck, he hadn't abandoned me. He would be ashamed to know how close I had come to abandoning him.

CHAPTER 13

THE UNNATURAL MIST swirled at my feet and tendrils crept around my knees as if trying to pull me back. The smell of rotting compost was strong enough that it would take three baths to rid my pores of the smell. Ten men stretching at arm's length wouldn't be able to encircle the trunks of the massive Faengsel trees. The complicated root system threatened to trip me or twist an ankle if I moved too quickly. No plants or undergrowth grew beneath the towering giants. The squish of my boots in the muddy soil echoed through the stillness.

The silence played tricks on my ears. There were no bird calls or chirping crickets. No drips of water, which was strange. A damp mist hung in the air, so thick toward the ground that I couldn't see where I placed my feet. Yet the water that dripped from the trees made no noise as it fell to the hidden earth. The atmosphere unnerved me. I pictured Jaimeson's relentless teasing for running from my own imaginings to keep myself moving forward. So far, I had heard nothing, seen nothing that would hint at danger.

I moved for several hours through the dank trees. When I heard the voices, I thought it was my mind playing tricks on me. It was muffled at first, but as the noises grew louder, they broke through the thick atmosphere of the forest. And from the volume of their voices, they were either not afraid to get caught or they didn't believe another soul would be within a dozen leagues.

My curiosity was piqued. Only extremely desperate humans would be here. I could not sneak up on anyone through these trees, with a lack of ground cover and the mist shifting about me like it was announcing my presence. I looked up. The branches were high, over three times the height of the branches in the Shirewood, but they were thick, covered in leaves, and they intertwined with the next branch like friends holding wrists.

I shouldered my bow that I had been clinging to nervously, fingers twitching for an arrow with each step. I gripped the white and black spotted bark of the faengsel tree. It was like the trunk had been stained with the shadows of this place. There were no lower branches to lift myself up so I had to use the rough ripples in the bark as handholds and shimmy up with my arms wrapped around the tree as far as I could reach. I was among the branches just as the voices became clear.

"Do you think we're close?" said one voice, friendly and playful, though not without a hint of nervousness.

"Close to what?" This voice was pitched slightly high, arrogant, or perhaps covering their fear.

I shifted, taking care not to make the branch groan or shudder. It was an unnecessary worry. The branch was a solid as a stone floor. I leaned forward, peeking through a break in the large, flat leaves. I almost fell off my branch when the Prince of Tuleves stepped into view. He looked nothing like the posters. Those made him look older, regal, a man in command. The prince below me was not much older than me, with messy blond hair and a mischievous look that made him impossible to match with the sharp-chinned image distributed throughout the kingdom. I recognized him mostly by his royal purple cape and unmistakable crest on the breast of his shirt.

Iranus the Tracker had taken the contract to bring in the prince and his companion. He would be looking for these two once he'd delivered my brother. I had found them first. And if this was the prince, then the other voice belonged to the Grand Councilor's son. I watched as the second person came into view. Two royals, cloaks splattered with mud, up to their knees in mist, looking about like two frightened children sneaking into the kitchens after dark.

The second traveler's head appeared, framed in the gap between the green spines of the forest leaves. I had the sensation of falling and had to grip the branch, digging my fingernails into the bark. The face was familiar. Not from poor likenesses on announcement posters. No. His face was one that I knew. One that I had touched, caressed, kissed, loved. The young man accompanying the prince, wearing a soldier's uniform, was Marion.

Iranus had said he hunted two boys, the prince and the Grand Councilor's son. If Marion was the traveling companion of the Prince of Tuleves, that meant he was the son of the Grand Councilor. In the time we had been friends, and then more, he had never told me who his father was. He had led me to believe he had no parents and was embarrassed about it, but thinking back, I had assumed, and he had never taken the time to correct me.

The Prince of Tuleves wore a purple riding cloak, fine gloves, and a feathered hat that reflected the ridiculous fashion trend among royals. Jaimeson had stolen one from the last caravan and worn it for three days. I'd had a stomachache from laughing so hard.

But Marion, my Marion, wore a soldier's uniform, undecorated, heralding the dark blue and red pinstripes of the Tulevesian army. He'd been in training when I knew him, but he had never wanted to be a soldier. He was taller now, with a more defined chin and slightly sharper cheekbones. A year had turned the boy I had loved into a man.

"You can drop the act," said Marion. "You may have the rest of the council fooled, but I know your random acts of rebellion are more than tantrums. You're looking for something. I could help you find it if you'd tell me what it was."

"This forest is getting to your mind," Prince Garreth said. "You might even be starting to hallucinate. And that smell has rattled your sense of reason. You know I like to give the council something else to talk about besides taxes. Now they will have to decide whether to make me king or behead me. It will be quite a conundrum."

Marion sighed and shook his head. "Well, I guess you've proven your point. There is nothing the rebellious Prince of Tuleves won't do. Can we go home now?"

Even from high up in the branches, the forest smelled of dank, rotting compost, a thousand years of deadfall and animal dung without a spark of sunlight to dry it out. It wasn't somewhere a prince would go to cause a scene. Sure, he liked to break rules and embarrass the council, but he had never traveled this far from the capital. There were no witnesses here of his crime. And, as I heard it, he usually preferred a crowd.

The prince passed beneath me. I focused on Marion, the son of the Grand Councilor. That meant he was a Lavante.

He had never told me his last name, not on that first visit to commission a bow from my father when I was twelve, nor in the last days before my life was destroyed, when he gave me a willow ring and a promise.

I had never told Jaimeson of Marion. Our promise to each other was to be a surprise at dinner. I never had the chance to announce it, to introduce my family. My brother mourned the loss of Mother and Father, of his future dreams to join the royal court in Father's place. Jaimeson never would have understood the loss of a mysterious boy who taught me that kindness and compassion still flowed in the hearts of men.

I'd told myself Marion would hate me for disappearing without a word, without explanation. I was sure he would move on, but I'd kept him in my heart.

Now that childhood crush twisted and mutated into something unrecognizable. My love for him hadn't waned from time, but his lie doused the glowing coals I'd been protecting. He wasn't the boy I believed he was. And now I wasn't just angry. I had to hate him for being the son of the man who ordered my father's arrest.

CHAPTER 14

"IF YOU'RE HERE to break a rule, we need a witness." Marion had never been one to leave things alone.

The prince didn't answer. He continued forward, his steps squelching in the muck despite the fact that he moved with the confidence of a trained hunter. Marion followed, his panther-like stride allowing for a silent stroll behind the prince, a skill that went beyond training. He'd always been able to sneak up on me.

I carefully moved across the branch, following them overhead, thankful I no longer had to creep along the unpredictable root systems that crisscrossed the ground.

"I'm here to defy the decrees of a tyrannical father, to make him regret. . ." Prince Garreth paused, the muscles in his jaw flexing. "Everything. When he comes back, he'll regret ever leaving."

"Sure," Marion said. The question in his voice rose up into the trees. "But that isn't the only reason. I've been with you as you entered every forbidden room in the castle, broke into sealed archives, and even tried to find a way into the ruins of the Oracle Temple. And every time you do it so loudly that you make sure you get caught, after you've made a meticulous search."

"I want the council to feel the embarrassment. No use being a reckless, arrogant prince if no one knows about it. If I hadn't done things publicly, can you imagine how the council would have painted me before the public?" Prince Garreth's voice went high and mocking. "As a wise and generous and perfect leader."

"Not a bad excuse," Marion continued, as calm and unflustered as if he were on a stroll through familiar castle hallways. "Except that you've brought me here with no audience, no fanfare. You'll have no proof you've even been here. I know this isn't just about disobeying your father or proving that you are such a spoiled prince you'll make a terrible king."

"I could have you beheaded for that comment," Prince Garreth said wryly.

"No, you wouldn't," Marion said. "You wouldn't survive a day without me. You need me and you know it. That's why you should tell me."

"Tell you what?" Prince Garreth paused to pull his sword from his sheath and strike through some vines that had grown thick and entwined between two trees.

Marion's voice was even and patient. "Tell me what you're looking for."

Prince Garreth turned, the mist twisting around his knees. A moment seemed to pass between the two of them and I wished I could see their faces instead of the tops of their heads. Their exchange pressed on an old wound. A deep longing rose up. Friendship. I felt the loss of Dawn as fresh as if it had been yesterday. We could always talk like this, without fear of dismissal or judgment.

A scream echoed through the forest. Animal. Feral. It was so loud and shrill I wanted to cover my ears, but I couldn't risk moving with them right beneath me. I had never heard a cry like that. Perhaps the tales of Faengsel monsters had not been exaggerated after all.

Both boys flinched, crouching down. Marion gripped his sword.

Once the echo of the animal scream died away, Prince Garreth surprised me by replacing his sword and pulling a bow from his shoulder and an arrow from a large quiver. The bow did not fit him correctly. It was too long for his height and the grip looked large for his hand, but he held it with confidence, notching the arrow and turning in a slow circle.

"That sounded like a wildcat," Prince Garreth said.

My ears were tuned to every sound, to every creak of a branch or rustling of leaves. Wild cats hunted from the trees and the last thing I wanted was to be caught up here with a hungry wildcat, especially as large as that one sounded.

"It might be a scarlett," Marion whispered, the first crack of nervousness entering his demeanor. Scarletts were rumored to be ancient wildcats the color of a mix of fresh and clotted blood, older than the seven immortals.

His voice was so familiar, as if our year apart had only been an instant. His obsession with beasts of legend had always been so endearing to me. While other men feared fire or war or death, Marion feared only upsetting ancient beasts who roamed the lands where humans could not travel. The bounders and scarletts of Faengsel Forest. The komdors and pythons of the Swamps of Gorgeon.

Stop it. I could not let myself become enamored again. Despite the goodness I thought I had seen in him, he was a royal. And a liar.

"Don't be ridiculous." Prince Garreth swept his weapon around him with the trained movement of a bowman. "There has been no recorded sighting of a scarlett for over a thousand years. And even those were the scribblings of a half-starved madman."

A rushing sound came through the forest, an empty wind that moved nothing, but roared in my ears. A flash of red moved at the edge of my vision. I turned, but there was nothing there.

I kept still, examining the branches on all sides of me. The leaves were thick and blocked any good view save for a few feet in front of me. When I turned my attention back to the ground, Prince Garreth and Marion had moved on. I stood and stepped onto another branch to follow them. A huge shadow moved toward the royals on the ground.

I crouched lower to try and get a clear view through the branches. It couldn't be what I thought, but my eyes could find no evidence to the contrary. A majestic form stepped out of the shadows. The leaves above it seemed to part, letting droplets of light through the foliage to land on the back of the magnificent creature.

It was a bounder. Sixteen handspans high, with a chest three times as wide as any horse, a rack of horns on its head that rivaled the branches I stood on. The gaze of the beast stared directly at the royals below me. No fear. No surprise. The black eyes seemed to drill into Prince Garreth. If those eyes had turned up toward me, I would have felt completely naked and exposed.

Prince Garreth did not shrink. To his credit, he squared his shoulders, took a deep breath, and aimed his arrow for the bounder's heart. My shout was echoed from below.

"Wait!" Marion's shout was louder, closer, as he lunged forward to stop Prince Garreth.

I watched the scene below as if time had been robbed of spark, causing it to slow and warp. Marion's hand landed on the prince's shoulder as the arrow sped along a perfect line toward the bounder. The arrow slowed and stopped, hovering in the air an inch from the bounder's hide.

The bounder's head shifted, a slight shake of disapproval. The arrow turned, snapping back in the prince's direction with the strength of a bowstring behind it. Prince Garreth dove out of the way, causing Marion to stumble straight into the path of the arrow.

This time, there was no one to echo my cry.

CHAPTER 15

PRINCE GARRETH ROSE UP out of the mud, sputtering and brushing himself off. He failed at recovering any dignity, but I was focused on Marion.

I pushed my mask into my mouth, stuffing my fingers between my teeth to stifle a sob before the prince heard me. The bounder melted back into the forest as if it had never existed. The only evidence of its presence was the swirling fog where it had stood, and the arrow fletching sticking above the mist where Marion had fallen.

I couldn't believe what had just happened. A beast of legend had stepped from the forest, used a gifting, and left an innocent—well, not completely innocent, but not the one guilty of shooting the arrow— to die.

My instincts told me to disappear the same way the bounder had, to be on my way. I was losing precious time to get to the Tournament of the People, but I couldn't pull my eyes away from the scene below.

Prince Garreth stumbled toward the arrow, brushing the mist aside with his hand. I leaned forward, lying flat on my belly to see more clearly. If the prince ran, leaving Marion behind, it would confirm everything I believed about royals. I wouldn't leave Marion to bleed out on the forest floor.

There was a small groan. Marion's face was a shadowed outline beneath the thinning mist.

"You missed." He coughed with the effort of forming words. "How bad is it?"

Prince Garreth cleared his throat. "Uh, not bad. Well, it's bad, but it could be worse."

The wild scream sounded again, closer than before, bouncing off the trees, making it impossible to tell which direction it came from. If bounders existed, then this sound could truly be coming from a scarlett of legend. It would smell Marion's blood and be drawn to the weakened prey.

"Do tell, how could this be worse?" Marion echoed the thought in my own head.

Two spoiled royals half a day's ride from the nearest village, one of them wounded, their horses at the edge of the woods or farther, wild animals surrounding them, and Iranus the Tracker on their trail. I waited to see how the prince would put a positive spin on their situation.

"It's only buried up to the head." Prince Garreth was surprisingly calm and matter of fact. "Most of the shaft is still free. The leather armor you insisted on wearing slowed the impact. So that's some good news. I could pull it out, but that could cause more damage. It might be better to break off the shaft and leave the head in until we can get to a healer."

"I'm going to die," Marion groaned. "Slow and painful. That's what I get for following a pathetic excuse of a prince."

It seemed he and I still agreed on a few things.

"No need to get sore about it." Prince Garreth removed his coat, ripping along the seams of the arms. He took off his belt and set everything within reach. He was moving with precision and expertise. Perhaps they had given him some useful schooling during his plush life.

"Remember what we learned about self-fulfilling prophecies," the prince said, moving to Marion's midsection. "If you believe something, it's more likely to happen. That's how the Oracles controlled the people. It's why my father said they had to be destroyed. Don't believe something will happen that you don't want to happen because then it will happen because you made it happen."

Rough bark pressed into the palm of my hands. Prince Garreth spouted Jaimeson's theory of self-fulfilling prophecies, although twisted. I'd never heard the reasoning behind the desolation of the Oracles, only that they had betrayed Kadasha. My heart wanted to deny the idea of the Oracles controlling people, but then I remembered Captain Tevya's face as Jaimeson forced her to give him the blood jewels.

"Philosophy," Marion said. "I'm lying here after you shot me with an arrow and all you can do is spout philosophy." His voice was weaker. I could sense the heat spreading through his clothing. Blood. And a lot of it.

Prince Garreth steadily placed his hands at the point where the arrow disappeared into Marion's stomach. He meant to pull it out.

Marion seemed to realize this at the same time. "Don't touch it." His words slurred with panic or delirium. Or both. "Just don't touch it. Go get help and bring them back."

The same animal scream sounded again, so loud that the vibrations of the noise moved through my head and into my bones. The prince jumped to his feet, hands clenching and unclenching. If he left, I would have no choice but to reveal myself. I couldn't leave Marion to die alone, not even as the son of the Grand Councilor.

I peeked down the branch, expecting the scarlett to be standing directly over me. There was nothing in the shadowed leaves.

"I didn't mean it," Marion said. "Don't leave me. If you can help me to the horses, I'll make it home." He reached out of the mists and gripped Prince Garreth's legs. The prince hesitated, considering for a moment.

Prince Garreth crouched back down. Surprise shot through me like I was taking a dip in a half-frozen stream. It seemed the prince battled his selfish nature the same way I did. "Positive thinking. Bet they didn't teach you that in military school."

He checked the supplies that he'd prepared and then moved his hands back into position to remove the arrow. His surety and confidence surprised me almost as much as his decision to stay. Perhaps I would not have to reveal myself after all.

That's when the vines in front of the prince and Marion parted. A scarlett larger than a tax wagon stepped out onto a raised root facing the two royals. The scarlett opened its mouth and let out a low reverberating growl that was almost as heart-stopping as the scream.

Prince Garreth fell back, crab crawling away from the scarlett, leaving Marion and his bloody wound exposed to the gigantic wildcat. Without thinking, I dropped from my branch, landing between Marion and the scarlett. Instinct had my bow drawn; my arrow nocked before I finished standing. I looked right into the eyes of the scarlett. The filtered light landing in its red fur gave the appearance of dripping blood. Its entire coat moved, shifting over raw muscles. Its eyes burned like glowing embers, full of intelligence.

My bow fingers twitched, but I didn't release. I'd seen what had happened with the prince's arrow.

The thunder of large hooves begged for my attention as the bounder reappeared in the clearing at the same moment Prince Garreth tried to exit. I didn't take my attention from the scarlett, but in the edge of my vision the prince nearly collided with the antlers. The prince slid to a stop, dropping to all fours before the magnificent creature. If I hadn't been waiting to be disemboweled by an ancient wildcat, I might have smiled at the humbling position.

The bounder pawed at the ground, swinging its great head from side to side. Prince Garreth turned, surely looking for an escape, but his eyes fell on me.

"Who are you?" Despite his prostrate position on the ground, mostly covered in mist and mud, his voice had lost none of its arrogance.

The scarlett's tail twitched and I almost lost my grip on the bowstring. The key to an accurate aim was to release quickly, without hesitation. My arm was already shaking with the pressure of holding the string anchored to my cheek. It was pointless to release the arrow, but I was too scared to lower my bow, frozen in a struggle of will between my muscles and the deadly glare of the scarlett.

Marion groaned. The scarlett licked its lips, lowering its haunches, shifting back and forth, shaking the vines on either side of it.

I was out of time. I knew if I let the arrow fly it would do no good against the beast in front of me. I could shoot over its head in warning.

The cat would not heed such a small gesture. I needed to startle it somehow.

The movement of the vines extended down into the mist, swirling the moisture between the scarlett and my legs. I shifted my foot to the side until it was stopped by something solid. I wasn't sure if it was a vine or a root, but I took the gamble. I sucked in the heat, pulling as quickly as I could. White frost crept up the vines on either side of the scarlett. The leaves froze higher as the vines became solid. My arm shook, my muscles straining. I sucked in one last surge of spark, the pain flaring in my chest and let the arrow fly.

It hit a length of frozen vine a handspan above the animal's left ear. There was a shattering sound like the dropping of a crystal goblet on a stone floor. The vines cascaded down over the head of the scarlett in a fall of ice shards and frozen green daggers. The scarlett flinched backward with a growl of frustration and then disappeared into the mist.

I took a deep breath and as I let it out, the mist fell to the ground in a perfect circle around me, the tiny droplets of water in the air now frozen solid.

Marion's entire body was now visible, his hand gripping the arrow protruding from his stomach, his weight supported on the opposite elbow like he was ready to pull himself to safety. His eyes were locked on me.

I wanted to run, disappear into the forest. But I also wanted to drop to my knees beside him and wipe the frost from his brow. One year since I had been lost in those golden-brown eyes. One year since I had touched his chiseled chin, now with sharpened angles, his jaw a line of strength.

The bounder huffed at Prince Garreth, pulling my attention away from Marion. It lowered its head in what felt like a bow of respect, but then the enormous horns caught the prince under the arms and shoved him toward us. The prince stumbled to his feet, straightening his frilly sleeves and smoothing his hair back as if he could save an ounce of his royal pride. The drip of frozen sweat on the end of his nose hung like a drop of dew caught in an early morning frost.

The bounder lowered its head one last time in my direction. I sensed a promise and a deep longing. Then it turned and disappeared into the shadows of the forest.

Both royals watched me like they were waiting for a courtier to provide introductions. No time for formalities. I moved to Marion's side, helping him lie back down without disturbing the arrow. Our eyes met.

"Ari?" He breathed out. Though only my eyes were showing above my mask, he had recognized me. I panicked and reached for Marion's spark. I sucked in, slowing his heartbeat until his eyes fluttered back in his head.

Prince Garreth kneeled on the other side of his body. "What happened?"

"He passed out. Probably from loss of blood. We need to get him out of here and find help."

The prince's eyes darted to the shadowed trees around us. He was afraid and I didn't blame him. We had no cover. The animals were arrow proof. Marion's wound was severe. But I wouldn't leave him to such a fate.

I reached across Marion and placed my hand over the prince's gloved fingers. "I will help. You don't have to do it alone."

The words seemed to snap him back to the present. He opened his mouth like a thousand words were trying to escape. Instead, he nodded. This wasn't what I should be doing. I needed to get to the Tournament of the People. I needed to focus on a plan to save my father and my brother. But Marion had said my name. He'd sounded happy, full of hope. Not angry. It had ignited a spark of hope. That selfish emotion made me reconsider my position.

It was Jaimeson's voice that echoed in my mind. *This is an opportunity. You are doing the Prince of Tuleves a favor. You could ask for one in return.*

Prince Garreth pulled off his riding gloves and tossed them to the side. The frozen layer of frost was already beginning to melt, steaming off the ground in thin tendrils.

"We have to remove the arrow. Moving him with it in will only cause more damage, but it should be much easier now that I can see." He looked at me as if he wanted an explanation. I didn't give him one.

"Don't either of you have a gifting that could help?" I asked. Surely a royal would have a useful gifting.

"I don't think the ability to talk so loud for an hour that I lose my voice for a week is going to be very helpful in this situation."

The gifting of sound. Not very useful right now.

I already knew Marion's gifting. He had the gifting of strength. It wouldn't do us any good for him to give away his own strength when he was losing it in the pooling blood around him.

"Marion's gifting won't do us any good. Punishment for sleeping on the job is twenty lashes." Prince Garreth flicked him on the nose.

No response.

The prince took a breath, and to my surprise, became completely focused. He handed me his makeshift bandage he'd made from his coat. I recognized the movements from assisting Orblee.

"As soon as the arrow is out, press down with this, firmly, don't hesitate." He placed one hand on the shaft of the arrow and the other on Marion's stomach. He glanced at me once to see if I was ready and then pulled the arrow out in one smooth motion.

I pressed the coat against the wound, using my weight to add pressure. I had little strength left in my arms after holding the bow taut for so long. Prince Garreth grabbed the belt he'd removed and wrapped it around Marion's middle to hold the coat in place.

"I don't know if it will be enough to stop the blood," he said.

I couldn't tell him that Marion's heart had very little spark, pumping only enough blood to keep him alive, but I reassured him. "It will be enough."

CHAPTER 16

I WARRED with my decision to keep Marion's spark low as Prince Garreth and I struggled to carry him through the fog of Faengsel Forest. The air had gone still. A pressure weighed down on my ears with the same intensity as if I had dived to the bottom of a lake. No more animals appeared, although I felt eyes watching us from the branches and shadows. The sight of the Prince of Tuleves and a wanted thief stumbling across roots dragging a wounded man between them must have been quite the show.

Marion had recognized me. If he connected my family name with the Hooded Robber, I would never get Father or Jaimeson back. We'd all be charged for my crimes and hung from the gallows.

I carried him with my arms wrapped around his chest, his hands dragging through the fog. Prince Garreth carried his feet. My size and strength were an advantage on this occasion. Fortunately, I had traversed most of the forest, and the prince and Marion had only entered a short time before from the opposite direction. Despite that, it took three glasses for us to travel the short distance to their horses.

We finally broke through the edge of the forest and found the horses tied in a slight depression. The sun hovered above the tree line like a golden tear about to fall off the edge of the world.

I set Marion's head down gently. Prince Garreth dropped his feet like a sack of rice and fell to his knees. I supposed the royal training wasn't as physically intense as carrying a body through an invisible maze of tripping hazards. I stepped back, knowing this was my chance to make Jaimeson proud.

I turned away. "It's almost dark. I need to find a safe place to set up my camp."

"You're not leaving." It was said as a command from the Prince of Tuleves. I hesitated. He took it as a sign of compliance. "Help me get Marion onto his horse."

"I've already risked too much. I have my own skin to worry about."

"I can't do this without you." His sincerity made my next words catch in my throat, but I pushed them out anyway.

"What is my help worth to you?"

"A reward? I'm not carrying any coin on me."

"I don't want money. I need your influence." Jaimeson's voice chided me. *Too soon. You showed your hand too soon.*

The prince let out an exhausted bark of a laugh. "Influence. That's rich. Did you hear that, Marion? Oh, no. I guess he didn't. Not a problem. His sense of humor isn't much better when he's awake."

His reaction threw me off balance. I didn't understand the joke. "You're the Prince of Tuleves. In return for my help, I need you to pardon my family."

"No problem." The sarcasm in his voice made me feel like a small child at the butt of a joke. "I'll just walk into the King's Council and say, 'Excuse me, but this young man who likes to run around dressed as an enemy of king and country would like me to release his family. Let it be done." He pranced past me and made a ridiculous wave of his hand. "Sorry. I think you've confused me for a respected member of the council."

"You're the prince."

His answering glance felt like a bucket of cold water had been dumped over my head. He had no power. He was a despised figurehead who was more of a problem than a royal. Even if I'd played my cards better and made the Prince of Tuleves want to help me, he couldn't.

"Now help me get the powerful son of the Grand Councilor on the back of my horse and I'll promise not to turn you in for impersonating the Hooded Robber."

I almost told the high and mighty Prince Garreth where he could stick his oversized head, but a new idea came to me. Maybe there was a way to get Father and Jaimeson back. Captain Tevya had commissioned Iranus the Tracker to bring in the Prince of Tuleves and his companion. And the spoiled royals were right in front of me. If I could trade the prince for Jaimeson and then use the tournament to get Father pardoned, I could help them both. And maybe in Helefount, I could plead before Kadasha's throne for my gifting.

I would do as the prince asked, but it would be his own undoing. He deserved to be turned in to Iranus and whatever fate awaited him. He'd chosen his own path of being a bane to the council instead of finding a way to use his privilege. I approached to help lift Marion, but Prince Garreth raised his hand.

"Take another moment to rest." He said it like I was the one who needed rest. "I thought it would take more time to convince you. Who are you, anyway?"

"No one," I said.

"All right." The prince leaned back on one arm, pulling a long grass and putting it between his teeth to chew on. So casual, like he wasn't worried about the setting sun or the tracker on his heels. So informal, like he was born on a farm instead raised in a palace. "I like a good puzzle. You've dressed yourself like the Hooded Robber, so you are either illiterate or daft."

"Pardon me?"

"Every announcement board in the entire kingdom has the reward amount for the real Hooded Robber. If you thought it was safe to dress up like a wanted criminal, you either didn't know about the reward on his head or you were stupid enough to think it would scare people away. Not a safe bet."

His insults were aggravating, but his misjudgment was to my advantage. I had spent enough time around Jaimeson to recognize an opportunity.

I sat down, sighing like I had been caught in a lie. "I'm not daft."

"A runaway apprentice," Prince Garreth concluded like his brilliance was unrivaled. "A boy who's been gifted with strength or heat, forced to become a laborer. It would be a terrible fate. You smell too clean to have been a runaway for long and your eyes are too kind. If you're thinking of becoming a thief to survive, we brought no money with us. If you were going to take our horses and leave us stranded, you might as well have left him to die in the forest."

He leaned closer to me, our heads almost touching. I resisted an impulse to headbutt him and break that perfect line of a nose. He smelled of horse manure and death. How long since this royal had taken a bath?

"Well, then. Tell me, am I right?"

I tried to follow his line of thinking back to his conclusion. "A runaway apprentice?"

His brows came together at my confusion. "I'm wrong. Does that mean. . ." He looked me up and down as if considering for the first time that I might be the Hooded Robber.

"No," I said. "You're not wrong, just a little off. I'm a runaway." I turned away from him as if filled with embarrassment. "I cannot tell Your Highness what I've run away from."

"You can't tell me?" He leaned back, a brilliant new realization lighting up his face. "An indentured servant? You're a tax evader."

The truth slipped in too easily. "My father, sir."

"Don't you dare call me sir, or sire, or anything of the kind." He stood up and offered me his hand. "You can call me Garreth. And please don't lump me in with those who would punish people who can't make enough money to survive, let alone support a fat and lazy council."

It was my turn to be surprised. I let him help me up and he held my hand.

"Will you help me? Your secret is safe with me," he promised.

"I will make sure you get your friend to a healer." It was the best I could do. I wasn't about to help the Prince of Tuleves. I was planning to trade him for my brother. But I somehow his casualness with a dash of sincerity made it easy to stop thinking of him as a prince.

We grunted and groaned as we shifted Marion onto his horse. There was no way to get him to balance himself, so Garreth rode behind him. I straddled the grandest horse in the kingdom. I stroked the fine beast's neck as all my days of riding lessons with Dawn and Jaimeson came back in a flash. I urged the horse forward, thrilled at the strength beneath me.

"You don't ride like a peasant. Was your father a landowner?" Garreth struggled to keep Marion's horse at pace with the one I rode while keeping him balanced.

I slowed and slouched, letting him pull out in front. Perhaps this was a mistake. The longer I stayed with the prince, the more he would learn about me. But I could not give up on the hope that there was a way to save Jaimeson and Father.

"Have you ridden with many runaways?" I asked. "You know nothing of me and where I come from. Plus, your own lack of personal hygiene would suggest royals are no better than highway brigands."

"Touche." He showed no sign of being offended but sniffed his own shoulder as if testing my theory. "I do smell bad, but I have a good excuse."

We rode in silence as the stars shifted overhead. The constellation of the Hound of Armen set while the Great Bounder rose in the east. Mother had taught me the stars. It did no good to track your prey so far that you couldn't find your way home. I could tell the time of night and my location based on the visible stars.

Time was a commodity we didn't have. I still held some of Marion's spark, but his wound trickled blood down his leg, soaking Garreth's sleeve.

A quarter watch into the night, Garreth's head began to bob. My own eyelids were heavy after a full day's travel, but Jaimeson and I had sat up through many nights, waiting and planning. I had plenty of tricks for staying awake, but Garreth looked as if he might topple from his horse. I pushed my horse into a trot to ride next to them.

"We will not make it back to Tuleves City tonight," I said.

"The Grand Councilor's healers are the most powerful in the land," Prince Garreth responded. "If he has a hope of recovery, it lies in the Sanatorium."

The Sanatorium was famous for their healers. But it was a place reserved for royalty. Even my father, before he was accused and stripped of his wealth, was denied access when Jaimeson had been sick as boy. For three years my brother had had unpredictable and unexplained seizures.

The local healers had offered herbs and advice, but nothing had helped. He had eventually grown out of them, but there had been a deep bitterness in my heart toward a kingdom that would let their people suffer when it had the means to help them.

Garreth was not wrong. The Sanatorium would be the best place to heal Marion, but we wouldn't make it there in time. We were still a full day's journey from Tuleves City. I tried to picture the maps in my head, placing Faengsel Forest behind me, Mount Ariantum to my left on the horizon hiding the great red star, and to my right was Shallow Lake. That meant that we had no options. We were traveling through the Cracked Plains, a barren part of Tuleves where the dry cliffs and canyons prevented villages from being viable.

The overgrown road we traveled looped through the Cracked Plains but was never used, abandoned since the Desolation of the Oracles. The road was built to guide people to the Oracles. Now that they were gone, no one traveled this road. And as far as I knew, no villages survived. As the road slanted downward into a valley, Garreth's horse shifted and both royals almost fell off. I moved forward and supported the prince as he got resettled.

"I can't feel my legs." He said it as a fact. "You might be right about not making it to Tuleves City. Do you have another suggestion? I'm not sure Marion will last the night if we don't get him help."

I scanned the area and noticed a star twinkling below the horizon. No, that was impossible. I looked closer and could make out several different lights. It had to be a village, but I could not think what village would be out here. It was in the direction of the ruins of the Oracles, mostly surrounded by Shallow Lake.

We approached a crossroads. The overgrown road we currently travelled on turned off into an almost invisible one, but there were ancient cobbles beneath a layer of dirt and weeds.

Garreth turned to look at me, but his movement was a mistake. Pain distorted his face in the light of the moon that shone full and bright on his features. His fingers gripped the saddle tight enough to look white as bone as he struggled to maintain his balance. His royal thighs had to be burning, gripping the wide part of the horse's back, keeping his friend from slipping off the saddle.

"We turn here." Garreth moved Marion's horse slowly and painfully onto the abandoned road. I leaned forward to seem like I was worried about them falling off the horse. As soon as his back was to me, I pulled out my knife and cut a decorative strap that had the royal seal stamped into the leather from the saddle. I tied it to the end of an arrow and shot it into the crossroads sign.

Iranus the Tracker would know where to find the prince now. And he would recognize my fletching.

I had officially kidnapped the Prince of Tuleves.

Chapter 17

The moon had followed its course across the sky and set before we reached the small village. I was grateful it existed, but I'd never seen it on maps. Never heard of people living so near the ruins of the Oracles.

The darkness of the night made the stars' light feel generous. The chill of predawn settled into my bones. Garreth's teeth chattered in an unprincely like way, his coat sacrificed to staunch Marion's wound. He stayed slumped against Garreth, a grunt escaping whenever the horse shifted to adjust to the uneven road.

The power to absorb spark was useless when one needed heat. If I could send a little heat their way, it might make them more comfortable. Of course, I reminded myself that I intended to turn them over to Iranus, and prisoners were not meant to travel in comfort.

A shiver that had nothing to do with the cold air played down the bones of my spine as I thought of facing Iranus again. This time I would have the upper hand. I would not be taken by surprise again. I had time. Once I traded Garreth for Jaimeson, I would win the Tournament of the People.

It wasn't until a dark shadow loomed up beside me that I realized we were in the village. There were few fires or candles left burning this early in the morning, even with the chill of the air. Only one light was left, high up on a hill as if calling to me.

The horizon followed the outlines of small shacks leaning against one another like a child had stacked blocks in a line and then knocked them down. I heard the dripping of water up ahead and could barely make out the white stones set in a circle. A community well.

"Where do we go from here?" Garreth asked. His voice was gravelly; his face twisted with pain. "Are we close? I've lost all feeling in my feet."

"A healer will leave a lantern on her door even at night so she can be found in an emergency." I knew this because I'd lived with a healer for the last year. Many nights had us roused from our beds to help some poor soul who had knocked on Orblee's door. A mother whose baby had stopped breathing. A child whose father who had gone delirious with fever. They came and Orblee never turned them away, no matter the hour.

I clicked my tongue and walked the prince's horse slowly around the well, checking down the streets to my right and left. There, where a street jutted sharply up a hill, was a path to the light.

"Come," I said to Garreth, enjoying giving the Prince of Tuleves an order. "The healer lives up this way."

He followed without complaint, but I misjudged the steepness of the street. I leaned forward into the horse's neck to keep my balance, but I heard a curse behind me and turned to see Garreth and Marion slide off the back of their horse.

A pile of royals lay below the horse's rear end.

I saved the image of the prince flailing underneath Marion for another time. I jumped from my horse and pulled him off Garreth. The freezing touch of Marion's skin made me flinch. I had taken too much energy.

I felt below his chin, the way Orblee had taught me. There was a pulse, weak, but there. Garreth did not rise. He moaned. He wasn't dead yet.

"My legs don't work anymore," Garreth said. "It's like there's nothing there."

"Your legs will recover," I said. "But I don't think Marion has much time."

Garreth paused. "Are you on a first name basis with my personal guard?"

"He's the son of the Grand Councilor," I said, remounting the horse. "It's not like he has an official title. Stay here. I'll fetch the healer."

I pushed my heels into the horse's flank, the hooves moving into a quick clop up the cobbled street, echoing in the silence that followed behind me.

Garreth would come to his own conclusions about why a runaway would break social protocol with a first name. Hopefully, he would write it off as exhaustion. I rode the horse hard up the hill and pulled to a stop in front of the light. The lantern hung on a large nail pounded into the frame of the doorway. The doorframe was the only part of the small cottage that looked stable.

The healer's hut was the last on the street. The steep hill ended at a dead end, blocked by a wall that extended up into the darkness, disappearing beyond the light of the lantern. But even in the dark I knew what it was, realized why this village was down an untraveled road, avoided by travelers and soldiers alike. One side of the healer's shack leaned against the great wall that surrounded the ruins of the Oracles.

This was where one thousand Oracles had worked and lived, where one thousand Oracles were slaughtered for betraying their faith. Only the truly desperate would live this close to the condemned city.

There was no time to ponder it further. Marion was running out of time.

I pounded on the door, shaking dust down from the straw roof, the lantern jingling against the door frame.

The door opened before my fist landed a third time. A face appeared in the lantern light, not wrinkled and aged like Orblee's, but a young face with sapphire eyes and long thick hair nearly to her waist. A face I knew even better than my own.

I stumbled back, tripped over a cobblestone and landed beneath the horse's belly. I shielded my eyes as if the light of the lantern blinded me. I could not believe what I was seeing, what I should not be seeing. Yet, I had wished to see her for so long.

Dawn stood in the doorway of the healer's hut. My best friend.

Do not follow.

Her last words. And now she was here, in front of me.

"Are you okay?" Dawn leaned forward.

I scrambled to make sure my mask was in place, covering my face, my identity, my betrayal. I had left a sign for Iranus. I had led him here. Dawn was a healer in this hidden village on the edge of the ruins. She'd always been a powerful healer. Captain Tevya had said there was a healer with a concealed location. She was protected. I had exposed her.

"No," I said, waving her away, coughing so my voice sounded lower, gruffer. "It's not for me. There are others."

"I'll sound the alarm." Dawn grabbed a string attached to a bell I hadn't noticed before. It was a solid iron bell, one that farmers used to call in the pigs for dinner. It would wake the whole village.

"Wait!" I pulled myself up, reaching to stay her hand. She paused before I touched her. "It's only one boy. You don't need to wake everyone."

Her hand hung on the rope, the clacker swinging inside the bell. I could never lie to Dawn. Her eyes pierced me, seeing past deceit like she had always done.

"We need to bring him here, quietly. Without alerting the village."

"Have you brought me an outlaw?" One eyebrow quirked up. She could always make me laugh with her silly faces. Any humor in me hung limp and lifeless as a dried piece of meat. I had brought her an outlaw, but it wasn't the injured. It was me.

"No," I said. I dropped my head lower, keeping to the shadow of the horse. "But they may not be welcome here and I want to avoid any. . . violence." The words were said with sincerity. In a village of people desperate enough to hide, the prince and the son of the Grand Councilor would be public enemies.

"Not welcome?" Dawn said in a tone of disapproval.

I sighed. "It's the Crown prince and the son of the Grand Councilor." I could not say his name for fear she would hear the emotion in my voice.

She stiffened and checked down the street as if a crowd might have gathered in the last quarter of the night. She even looked toward the wall as if ears could hide among the stone blocks.

"How far?" she asked.

"At the bottom of the hill, near the well."

"Come."

She reached back into her hut, pulled out a soiled cloak, and strode down the street. She was shorter than me by almost a head. She wore a nightdress of heavy fabric with short sleeves, but she didn't shudder at the cold night. And the cloak remained draped over her arm. I followed Dawn, leaving the horse tied to a post so the animal would not have to travel down the steep street in the dark.

Fear leaped into my throat, almost choking me when I didn't see the prince where I had left him. But then I saw him pulling water from the well. He placed the liquid to Marion's lips. Garreth startled, spilling the water when Dawn approached him.

"Your Highness." Her words were crisp, almost an accusation. "We must get indoors as quickly as possible. Are you injured?"

"No," Garreth said. He attempted to stand. He made it to his feet, but his legs stayed bent, his muscles so stiff from the long ride that he couldn't straighten them. Dawn stood as straight as a warrior in front of him, her white gown visible in the simple starlight. A light breeze pulled her hair back from her face.

The Prince of Tuleves tilted his head far enough to see Dawn's face and his jaw dropped open; his immense royal vocabulary momentarily stripped from his mind.

I knelt by Marion's side. His breathing was labored, sporadic.

"You injured him worse when you fell off the horse," I accused Garreth. He was slow to take his eyes from Dawn.

"There was another horse?" she asked. Concern flashed across her face. "Where has it gone?"

"Not far," he said, pushing himself a little straighter with a grunt of pain. His voice regained some of its arrogance. "It's as tired from the night's ride as we are. Do you have lodging for us?"

"Did it have your crest on the saddle?" Dawn stopped only inches from Garreth's. To his credit, he did not step back but held her gaze with defiance.

"It was Marion's horse," he said, his eyes even with hers, though his back was still hunched from his tightened muscles, his knees bent and bowlegged. "But, yes, his saddle carries the seal of the Crown."

"Well, then," Dawn said. "You will go and catch it. We can't risk anyone seeing it. Bring the horse to my hut and hide the saddles and bridles under the straw beside the house. Do it quickly. The sun is not far from rising."

She turned toward me, her hair flicking the prince in the face. He stared like he was being stalked by another scarlett. Garreth's muscles were coiled, his eye twitched in a fight or flight battle. As much as I enjoyed watching Dawn effectively put a royal in his place, I needed an excuse to slip away, find a moment alone and regroup. My plan was uncoiling faster than a runaway spool down a cobblestone street. I couldn't think how to reel it in. I needed time.

"I'll go after the horse," I said. Maybe I could find the horse and ride away, leaving this tangled mess of princes and jewels and trackers far behind me. Jaimeson could talk his way into a private wedding celebration. He could surely talk his way out of prison. And Father was strong, but he would not survive a march to Helefount. I also had to consider the danger I'd put Dawn in as well.

"Yes," Garreth said. "Send the runaway. He travels well in the dark, sneaks up on people, and can fight off giant cats. Send him after the horse."

"You must go." Dawn's declaration stole my breath and my resistance. She had raised her eyebrows in question at "runaway," but did not ask for clarification. Despite my skill with the bow and my height, Dawn had always been the stronger of the two of us. "I cannot carry the Grand Councilor's son by myself, and you can hardly carry yourself."

It was true.

"And what if he's seen?" I asked. "If it would be dangerous to see the seal, surely seeing the prince himself would be worse."

Garreth motioned at me and nodded.

Dawn straightened her arm, the soiled cloak dangling from the crook in her elbow like the skin of an animal. Garreth wrinkled his nose at the fabric, but, after one glance at her, he took the cloak and threw it over his own shoulders.

He gave a grand effort to straighten his legs and his back so he could stand over Dawn, but his body refused, tightening against the force. He collapsed back with a grunt against the side of the well.

"I don't chase after horses in the middle of the night." Garreth's attempt at indignation fell into the darkness of the well. A slight desperation crept into his voice. "I need to rest until the stiffness goes away. The horse will be fine."

"I'm not concerned for the horse," Dawn said, taking me by the elbow and guiding me to the other side of Marion. She lifted one of his arms over her shoulder and motioned for me to do the same with the other arm. "Imagine that a horse with the Crown's seal is found wandering around the edge of the village. How long before the entire cavalry arrives to find the horse's master?"

Dawn and I lifted Marion to his feet. His head lolled onto my shoulder and the warmth of his breath seeped into my neck. He smelled of sweat and leather. Mud clung to his cheek.

"Besides," she said as we turned our back on the speechless prince, "walking will do you good. If you rest now, your muscles will seize, and you'll be bedridden for days. Walking it off now will work some blood back into your legs."

Marion's weight was as great as a wet pelt of a bear while the compost smell of Faengsel Forest clung to his hair. Dawn and I moved slowly up the hill, steadily, my heart beating triple-time, not from the physical exertion, but from his nearness. And hers. My two greatest friends in the whole world, both of who I'd believed lost, were here. I could not have asked the goddess Kadasha for a greater gift, and yet, it was a curse. Dawn was now in danger as well. If Iranus found us here before Marion recovered, he would discover the secret healer. I doubted the tracker would simply reveal her location so the good Captain Tevya could bring her sister to be healed. Powerful healers were taken to the Sanatorium to serve the royals.

Still, their presence warmed my heart in a place that I had left for dead, hopes and dreams shut in a box and frozen in time, sealed with pain. The box was opening, and hope and joy were seeping into a dry and barren wasteland. But the danger dashed in like a flood, drowning out the gladness.

I had the Prince of Tuleves and the Grand Councilor's son. I had found Dawn. Iranus the Tracker had my brother, my signal, and my scent. I would lead him to his prize.

CHAPTER 18

MARION'S HEAD shifted slightly with the rise of the street. His lips turned toward my face. I had to turn away. I imagined touching those lips again. I could almost hear his voice in my ear.

We reached the step to Dawn's hut. It was not the place we would set him down. "You can release him now," she said. There was no question.

She knew. She spoke of the spark that I was taking, that I held to keep his heart slow and his bleeding to a minimum. I barely realized I still held it.

I relaxed, releasing the small but steady pull, unable to return the energy I'd stolen. Marion's heart quickly accessed its own spark, speeding up with stronger and stronger beats. He groaned as we squeezed through the doorway. His head lifted off my shoulder. A small wet spot of drool soiled my already dirty robes. Not attractive, but the small imperfection made my lips twitch, a rebellious smile, like a twelve-year-old with a crush.

"Where am I?" His voice was groggy. "What happened?"

We entered the main room of the hut. It was bare of furniture except for a single rocking chair in the middle of the room, two shelves, and a small cooking stove. Other than a few pots and pans, the shelves were covered with medicine, herbs, healing stones, and powders of all different colors in glass jars. I could see no actual food.

Marion's legs flexed as he took his own weight. I slipped out from under his arm, but Dawn continued to guide him to a smaller doorway off to the side.

"You're in my hut." She was calming, confident, the way I remembered her talking to small animals she had saved from the field and forest around the house. "You are safe here."

The doorway was bare, covered only by a hanging blanket. She pulled the blanket back to reveal a tiny space with a cot, barely enough room for someone to stand in the floor space between the cot and the walls.

She had so little. When Dawn lived with us, we shared a bedroom larger than this entire hut. Our beds were feather and our pillows down. Our food was brought to us on trays when Mother hunted into the morning and Father had already started working in his shop.

I often slept in after hunting with Mother most of the night, then worked with Father in the afternoons. Dawn would wait patiently for me to finish my chores, never complaining, often finding paints or clay to entertain herself. She never showed interest in hunting or bow making, but the free hours we had in the evening between dinner and sunset were always filled with laughter and adventure. When she began classes in the evening I missed her company. Marion had filled that void.

Father and Mother had made sure she never wanted for anything then. Now I could see the thinness in the fabric of her homespun, but clean dress. Her cheeks were slightly sunken, her skin pale in the lantern light that stole into the room through the still open door.

Dawn tried to gently lay Marion onto the cot.

He resisted, turning and leaning toward the door. "Where's Garreth? Did he run off into the forest? I need to go after him." He gripped his middle where the coat still pressed against his wound. When he pulled his hand away, it was red with fresh blood.

I slipped through the door to help Dawn get him to lie down.

"Be still," I said and succeeded in getting him to sit on the cot. "He did not leave you in the forest. He helped bring you here."

"He did?" Marion sounded doubtful. "He's afraid of the animals.

He doesn't know the prophecy. The beasts of legends will rise. The immortals' time will come to an end."

"That's not a prophecy," I said. I hadn't realized he'd studied beyond the legends. "Kadasha is our immortal, and she watches over us from Helefount."

Marion met my eyes again. "I saw a bounder. Garreth tried to shoot it. Can you believe that?"

I nodded, not able to find my voice with him so close. Dawn didn't answer. Her head was tilted to the side; her eyes half closed like she was listening to something. She stepped from the small room and leaned against the stove.

"Yes," I said. My face had ended up much too close to his as I tried to get him to relax. Instead, he tried to stand up again.

He succeeded in getting to his feet, pinning me between his chest and the doorframe as he collapsed with exhaustion. "You saved us from the scarlett. And then. . . nothing." He put his hand to his head. "Why don't I remember anything?"

"You're okay," I said. "You're suffering from. . ." The truth was he was suffering the effects of me draining his spark. It could either leave someone lethargic or give them a surge of adrenaline as their body tried to recover. He was obviously in the second category. His chest was toned; his arms muscled. His neck flexed as a vein twitched. "Shock," I finished lamely. "You were injured, and you've lost a lot of blood."

I used the one arm that could move in the confined space and placed it on his chest. The move felt so natural, so familiar, that I couldn't help circling my hand around his shirt. "If you lie down, I'll explain everything. I need you to relax so we can clean your wound."

He looked down, confusion still creasing his brow. I glanced at Dawn, but she paid us no attention. She dipped a cloth into a pan on the stove.

Marion looked up and found my eyes. The fog cleared from his complexion, his body relaxed, his breathing evened out. He lifted one hand and placed it over my own, the one on his chest. He didn't seem to be aware of the small space we were trapped in or the fact that we were only a hair's breadth apart. He leaned his head forward until our noses nearly touched.

There was no air in the room. His body squished the breath out of my lungs as he pressed me more firmly against the doorframe. I couldn't take in air to protest, not because I was hurting or the pressure was so great I couldn't manage. It was his nearness, the bright hope that burned behind his face as he studied my eyes. His hand came forward, brushed the side of my hood. I knew I should stop him, protest, kick his legs out from under him and take him down, but I was frozen with a deep desire I had never imagined feeling again.

He pulled my mask down. "Arianna."

I had been exposed.

CHAPTER 19

MY CONFIDENCE DRAINED OUT of me with my features exposed.
My true identity on display. I glanced at Dawn who had stopped stirring
the pot on the stove. Her lips turned up on the edges. Her eyes softened.
"It's good to see you again, my friend." There was no evidence of
surprise.

"You knew it as me?"

"I've always known you would knock on my door someday." The
smile kept up into something real, something brighter. Despite her
words, there was a part of her that was sad this was the someday I
knocked on her door. "The outfit was a surprise, though."

"I'd recognize your eyes anywhere." Marion still leaned against me.
His words slurring with a delirium build of pain and exhaustion. "Of
course, I knew it was you." He acted as if I hadn't been addressing
someone else. Dawn let out a breathy laugh and pulled her pot from the
stove, pouring the contents over some green leaves in a bowl.

I tried to shift Marion so he would stumble back toward the bed,
but his attention was riveted on me, and my efforts were like wind
against stone.

"I've missed you." He mumbled the words so that his chest rumbled
from the vibrations. His lips were inches from mine.

"I . . . I missed you, too." The depth of that truth resonated through me, a secret I hadn't been able to speak for a year. I thought for a moment he would kiss me right there in front of Dawn, but he looked into my eyes for another moment before pulling back.

"Things have changed." He gripped his side. "I've pledged my life to protecting the prince. Helping him . . ." His words died for a moment. Then a shallow breath. "Means everything."

Before I could response, his weight increased against me and his head sagged forward. I didn't have the strength to hold him up as his eyelids fluttered and his strength seeped out of him.

"Did you do it again?" Dawn approached us, a wet cloth and the bowl of steaming mixture in her hands.

"No." I grunted as I shifted to aim his weight backward, letting the cot catch him in the knees so he could sink down to the bed. It wasn't as graceful as I would have liked, his head bouncing off the wall twice before I could get him situated. "He ran out of adrenaline."

Dawn nodded. "Remove the belt and the coat and then take his shirt off."

I had helped Orblee many times and this was no different. Shouldn't be any different. I refused to notice the lines of Marion's muscles perfected from a soldier's workout; his arms larger, biceps curved and solid as I removed his leather armor. I refused to stare at his jaw, his lips, or his thick eyelashes that I used to run the tip of my finger over after he would kiss me. I pulled his shirt, stained with dried blood, over his head, then washed the blood from his stomach, focusing on the gash in his side where the arrow had pierced.

Garreth had done a decent job of removing the arrow without tearing more skin, but the arrowhead had been wide and fat to inflict damage even if the shot was clumsy. It hadn't been the small sliver heads I used to pierce an animal's skin with accuracy enough to cut a single vein.

Dawn worked beside me, her movements confident as she pressed her fingers into the wound. I continued to clear away the blood. Our shoulders brushed, our breaths matched each other's in the silence. I could stand it no longer.

"This is where you've been? This is where I could not follow?"

She gave a curt nod. "We both had a journey to travel. I know that yours was hard."

"Yours doesn't look like it was much easier." I hissed the words. My anger flared despite the fact that she had had little choice when the soldiers came. She could have hidden with us or been arrested with my father. I hadn't lived a life better than this. An outcast in a poor village, robbing caravans at night and pretending to help people during the day. Still, I would have done anything to have her with me. "We could have faced it together." I picked at the wet cloth. "I missed you."

There was a beat of silence and then her cheek rose with her sideways smile. "Life has been a bit boring. It's about time you showed up and brought some excitement."

"It might not be the kind of excitement you want."

"Trouble follows you like a hungry tracker. Can you blame me for avoiding that for a little bit?" She pulled her fingers up; a tiny shard of arrowhead pinched between her two fingers. Even Orblee would not have been able to do that without her triple thick looking glass and a pair of tweezers.

Marion gasped, his eyes opening. I moved to his head to hold him still. I didn't have a response for Dawn. Guilt ate at me. She didn't even know how true her words were. I focused on the patient. The man beneath our fingers.

Dawn took the rag and dipped it, wiping the wound clean and pulling a thread and needle from a bag beside her. "Distract him."

I pulled both of his hands across his chest, leaning on them to keep him from flailing. Our faces were inches away again. I let the weight of my body hold his hands and moved my fingers to the sides of his face. "Just look at me. I'm right here. It will be over soon."

He flinched as Dawn inserted the first stitch, but his eyes stayed glued on mine. "They told me you died, that you were in the manor when it burned. I thought you were gone."

"Burned?" I remembered fire, the sensation of needing to run, burning from the inside as the fire consumed the room around me. I remembered my arm pressed against Jaimeson's neck. It was a blur, an unfinished painting. I couldn't remember exactly how we got out to the leather tanning shed. I couldn't remember anything until the moment Iranus killed my mother.

"No. I wasn't burned with the house."

"Where have you been?" He asked the question I couldn't answer.

"I had to run. I stayed hidden after my father was arrested."

"Your father was arrested?"

"For tax evasion. Do you know of his fate?"

Marion flinched as Dawn pushed the needle into his skin again. "I'm sorry. I did not hear of his arrest, only that the home burned with the family inside. I was devastated that I'd lost you."

When I looked away, he tried to sit up. I pushed him back down and changed the subject.

"Tell me about the army," I said. "When did you decide to enlist? I thought you wanted to be a politician. Sit on the council."

His flinches stopped, but Dawn still pricked his skin over and over behind me.

"I couldn't assign boys to a draft or send a legion to the border, if I didn't understand, if I had never experienced it. And you were gone. The risk seemed worth taking. You're more beautiful than I remember." I wondered if the pain and loss of energy made him drunk, saying things he didn't mean.

"I thought you'd hate me for running."

"I hated you for dying. Maybe I hate you for letting me think you had died. But I'm too tired to be mad. I thought I'd never see you again."

"It doesn't matter now, does it? There's a reason you lied. A reason you never told me who your father was."

Dawn tugged the final knot tight. "All done. He needs his rest."

I stood, but Marion caught my hands as they left his face. "Don't leave me again." His words were slurred, his eyes unfocused again.

"I'm not leaving." It wasn't a promise. I couldn't form the words correctly. He was the son of the Grand Councilor, not Marion, my childhood sweetheart. "Not yet."

"I will take care of things here," she said. "You're needed elsewhere."

"Elsewhere?" A pulse of desire shot through me, to run, escape, but I pushed it back. There was nowhere else I wanted to be in this moment, close to Marion, next to Dawn. Two people I had loved and lost. Despite the urge to run, I didn't want to leave.

She only gave a grunt of confirmation. The cot creaked as she coaxed Marion to a more relaxed position.

"Take your bow and put your mask back on," she said. "The Prince of Tuleves has run into some trouble."

CHAPTER 20

THE VOICES CAME from a grove of trees a stone's throw from the main path.

I'd left Dawn's hut quickly after Marion had tried to rise, insisting he come with me to help. Despite his exhaustion and pain, he'd been determined. Dawn had used an herb to calm him, but he'd still looked at me with desperation.

"Promise me you'll help him."

What else could I do? I'd promised. I'd promised the son of the Grand Councilor that I would help the Prince of Tuleves. I'd come a long way from robbing caravans.

I turned right at the well. There were signs of shod hoof-prints. Marion's obvious trail followed behind. He wasn't even trying to cover his tracks.

The grove of trees blocked my view but provided cover. It would be difficult to approach without disturbing the bushes. I could have climbed a sturdy branch on a gnarled old tree that twisted into the grove at an upward angle, but I was starting to feel like I was half marmaton. Marion had once tried to make a pet of the child-sized hairy creature.

I was sick of climbing trees, so instead, I crawled on my belly, keeping my bow and an arrow in front of me as I slid along the ground like a caterpillar.

Garreth had run into trouble. How Dawn had known I wasn't sure, but it had probably been a safe bet. He had crossed paths with a Burgher Squad, men hired to protect small villages on account of their deformities as much as their ability to fight. Since soldiers were reserved for the borders or the cities and suburbs of Tuleves, smaller towns and villages often had to find their own ways to keep the peace.

Burgher Squads, desperate men that had nowhere else to go, were paid with a place to sleep and food to eat, and few received more than that. There were three men in the clearing surrounded by trees. A fresh spring trickled between the roots, explaining the circular grove.

One man held a lantern on a pole, casting a ghastly glow. The light revealed distorted features, a chin stretched and scarred, a nose twisted into a cheek, eyes misaligned. He leaned over Garreth, who was on his knees, hands held behind his back by a second man. A third, the tallest of the three men, held the reins of the horse. He wasn't just taller than other men, his head would have been level with someone mounted on the horse. He was skinny, his arms like willow branches, and his neck seemed stretched so thin it could barely support his head.

If the third man was the branches, the first was the trunk, as solid and stocky as a stone wall. His features made me cringe. He leaned in toward the prince, one eye rolling out of control. His breath, fogged from cold, reached Garreth's eyelashes.

"We found the horse first."

"I think we've all outgrown the finders keepers, losers weepers mentality of children." The calm in the prince's voice surprised me. I don't think even I could have maintained my calm in that situation.

"Children," said the second man who had Garreth's hands pinned behind his back. "Are often the wisest of us all." He pulled Garreth's elbows up in an awkward, painful way. Garreth hissed but didn't cry out.

"True," he said. "So true. Someone should tell the council we could solve all the kingdom's problems if we let a couple of kids advise them."

The three men shifted without smiles, impervious to Garreth's dry humor.

Still, the situation didn't bode well for me. The prince was my collateral, and I needed the horse to come as well, being evidence of the prince's identity and location. The problem was these weren't soldiers. These were my people. Outcasts. Wanderers. Maybe even outlaws.

If Jaimeson had taught me anything, it was that there were other ways to negotiate. I checked to make sure my mask was back in place, my heart warming at the memory of Marion's fingers brushing my cheek. I wanted to suck the energy from my own heart. I had grown up in the last year, far more than I should have. I was beyond childish romance. This was no time to get distracted.

"What should we do with him?" asked the tree-like man. His fingers twitched nervously around the horse's reins.

"That's a simple answer," Garreth said. I would have smacked his arrogant mouth if I hadn't been on my belly ten handspans away. "You hand over my property and send me on my way with a little wine and cheese."

"Your *property*?" The man who held Garreth had one wooden leg and arms as thick a cathedral pillar. "Are you claiming to own this horse?" His suspicion raised my hackles. They had seen the insignia on the saddle. If Garreth claimed to be the owner and exposed himself as the Prince of Tuleves, these men would not hesitate to throw him into the Haltic Sea with a boulder tied to his waist. The people feared the council, but everyone hated the rebellious, spoiled son of the missing king.

Garreth wore Dawn's cloak which covered his lace and frills. His face was haggard and dirty, and his hair stuck to his head, slick with sweat from the ride. It would probably take his own mother to recognize him.

"In a certain sense of the word," Garreth said, his voice more careful, hesitant. Even he must have felt the charge in the air. "I went through a lot of work to get this horse and have earned the right of claim."

The man as thick as a tree trunk thumped Garreth on the back of the head. "Are you saying you *acquired* the personal horse of the prince?"

Peg-Leg loosened his grip on Garreth's shoulders. Fools. All of them. They played their hand too early. Even the inexperienced royal could tell what the men wanted to hear.

Garreth added a poor imitation of a back country accent. My eyes rolled as he overplayed his hand. "That's right. I caught myself a horse while the prince's back was turned. Borrowed it right out from under his nose."

"Do you work in the stables in Tuleves?" asked the willowy man who swayed like long branches in a strong wind.

"No." Garreth pulled against the man holding him so he could use his hands to tell the story. Peg-Leg relented but touched a rusty sword tied to his waist by a strip of cloth. "Haven't you heard the prince is at it again? On the run. Got the whole castle guard and the city sentry on his tail. And guess who found him first? Yours truly. Took his horse while he relieved himself behind a tree."

It was time to save the prince from himself. I prepared to rise as the peg-leg man spoke. His words turned my insides to ice.

"So that's what the tracker was after."

All my senses went on high alert. There was only one tracker who demanded that kind of reverence. Iranus had already come to the village. He'd come possibly before I'd left my sign. I hadn't been watching for his trail in the dark. I had let down my guard, giving in to surprise at finding Dawn, distracted caring for Marion. There was no way Iranus could have already delivered my brother to Tuleves and returned. I was sure I had at least another day. He must still have him with him.

Iranus had had a half-day head start. With a horse he would have had to stay to the roads, riding toward Renathath. I could not imagine when or how Iranus had come through this village. Perhaps they spoke of another tracker.

Either way, I needed to get the drop on the tracker, and when I did, I needed the Prince of Tuleves to be in my control, not with this Burgher Squad.

I took a quick sweep of as much as the landscape as I could see. The fact that the shadows were becoming more defined told me the eastern sky would be lined with the light blue of morning soon. The night was almost over.

"The tracker?" Garreth sounded as concerned as I felt, but there was no reason for that. He was the Prince of Tuleves. The worst thing that would happen to him was to be dragged back to his luxurious chambers and forced to eat a seven-course meal. "You saw him here? In the village?"

"He will be interested in speaking with you," said Peg-Leg. The more he spoke, the more I recognized him as the leader. "If you were the last person to see his quarry."

"It has been a pleasure, but I think it is time I went on my way." Garreth stood and reached for the reins.

The three men moved with precision and speed as if of one mind. Peg-Leg's pillar-sized arm seized Garreth around the neck, the willowy man aimed a knife at Garreth's gut, and the trunk-like man pulled a crossbow from under his cloak and pointed it between the prince's eyes.

Chapter 21

Only Garreth could raise the tension level to the extreme so quickly. My promise to Jaimeson nagged at me. Father believed all people were worth saving. Personally, I wouldn't have lost sleep over the loss if a spoiled prince, but somehow, I saw him as more than that now.

I pushed to my feet and stood directly behind the leader, releasing two arrows less than a breath apart, hitting the crossbow Trunk held and the dagger blade the willow-man had held. I hit the metal on both pieces, sending them flipping into the brush. The horse flinched as my arrow just missed its haunches. My second arrow that hit the dagger had whizzed past Peg-Leg's ear. To his credit, his grip only tightened on Garreth's neck. He turned slowly, swiveling on the point of his wooden leg.

"What have we here?" Peg-Leg's features came into view. A hardened warrior's jaw, eyes cold from seeing too much death, and a soldier's scar where the king marked his infantry above the eyebrow. With all that, he wasn't far past his twenties. The young man had been cast aside and abandoned after giving his loyalty and losing his leg in the name of the king.

"I'm sorry to interrupt," I said, part of me sincere. Garreth tried to say something when he saw me, but he could only sputter and choke with the pressure of the arm on his neck. It was good for the Prince of Tuleves to taste his own humility. Again. I wondered if he would have any pride left by the time he was returned to the castle.

I kept my voice low and gravely. "But I believe we have some things in common. While we'd all love to have a horse, it would be difficult to trade such a fine animal without raising suspicions, and even harder to ride her around without turning a few royal heads. I could leave you with a more usable prize if you'd be willing to leave me the boy and the horse."

"It's him!" To my surprise, Trunk, the man who'd lost his crossbow, only had a look of confusion for a moment. He leaned forward, tapping Peg-Leg's shoulder like a young boy vying for the attention of his distracted mother. "It's the Hooded Robber."

It felt as if the time had been sucked from the grove as surprise paused everything. I forgot to draw breath. Even Garreth stopped struggling and sputtering, looking at me with new interest.

Willow Tree stepped forward with a flourish, going down on one knee in front of me. "I owe you more than my thanks. You saved my daughter as well as my wife. It is an honor to meet you in person."

"I've saved no one." I almost forgot to keep the squeak out of my voice. I was a thief, an outlaw. I'd only wanted to survive. To make it to Helefount to ask for a gifting. I had never met this man or his daughter.

"My nephew avoided arrest earlier this year." Trunk stepped forward, his crossbow forgotten. "Thanks to you."

The glowing gratitude in the man's face made me step back. There was no enemy that could intimidate me with my bow in hand, but this, the adoration, made me want to melt away and puddle under a rock. It was the choking noises from Garreth that reminded me why I wasn't running.

"Not. . . he. . ." Garreth's face was red, but even as he fought for breath there was an air of disregard, like even with a pillar wrapped around his neck like a snake, holding him on his knees. He was still better than me.

"You want this boy?" asked Peg-Leg.

"And the horse."

Peg-Leg paused only a moment, then he flicked his shoulder forward and released the prince's neck. Garreth fell, rolling until he hit my feet. He coughed, staying on his knees to catch his breath. He tried to say something, but I stepped on his hand and his words turned into a grunt.

"This may bring more trouble than you bargained for," Peg-Leg said. "He has Iranus the Tracker on his trail. That man is more persistent than a bloodthirsty hunting hound and more heartless than the council. If he is anywhere near this boy, I would run the other way. You do not want to cross scents with the tracker no matter how good your reputation is. Or perhaps because it is so great."

The way Peg-Leg spoke with such logic and sincerity reminded me of my father and his lectures. He was always telling Dawn and me to act with more caution. *No one ever died from too much wisdom. The two of you would do well to acquire some.*

Garreth managed to pull his hand from under my boot but had the intelligence to stay silent.

"How did you get help from me?" I asked.

"The healer Orblee gave me money to purchase an herb only available at the Sanatorium."

"That would have cost a fortune," I said, disbelieving.

"We had to pay a bribe as well as for the medicine, but my Ella would have died without it. Everyone knows Orblee helps in your name. She shows us your extreme generosity."

"I steal it," I said.

"And give it to those in need." The willow-tree man refused to see reason. I had robbed caravans in an act of defiance, attempting to right the scales of justice, but never believing I actually could. I guess I hadn't realized how much we had collected over the last year. "The council doesn't realize that no reward will be enough for the common folk to turn you in. You've done too much."

I blinked to give myself a moment to think. The pressure of my eyelids held back the emotion that was building there. I had done something that made a difference. Without a gifting. The realization should have been relieving, exciting. Instead, the urge to run only intensified. I wasn't who he thought I was.

Peg-Leg held up his hand, offering me the reins. "Take him and go. Be careful."

"Thank you," I said. I bent over to help Garreth to his feet. He was still recovering his breath.

The horse tossed its head, ears laid back. A tingling sensation lifted the hairs on the back of my neck. Someone else was coming.

I barely had time to grab Garreth by his frilly collar and roll us under the bushes as Iranus the Tracker pushed his horse through the branches.

I ended up on top of the prince, his breathing still raspy. I covered his mouth to stifle the sound. I blinked, not wanting to believe my eyes. Iranus had found us already.

"Gentlemen." His voice grated on my nerves enough to make me shiver. Garreth hadn't moved, his eyes toward the clearing. I hadn't stopped to contemplate his motivations for avoiding the tracker, but he seemed as determined as I was. "We meet again. This seems an odd place for the village patrol."

Willow Tree and Trunk shifted their feet. Peg-Leg didn't move.

"We found something interesting," said Peg-Leg, his voice calm, soft. I was impressed with his wisdom in dealing with the tracker. "Perhaps it has something to do with what you are searching for."

I couldn't see above their ankles, but their feet shifted enough for me to know they'd turned to look at the horse. Peg-Leg was using the horse as a distraction from us. I didn't dare move, though my limbs were aching to run. When I planned on meeting the tracker, I wanted it to be on my terms, with three escape routes and a dozen backup plans. From the glimpses I got through the leaves, Iranus was on the horse alone. Jaimeson wasn't there. I couldn't use Garreth as a trade without my brother here.

"Yes, I thought I smelled the prince down this road," Iranus said, "but he is hard to smell over the stink of the three of you. Were you hoping to take the horse for yourselves? Try to sell it?"

"The only way this horse would benefit us is if we fed our families with it," said Trunk, more impulsive than Peg-Leg. "We found it here getting a drink. We were going to return it for a reward."

"I don't think this horse will lead you to the prince," said Willow Tree, his voice shuddering like branches in a gale. "It was brought to our town by a thief. We scared him so badly he ran off without the horse. We'd be happy to help you hunt him down."

My proximity to Garreth was uncomfortable, especially when he turned his head toward me and our noses nearly pressed together. I slid my hand from his face, putting one finger to my lips for him to be quiet. His response was to roll his eyes. I tried to slide off him, but his arms tightened around me, pinching me to him. He kept his eyes on mine, shaking his head slightly.

"Is that so?" Iranus asked. "A thief brought the horse, but you found it drinking water?"

There was no sound from the men, but I hoped there was nodding. Then I heard the long, slow sniffing that I had come to associate with Iranus. He made a high, barely audible whistle as he sucked in air. My skin went cold.

There was the whirr and thunk of a boleadora and Willow Tree fell to his knees, the boleadora wrapped around his neck. The thick rope with the heavy balls on both ends of the string cut into the skin. Willow Tree folded over, his head nearly touching the ground, grappling at the strings cutting into his windpipe.

Peg-Leg drew his sword, but it fell to the ground as a throwing knife hit flesh. Iranus would show these men no mercy.

"Tell me another lie, and it will be last time you use your tongue."

I couldn't stay hidden. Mother had taught to me be invisible while hunting, but never to let others take a hit for me. *Stand up for others and you will find you never stand alone.*

I only had one advantage, and he was holding me like he thought he could keep me safe. Like I was the one who needed protecting. Well, hopefully the shock of what I was about to do next would keep his mouth shut.

Pulling a dagger from my boot, I rolled back into the clearing, pulling Garreth with me. I used his weight to twist myself around. When I came to a rest facing Iranus, I pressed my dagger Garreth's throat.

CHAPTER 22

"I'VE GOT what you want right here." I held my dagger steady, but it shifted as Garreth swallowed. "And I'm willing to make a trade."

Iranus dismounted, the furs coving his horse's back shivered, droplets of water cascading to the ground.

"This didn't work out for you so well last time."

"I've brought you exactly what you want," I said. "Let these men go and we'll discuss the life of the prince."

"There is no bounty on these men's heads." Iranus never looked away from Garreth and I like he was afraid we would disappear in a cloud of smoke. "I have what I want right in front of me and they've been punished for their lies. They're free to go."

"He *is* the prince." Trunk helped Peg-Leg to his feet. "Right in front of us the whole time."

Willow Tree unwrapped the boleadora, but stayed on his hands and knees, coughing. "I knew it. Not a thief at all."

"Take him to the healer," I said. Peg-Leg had been hit below the collarbone. It would be fatal if he didn't get help quickly. Willow-tree and Trunk lifted Peg-Leg between them and moved out of the clearing. They only hesitated a moment on the edge of the brush to see if Iranus would call them back, but his attention was entirely focused on me.

"You think you can bargain with me?" Iranus asked, flipping a throwing knife up in the air. He dared not throw it. I had Garreth in front of me. I crouched behind him so that barely the top of my head was exposed. He knew I was fast enough to dodge his knife and put Garreth's pretty face in the way instead.

"Where's my brother?" I asked. "I will give you the prince unharmed in exchange for my brother's freedom."

"I left your brother abandoned without food or drink on the edge of the Cracked Plains." He flicked the knife even higher, as if daring my gaze to follow it into the air. "But if I had the gifting of time, I would predict that he's already found his way to the dungeons of Tuleves." If I had had both hands free, I could have drawn my bow and knocked the knife from the sky.

"You wouldn't just leave him. He stole the blood jewels."

"Only the Hooded Robber has been blamed for that. Now I have two prizes right in front of me. The other one is missing. I saw a trail of blood. Perhaps you've found a healer here with extraordinary strength."

The cold truth seeped into me like blood soaking into the ground during a battle. Iranus had killed my mother. Taken my brother. Threatened my friend. I had failed everyone. My only chance now was to run while Iranus captured Garreth. If I ran fast enough, I might be able to warn Dawn.

I threw my dagger just as Iranus tossed his throwing knife again. He had reflexes like a wildcat, almost as fast as me, and shifted to the side to let the dagger go by. I had not been aiming for Iranus, but for what was just behind him. My heart fell to my toes as Iranus' horse screamed.

The tracker cursed.

I turned and ran. The last thing I expected was for Garreth to follow right on my heels.

"What are you doing?" I hissed as we ran out of the grove and up the hill.

"I've been avoiding that guy for days," Garreth said. "I'm not ready to go home yet."

"He has your smell," I said. "There's nowhere to hide."

Another horse neighed. Iranus had mounted Garreth's horse. I pulled an arrow from my quiver and stopped running. I turned and went down on one knee. I pressed the tip of the arrow against my lips and pulled with all of my sorrow. I sucked in what felt like the whole world, the pain of losing Father and Mother, the anger of imagining Jaimeson behind bars in a filthy cell. Marion wounded. Dawn hunted by the tracker. The arrow turned a frozen blue, glowing in the gray light of dawn.

I nocked the arrow just as Iranus burst out of the clearing. I aimed for the fur on his shoulder and released. The arrow flew true and caught Iranus to the left of his neck, catching onto his fur coat and burying itself into the trunk of the tree behind him.

The horse kept running, but Iranus fell back, stuck to the arrow. Then the cold spread. From the arrow, down the trunk of the tree, up Iranus's neck, through his chest, down his fur-lined pants, all the way down to the tips of his boots. The pain blossomed in my chest and spread through my body the same way the ice spread over the tracker's face.

He froze over, completely encased in ice.

"How long will that last?" Garreth asked.

"I don't know," I said. "I've never done that to an enemy before."

"I suppose you have a lot," he said as casually as if he'd remarked on the cloudless sky.

"Have a lot of what?" I asked.

"Enemies." He smiled. It was silly. Poorly timed. And ridiculously childish. I couldn't help smiling back.

"I have a few, I suppose."

"Let's get back to Marion," he said.

"We can't," I said, grabbing his sleeve. "He will follow us there. We have to leave, get as far away from this place as possible. We can't lead Iranus to. . . the village."

Garreth paused. "Or Marion?" He looked at me skeptically. "Are you always this altruistic? What is your angle in all of this?"

"My angle?" I had just tried to bargain his life for my brother's. "I was going to trade you."

"After you saved our lives?" he said. "And helped all those men's families?"

I turned away from him. He didn't know what he was talking about. "That wasn't me." That had been the Hooded Robber.

A movement caught my eye. Iranus's hands, stretched out reaching for us even as he froze, were starting to twitch. The first rays of the sun touched the tips of Iranus's fingers as it rose above the mountains. The light glistened on frozen branches.

"Come on," I said. "We're out of time. Let's catch that cursed horse and get as far from here as we can."

"What if we just make him think we left?" Garreth asked.

"He can smell us if we stay. It doesn't matter where we hide."

Garreth gave a shrill whistle, and his horse came up the rise onto the road. He grabbed its reins and patted its nose. "Shhh. It's alright. It's time to go home."

"I'm going to need your clothes," he said. He pulled off Dawn's cloak and then tugged at the collar of his frilly shirt, shrugging it over his head.

"Over my dead body." I hugged myself like my cloak was more than just a source of warmth. It was. It was my protection. My shield. My safe place.

"That's a little dramatic. I don't need all of them. Just your costume. If it comes to a choice between your cloak and your life, would you really choose that unflattering piece of cloth?"

Garreth tied the sleeves of his shirt around the horn of the saddle and then put his hand out expectantly toward me. The sun's light bounced off his bronze skin, his muscles smaller than Marion's but toned and flattering. Goosebumps rose on his arms and chest. It was colder now than it had been when it was dark.

A cracking sound echoed through the valley. Iranus's arm flexed making a fissure through the ice. Garreth pulled me down into the ditch and ran along the side of the road until Iranus was out of sight. "It's now or never."

I pulled off my cloak, my mask still attached to the hood and handed it to Garreth. Our hands met as he took the coat, He paused, staring at me, at my exposed face.

"You're not an escaped, indentured servant or a runaway boy," he said. "I was wrong. You are the real Hooded Robber. And he's a girl. I mean you are. A girl." His words had a slight hint of something I had never expected to hear. Admiration.

I turned away and tied the cloak to the back of the saddle with a strap of leather.

Garreth slapped the horse on the rump. He grabbed my hand and pulled me in the opposite direction the horse was running. We were headed back toward the village.

I realized why I had felt so bad when the men had thanked me for my actions. I hid behind a mask to right the scales of justice. I deserved no thanks. Now, I'd sent my mask off on the back of a horse. Like this, as Arianna, I had no power. The scales would stay unbalanced.

CHAPTER 23

"Our own smells are much stronger than a couple of pieces of clothes." I wished for the shadows of night to return. We were off the road and out of sight of the place I'd left Iranus, but I felt exposed. I had not Hooded Robber mask. I wore a simple tunic with loose pants. I'd wanted a gifting, not to be remarkable, but to be able to be useful. The mask had given me that and I'd never realized how much I had grown to depend on it.

"Not if he can't smell us at all." Garreth's muscles worked as he ran. I kept my eyes on the road. Seeing him exposed like this made him feel less royal. His fingers still held my hand. "I did some research before we left. There is one way to cover your smell from Iranus the Tracker. Come on. I saw a graveyard outside the village."

"A graveyard?" This plan sounded worse than Jaimeson's. "We don't have time to dig a hole and bury ourselves. And he could still smell us through six feet of dirt."

"But not over six rotting bodies."

I didn't have a response. My mind flashed back to the night a year ago Jaimeson and I hid in Father's leather tannery. Uncared for in the weeks leading up to the raid, it was full of the smell of rotting meat.

Small, dark shapes lined up in rows came into view. Grave markers, most of them simple crossed sticks, tied at the center with a vine or rope. I touched my chest as I ran. A dull, throbbing pain remained. I hadn't had a chance to look at the small tattoo, but a part of me knew it was growing.

"We are out of time," I said, desperately, tugging against his grip on my wrist. "This won't work."

He led me toward a building in the center of the graveyard, larger than Dawn's hut, built with more care. It was a charnel house, the place bodies were kept before burial. During a plague, charnel houses could fill up completely before anyone got around to burying them. In good times, there were usually two or three deceased waiting on a proper burial. The dead were always buried on Oplana, the first day of the week.

I pulled myself free. "We have to lead him away from the village."

Garreth turned, moving faster than I expected and gripped me by the shoulders, not hard, but with a firm pressure used to calm a frightened child. "It will work. Trust me."

His eyes were the light royal green of the ruling line. I had not noticed the color of his eyes until now. Marion's were brown, as deep as a well, always simmering with thoughts. Garreth's were clear I felt like I could see to the bottom of his soul. It could be that his eyes exposed his shallowness.

I didn't trust him, but it didn't matter now. Either this worked or it didn't. I nodded.

The door to the charnel house was latched but not locked. We opened it and slipped inside. Garreth used a small stick to pull the latch back in place.

The smell was awful. Several bodies were laid out on bunk style shelving on the walls. There were enough planks to stack the bodies six high. The two lowest shelves were full of bodies all the way to the back of the building, probably a dozen in total. It had been a while since someone had come to bury them.

I covered my nose and sent Garreth a glare that could have burned holes in his skin.

"This is your grand idea?" I asked. "Sit somewhere that smells worse than you and assume that it will confuse Iranus the Tracker? He's discovered people in places that smell far worse than this."

He wrapped his arms around himself and rubbed his arms, the first sign he'd given that the cold was bothering him.

"It's not the smell," he said, stuttering on the letters as he shivered. "There's an herb they rub on the building wherever there is a good healer. It blocks the smell of the rotting flesh and any other smell inside the doors. I read about it in an old history book."

A good healer. Dawn was the healer of this village. He had met her for barely an instant and he was already betting his life on her.

Morning light chased the shadows of the charnel house back into the corners. I had expected it to stay dark, but there were vents in the roof that allowed the heat of rotting bodies out and slanted rays of light in. The smell remained trapped. My anger was tempered by my surprise as I imaged the prince reading an old historic tomb.

"History?" I asked. "Something you do in your free time?"

"It was illegal, of course," he said. "I only read books that have been b-b-banned." He smiled at his stutter. He smiled way too easily. "It's a lot easier to stay warm when you have to keep moving."

"Don't look at me," I said. "You took my cloak." I gagged a little when I forgot to breathe through my mouth. The smell of rot and decay filled the room, making it feel like a prison, not a haven. "Here." I threw an old blanket at him from an empty shelf. The blanket smelled of dust and mold, but at least it didn't have a rotting corpse underneath it.

Garreth wrapped the blanket around his shoulders. "It's big enough for two. It will take a couple hours before Iranus follows the horse far enough for our smell to be less than the clothes. You look cold."

I'm sure I did. I was hugging myself the best I could while keeping one hand over my nose. It wasn't easy, but there was no way I was sharing a blanket with the spoiled, not-so-shabby-looking, tougher-than-I-thought Prince of Tuleves. He leaned toward me. I backed up and hit a shelf with a man who'd been dead at least a week. The whole body shifted, sending out a new wave of odor. I could taste it as well as smell it.

Garreth's smile had melted, curiosity replacing it, making his light green eyes deepen to almost blue. "Do I know you? You seem so. . . familiar."

"Nope," I said, spinning away so I wasn't pinned between him and the dead bodies. "I'm not from Tuleves and I haven't been there in years." Not a lie.

Garreth took a deep breath, coughed from the smell and then shrugged. He leaned against the door and slid down to the floor. "We've met somewhere, I know it. I'm just so tired I can't think straight, but it will come to me." He squinted at me one more time, even though my hand still covered my nose and most of my face.

"Here," he said, shifting against the door and pulling the blanket open to make room. "We have at least three hours before Iranus is out of sniffing range, and we can rub the herb on ourselves on our way out. I know you're as tired as I am."

The exhaustion of the last three days and the chill of night seeped through my last layer of resistance. I sat beside him but wiggled my way under the blanket, so it didn't wrap around both of us. He shifted under the blanket, and we sat back against the door, blanket pinned behind our shoulders.

He laid his head on my shoulder like a young boy might do with a friend. If he attempted to put his hands on me, I would break his fingers, but there was no other movement. No other sign of ill intent. I was about to push his head off me. I was no pillow. Then I remembered how he knew me.

We had met once before on my ninth birthday. I had been denied the gifting for the first time and after the ceremony, I escaped into the fields. I'd collapsed to the ground and was about to let my tears fall when I had heard someone else crying. A city boy, dressed in ridiculous finery, ran across our field. At nine, the surprise of seeing a strange boy crying had dried up my tears and pushed curiosity to the surface. I followed him a short way until he tripped and fell. He didn't seem to have the energy to rise, so I had knelt next to him.

"What's the matter?" I had asked.

He'd turned those light green eyes toward me, red-rimmed from tears. Now that I remembered, I don't know how I hadn't recognized it earlier.

"He let her die," the boy had said. "Father didn't even come and see her. He just let her die alone."

"Who?"

"My mother!"

The queen had died. Prince Garreth had been a sad little boy, not a royal. Not then.

All I had thought to do then was give him a biscuit from my pocket and hug him like a rag doll. He'd cried on my shoulder until Mother called me from the porch. I'd never even bothered to find out his name, but now that I knew, it meant much more.

Garreth was the Prince of Tuleves. That meant that his father was the king.

The King of Tuleves had let his wife die. Alone. And I was sure, since it had been my birthday, it was only a week before King Tyndall had left on the crusade he had never returned from.

Garreth had lost both his parents within a week's time. I hated that this royal had more in common with me than I wanted to admit.

CHAPTER 24

"I REMEMBER." I never expected to feel save in charnel house surrounded by the smell of death. But the urge to run was gone. The years melted away and I felt nine years old again. I let my cheek rest lightly against Garreth's head. My eyes closed. "We met the day your mother died."

I expected him to stiffen; to deny the moment his weakness was displayed in all its glory in front of a nine-year-old girl. But he barely moved. His lips parted and he let out a soft, "Ah. That's it."

Sleep pulled on me. We'd both been up all night, but I'd wondered since that day, and I doubted I'd get the chance to ask again. "Why? Why did your father never come? Why did he let your mother die alone?"

"Because he discovered she had the gifting of time." Garreth's head rolled so that his temple balanced on my shoulder. The back of his head rested against the wall of the charnel house. We were perfectly balanced. Holding each other up while every muscle relaxed. My heart ached at his words. Orblee had shared her secret with me. That she had the gifting of time. How cruel to make a law against a gift that couldn't be helped. No one chose their gifting.

"Did he kill her?" It was the law, but I couldn't imagine Garreth's sorrow if it had been murder. That wasn't the sorrow that I'd seen in him.

"No." Garreth tugged the blanket tighter around his neck. "She was already dying. He turned his back and did nothing to stop it. He said he'd brought a curse on Tuleves, and he had to go to Helefount and regain Kadasha's favor."

"The crusade."

"He meant to save the kingdom, but he failed to even save himself."

"I'm so sorry." I took a deep breath despite the putrid air. "That must have been so awful."

"He would have known it was pointless if he'd listened to Mother's prophecy. She told him he would never return."

"Prophecies." That word again. I scoffed. "People put so much faith in a small glimpse into the future. They could mean anything. I could tell you that you were going to die. And guess what? There is a 100% chance I'd be right."

Both our shivering had stopped. The blank was rough against my skin, but I was grateful for the warmth.

"You're a prophecy skeptic." He let out a huff of air. An attempt at a laugh with exhaustion weighing him down.

"They're always so vague and cryptic. Maybe if the Oracles had just told people what they saw in the future instead of partial explanations." I raised my voice and spoke in a squeaky impersonation of an old lady. "There will be dark times in your future. Watch out for men with long noses. Your ability to hold your tongue will save your life someday."

This time his laugh was sincere. "You didn't tell me you had the gifting of time. I've heard all those exact prophecies. Especially the one about holding my tongue. Never was able to follow that advice, but I haven't died yet."

"You agree with me?" I was surprised he hadn't argued. People either hated or revered the Oracles. No one ever let me explain my theory of vague prophecies. Especially Jaimeson. He'd wished for the Oracles to return so he could get guidance for his future. "I thought you said the Oracles were destroyed because they were manipulating the people."

"That's what kept the people from revolting. Many of them had felt the confusion of the prophecies, just like you said. But the real reason was Kadasha commanded it or she would revoke the gifting. Take them all away. My father sacrificed the Oracles to protect his people."

"You sound like you respected him."

"I did. Once." His voice changed. A closed conversation. "What about you? How in the name of the seven immortals did you become the Hooded Robber?"

"My father was arrested for tax evasion, that was the official accusation, but they destroyed everything, burnt our house to the ground. They didn't have to do that. My brother and I hid and then ran for two days. We were about to drop from exhaustion when a kind farmer took pity on us and gave us a meal. While we were there the tax collectors came. They asked for more than the farmer had and when they went to arrest him, the wife stepped between them. She was sliced through the belly. Right in front of their children. One of the children found some coin, hidden away for the replanting season. She gave it to the soldiers, and they went away, leaving the woman to bleed out on her own porch. We helped the farmer carry his wife to the nearest village. While the healer was helping the woman, I got mad. I retraced our steps, despite my two days of travel, and found the soldiers. It was night. Mother had trained me to walk silently and move unseen. I took back the money while they slept, and a few other bags of coin as well. When I returned to the village and gave the money back to the farmer, the healer, her name was Orblee, took me aside and offered Jaimeson and I a place with her. She said the people needed a thief. She made me my cloak and the mask. Jaimeson said he'd come up with better plans. We've been a team ever since."

I became the Hooded Robber. The Hooded Robber had made a difference. The Hooded Robber wasn't a helpless girl running from the tax collectors. Running from her past. From her weakness. From the feeling of helplessness I'd felt when I'd watched my mother murdered in front of my eyes.

I don't know how much of the story I made it through before we were both asleep, but I finished reliving those moments in my dreams.

CHAPTER 25

A LINE OF DESPERATE, dirty people waited outside of Dawn's hut. A woman rocked a baby back and forth with a glazed look in her eyes. She didn't even seem to have the strength to bounce the baby anymore, only hold it and keep from falling. An old man leaned on a cane; his muscles caught in a constant shake. A man held between two friends, a gash in his head that had a congealed scab, dried blood crusted on his face. All had obvious signs of needing a healer.

Garreth and I had slept part way into the morning, rising as soon as the sun had made it a third of the way into the sky. He showed me which plant hanging by the door was the correct herb, and we rubbed it on ourselves like lye soap, covering as much as our bodies and clothes as we could. We watched for Iranus on the walk back but saw no sign of him.

I wondered how Marion fared this morning. Garreth and I passed the line of people who watched us with glares and curses. Seeing the healer was a privilege earned by waiting, and we were skipping ahead. I shrugged apologetically, but, even without his coat and a ripped and bloodied shirt, Garreth gave off the impression of not waiting for anyone or anything.

He stepped up to the door and the old woman in front grabbed his arm. It was quite a sight. The prince, still wrapped in a smelly blanket, stinking of death, towered over the woman who showed no sign of intimidation.

"Wait your turn," she said, exposing a mouth with fewer teeth than ears. "We all have to wait. Isn't nothing special 'bout you, boy."

"Actually. . ." he said, puffing out his chest.

"Actually," I cut in, placing a light hand on the woman's swollen hump on her back. Orblee had a medicine for this kind of hump, but I didn't know what it was. "We're here to help the healer. We don't need her services."

The woman's scowl didn't lessen, but she stepped back, glancing between Garreth and I like she was watching the long arm of a grandfather clock. We pushed through the door only to be greeted by another glare. Dawn narrowed her eyes at us. She sat on the rocking chair, her skin pale and hands shaking as she held the arm of a young boy. His hand curled awkwardly into his arm, his shoulder pulled high into his neck, and his head leaned to the side.

"There have been small improvements since the last time." A woman stood behind Dawn, one hand gripping the back of the chair with bloodless fingers. "Show her, Yoself."

Yoself lifted the crippled arm and wiggled a few of his deformed fingers.

"That's wonderful," Dawn said. Her voice was strained. "I have more medicine. Are you doing your exercises I showed you?"

He nodded his head. His eyes squinted in pain at the movement.

"Without your gifting of speed?"

"The exercises hurt," Yoself said, his eyes on the ground. "I like to do them really fast to get them over with."

"You must not use your gifting for this." Dawn sat forward on the chair, placing her hand around the twisted limb. "The exercises need to be done slowly. Focus on doing them correctly and then they will start to help."

Garreth dropped his blanket. "How can you waste time with these peasants when you have the son. . ." He waved toward the back room.

Dawn's head snapped in his direction, her lips pressed together until they almost disappeared.

He gulped but continued. "When you have a more important patient with a more serious condition. Are you even caring for him? Send these people away."

The woman pulled Yoself into her skirts. Dawn stood, catching herself on the handle of the rocking chair for a moment before pushing herself to her feet. I reached out a hand to steady her, but she waved me away. A healer had their limits, and I had seen Orblee reach hers often enough. I'd never seen Orblee as drained as Dawn looked. But when she spoke, there was no tremor or weakness in her voice.

"If you knew the value of these people you would be serving them rather than stealing from them," Dawn said. "One of them is worth all of the wealth in the treasury of Tuleves."

Garreth stepped back even though the top of her head barely reached his chin. I'd seen the prince held down by a giant bounder, chased by a scarlett, and curled up in a tomb, but this was the first time I had seen him intimidated.

"They are peasants," he said. I was surprised he was able to find his tongue. "You will never be able to help them all, but Marion could change all our futures."

I glanced at him. At his words. They had the ring of a vague prophecy. Just like we'd talked about in the charnel house.

"These are your people. Each of their lives affect the future in ways you could never understand." Dawn turned and knelt in front of Yoself, touching his face. The mother watched Garreth like a cornered animal. Dawn kept her hands against Yoself's cheeks, looking into his eyes for a long moment. "I know the exercises hurt, but they will make you strong, stronger than all of the other boys, stronger than the Prince of Tuleves. Today, I will help a little more, but you must promise to keep working hard."

"I promise."

Dawn moved her hands, one onto the boy's crooked neck and the other on his raised shoulder. She pressed the two apart. Yoself gasped. Dawn grunted with effort and her lips went colorless. "The prince will need your strength before the end."

When she pulled away, Yoself's head stayed straight, his shoulder even with the other. The mother's fingers flew to her mouth as she began to cry and speak rapidly in a language I didn't recognize. She fell to her knees and examined Yoself's neck and shoulder.

Dawn stood, wiped dust from her skirt, and pulled from the shelf a small bag of skins tied with a leather strap. "Give him this once in the morning and once before he goes to bed. Mix a small amount with boiling water and let him drink it slowly. Bring him back when the medicine is gone." She looked at Yoself. "And don't skip your exercises."

The mother, with tears flowing down her face, took the bag with both hands, trapping Dawn's hand long enough to kiss her fingers several times, then backed away in repeated bows.

I had to push up against the wall to let the mother and son pass. Their gratitude pulled at my heart. Dawn had helped that family, but she'd left mine to burn. No. No. She'd been a frightened girl, running to save her own life. I shouldn't, couldn't blame her. Iranus and the Grand Councilor were to blame.

Besides, one look at Dawn told me she couldn't possibly take care of all those people on her own. If she was anything like Orblee, she wouldn't stop until she'd helped every person at her door. I had to find a way to get her out of here. We may have fooled Iranus for a time, but he would be back.

"We have to leave." I swallowed, realizing the urge to run had risen to a pounding pressure in my head. As weird as it sounded, I missed the peace of the charnel house.

Dawn met my eyes. She didn't ask why. She didn't even seem surprised at my declaration, just simply shook her head. "I cannot leave now. How much time do we have?"

I hated how she always knew what I was saying without even asking for an explanation. "It will take Iranus until late tonight to catch up to the horse at Tuleves City. When he realizes we aren't there, he may not even take time to rest. He could be back by morning."

"Iranus the Tracker?" she asked.

"Were you expecting someone else?" I couldn't control the waspishness of my voice. I had gone almost two whole nights without sleep, been chased by a wildcat, and holed up all morning with the dead.

"Look," Garreth cut in. "If we take Marion and go, we'll be out of your way. We can get a head start on Iranus." I didn't know if I was included in the "we," but I couldn't leave Dawn here now that I'd led the tracker straight to her.

She shook her head, and even that small movement was a struggle for her. "Marion cannot be moved. The healing I was able to do is just enough for his body to hold together to give him time to heal. Like stitches in a gash. If he moves, his wound will tear back open. And there was bleeding inside. He will not survive movement today. Besides," she paused, looking at me, "it sounds like we have a little time. We will be ready to move tomorrow morning."

She also referred to a "we." My heart floated with happiness at the thought of Dawn coming with me. Iranus's words came back to me. *Absorb all light.* I brought sorrow to everyone I loved. "Maybe it would be better if I left and tried to lead him away from here."

I turned, grabbing the door handle. My breath came in short gasps as the effort to stay became a physical exertion. I didn't want to leave Dawn and Marion again, but I didn't know what would happen if I stayed. I could put all of them in more danger.

Garreth put a hand on my arm. Surprised, I flinched back. He had a pleading look, one that didn't belong on his proud face. "I can't leave him. And you can't leave her like this."

"What do you care?" I asked. "So what if you get dragged kicking and screaming back to your palace? You'll get a slap on the wrist. I will hang from the gallows. Dawn will get taken to the Sanatorium. I've doomed us both."

"I'm not ready to return to the city," he said. "If you stay for today, I think we can help each other. Please."

My mouth hung open. I didn't know what he needed from me. I had to save my brother and my father, or at least one of them. But I couldn't leave Dawn and Marion, possibly to die. What was saving one life if I had to sacrifice another to do it?

I still had three days to get to Tuleves City for the Tournament of the People. It was my only plan at the moment. I closed my mouth and took a deep breath through my nose.

"Fine," I said. "But we leave before first light tomorrow morning. All of us."

The prince stepped back, his shoulders sagging as if in relief. Dawn nodded and tried to stand, but the shaking in her muscles forced her to sit back down.

"You need to rest," I said. "You sit and tell me what to do. I can help."

"I've got training, too," he said. "You won't make it through the day like that."

Dawn nodded at me gratefully and then glanced at Garreth. "Let in the next person," she ordered, perching on the rocking chair like a queen ready to rule her kingdom. She placed one hand on Garreth's forearm. "You will find what you seek, but for now, stoke the fire until the water boils. There is a shirt to cover yourself on the line in the back."

The Prince of Tuleves obeyed, pulling on a cloak that hung by the door and placing wood into the small stove. He hadn't wanted to go back to Tuleves City. He'd helped me evade Iranus the Tracker and done it with a sense of purpose. He had a goal, and I didn't know what it was. If Marion and Dawn were right, then Garreth was looking for something. But what could he possibly be searching for when he had everything in the walls of the castle brought to him on a silver platter? Perhaps he longed for his mother the way I longed for mine, but they were both gone. Neither could be found hidden at the heart of Faengsel Forest.

CHAPTER 26

GARRETH and I were able to give Dawn a short break while we cared for some of the general health concerns. I knew how to mix a poultice for a fever. Garreth knew how to set a broken bone. At mid-day, I took a small bowl of soup and a slice of habala bread to Marion.

I moved the stool next to Marion's head. It was the only spot to take the weight off my feet, but I choose the small amount of floor beside the stool. Marion's eyes were closed. A small rasp accompanied his breathing. I balanced the soup and bread on the stool and let myself relax against the wall for a moment.

I felt like I had when Jaimeson and I had run for two days, afraid we were being hunted by the tax collectors. They had come for my father, but they'd tried to take us all. I'd overheard the captain in charge telling his men to bring us all. My father's debt was bigger than coin. They accused him of treason and were determined to bring us all in for punishment. My father gave himself up, begged for them to take him and leave us. The captain had ordered the house burned to force us out. Mother returned from a hunt in time to see the house in flames and her husband in custody. She'd come running for us. She might have even saved us, saved Father at least. She was a warrior of renown. There weren't enough soldiers in the Tulevesian army to stop her.

But one tracker, hiding in the grass, was able to rise from the ground and stick a dagger in her belly while she tried to save her family.

I sagged against the frame of the cot and an uncomfortable lump dug into my leg. The bags of the blood jewels were still in my pocket. Good thing these were men trousers. No women's skirts had pockets this deep and protective. If I ever balanced the scales of justice, equal pockets for women would be my next mission. An uneven board beneath the cot caught my attention. I used the dagger I kept in my belt to pry the board up and slip the jewels beneath the floor. I pushed the board back into place and leaned back. The wall became my pillow. Exhaustion pulled my arms toward the floor.

"You must have had a hard night." The voice was barely a whisper. The sound still made me jump.

"Can't be as hard as the one you had." I shifted to my knees so I could lift the bowl. "You almost didn't make it. I brought you some soup to keep your strength up. We need you rested and ready to move by tomorrow." I bit the inside of my lip. Marion. He wasn't the boy I'd fallen in love with. And I definitely wasn't the same girl he'd kissed in the orchard. A lot had changed between us. But he was still here, talking to me. I'd never imaged being gifted such a moment.

"I've had worse." He moved to sit up and take the bowl from me, but he groaned and gripped his side. "Nope. I take it back. That was my worst night by far. What even happened?"

"Let me help you." I shifted the small down pillow to tilt his head. Then I spooned the soup into his mouth. A small amount of liquid escaped and dripped down his chin. I used my thumb to wipe it away without thinking. "Two foolish royals went hunting ancient creatures of legend. And you found them."

After three slow spoonfuls, Marion took the bowl with both hands, trapping mine beneath his, and tilted the rest of the soup into his mouth, gulping like a man dying of thirst. "Thank you for that. And we weren't hunting for the ancients. At least Garreth wasn't. I was hoping we'd run into one, but not like that."

"Only you would hope to come face to face with a Scarlett with claws like swords that could chop you in half with one sipe." I set the soup bowl down and waved my hand at his boyish silliness.

He caught my hand in the air and gripped in with a passionate intensity. "They exist, Arianna. They exist. That means that the forbidden manuscripts are true. The tomes taken from the Oracles speak of the ancient creatures who lived even before the seven immortals. The manuscripts speak of a great division of the earth, a rending of continents, that can only be stopped when the ancient and mortal are brought into balance."

I scoffed. "Sounds like another useless prophecy to me."

"You are skeptical of the gifting of time?" Marion waved away the habala bread I offered him. His color had drained and the circles under his eyes seemed even more pronounced.

"I am not skeptical of the gifting." I rearranged his pillow so his head could fall back. His eyes blinked and I knew he would not stay awake much longer. He needed his rest. I needed to get back to helping Dawn. "I am skeptical of the interpretation of their prophecies. They told the citizens of things to come, but no details that might be helpful. They described the possibilities, but not how to bring it pass. The spoke of destiny and fate, but never how to change a negative fortune. What use was the gifting of time other than to comfort people or scare them into submission?"

Marion fought the exhaustion as it pulled on his eyelids. His fingers found their way out of the blanket and touched my knee with a light pressure. "Then you believe they deserved what Kadasha commanded? They deserved their fate?"

I stood, jerking away from him. "No one deserved that blood bath. That's not what I said. That's not what I meant." The fact that he could accuse me of such a thing made my chest constrict with images of the train of sorrow. People being arrested for having too little. No one deserved the sorrow of unbalanced scales.

"I'm sorry." Marion pulled the blanket tighter to his neck, flinching at the pain that small movement caused. "I know you better than that. I just. . . I think understanding the gifting of time might be what saves us, what gives us the understanding to choose the right path. A prophecy from someone with the gifting of time is our only glimpse into the unknown but unavoidable future." He had changed. He'd always talked with me about how to be better. How to prepare for the future. How to follow a path that led to the intended destination. But he'd never been dependent on prophecies to do it. I had loved the way his mind worked. I also loved how he struggled to explain faith to me now.

"You almost sound like you've visited the Oracles yourself."

"Not all of the Oracles were inside the walls of the temple before they fell. Somethings that are forbidden are still accessible. I was given a prophecy." His voice was getting weaker. Despite his passion for the subject his physical body was telling him to rest.

"Were you told you would one day find the woman of your dreams in a damp forest and fight for your life against creatures of legend?"

His head flopped to the side in an exhausted head shake. "No. I was told that my kingdom would fall into chaos and destruction if I didn't protect the prince. He is my responsibility. My charge. And he is my friend."

His eyes fluttered closed.

I reached out and felt his forehead. His head was damp with sweat, but I sensed no fever. Still, he ranted like a delirious man on his death bed. He had been a child when the Oracles were massacred. And anyone using the gifting of time after that were untrained and in hiding. "Let me check your bandages."

His eyes didn't open, but his hand waved in the air. "Not now. I'm fine. I just need a little more rest." His hand bumped against mine and he gripped it with a strength that belied his exhaustion. "Just promise me you'll be here when I wake up this time. I know I said last night was my worst ever, but it was nothing compared to the night after I discovered you had died in a fire."

CHAPTER 27

THE SUN HOVERED above the high plateau like a child dipping his toe into the cold waters of a lake, heat clinging to the day the way I clung to the rag in my hands.

The last of the villagers had been seen. Garreth hung the sign that the village healer was out and went in the side room to check on Marion. I wrung the cloth, cleaning the last of the blood into the water so that the red swirled in the once clear liquid. No one had died today.

My plan had failed. Garreth was supposed to help me. I had kidnapped the Prince of Tuleves to trade for my brother's life. But my brother was gone. I'd thought I could convince Garreth to use his influence to save my father, but the prince was helpless. He had no power in his own kingdom.

I didn't know what to do next. I still had Garreth and Marion. I could try holding them for ransom against the Grand Councilor. I wasn't exactly in the position to bargain with a man who controlled armies. And where would that leave Dawn? I'd led Iranus to her hiding place. The tracker would find her when he returned.

I could continue to the Tournament of the People, but the Prince of Tuleves knew I was the Hooded Robber. I did not trust him to keep my secret. And that stupid tournament would only allow me to save one person. My mistakes were piling up, and with each one, another person's life weighed on me.

Father was in debtor's prison because I didn't have the courage to help him. Jaimeson was beyond my reach, because I had hesitated. Marion lay in a bed wounded, because I hadn't stopped Garreth from shooting the bounder. And now Dawn was in the path of Iranus the Tracker, because I had led him straight to her.

I wasn't even sure I could save myself, let alone each person I loved that fell into my shadow. I could run, but Iranus would track me, follow my scent to the ends of the land. He was not one to let an offense go. Not after I had trapped him in ice. Maybe that was the answer. Maybe I needed to run and let Iranus track me down. I could lead him away from here. Away from Dawn.

It wasn't a long-term solution. Iranus would catch me eventually and turn me in for the reward. Then return for Dawn. It would all end the same if I ran.

I squeezed the rag until every drop had fallen.

Dawn was worse off than she had been this morning. While we had done most of the work, she had used her spark several times to scatter infection before it reached the heart, bind muscle that was torn beyond the help of a needle and thread, and once, to calm a woman who had gone mad from internal pain.

I dumped the bucket and watched the sullied water run down the street. The shadow of the Ruins of the Oracles stretched over me, the wall so tall I had to crane my neck to see where it met with the blue sky. The Oracles had been granted a gifting by Kadasha. Even they had been favored once.

I had not been chosen to bear a gifting.

I couldn't give of my spark. I could only take the spark of things around me. I sucked it into that dark turmoil inside me without consequence. I didn't grow weaker or confused or listless. I was an abomination that sucked without remorse, a hunger that could never be satisfied.

Those who had the gifting had to use their own spark to increase specific natural reactions. A healer used what was in them to increase the natural healing of a human body. An Oracle used their energy to increase the spark of time. They would get glimpses, images of the future. Orblee had claimed to have the gifting of time, but her vision of my future had been no help. *My story would not end as my mother's did.*

I lifted my face to the wall and held up my hands. "What does that even mean? What is the point of the gifting of time if the prophecies don't give us a hint, a clue as what to do? Tell me what to do. Give me a direction that I might save my family in the end."

The walls were silent.

I dropped my hands. I hadn't been expecting anything, but somehow, the silence mocked me.

I put the rag over a hot stone to dry and went back inside, kneeling down beside the rocking chair. Dawn seemed to have aged thirty years and yet it was still the face of my friend.

Garreth came out of the room, throwing back the curtain. "His fever spiked. He's not responding."

"I checked on him mid-day." But I hadn't changed his bandage. I hadn't checked on his wound. I cursed myself for not being more thorough.

"He's not now." Garreth paced back and forth in the tight space. "How could we have spent all day working on others when Marion needed us? How could you?" He turned on Dawn and I stepped between them, his finger an inch from my nose. Garreth's intensity surprised me. This was more than a spoiled prince upset that his guard was not at his post. Was it the fear of losing a friend? Or was there more?

Dawn stood, fighting the fatigue. She refused help as she moved to the curtain and pulled it back. She bent to shift the blanket off Marion's torso and gasped.

I raised up on my toes so I could see Marion's wound over Dawn's head. It had festered, a green pus coming from the center, blue and black lines stretching from the wound in all directions, the darkest line headed for Marion's heart.

"It's infected," whispered Dawn. "An unnatural one. Did you poison the tip of your own arrow?"

Garreth stepped back even though Dawn had not looked at him. He almost tripped over the rocking chair. "How did you know it was my arrow?"

Dawn waited for an answer.

"I didn't poison my arrow tips, but they weren't covered. They could have brushed against the plants and leaves of the forest."

"Tell me how this happened."

"It was a bounder," I said, filling in as his mouth opened and closed like a fish testing the top of the water for food. "Garreth tried to shoot a bounder in Faengsel Forest. The arrow turned and. . ." I waved at Marion, not wanting to finish the story.

"Saints of Ashanti." Dawn cursed, calling on the seventh immortal associated with the gifting of reasoning. "Why didn't I see that?" Neither Garreth nor I had answers for her.

She closed her eyes, gingerly touching and probing the wound. She coughed. "I don't have enough spark left. I can barely slow the infection, let alone stop it."

"What do we do?" I asked.

"We go to the gardens," she said.

"Is there a garden nearby?" I said. "I can go. I'm good with plants. Tell me what you need."

"This you cannot do alone." Dawn stood and pushed both of us back through the doorway into the small main room. She pulled the curtains shut.

"We can't leave him here," Garreth protested. "What if someone breaks in?"

She raised an eyebrow at him, her condescension as regal as any royal. "And what would they be breaking in to steal?"

He withered like a plant with too little water, but he didn't give up. "Your. . . chair. The medicine. I'm sure that's valuable."

"My home is never unprotected," Dawn said, opening the main door to the street.

Her words pierced like a sharp needle into my heart. My home had been hers. And it had gone unprotected. Her movements were slow, painful, her strength wasted away from the labors of the day.

Garreth hesitated a moment, his fists clenching and unclenching as if he searched for a grip, a way to find some semblance of control. Finally, he shook his head. "She is the most aggravating. . ."

"You'll get used to it," I said.

I pulled the door shut and turned, expecting to follow them down toward the village, but instead, they moved up the hill to the place where the hut leaned against the high wall surrounding the Oracle ruins. Dawn slipped into a small space behind the hut. Garreth shrugged his shoulders and followed. I pushed in behind him.

"You need a bath," I said, bumping into him when the cloak he wore caught on a sliver of wood sticking out from Dawn's hut. He wrestled the cloak free, hitting his head on the rafter above him and scratching his cheek against the rough stone of the wall. He swore. "And some patience."

"You smell worse than the dead."

"Whose fault is that?" I asked.

"Through here," Dawn said. She motioned forward in a space where forward was not an option. She stood at the back wall of her hut, but there was no exit. Boards covered the small opening that had been there, closing us off.

"Inside?" Garreth looked at the wall with new interest. "No one is allowed inside. Besides, all the entrances were collapsed. There hasn't been a way inside for over a decade. Believe me, I've tried. Anything my father has outlawed is a source of entertainment for me. But this. . . was impossible."

Dawn placed a hand on his shoulder and pushed him. For a moment, I believed his head was going to slam into the ruin's wall, but he disappeared, headfirst, straight into the stone.

An entrance into the forbidden ruins of the Oracles. Many had tried to find an entrance. Others thought to climb the walls with ropes or ladders, but there was more than the king's law against trespassing. People believed it had been cursed. Ropes snapped. Ladders crumbled. No one had found an entrance.

Dawn put one arm in front of me. I thought she meant to keep me out. Instead, she pulled me to her, wrapping her arms around me in a tight hug. "I've missed you so much."

Her words threatened to crack a dam inside me. Oh, how I'd longed to see her. How many nights had I laid awake, wishing things had not changed, that we could have continued growing up together as sisters? As friends.

"I'm sorry I could not say it before," Dawn said, loosening the hug slowly, as if her very being resisted separating again. "But the prince cannot know our connection. Not yet."

I wanted to ask why, but her gaze prevented me. She had always been so sure of herself, always right when I was wrong. Garreth knew I was the Hooded Robber. A connection to Dawn and the Hooded Robber would be unwise. Of course she would realize it first.

A cool breeze from the wall behind me brought the scent of ash. I had so many questions, but before I could say another word, she pushed me as forcefully as she had Garreth through the wall.

I sidestepped until the wall disappeared and I tripped. Garreth caught me and I fought for my balance while pushing his hands off me. Dawn stepped through the wall, and even with my eyes on her, I could see no gap, no opening in the stone. Moving closer, I realized that the opening was not from side to side like a door, but a gap where the wall that had appeared unbroken actually failed to meet, overlapping for less than a horse-length before ending in a perfect match to the wall behind it. It was seamless. I had to touch the wall in order to see the difference in distance.

"Amazing," I said. All this time, there was no gate, no lock. Just a simple illusion covered by the home of a poor healer.

Dawn nodded as if the effort to speak was too great for her. She ran her hand along the stone, pausing a moment.

The wall of the ruins had been deceiving. The outside showed no sign of deterioration, but the temple within was barely recognizable as a building. Huge piles of rubble filled a courtyard as if the structure had been torn down. A side door stood alone without walls to support it. Despite the devastation, I could imagine the scene as it had been. The exterior wall enclosed an enormous amount of land, a huge courtyard. The workmanship of the stone on the ground had been placed in an intricate swirling pattern. The architecture of the columns that remained standing testified of a craftsman more skilled than any I had ever witnessed.

Dawn sat on a boulder, her hands shaking as they rested in her lap. Her breath came in short, hungry gasps.

"Are you sure you have the strength for this?" I hated to ask. I feared what would happen to Marion if she said no. But she looked so frail, so much older.

Despite her exhaustion, a look of triumph crossed her face as she gauged Garreth's reaction. I turned to look at the prince.

"It's incredible," he said, appearing to try to retain some dignity, but sincerity snuck into his facade. "It must have been a sight during the time of the Oracles. What could cause so much damage?" He picked up a stone stained black.

"Men," Dawn said. "Evil men with jealous hearts."

For a moment, I thought I could hear it, the mob of soldiers yelling, the cries of Oracles as they were forced to their knees, the cracking of stone as the walls were pulled down. I could hear screams echoing out of the stone as torches were thrown into the temple, as fires filled the remaining windows and devoured the carpet and drapes like a hungry beast.

Garreth dropped the stone like it had burned him, like he had heard the sounds I had. He wiped his fingers on his shirt leaving black streaks. The black was not a natural part of the stone but a testimony of the destruction that had happened here.

CHAPTER 28

DAWN SHUFFLED TOWARD THE TEMPLE. Each time a stone turned beneath her foot, I was afraid she would fall. Garreth stood close enough to catch her, but she refused to let him touch her. She seemed so fragile and so strong at the same time.

We approached the frame that marked the temple entrance, but once we got closer, she motioned for us to walk along the foundation wall. We reached a freestanding arch of stone; a single mark of strength left in a world of shattered beauty. She led us under the arch and around a half-wall.

We entered an interior courtyard, and the sight sucked the breath from my lungs.

In the center of the destruction, in the middle of ruins as black as death, was a garden of color. Plants crawled among the stone. Flowers opened to the sky: pink, purple, red. The contrast was so intense I felt the urge to cry. Garreth turned and dabbed at his eye. Perhaps he was not as cold as stone.

I traced the curving indentations with my finger along a small section of still-standing wall, admiring the talent it would take to carve such perfection into stone.

When I pulled my hand away, my finger was stained black. I wiped it on my shirt, disgusted, trying to remove the stain that tarnished the stone. I turned back. Dawn was on her knees next to a small yellow flower.

"That?" Garreth said, a gruffness in his voice. Perhaps a way to cover for his moment of emotion. "That is the least glorious flower in the garden. If I were a gardener, I would pull that one out like a weed."

"True power does not display itself for everyone to see," Dawn said. "True power is satisfied with being invisible to the world."

"What is the point of power if no one sees it?" He sounded truly confused.

"Crush this," she said, handing each of us two leaves. They were small, four pointed, and thin as parchment. "Press it into your palm like this." She took Garreth's hand, showing him how to use the pad of his thumb in a twisting motion.

Color rose on his cheeks. I didn't know if he was blushing at Dawn's touch or was embarrassed to be instructed by a village healer.

I turned my attention to my own two leaves and used the same technique to crush the leaves into my palm. A small amount of white liquid squeezed out from under my thumb, sticking to my skin.

Garreth brought his hand to his nose and sniffed. "Ah, that's terrible. It smells like the odor of a snotle. One spray from them and you'll be friendless for a year."

Unable to resist, I put my nose closer to the leaves. He wasn't wrong. I gagged as the smell filled my nose and worked its way down to my throat. The smell was so rancid I could taste it on my tongue. Snotles were spiny creatures that lived in the Swamps of Gorgeon and lived extremely long lives. No predator would come within a whip's length, let alone try to eat one.

Dawn used a bent sewing needle to scrape along the outside of the crushed leaves on our palms, rolling the white, sticky substance into a rounded droplet. It was smaller than a drop of dew. I had to cover my nose with my other hand. The smell intensified as she worked the liquid. Once she had the drop on the end of the needle, she lifted a canteen of water and let the drop fall inside.

She brought the canteen to her lips and drank.

Garreth made a gagging sound. "I can't watch."

"How can you stand to drink that?" I couldn't hide the fact that I agreed with him.

The sun set behind the walls earlier than outside the ruins. The temperature dropped with the fading light. Neither Garreth nor I moved as she slowly sipped the snotle-flavored water.

The change in Dawn was as gradual as her drinking. When she looked up, Garreth stumbled back, tripping over a small stone and taking a hard seat on a boulder. I wanted nothing more than to run and wrap my arms around her, but I pinned my arms to my side and bit my lip, hiding the fact that I felt like a child. Dawn's face was young again, her shoulders straight, hands stilled. No more tremors.

Plants that could restore spark? Why did not every garden in every village have such a plant?

The sun was setting, touching the wall and leaving streaks of light racing through the ruins. Dawn stood, as regal as any queen, and the light fell across her face. I had the strangest urge to kneel and I wondered if, here, in this garden of Oracles, many people had fallen to their knees to worship those who could touch the spark of time.

I dropped my eyes and studied the plant at my feet, the simple yellow flower that had seemed so out of place in this garden of fantastic color. How could a plant have such a stunning effect? Impulsively, I reached out to touch the yellow petals. Dawn grabbed my hand, stopping my fingers an inch from the petal.

"The flower is as deadly as the leaf is effective," she said.

She finished drinking the rest of the water in the canteen and let out a small sigh of relief.

"What is it?" Garreth asked.

"A very rare herb, one that should be used with caution. It can restore a healer's spark."

"Why was it here, in an Oracle garden?" I asked.

"Much of their wisdom has been lost. . . or destroyed."

Dawn snapped off a stalk from another plant that was as stiff as bark and handed it to me. "A tea made from thembus will help Marion heal on his own."

A thembus reed. Orblee had spoken of the healing power of thembus, but it was a lost legend. A sharp smell stung my eyes as I worked the reed between my palms. I squeezed a single drop of sap, thick and black, into a clear flask. Impatience to save Marion made my fingers clumsy as I pushed in the stopper.

"I didn't come here to garden," Garreth said. "If this stuff will help, let's go." I hated that he voiced my thoughts. We were nothing alike.

Dawn put a steady hand on his shoulder. "True friends are rare. It's good you want to save yours." She motioned for him to exit the garden, but she paused next to me.

She plucked a petal from a purple flower, releasing a scent of lemons that reminded me of Mother. She rubbed the petal along my arm. "This will cover your scent for three days." The cool line of dampness felt like freedom. Iranus would not be able to track me. I could run.

Dawn wrapped my fingers around the flask of thembus sap. "Dilute this in a full kettle and give it to Marion. He will die if he doesn't get this before the sun rises in the morning." She raised her eyes and put one hand against my cheek like a mother sending her child to war. "For good or ill, it's time to show your face. One person has the power to tip the scales. Imagine the power of a hundred. Or a thousand. An avalanche started by a single stone."

CHAPTER 29

I FOLLOWED Garreth out between the walls. He shimmied between the shack quickly. Dawn followed behind. His form disappeared a little too quickly, like he'd been pulled. I stopped and listened. And then I knew. It was like I could smell him.

He's here. A burning sensation started behind my eyes. I had led him here. I had put another person I loved in danger. I didn't know what Dawn had meant about showing my face, but there was no time for questions. Now that I had stopped to listen, I heard the creak of shifting leather, the huff of impatient horses, the clop of more than one set of shoed hooves.

"Search these homes," called a commanding voice. "Find the healer."

My heart froze. Wood splintered as soldiers broke down doors. A woman screamed and there was the sharp sound of a slap. The scream stopped. The noises grew and increased as more doors were shoved open and more villagers were pulled from their homes.

Dawn tried to push past me. I held her back, blocked her way with my body. Her breath caught as a baby began to cry.

"They're here for you," I said.

"I know." I had never heard her so desperate. "I can't let them get hurt. They're my people."

"I'll stop the soldiers," I said. "But you must hide. Promise me you will stay hidden until they are gone."

"I'll come with you," she said, her hand on my shoulder. I pushed her back against the boards at the end of the tiny alley. "If you ask me, we can do this together. You've traveled a lonely journey for so long. I wish it wasn't your burden to be alone for a little longer."

I blinked once, a traitorous tear slipping down my cheek. If I had thought for a moment that Dawn meant we could hide together, that she would run away with me, I would have said yes. I wanted to run. But I saw the bravery, the determination in her eyes that I had always envied. And I knew she meant she would face the soldiers with me. I couldn't have another person taken because of me.

I shook my head. "You can't this time. Stay hidden. And promise me, no matter what, you'll get away from here. Run as far and as fast as you can. I understand now why you asked me not to follow. I'm sorry. I've should have listened."

"Neither of us are very good at listening to what fate has in store."

A scream sounded from beyond our view. Dawn stared straight into me for an entire heartbeat, one that stretched from the beginning of time to the folding of the world. Then she nodded and slipped back into the ruins. I took a deep breath and wiped my face. I only had the small dagger in my boot, having left my bow and quiver in the hut. I didn't know how I could fight off Iranus, let alone others.

I pushed to the end of Dawn's hut, took a deep breath, and peeked around the corner. I expected to duck a swinging sword or dodge a blade thrown at my head. No one noticed. My appearance was the least exciting thing happening. A dozen soldiers moved down the street, tossing people from their homes. They held torches high, battling black shadows, lighting the night with flickering orange and red.

I closed my eyes, remembering the soldiers ransacking our house, throwing furniture from the upstairs windows, ripping curtains and confiscating anything valuable. No. I did not know what Kadasha wanted from me. I had no Oracle to tell my future, but I could not leave now. I had only wanted two things. To save Marion and my father. But now, I wanted to make these soldiers stop. I would do whatever it took to make them stop.

Make a plan, Arianna. Don't hunt a prey that you don't understand. Outsmart the animal at its own game.

They wanted the healer. They would not stop until they found Dawn. Or until they thought they had found her.

In the dancing shadows, Garreth stood stone still in front of a tall man who had dismounted from his horse.

"Thank Kadasha you're safe," the man said. I couldn't ignore the similarities between the tall man and Marion. This man wore a riding cape with jeweled hems made of the finest fabric I had ever seen. It was a deep purple and hung with a purposeful fit. Light fabric that would allow for movement despite the finery it displayed. A sword hilt poked out from his side, and the gleam of armor could be seen through the fabric on his chest. He stood in front of Garreth with the authority of a superior.

This was the Grand Councilor of Tuleves. Marion's father and the man who'd ordered my father's arrest. "When we found Marion, I feared the worst."

Garreth and the Grand Councilor faced each other for an awkward second, and then the Grand Councilor reached out and pulled him into a hug.

Iranus stood behind the Grand Councilor, his mouth twisted as if he'd bitten into an unripe fruit. I wanted to turn and run, to hide with Dawn in the ruins of the Oracles, but the flickering light fell on the men moving out of Dawn's hut, Marion's arms thrown over the two soldier's shoulders as they assisted him. He wasn't ready to be moved. They were going to kill him!

"Stop!"

The soldiers continued toward the horses while others gathered more villagers, pushing women to the ground, beating men who didn't move fast enough. One threw a child over his shoulder, packing him to the top of the hill like a sack of grain.

No one had heard me over the din. I moved closer to Garreth as the Grand Councilor released him. In the forest, he'd told me he had the gifting of sound. I'd never seen him use it, but we hadn't needed it until now.

"Use your gifting. Tell them to stop."

Garreth glanced at me and then at the Grand Councilor who had turned his attention to two soldiers dragging a woman toward him. The woman was in her fifth decade. The Grand Councilor shook his head. "That's not her. That woman has the gifting of heat, not life."

I grabbed Garreth by the arm and shook it. "Please. I know you think you don't have authority, but you are the prince. Surely, they have to listen to you."

He took a deep breath and held it for heartbeat. Then he parroted my command. "STOP." I should have covered my ears. His gifting of sound was strong and echoed from the wall of the Oracles to down to the city well. There was a pause in the commotion, but the attention wasn't on Garreth who'd given the command. Every attention turned their attention to the Grand Councilor for confirmation. Garreth hadn't been exaggerating. He had no authority even with his own soldiers.

The Grand Councilor looked at Garreth for a moment and then raised a hand. His silent hand movement had the effect of a cracked whip. The soldiers straightened. They turned from the other huts. They released people from their grips. They turned and closed in on us with their glowing torches.

I ran to Marion's side. "Put him back. He's not ready to be moved." I stood nose to nose with one of the soldiers who held Marion. He didn't flinch.

My arms were pulled behind me and I was forced to the ground with a knee in my back.

"She's right." Garreth's voice was still loud from his gifting so all could hear him. "He'll never survive the ride. Take him back inside."

The pressure on my back lightened but wasn't removed. A sliver of fear shot through me. The only response to Garreth's words was a shifting of attention to the Grand Councilor again. I could feel it more than see it, since my view was of the cobblestone and the toe of a shiny black boot.

"I'm taking him to the healers at the Sanatorium," said the Grand Councilor. A shaft of steel had replaced the warmth in his voice from a moment before. "We must get him back to Tuleves. Your decisions have finally caught up with you, and those closest to you are paying the consequences. Get him on a horse." The last part was a command to the soldiers. They moved Marion forward again.

I shifted beneath the loosened grip and kicked out, buckling the knee that wasn't pressed into my back. The soldier toppled and I jumped to my feet, pulling my dagger from my boot and pointing it at the neck of one of the soldiers taking Marion.

"Wait," I said with more command in my voice than I felt. "Let me help him first, and then you can take him. Please. I just want to help him."

A cold blade pressed against my own throat from behind. The smell of smoked leather and animal fur wafted to my nose. Iranus the Tracker was right behind me. I could not imagine how he had returned so quickly. Perhaps he hadn't followed the horse to Tuleves City. This man was harder to get rid of than lice in thick hair.

I had a plan, but for a moment, fear clogged my throat. I swallowed.

"I'm the healer!" The words were out of my mouth before I could process the consequences. The sound bounced off the wall of the Oracle ruins and died away. I knew this was what I had to do to protect Dawn and to save Marion. "I am the healer." I said it with more conviction.

A sting bit my neck as the blade pulled away and Iranus the Tracker grabbed my arm and turned me to face him. Disbelief and confusion warred in his eyes, so dark and deep that I could have been looking into a well. He sniffed and my entire body tensed. If Dawn's plant wasn't strong enough, Iranus the Tracker would know my smell as the Hooded Robber.

"She smells of healer's herbs," he said. He let my arm go and stepped back with what might have been a half-bow of apology. My heart stuttered back to life.

"The healer?" I almost rolled my eyes as Garreth failed to keep his royal mouth shut. "The healer. Yes. This is the healer and she's the one that saved Marion and knows what she's talking about."

I didn't know which was worse, the doubt at the beginning or the dribbling confidence he now spouted unnecessarily into the night. He needed to stop talking. I turned and placed my hand on Marion's cheek.

His face was slick with sweat, his breathing labored. His eyes fluttered at my touch, but there was no comprehension in his gaze. He needed a true healer with the gifting. All I could do was steal the precious spark that was fighting to keep him alive.

Grand Councilor Levante stepped up beside me, inspecting both me and his son. "You are the healer of this village?" He looked around at the destruction. Soldiers had ripped a pillow, leaving limp and dirty feathers speckled on the street. A hay bale had broken open, clogging the gutters, and a crowd of villagers had gathered, kneeling next to the crying woman and her child. Others looked at the soldiers with tensed muscles and hate in their eyes.

"Yes." I turned to face him, licking my lips to moisten them and pushing my shoulders back to look more confident. That was a mistake. Healers rarely grew to their full height. I was already much too tall for an average girl, let alone a healer. Still, at my full height, the Grand Councilor glowered down at me.

"I've come to invite you to join the Sanatorium," he said. "Your acts and achievements in the realm of healing this last year has reached even my ear. I've come personally to extend the invitation." His eyes flickered toward Marion, who hung limp and pale between the two soldiers.

An invitation to the Sanatorium. A place where healers were kept for the royals only, to serve the upper class. I'm sure their healers were treated with the best food and clothes and equipment royalty could offer. Far better than here. But it was still a prison. A way to leave the scales tipped in the royals' favor.

Dawn's people were here. I had seen her love for them. Still, she might be better off in a posh prison than draining herself of spark day after day in this depressed village. I might be ruining another person's life, but I still couldn't douse the anger that flared up inside me.

"What about them?" I asked, motioning toward the gathered villagers. "They need a healer. You have plenty of healers and these people have so little already." I remembered holding Jaimeson's hand as he shook through his tremors, tears falling down Father's face, Mother pacing like a caged animal. All of us so helpless.

I knew, without having to ask her or see her face, that Dawn would never have accepted an invitation to the Sanatorium. I needed to go to

Tuleves City. This could get me into the tournament that I needed to win. I could escape a healer's prison once I got there.

Just as I took a breath to accept the invitation, another soldier stepped out from the hut, holding my bow and quiver. I barely kept myself from jumping forward and ripping them from his hands.

"Grand Councilor," the soldier said. "I've found these in the hut."

Iranus moved forward like a hunting hound and sniffed the bow. "These belong to the Hooded Robber. I told you he was close. I told you he was here. He was with the prince one night ago."

I felt as if my head had been placed in a guillotine.

Garreth scoffed. "The Hooded Robber is too smart to get caught by a noisy, stinky bunch of soldiers. Sh. . . he left at first light this morning."

I kept my head down, but my eyes flickered involuntarily to his face. I didn't know his motivation for protecting the Hooded Robber or playing along that I was the healer.

"Without his bow?" Iranus asked. He was right. I would never have left without my father's bow.

"The Hooded Robber is a friend to the people," said Garreth with a little too much conviction. He was overplaying his hand. "He gives back what he takes from you. He must have seen the healer's need and made a gift of all that he had. I'm sure he could make another."

Ignorant and stupid. I could never remake that bow with the craftsmanship of my father. I could never replace it.

"You helped the Hooded Robber?" the Grand Councilor asked me. "He's a wanted criminal."

I heard Orblee's voice in my head. "All are welcome at a healer's door."

"Break it," the Grand Councilor said. "And find his trail. The reward will be doubled if you find him before tomorrow."

Before I could process the words, the soldier held my bow against the ground, and with one foot, snapped the bow in half. I let out a cry before covering my mouth, but the sound was drowned out as most of the soldiers spurred their horses down the hill, following the order to find the Hooded Robber.

Iranus hovered at the edge of the remaining torchlight. Our eyes met. For a moment, I thought he would call me out on my lie, denounce me as the Hooded Robber. His mouth opened, then shut. He dropped his eyes and stepped back, disappearing into the shadows of the night.

Iranus was too close. Dawn was right here and Iranus would know that the healer had returned. Going to Tuleves for the Tournament was just another way for me to run away. I would find another way to save my father, but for now, I needed to make sure Dawn wasn't discovered by Iranus.

"I won't go. I'm needed here but let me help your son before you go." I almost slipped and used his first name.

"I'm afraid the invitation is not optional," Grand Councilor Levante said, turning away from me. "You are now a guest of Tuleves City, whether you like it or not."

The soldier that had remained approached me, light from the torches bouncing off the silver shackles in his hand.

CHAPTER 30

"I'LL COME," I said, raising my hands and backing away from the soldier with the shackles. If I was taken as a prisoner, I wouldn't be able to get Marion the thembus extract before we reached Tuleves City. I didn't know if I would have another chance.

The villagers grumbled at my words, shifting like the haunches of a scarlett ready to pounce. The soldiers felt the shift, nervous now that most of their comrades had gone to hunt down the Hooded Robber. I was sure if the soldiers had tried to take Dawn, the villagers would not have held back. As it was, there was an undercurrent of tension, like a set trap waiting to be tripped.

There were six soldiers left: the two that had Marion between them, two on horses holding torches, the one holding shackles in front of me, and the one snapping Father's arrows into pieces too small for kindling.

"Get the horses," Grand Councilor Levante said to Garreth.

"Uh, we actually only have one," he said. "Iranus was supposed to bring the other one back with him." Despite his casual tone, Garreth watched Marion nervously, glancing between us as if he expected me to do something. I didn't have time to prepare the thembus extract. It needed to boil for over an hour with several gallons of water to dilute it enough to be used. I didn't know the consequences of straight thembus extract. I didn't know what it would do to a man's body.

The soldier with the shackles moved toward me.

"I'll take the horse and ride with the wounded." I took the reins of Garreth's horse. She didn't spook at my touch. I'd ridden her half the night. "I can keep him alive until we get to the Sanatorium." Even I didn't know if that was the truth or a lie.

The Grand Councilor approached me, his eyes a fathomless pool of black water. Under his calm I sensed anger, though I couldn't be sure who the anger was directed at. As he loomed in front of me, the light from the torches faded and a darkness developed all around him, like light was being sucked into nothingness, unable to touch him, unable to escape his pull.

Then the moment passed, and the Grand Councilor tightened the saddle.

"Take him as swiftly as possible," he said. "I don't want to lose my son."

"Your Grandness," I said clumsily, not sure how to address him. "If I can have one hour, I can make a poultice. It will ensure he survives the journey."

The Grand Councilor shook his head. My heart sank as his face hardened to stone. "You will keep him alive. I hold no faith in the snake oil treatments of peasants."

The soldiers pushed me onto the horse unceremoniously, lifting Marion on the horse behind me and using ropes to tie his feet together under the horse's belly and secure his arms around my waist. His breath tickled my neck, warming the skin as he breathed out. He sucked air back in, leaving a cold sensation below my ear.

I needed a new plan. I had been tied to the saddle along with Marion. I could not make the poultice. And from the uneven beating of his heart against my back, he would not survive until dawn, let alone a full night's ride on the back of a horse. How I wished I could gift him something of myself. My heat, my strength, my healing. I would have even gifted him my reasoning if I had any wisdom to share.

I understood Jaimeson's urge to force people with his reasoning. I wanted to make the Grand Councilor see his son's precarious situation.

I would have shoved my gifting into his stone-cold heart. But there was nothing I could do to keep Marion alive.

The villagers parted for us, making a path down the hill. Eight horses, two carrying double riders, made their way out of the small village, away from the walls of the Oracle Temple's ruins. Away from Dawn. Away from my father's shattered bow. Away from the blood jewels I had hidden in the floorboards. I squeezed the vial with the thembus extract in my palm, Dawn's words echoing in my head. *He won't survive if he doesn't get this before you reach the city of Tuleves.*

We splashed across the shallow lake. The stars reflected in the water rippling out from the horses' legs. At the crossroads, I began to understand the prince's complaints on our last trip. I was losing feeling in my legs, my back was beginning to ache, and even the slightest shift had me worried I would lose balance and pull the horse on top of us.

At the crossroads we joined a larger caravan, one that I would have loved to rob with Jaimeson. But my mind was too distracted to take in all the details, only the fact that there appeared to be no fancy wagon carrying royals and the food cart was still mostly full.

The captain, a woman with a square face and a no-nonsense posture, rode up to me, watching me out of the corner of her eye like I might be a snake with the ability to slither right out of my bonds. She pulled her horse to a stop in front of Garreth's.

"What game do you play?" Her accent was thick, her *g* spoken deep in her throat. Her words were said with such force the spit nearly landed on Garreth's face. "You have found plenty of ways to displease the council, but never have you gone this far. Never have I seen you risk the life of another. Until now. And being found in the same hut as the Hooded Robber and in the presence of the dying son of the Grand Councilor. You should have a noose around your neck." She paused, leaning back on her horse, looking up at the sky as if her question could be cleared up by the stars overhead.

"What game does he play?" she said to the open expanse. She shook her head like the puzzle had her stumped and then lapsed into silence.

The captain had planted a question in my mind. It circled around like a donkey tied to a grain mill. Over and over. What game does he play? The Prince of Tuleves was searching for something, and the

Grand Councilor treated him like a son. Marion was dying slowly as he leaned against my back. Was it all a game?

Was Garreth playing with fate or was I the pawn in someone else's game?

The twang of a bow string and a swish of an arrow flying through the air brought me out of my reverie. The soldier on the horse in front of us fell to the side, an arrow in his back.

Then came the flames. Arrows with burning pitch arched above my head like shooting stars falling to earth. The soldiers erupted into chaos. The captain beside me drew her sword and began shouting orders. My heart stuttered. We were under attack. I recognized the signs of a small force designed to confuse a larger one. There had only been three flaming arrows. Only one soldier had been shot. If I had to guess, two, maybe three, people were attacking a caravan of at least forty. It seemed like something Jaimeson and I would have done.

I struggled against the reins as my horse danced in circles. Marion shifted and I was barely able to stay upright. The riderless horse in front of us reared up as another volley of burning arrows lit up the scene. One of the arrows landed in the food cart while another sank into the saddle of a soldier. The final burning arrow landed next to the road. The dry grasses and plants caught the flame and fed it. My horse reared up in fright.

I couldn't fight the pull of Marion's weight behind me. I sucked in the spark from the ropes that held Marion to the horse's saddle and the weight of both of us falling snapped our frozen bonds.

We rolled off the back of the horse and landed in the steep ditch next to the road. No enemy had appeared to fight, but their distraction had worked well enough that the squadron and caravan guards were struggling to form a solid line of defense, unsure of which direction the next attack would come.

We rolled down the steep incline and I lost my grip on Marion as we were pulled apart. The fire blinded me as much as it provided light and I had to feel along the bottom of the ditch to find his body. He was curled up, one hand stretched forward. He was moving, attempting to crawl as the fire spread around him.

I sucked in the heat. Ice crystals formed on his hair as the fire dampened around us. I turned him over on to his back and covered him with my body to protect him from the flames.

His eyes were open, glazed with pain. His torn shirt exposed the black lines coursing up through his torso, almost to his heart. His hand reached up and cupped my cheek.

"You have the face of an angel." He smiled as if the pain had gone. "Don't leave me again. I never got to tell you. . ."

"Shhh," I said. I pulled the glass vial from my pocket, the cold freezing it to my palm. The black lines of infection under his skin could reach his heart at any moment. He would die. I did not have time to prepare the thembus sap and I did not know the consequences of giving him such a pure dose, but I knew what would happen if I did nothing.

My hands shook as I tried to make the small drop of the almost frozen liquid roll to the end of the tube. Its progress was painfully slow. I leaned closer, holding the vial over Marion's mouth.

He lifted his head, pulling my face down as our lips met. Of all the times for a kiss, this was the most inconvenient. He'd never had great timing. I let myself enjoy the warmth of his lips for three heart beats, steam from the frost I had created around us rising like an offering to the gods watching from above.

I pulled away and watched his eyes roll back in his head, a final sigh as a last grimace of pain crinkled his brow. I pushed the vial toward his mouth, the drop of liquid finally warm enough to roll to the edge of the glass tube.

Just as it fell, someone grabbed me from behind and pulled me backwards. My last image of Marion was with a tiny glimmer of liquid hovering on his lip. I did not see if it rolled into his mouth or fell onto the ground and was wasted.

My view was blocked by the Grand Councilor. The fire around him withered like a force called it into the ground. I grabbed for my dagger, but as I stood, a loose horse, frantic and wild without a rider, jumped over the ditch.

The last thing I saw was the torso of a horse as it collided with my head.

CHAPTER 31

I'M FLOATING on a cloud above a beautiful city, excitement filling me as I try to get closer. A vine grows out of the clouds, slapping me with a stinging nettle. I fall back into the cloud. My hands sink into the softness. I struggle with all my might, but there is no pressure against my palms to allow me to free myself from the fluffy clouds. Each time I make an inch of progress, a vine grows up and wraps around me, my ankle, my wrist, my waste, my neck.

I'm so close. Helefount spreads out before me as the clouds thin and I see two figures below me, walking along the road that leads to the large golden gates of the city. Jaimeson and Father, arms over each other's shoulders, push forward along the ground. I want to catch up with them, call to them, but my arms won't move and my mouth fills with clouds. I fight against the growing vines, breaking one, then another. Wait. Wait for me!

"Calm down. For Kadasha's sake, wake up."

My eyes opened and I tried to sit up, but my hands were being held down by a woman dressed in a gray smock. I stopped struggling and she released the pressure. I could move. I wasn't on a cloud.

"Father. Jaimeson." The vision of them moving forward without me wavered in my mind.

"Is that your name?" the woman asked me. "Strange name for a girl."

"Help me with her." Another voice in the room with plain walls. Nothing to identify where I am.

I sat up to see two more women. One was out cold on the floor, her head covering askew, her eyes closed. She looked young, maybe ten years younger than me. Just a child. The other woman tapped the girl on the hand, trying to wake her up.

"What happened?" I asked.

The older woman kept a hand on my shoulder, pushing me down. I shoved her hand off. Wrinkles collected around her eyes. Her lips thinned and pursed with disapproval.

"She used too much spark when she healed you." I didn't see which woman had answered me. My eyes had been drawn to the ceiling.

Above me, the entire roof was shaped into a dome, painted with detail that gave reality a dull quality. It was the image from my dream—a city laid out above me, painted into the fresco ceiling, perfect and glorious with a shining golden gate and tiny specks for people milling about the streets. A view of Helefount from the air, the streets and buildings in perfect scale, matching the maps I had spent so much time studying.

"Where am I?" I asked.

"This is the Sanatorium, of course," said the older woman still next to me. "We have the best healers in all Tuleves. Wake up, Polisha. It was a simple job. How do you expect to become a healer when you have so little spark?"

"She healed me?" I asked, bringing my attention back to the girl. It was difficult to pull my eyes back to the floor. The ceiling was high above me, but the walls of the small room only extended a little way up, like some large room had been broken up by temporary dividers, allowing me a view of the landscape painted above me, but providing small areas of privacy.

I touched my head and found a still tender spot. I could also sense the darkness in me, empty and hungry as always. Poor girl. I must have sucked more of her spark than I needed. I was surprised I healed at all.

"It wasn't her fault," I said. I grabbed the edge of the bed for balance as the blood rushed to my head. I knelt next to the girl and the other woman moved back. The grumpy matron might have blamed the girl for giving too much spark, but this one knew the problem had been me. I could see it in her eyes. "I must have had a worse injury than you thought. Deeper. Inside."

The night before came to my mind, the horse, the fire, Marion.

"Is Marion all right?" I asked. If my head hadn't already been spinning, I would have jumped up.

On the names of the seven immortals, please let him be alive.

"The son of the Grand Councilor," I said the words slowly. "He would have come in with me, at the same time."

The women's eyes grew large. They looked at each other.

"Please," I said. "He has to be all right."

I felt a squeeze on my hand and looked down. The girl named Polisha had finally opened her eyes. She had an apologetic look on her face.

"He's alive," she said. "But. . ."

"Hush," said the older woman. She came around the bed and pulled Polisha up by the scruff of her robes. "To the furnace with you. You'll be shoveling coal for the next four hours."

I scrambled to my feet. Polisha felt like my only ally in the room. The other woman bowed and backed out the door. I wanted to tell the older woman that Polisha needed rest, that her spark was weak, but I thought I would get a better reaction another way.

"I need someone to stay with me," I said. "In case the healing wasn't enough." I pitched my voice high and whiny. If I was in the Sanatorium, then they were used to dealing with royals. And if they didn't know who I was yet, they might think I was a spoiled girl craving attention to keep her happy.

"I don't have time for this," said the older woman. "Polisha, stay and help where you can. Just don't pass out again."

With a huff of annoyance, the older woman left with one final glance back.

I motioned for Polisha to sit on the bed with me. "Are you hurt?" I asked.

Her eyes widened. She was even younger than I first thought. "I don't know what happened. I could feel your injuries, but once I started healing, I couldn't stop. Did I do enough?" She reached out to touch me again, but I caught her hand.

"You did fine," I said. "I don't need any more and you've spent enough. Are you a healer here in the Sanatorium? You seem. . . young."

The girl's eyes dropped. "I'm only in training. They rarely let me help with healing, but the others were either busy with those injured in the attack or already drained. They didn't think your injuries were severe, so they called me in." She shrugged. "Probably the last chance they'll give me for a while."

"I'm sorry." I meant it. From the authority the older healer carried like a crown on her head, I imagined politics here at the Sanatorium were competitive. "You're stronger than any of them know." I could feel her spark already flaring back to life as I let go of her wrist.

She folded her arms in front of her, but the smile grew on her face. "I'm almost nine."

I hadn't known they brought healers here so young.

"Could you tell me about the Grand Councilor's son?" I asked. "He was with me when we were attacked. I would really like to know if he's okay."

Polisha's eyes were round, deep brown, and shining with curiosity. She checked the open door before she went on in a whisper. "They've never seen anything like it. He has no injuries, no scars, nothing wrong with him that we can tell. Or that we can heal. But he burns like an oven filled with coals and he won't wake up."

My stomach twisted. "No injury at all?" What about the arrow wound? What about the black infection seeping through his veins?

Polisha shook her head with a serious look. "The older healers are baffled. The Grand Councilor is angry."

"Can you take me to him?"

She hesitated and then nodded. "He's in the healing room next to this one."

I slipped out the door, holding the full length shift the healers had covered me with. The room was twice as big as I had imagined, with circular exterior walls and a dome ceiling. The center of the room had a single tower that reached up to the exact place in the Helefount painting where Kadasha's sanctuary was located. The tower had a door in the bottom with solid walls that must have hidden a spiral staircase. The top of this circular tower had a terrace where someone could look out at all the smaller rooms below. I shivered. The wealthy had access to the best healers in the land, but someone seemed intent on watching it all happen. There were no windows to the outside to tell me if it was still night or if the sun had risen.

I gawked for a moment at the image of the city floating above me. My goal was to march into Helefount and ask Kadasha for a gifting. It was right above me, if I could only reach high enough.

The outside circular hallway was busy with more women and men in the same simple gray robes that Polisha was wearing. Healer's uniforms. At least two dozen healers rushed in different directions. One sped by me pushing a soldier laid out on a rolling cart. His uniform was scorched down the entire left side of his body. Memory of the fire and the image of the Grand Councilor standing tall returned to my mind, the flames withering around him.

I slipped into Marion's room and shut the door softly. Even without a closed ceiling, the bustle and call of the healers softened. He lay flat on his back, his face straight up toward the city overhead. His chest rose and fell below the white sheet. My heart fluttered with excitement. He was alive. He had made it to Tuleves City alive.

His eyes were closed, but his features weren't relaxed. The corners of his eyes were strained and there was a furrow between his eyebrows.

I placed my hand against his cheek. My mind filled with visions of fire, flames surrounding me, heat consuming me. I pulled back with a gasp. I'd felt fever from infection and illness, in babies to old men, but I'd never felt the feverish pulse coming off Marion in waves. With a tentative motion, I placed my hand on him again.

He was as hot as a sunbaked cobblestone, but he wasn't dying. He wasn't sick. At least, not in any way I'd seen before. The spark of the sick and dying were like weak flickering candle flames.

His spark was brighter and more brilliant than anything I had ever felt before.

And it was burning him up from the inside.

CHAPTER 32

I BACKED up into the corner behind the door, away from Marion, out of sight of the center tower. The empty windows seemed to have eyes that stared right through me, condemning me. I had put Marion in this place. Garreth may have shot the arrow. The Grand Councilor may have been the one to bring him to Tuleves, but I had given him the thembus extract. I had saved his life only to condemn him to hell.

Marion. I had never meant to make him worse. If his body couldn't contain the strength of his spark, he would go mad.

I looked down at my hands. It seemed every time I tried to help or do something good; I made things worse. I couldn't heal, couldn't give Marion my spark, but that wasn't what he needed. He had enough spark for twenty men. Fifty. Too much spark.

My hands shook a little as I looked at them. For the first time that I could remember, these hands that had never been able to give, only take, were needed for something other than stealing. I glanced up at the darkened terrace at the top of the tower. I couldn't tell if someone was watching, but if there was only one guard he couldn't possibly watch in every direction at the same time.

Kneeling next to Marion, I lifted one of his clammy hands, placing the back of it against my cheek. His fingers were curled in, muscles tight with unconscious agony. What had I done to him? With my other hand I pulled down the sheet enough to expose his bare chest and spread my fingers out, palm flat against the skin right above his heart. His spark almost made him too hot to touch.

I sucked in, pulling the spark into me. I started slowly, hesitant, watching for any signs of distress, hoping I didn't damage him from taking too much, too fast. Even with my hesitation, the effect was immediate. The tension in his face drained away, his fingers slackened in my grip. His breathing evened out and deepened as his entire body relaxed.

My head dropped as I continued to pull. He had so much spark, I wondered if I might finally be able to fill the emptiness inside, but his spark was already down by half. I felt no change inside me beside the pinch beside my heart, the pain stinging my skin. Even this was making the vine tattoo grow. I could feel it. I pushed that fear aside for another time. I thought of our year apart, of the pain I had caused him, both leaving his life and now coming back into it. I wasn't a safe person. I would eventually destroy the lives of everyone I loved.

"I'm sorry." The words slipped unbidden through my lips.

"For saving me again?" Marion's voice startled me so much that I my hand flew off his chest and caught him in the nose. He didn't even flinch even though it felt as if I had punched stone.

"Sorry," I said, rubbing my sore hand. "I didn't mean to. . . I only wanted to. . . You're awake."

He reached out to me, pushing up on his other elbow. "And you're alive." His smile was as strong as the pull of a waterfall dropping off a cliff. I knew I shouldn't, but there was no resisting the current. I moved closer and let him wrap his arms around me. His arms were warm and strong, his smell masculine and alluring. I sat on the bed and snuggled into his embrace. It had been over a year since I'd been hugged.

Jaimeson would give me a pat on the back sometimes, but he always pulled away quickly, nervous, like he was afraid I would hurt him again. I wouldn't hurt him again. I'd promised. I was here for a reason, and as good as this felt, this was not it.

"Listen," I said, pressing both hands against his chest to push him away. I pushed hard, harder, but his arms were like a vice, his chest a wall of iron. He had a new strength, incredible power. A flash of fear jolted through me as I imagined being crushed in his grip.

Then he let go.

"You're stronger than I remember," I said.

"Yeah," he said, touching the muscles on his arms like they were made of a strange new material. "I feel weird." His muscles stood out, large and shaped with precision. I wanted to reach out and touch them, too.

Focus, Arianna.

"Things are a little weird," I said. He raised an eyebrow while poking his own arm.

"More than a little, I would say."

I stared at my hands, trying not to think of his bare chest, his rock-solid body. I could do this.

"I need you to promise not to tell anyone who I am." I'd woken up the one person who could ruin everything. He knew who I was, who I had been. He could ruin things for me in more ways than one.

"Are you in trouble?" The concern in his face, the way he sat up straighter like he could fight off some invisible foe for me, pulled me toward him. I missed the afternoons we had spent together, target practicing side by side. The first to get three bullseyes in a row got a kiss. Both of us always enjoyed the prize.

Before I could answer, the door of the small room swung open with a force that shook the walls. The Grand Councilor walked in, filling the room. A woman followed behind him, her eyes covered with a cloth. The lower half of her face was visible below the strip of cloth. It was beautiful in a way I had never seen. Perfectly shaped lips, high cheekbones. She wore a long white dress that hugged her body in exactly the opposite ways the healer's robes hung on mine.

Garreth entered the room behind her. Prince Garreth, I reminded myself. He was dressed in red silk robes and no longer smelled of death. We were in his castle. Despite our time together, a night with the dead, a day of healing the people, he was a prince. I'd almost let myself forget.

The room was beyond capacity. The air felt thin and there was no escape route. He stood as carefree as ever, leaning his shoulder against the wall, folding his arms like he had somewhere better to be. But I saw him glance at Marion. His eyes closed for an instant too long for it to be a blink. Relief. He cared but preferred not to show it.

"They've already set you to healing?" the Grand Councilor asked me. "Perhaps they should have discussed appropriate healer/patient relationships."

My face flushed with heat, and I jumped off the bed. The room was so small my back was against the wall in three steps. The only exit was blocked. I looked up, gauging the distance to the top of the wall. I could probably jump and grab the top since there was no ceiling, but they would grab my legs before I could pull myself up.

The Grand Councilor moved closer. I prepared to jump, but he reached out for Marion, wrapping his son in an awkward hug.

"I was so worried about you," Councilor Levante said. The same reaction, the same motions as when he had seen Garreth in the village. Either this guy really cared, or he had a funny way of showing his anger at them for running away.

He released Marion and turned to me. "The healers told me there was nothing they could do for him. But I see your reputation proves true. A healer of healers and at such a young age. We usually test the gifting of new healers, but it seems you've already passed your test. That wasn't something that could be done with the gifting of time."

"I don't have the gifting of time." I kept my knees bent, prepared to jump if needed.

The woman with the bandaged eyes nodded. "She speaks truth, but her future is cloudy." The woman in white spoke for the first time with an ageless depth, as if several voices spoke at once.

"Such a powerful gifting of life that you could do what trained healers could not." The Grand Councilor stepped away from his son and placed a hand on Garreth's shoulder. Marion and Garreth both looked at me. Marion's eyes were slitted like he was trying to solve a word puzzle the scribes had drawn too small. I was the puzzle. Garreth stared at me as if I were a jester about to perform an act. He expected me to do something. I had no idea what it was.

The Grand Councilor's words had sounded like praise. I relaxed my stance and curtsied clumsily as I held the edges of my shift together. "It was my honor."

"As it will be your honor to serve here the rest of your days for the newly crowned king." The way the lady in white stared at me, or at least kept her face turned toward me with eerie accurateness, made my skin prickle.

"Excuse me?" The urge to run had increased to a whirling windstorm and I could barely hold myself back from shoving the woman aside and barreling out through the door. There was no strategy in that. I would be surrounded by soldiers in a castle that I knew nothing about. I be thrown straight into a cell and then I would never find Jaimeson or Father. Even if this was a prison, it was at least one that I could explore.

Garreth pushed off the wall and came to stand beside me, putting his arm over my shoulder. I nearly elbowed him in the nose. "Direct as always, My Lady." He said it like a name, not a title. "But I'm sure our overaggressive invitation has once again shadowed the honor of working here."

The Lady's face showed no emotion, but her fingers twitched. Her posture straightened even more. A shadow moved across her features. The cloth, which looked like a bandage, seemed to sink into her eye sockets, making her look skeletal and ill.

The Grand Councilor did nothing to hide his disappointment and loomed over us, his face a dark cloud.

"You'll learn to show respect before the ceremony," he said. "While I'm glad you've returned, I cannot let your trespass go unpunished, especially since Marion was nearly killed. You're about to be crowned King of Tuleves. The life of everyone in this kingdom will become your responsibility."

"My father didn't take his responsibility very seriously." Garreth's voice was still flippant, but it had lost his carefree tone and was weighed down by a deep emotion. "What kind of king do you expect me to be when my father abandoned everyone for a pleasure trip to Helefount? Why should I have to clean up the mess he left us in?"

It was sudden. A split second. My eyes didn't even catch the movement until the Grand Councilor slapped Garreth's face. The crack echoed up to the painted ceiling. I imagined the healers out in the hallway pausing as the sound reverberated around the entire Sanatorium.

Marion stood, the legs of his bed screeching against the floor, the bed crunching into the wall, the frame breaking into the plaster.

"Father," he started.

The Grand Councilor held up his hand. Marion clenched his teeth. Garreth's fingers curled into my shoulder as if he was using me to hold himself back.

Grand Councilor Levante spoke to the prince, ignoring Marion. "Your father sacrificed everything for this kingdom, as have I. I will not have you insulting his name again. Or The Lady. She is the reason we have not fallen to ruin in your father's absence. You will learn to abide her council if you wish to save us all."

Garreth's fingers loosened and he took a deep breath. "You think I can save us? You think the council will listen to anything I have to say? Why even bother to make me king when you know I'm meant to be a pawn, my authority stripped by a blind woman and spoiled royals on the council?"

The air around the Grand Councilor shimmered and shivered, like the space above an open flame and then it was gone. Perhaps I just imagined it. He stepped away from us and offered his arm to The Lady. She finally took her covered gaze off me and turned her face up to the Grand Councilor, nodding slightly as if to reassure him of something. Grand Councilor Levante took in a deep breath to calm himself.

"You are meant to be king," he said. "And I have faith you will do what it takes to protect us from what is coming." He turned as The Lady led him out the door. "Ten stripes in the lower levels. To remind you that, as king, your actions will have far reaching consequences."

"Punish me," Marion said, but he seemed unable to move. "I'm as deserving as the prince."

"Rest," the Grand Councilor said. "You've suffered enough for your loyalty."

I pushed Garreth's arm off my shoulder where he'd been hanging on me as if he carried the weight of a kingdom. This was too much. I had no ability to help a prince save himself from his own stupidity. I had to find my brother and father and get as far from Tuleves City as I could.

"Grand Councilor Levante," I said, stepping forward, trying to show submissiveness even though that had never been a personality strength. I'd had practice in Prontwick, though. "I wanted to request a place in the Tournament of the People. I would love to compete at the prince's coronation."

"Like I explained to the prince," he said. "Honor and responsibility come with a price. You've been invited to serve in the Sanatorium. This is your home now. Healers live and work here. Learn the rules. Follow orders. And you'll find your new life can be quite rewarding." He guided The Lady into the hall.

"And if I'd had the gifting of time?" I asked. I couldn't help it. They acted as if the fact that I'd passed some test meant I was now cleared for a life of imprisonment. That could only be a good thing if the alternative was worse. If Orblee had been found as a girl as young as Polisha, she wouldn't have passed the test.

The Grand Councilor paused one more time. "It is a capital punishment unless endorsed by Kadasha herself."

"A public hanging?" I had never heard of a public execution for someone with the gifting of time.

"No." The Lady was the one to answer. "We waste no giftings here. The blood of those gifted with time would still be able to serve your kingdom. Even in death." They walked away as if they'd commented on the weather over the bay.

Thank goodness Orblee had remained free of this evil place. But now I was stuck here. Even if I could escape the healer prison, I wasn't going to be allowed to compete in the Tournament of the People. Not as myself. Dawn had been wrong. It wasn't time to show my own face. If I was to win the Tournament of the People, it would have to be as the Hooded Robber. That way, I'd have the people on my side. Even The great Grand Councilor wouldn't want to face the wrath of the people if he failed to keep his decree for the people's hero.

A moment later two soldiers came to the door. "Your Highness. We will escort you to your punishment."

Garreth walked past me, his head held high. He'd lost his swagger, but he still tried to act like he didn't care.

"I'll come with you," Marion said, finally moving forward. He stumbled, unstable on his feet.

"Not on your life," Garreth said. "You've done me no good so far."

My mouth fell open. How could he say such things after all Marion had done for him? Then I saw the pleading look that passed between them. Marion wasn't well. I didn't like the sheen of sweat that had returned to his face. Stress would not be good for him and watching his best friend get whipped ten times would do him no good when he was still recovering.

"I'll go with him," I said, placing my hand on Marion's chest and pushing him back toward the bed. "You need to rest. Healer's orders."

He allowed me to push him down reluctantly. This time his concern was directed at me. "You're not a healer," he whispered.

"You promised not to tell anyone," I said, even though it wasn't exactly true.

He shook his head, his eyes drilling into mine. "If they find out you're an imposter, they'll kill you."

CHAPTER 33

"Am I really not allowed to leave?" I asked Garreth as he strolled casually between the two soldiers. Neither of them had touched him, but Garreth had shown no sign of resistance. I wondered what the soldiers would do if he tried to run. Or if I did.

He gave a quick nod. "Healers caught outside the Sanatorium are brought back, punished, and put under extra supervision. Only two have tried that I remember. Neither of them tried again." A muscle protruded in his cheek, and for the first time since I'd met him, he looked truly sad.

"You know your healer history." I said lightly. For some reason, seeing the prince in a dark mood made the world feel off balance.

"I spent a lot of time here with my mother." He shifted his shoulders like he was taking off a heavy cape. He sucked whatever emotion had slipped to the surface back inside him, then winked at me. "The only way to leave is with an official invitation from royalty."

"What does that mean?" I asked.

The soldiers led us to a door, unlocking it with a key from their belt. We had walked halfway around the large room, the tower always gazing down on me with those empty windows.

"It means that it's a good thing you know a prince," he said.

Before I could respond, the soldiers opened the door and pushed me through. The smell of rot and soiled cloth hit me first. Then the sounds. It was as if the very walls groaned as I slipped down steps wet with moisture. A scream echoed up the stairwell, ragged and animalistic, but I believed it was human.

My lungs squeezed together like they were in a press. My heart hammered like a blacksmith's anvil. I turned to flee back up the stairs, but Garreth was right behind me. The soldiers shut the door, cutting off the light from the Sanatorium.

"Where does this lead?" I asked. There was a faint light coming from below painting shadows on Garreth's face.

"To the lower levels."

I moved down another step. His fingers tightened, almost holding me back. I wondered if the pressure was his own fear, rather than for my comfort. Garreth would have to endure being whipped ten times. I had heard forty could kill a man. Surely, ten would leave him unable to attend a coronation ceremony in a few days. Maybe that was his plan.

We reached the last stair. The floor spread out in a small open area. A single torch burned on the wall next to the stairs. Two soldiers sat at a small table playing cards. They stood at attention when they saw the prince.

"Jeffrey. Kahl." He addressed them by name. One of them even let a half smile slip.

"Back again?" the taller one asked, the one who had smiled. Garreth apparently attended the prisons enough to make friends with the guards. I imagined Garreth being whipped for every time he'd been in the village gossip for another act of defiance. He must have a strong resistance to pain.

"How long has it been?" Garreth asked.

"You almost made it six weeks."

"So, who won the wager?"

"I did." One of the soldiers who had brought us down the stairs put out his hand. "I wagered he'd wait over five weeks for the next run. I was closest."

The two standing by the table grumbled as they put their hands in their pockets and drew out two dinarah, placing them in the other soldier's hand. They bet on how often the Prince of Tuleves would visit the dungeons? And he encouraged it?

Garreth reached into his own pocket and pulled out a pouch heavy with coin. "My goal was less than two weeks, so I've definitely lost." He tossed the dinarah on the table. They spilled out onto the cards. My mouth dropped open. It was enough to buy two good horses and a wagon, enough money for me to equip my family for a journey to Hele-fount and be rid of this land forever. "Whose turn is it this time? Did they bring down Harley? He was on duty when Marion and I slipped past him."

Suddenly things made sense. The prince received no whips. He was the future king after all. Of course, the Grand Councilor would find a scapegoat to take the punishment for him. And Garreth gave these soldiers coin to ease his conscience.

"You watch people get whipped for you?" I turned on him, my anger rising to the surface. In the last few days, I had started to see him as a human being, but he was a tyrant through and through.

"Levante knows I hate it more than anything, but we've worked out a system. The healers come quickly. And the boys here get to take a little extra home to their family." He shrugged, but there was a catch in his words.

The soldier who had smiled now nodded. "I've taken the beating three times. Kahl here's only done it once. I got four kids and I'm saving up to buy a farm one day. Put my gifting of strength to real use."

The other three soldiers didn't respond, shifting and glancing at one another nervously. Garreth noticed, too.

"What's going on?" he asked.

"She said it was going to be different this time," Kahl said, shrugging. "We weren't told who it's going to be. There's a rumor it's one of the prisoners."

Garreth stiffened beside me. "A prisoner?"

Another door made of thick black wood, a small, barred window in the center, opened on the far side of the small room. The smell and the sounds intensified. The flickering orange of reflected flame danced on the back of the largest man I had ever seen. He filled the door frame. A short skirt of leather surrounded his lower half, while a belt as thick as a horse's neck held up the cloth and several weapons. His bare chest was sweaty and one of his eyes was completely white, the other so bloodshot it looked red.

"My prince," he said. "Your show awaits."

"Who is it, Yert?" Garreth asked.

Yert. He was on a first name basis with the prison master. I ignored the part of his voice that sounded like he cared who might be taking his punishment. Over and over again, Garreth had defied the orders of the council and the Grand Councilor, knowing that someone would be punished for him.

"If you knew someone was going to be hurt," I hissed at him as we followed Yert through the door, "why do you keep doing it? Why do you keep forcing people to be hurt for you?"

"It's not something you'd understand." His attention was focused on Yert who had yet to answer his question.

My entire insides seethed like a den of snakes that had been poked with a stick. I understood people getting hurt for me. I understood causing others pain. But letting people get hurt when I knew I could stop it? He was right. I couldn't even begin to fathom.

The floor tilted downward at an even slope, the smell worsening the lower we got. The walls were made of rough brick and stone, mortared together haphazardly, interrupted at uneven intervals with barred doors. It was too dark to see very far into the caverns, but behind the bars were slowly moving lumps in the shadows.

Then Yert's words sunk through the coiling and writhing inside me like they were reaching me through a noisy room.

"The Lady said he volunteered," said Yert. "Soldiers brought him in two days ago. He was accused of associating with the Hooded Robber, but the prisoner said it was a misunderstanding. He'd been in the wrong place at the wrong time. Stuck to his story even in the blood room. Brave man, not much older than my son. When The Lady said she couldn't trust him because he had the gifting of reason, he said he would do anything she asked to earn her trust."

My mind took time to examine each word Yert said, allowing me to notice odd things. First, his voice was mild and smooth. I would have imagined a gravely grunt as his chosen form of communication, but he spoke as an educated landowner, the tone slightly higher than my father's.

Second, I realized I knew exactly who had volunteered to take the prince's punishment.

"A young man?" Garreth sounded like he might be sick.

"No." I wasn't even sure the word made it out of me in a whisper.

Yert stopped. I wasn't surprised when I recognized the shirtless prisoner chained in the middle of an empty cavern, but I couldn't stop the gasping sob that slipped past my lips.

I'd found my brother.

CHAPTER 34

MY HEART STUTTERED and the floor seemed to tip sideways. I had to hold the doorframe, but I used the movement to put myself between Yert and Jaimeson.

"Leave me." The words came out with more command than I thought possible. Yert gripped the whip tighter. Garreth raised an eyebrow. "Give me a few moments alone with him. Please."

There was no escape. The good news was my brother, the planner, was here. I needed a minute alone with him so he could tell me the plan.

Garreth had no idea what I was doing, but he stepped back into the hallway. Yert wasn't as easily moved.

"Why?" he asked. "He has already volunteered."

"Because," I said, shifting to my full height. Yert was huge all around, but I tried to stand tall enough to look him in the eye. "I'm a healer from the Sanatorium. I need to make sure he will survive the whipping. The prince would not want to be responsible for the death of one of his own subjects."

"True," Garreth said. As much as I hated him right now, I was glad he was willing to follow my lead. "A healer checks every time."

Yert grunted. His blinded eye widened while the bloodshot eye closed to a slit. He stepped back into the hallway next to Garreth and shut the door. I had been so focused on my brother that I hadn't looked around. The room was made of smooth stone with whitewashed walls and floor. Spotless, as if it had been cleaned and repainted only hours before. It was nothing like the grimy cells I had glimpsed higher up in the dungeons. Chains dangled from the ceiling, holding Jaimeson's arms above his head. His head drooped forward, his chest muscles stretched, and his shoulders pulled back painfully.

Maybe he was already dead. I wished I was truly a healer with the gifting of life. At this moment, I'd even take the gifting of time. Even if it was a capital punishment, I'd turn back the rotation of the world. Change everything that had brought Jaimeson to this moment.

"Jaimeson?" I said his name. Hesitant. Frightened.

At the sound of my voice, my brother lifted his head. I rushed forward and wrapped my arms around him. His skin was slick with fever. He smelled of sweat and blood, but I couldn't help feeling a deep relief at being with him again. We were a duo. The two of us, together, could figure a way out of this.

"What are you doing here?" He pulled away from me, shaking like a dog ridding itself of fleas. He stared at me as if I were an unexpected annoyance, an unexpected wrinkle in his plan.

For a moment, I was the sparkless girl that the villagers looked down on, an insect to be squashed, a nobody. I had never felt that way with Jaimeson before.

"I came to the Sanatorium." The words stuttered out of me. "They brought me here and they don't let us out."

He raised an eyebrow. "Did the soldiers raid Orblee's? You're no healer."

He thought I'd been caught at Orblee's. Did he really think I had gone back to my daily routine while Iranus the Tracker rode off with my only brother? Did he think I would just leave him? Heat replaced the shame. Anger grew inside me like a fire fed by the spark of ten men.

"I came for you." The words hissed between my teeth as I fought to keep from yelling. "I was coming to save you. Did you really think I would leave?"

Jaimeson dropped his eyes to the floor. He seemed to sag even lower in his chains. "I was hoping."

Hoping? I didn't even know where to put the word. It hung between us, dangling like my brother. His body rotated slightly. I caught a glimpse of his back. Crisscrossed with scars, white with their newness. He'd been cut and healed dozens of times. I covered my mouth to stifle a sob.

I reached to touch the largest scar that ran from the top of his shoulder down to his last rib. He flinched. "What happened to you?" But I already knew. The Lady said they had questioned him. Cutting him and healing him just enough to keep him alive. And Jaimeson hadn't talked. He didn't tell them about me, or about the Hooded Robber. He had suffered all this to protect me.

Finally, he raised his head, shrugging and straightening as best he could. He used the tips of his toes to stop his body from turning away from me. "Well, you're here now. Tell me what happened. How did you end up in the Sanatorium instead of the dungeons?"

His strength gave me hope. "There's no time for the whole story. I'll tell you in song once I get you out of here. The important thing is that we're here together. We can get Father out and go to Helefount, just like we always wanted. Freedom. Safety. And. . ." I paused, excitement filling me at the news, "I found Dawn. We can take her with us. All of us together, to Helefount, the City of Kadasha."

He showed thoughtful interest as I spoke until I said Dawn's name. At the mention of her, his entire body stiffened. His face went blank. He had loved Dawn as much as I. Maybe more. Days before the soldiers came to take Father, he'd said he would spend the rest of his life with her. She had looked him in the eyes and told him he'd already chosen a path without her.

Dawn's disappearance after the fire was as devastating to Jaimeson as Mother's death.

"She's alive?" His tone was stony, emotionless, made of cracked granite.

I studied his face. "She's alive and well. She used her gifting of life to become a healer. I found her when I kidnapped the prince and the son of the Grand Councilor. Marion was injured. I intended to use him as a ransom to get you back, but that wouldn't work if he had died. Dawn helped heal him with herbs from the ruins of the Oracles, but then the Grand Councilor found us. I came here so Dawn could escape instead of being trapped to serve the royals." I never babbled, but the words poured out of me like they could wash Jaimeson's wounds clean. "But now we're together. I know you've got a plan. I know you can think of something."

"Enough" His words felt like a physical force. "No more. I don't want to hear it."

I reached for his face that had turned away from me. His cheek was hot, his jaw clenched. His entire body trembled. I had never seen my brother look so defeated. They had cut him, tortured him, and planned to whip him again. He could not bear it.

"We have to get you out of here," I said. "Make a plan and we will work the impossible, just like always. You cannot survive ten lashes."

"That's why you're here?" he said, realization bringing the light back into his eyes, though it didn't flicker with excitement like usual. This light smoldered with hunger. "You're in the Sanatorium because of Dawn?"

"I took her place so I could come find you," I said. "Now hurry up and tell me the plan." I checked the door. We didn't have a lot of time for planning. I was sure Yert was already cracking his knuckles and trying to convince Garreth we'd had enough time.

"I have a plan." Jaimeson took a deep breath, pushing his shoulders back.

"Great," I said. His voice exuded zero confidence, but I had to cling to something. "I can freeze the door while we dig a tunnel."

He shook his head.

"Tell me then," I said, waving my hand in a grand motion. "What's your plan?"

"I don't want to run, Arianna. That's never been what I wanted to do. I have a plan to fix things, to make it better. You'll have to run on your own. I want you to be safe. I want you to have your freedom, but I can make a difference. I have a gifting that could change everything."

His words stung, a lash across my soul. He had a gifting that could help while I had nothing. "I can help."

His face relaxed, sorrow and pity and love all mixed together. His fingers straightened above his head, reaching as he tried to pull on the chains to get closer.

I reached up, twisting my fingers with his.

"No."

Another lash. My soul felt gutted, spilling out hope all over the floor.

"I need you to be safe. Get as far from Tuleves City as you can. You are not part of my plan."

His words stung like a slap to the face in cold weather. "Jaimeson."

"Go, Arianna," he said. "You can't save me, but I can save others if you get out of the way."

"What about Father?"

"If I succeed, all will be well."

"I won't leave you."

"Yes, you will."

I tried to pull my fingers away, but Jaimeson tightened his grip until it became painful. My brother. My confidant and companion. His pupils expanded. His eyes narrowed.

"Run," he said. "Run away and don't think of me again."

His spark pushed into me, different than when I pulled. I couldn't stop it, couldn't push it back. I felt my mind complying. I wanted to run. As he let go of my hand, I remembered another moment from the night a year ago.

"We have to find her," I screamed. "We have to find Dawn before the house burns down."

"There's no time," Jaimeson said. "We have to get out now. The fire is spreading too quickly. She'll be fine."

"No." I turned and started to run up the stairs.

He tackled me, pulling me down and wrapping his arms around me. I tried to struggle, but all I could do was get one arm loose and push it up against his neck, trying to push him off me.

A curtain fell from the high windows, crashing on the stairs next to us. My instincts were to protect us from the flame. I pulled the heat into me.

Jaimeson screamed. His neck froze, instant frostbite where my arm pressed up against him.

"I'm sorry."

He placed his hands on either side of my face. "Run. Run to the shed and don't look back."

My mind screamed in protest as my body did exactly as Jaimeson commanded. Again.

I ran from the room, pushing past Garreth and Yert, unable to look back or change my direction. I ran down the slanted hallway, passing the human cages without a second glance. The snap of a whip echoed through the prison. Jaimeson's yell of pain chased me. But I couldn't turn around. I couldn't go back. I staggered, unable to walk in a straight line as my mind warred against my body. My hands shook as I slammed against a metal grate. My vision was blurry. I couldn't see where I was going as I turned random corners. My fingers scraped against damp walls. The air turned colder as I ran blindly.

Hot tears traced down my cheeks as I squeezed my eyes shut. I reached another passage with a single cell door at the end. A dead end. I fell to the ground, unable to go back. I fought the urge to keep running with every ounce of spark I had in me. Even with nowhere to go, I needed to keep moving.

I lay on the cool granite floor, the effort of resisting the urge to keep running making me twist and writhe. The swirling blackness whirled and warped, mocking me. I curled into a ball, rocking back and forth and hugging my knees.

Don't think of me again.

His memory slipped away like a homemade bar of lye soap. I grasped at it, fighting the gifting, fighting to keep the memory of my brother, fighting the desire to run like always. And now I knew why. For an entire year I had been fighting the urge to run because of Jaimeson's gifting. There was so much pain behind that realization, but along with it came a small sense of relief.

I wasn't a coward after all. Still, I had left someone to be whipped. The shame sat like a rock in my throat. I had left someone, again. I couldn't remember them, but I felt the shame of giving up, of giving in.

I was a prisoner of the Sanatorium without a plan. I could attempt to escape. I could stay and work my way into the good graces of the royals. I could continue to pretend to be a healer in the Sanatorium and rob royals while hiding in plain sight.

Whatever happened, whatever I decided to do, I knew that this time, I would not run.

CHAPTER 35

THERE WERE no clues to the passage of time. The dancing light from a few torches created moving shadows. The drips from condensation on the ceiling created an inconsistent ticking like a wind-up clock missing teeth in the cogs. My shaking slowly subsided.

I would not run. I would not run anymore. I set the cadence in my head to match the dripping water.

When I finally had the strength to stand, I pushed up onto my knees. A humming sound stopped me. I knew the tune. I used the bars on the final cell, the one that had blocked me from running any farther, to climb to my feet.

I pressed my face against the cold metal trying to see into the shadows of the cell.

The humming continued. My eyes adjusted to the different grays of the walls, the dark hue of the blanket, a lump resting on the ground in the corner.

The tune reached the chorus and I couldn't help saying the words. "No riches, no fame, no power obtained, are worth more than a lifetime with you."

The form on the ground shifted. The humming stopped.

"I'm sorry. I didn't mean to disturb you. That song was my mother's favorite."

The prisoner drew closer, crawling on all fours like a hunched animal until the blanket slipped from their shoulders. Torch light fell on a bearded face with sunken cheeks as he stood. His head touched the top of the small cell. He was tall enough that he still wasn't standing straight.

"Are you a phantom? A dream meant to torture me?" A hand whipped through the bars. His grip on my arm was feather light, his strength sucked away by this place. I almost pulled back, but he could do nothing to hurt me. And the small amount of torch light that reflected in his eyes, held me in place.

It couldn't be possible. There was no gifting that could defeat odds like this. There had to be a thousand cells in this maze of a dungeon.

"How is it that you carry my daughter's face to me in the depths of this darkness?"

"Father?" I felt the choking pressure in the back of my throat, but I would not let tears blur my vision of this man. I had meant to save him, not join him in the dungeons.

"Arianna? How are you here?" The question rang as an empty echo of another person's question. *How did you get here?* I could not remember the person or the context. But it didn't matter right now. I'd found my father. After almost nearly a year, I was face to face with him again.

"I came to win your freedom." I obviously hadn't worked out all the details yet. Not only was I a prisoner of the Sanatorium, but I was also lost in the dungeons. "There is an archery tournament, one meant for the people. If I win, the Grand Councilor will allow me to pardon one person. I will be able to clear our name. You will be free."

My father's hand moved from my arm to touch a strand of my hair that had pulled lose. The healers of the Sanatorium had pulled my hair back when they'd put me in these loose healer's robes, but my struggle to stop running through the dungeons had left my hair wild about my head.

"What would make the Grand Councilor keep such a bargain? You won't be allowed to win."

"I will wear a mask. I will be disguised as a hero to the people. They will have to keep their promise or risk the people's anger." The plan had holes. I was a prisoner of the Sanatorium and I had lost my bow. I felt the ache of the loss of it deep inside my gut. Even with my father standing in front of me, I knew that bow was gone forever. His skill might never be the same after this. I could steal one. I was the Hooded Robber after all. It would be more difficult to shoot with enough accuracy to win with a bow that did not fit me correctly.

"You do not need to wear a mask. Your greatest power lies in being who you truly are. Still, it sounds like a trick to me. Perhaps a trap. Your mother would smell that out in a moment." His lower lip shook. His eyes gleamed in the low light. I could tell he'd seen Mother's last moments as well. "How I've missed her. How I've missed all of you. I'm sorry I failed you as a father. I should have protected you and instead I put you all in danger."

"You were fighting for what you believed was right." I took my father's hand and pressed it against my face. The strong hands that had crafted bows with perfection, bent wood to their will, were as weak as bird bones. I felt if I squeezed too hard, I would crush his fingers. "I have never blamed you."

"There's more that you don't know." A cough cut off his words. It rattled in his chest as he struggled to catch his breath.

"You need a healer."

"Even if you find a way to pardon me, there are others who are more important. Your mother was an Arjodite. Her mission was to protect the Oracles before they were massacred."

"A healer told me. I knew mother was a warrior, but I didn't know she was an Arjodite. I didn't know I had Arjodite blood in me. But I know now, and I'll use whatever power I have to set you free. You were wrongly accused. You paid your taxes and were faithful to the king. You always taught me to support my country."

"I was accused of tax evasion to hide a deeper crime, one that I am guilty of. One that you all had to pay the price for."

I suddenly became aware of where we were. There were other cell doors on either side of me. No one seemed to be moving, but I was sure our conversation carried.

"Don't say any more." I would learn what he was talking about once I got him free of this cage. "I will get you out of here and we will go to Helefount."

"It isn't the paradise you imagine."

"But it is where Kadasha lives. And I want to ask for a gifting. I might have been able to make a difference. I wouldn't be so useless if I had a gifting."

"You are far from useless. You are my daughter. And you are the hope of the future."

I smiled against his palm. He always loved to spout poetic words for Mother. Making bows and writing love poems on the side. "I missed you so much. I have to get you out soon or they will send you to Helefount in a slave train. I cannot let you endure that."

"Don't risk the world on my account. There are other lives you were meant to protect. I am just glad I was able to see you one last time."

"Don't talk like that."

"Listen, when the time comes, I need you to be willing to make the right choice, even if it means letting me go."

"It won't come to that. I will not be forced to choose." It was my greatest fear. The nightmare that haunted me.

"Promise me."

Footsteps sounded from behind me. I whirled.

Three soldiers and the Grand Councilor came around the corner of the dungeon hall.

"Attempting to escape the Sanatorium through the dungeons is a poor plan. If you'd like a cell instead of a place of honor, that can be arranged." The Grand Councilor looked over my shoulder into the cell behind me.

When I checked for my father, he had slunk back into the shadows. I couldn't see him anymore. I hoped the Grand Councilor hadn't heard our conversation. I was still supposed to be the healer. My mask was still in place.

"I wasn't attempting to escape." I held my chin high and brushed my healer's robes off with a frustrated sigh. "I made a wrong turn and became lost. I would appreciate your help finding my way home." I swallowed hard after that last word. I didn't have a home. Not anymore.

"Escort her back to the Sanatorium."

One of the soldiers tried to take my arm, but I pulled free and motioned that I would follow him. I walked away from my father, leaving him in a cell. But I would be back. And one way or another, I would find a way to set him free.

CHAPTER 36

THE SOLDIERS ESCORTED me back to the small room with no ceiling of its own. This was where I had woken up. I still could not sense the time of day. I missed the sun and the stars, and I hadn't even been here a full rotation. If Polisha had not come in with a meal only a short time after the soldiers dropped me off, I might have gone mad from not knowing.

I tried to calculate how much time each event had taken that day, but a dizziness kept me from thinking clearly. It hadn't taken long to wake Marion. I wondered how he fared. Then I had gone to the dungeons with Garreth. I couldn't remember why or what I had done. I only remembered the urgency to run, to get away. Then I had found my father. Had it all happened before the midday meal, or had I missed the setting and rising of the sun?

I paced in the small room, slapping the walls with the palms of my hands every once in a while, to disperse the tension building up inside me.

The door opened with a rush of sound from the hallway. Polisha pushed in with a tray in her hands. I sprung toward he like she was a lifeline and I a drowning sailor without a ship. She flinched at my movement. I stepped back, hands raised.

"I've brought your evening meal." Her voice was soft. Her eyes lowered. I restrained myself from giving her a hug.

"Evening." I let out a sigh. "It's evening on the same day I arrived here?"

She nodded.

The grounding in time seemed to settle my world. The ship stopped rocking. My mind cleared of some of the fog. A deep ache remained. Something missing. Something lost. I'd found my father, but that had brought up the memory of the soldier shattering my bow. That must be it. I couldn't think of another reason for the emptiness that ate at me.

"Tomorrow you will start your duties. I'm to train you in the systems and processes of the Sanatorium. They already know you are a great healer and require no training. I think the others are afraid of you."

"Are you afraid of me?" She was the only person who really had a reason to be afraid. I'd drained her spark on our first meeting and left her passed out on the floor.

She finally lifted her eyes to meet mine. Her eyes were large for her face. Wide open and innocent. Her pupils were surrounded by a deep blue that reminded me of the pond next to my home.

"No. You don't frighten me. You talk to me like I'm a real person and not a rag to be tossed around. And I saw you help that soldier, the big one with all the muscles. You're here to make things better and I want to help."

I shook my head as I took the food from her. "I can't make anything better. I can barely manage a few minutes trapped in this room." I lifted the bowl to my lips and drank the soup. It was thin, but savory. The bread was soft and made fresh that day.

She perked up when I finished. "I get bored, too. They say it will get better as I age, but that seems so far away. Do you want to come to the training area with me? It is mostly for the soldiers' recovery, but the healers are allowed to practice, too. We wouldn't be very good at rehabilitating a soldier if we didn't know the moves they needed to be able to do."

I could have kissed the girl on her forehead. Anything to be out of this small room. And a training area could have the bow and arrow I needed to steal for the Tournament of the People. There was still hope. I could do this alone. For some reason, that thought made the pain of missing something flare up into my throat. I swallowed the lump.

Polisha led me to the far side of the circular courtyard beyond the dividing rooms. A large open area had targets against the wall, a rack filled with practice weapons, a sparring ring, and an observation area. Several healers were huddled together whispering while taking furtive glances toward the arena.

A single person stood at the end of the archery range, focused on the targets. His straight shoulders and soldier's stance sent a flutter to my already confused heart. Marion must not have been able to rest. He had looked for a place to examine his thoughts the same way I needed a place to come to grips with mine.

Polisha ran over and climbed up to the highest row of benches. She sat on her hands, feet swinging beneath her. She was a child who needed a childhood, not some healer trapped in this circular rat maze.

I pulled a bow from the weapons rack with more force than necessary. The weight was off balance, the string made of a weak material, and the grip was made for a hand three times the size of mine. The loss of my bow hit me with the force of a horse kick to the chest. I nearly stumbled from the pain of it.

Anger and frustration were my anchors. I felt a deep frustration with something, someone that I could not place, could not relieve. Marion was here, though, and he had some things to answer for.

I stepped up beside him at the top of the archery range, noting that the targets were less than fifteen horse lengths away. I could almost throw my arrow at them. I tried not to look at Marion as I set three arrows next to me and nocked the first one. The fletching was so tattered the feathers could have been taken from a drowned duck.

I failed at keeping my eyes off him. His head hung like the bow at his side, low and forlorn. His jaw muscle twitched and his eyes were closed. I wasn't even sure if he knew I was next to him. I let out a loud huff of air and released my arrow. I didn't usually breathe loudly while shooting, but I wanted to get his attention. I wanted him to see the anger I put behind my shot.

My first shot hit to the left of the bullseye because of the awkward weight of the bow. I adjusted. The next arrow hit high and to the right. My third shot hit the target's heart. Hardly an accomplishment at such close range, but I straightened my shoulders and raised my chin like I had proven my point.

I withered inside when his gaze turned to me.

"You always talked better with your bow than your mouth." Humor laced his voice, though it still sounded deep with sadness. He was trying to smile with the edge of his words.

I sucked in air, pretending it was strength and faced him, forcing the words out before his eyes could disarm me. "You didn't tell me. I didn't know who you were."

He betrayed no shock or surprise. Instead, he took in every detail of my face like a marooned man searching for water. "I still can't believe you're alive."

"We've established that," I said, trying desperately to cling to the anger, to see him as the enemy he'd become. "We've moved on to the fact that before you thought I was dead, you lied to me for a year." My voice rose in volume and the small circle of healers had stopped talking and now watched us. Polisha leaned forward like she was attending a local acting guild.

I spoke in a whispered hiss. "How could you tell me you loved me when you couldn't even tell me who your father was?"

His shoulders sagged even farther. He looked at something above me, his focus far away, much further than the edges of the room.

"It was so nice," he said, "to pretend I was someone else, to actually be myself. With you, I wasn't the Grand Councilor's son or a spoiled royal." A smile touched the edge of his lips as he raised his voice to impersonate me on the last two words. I had often spoken of spoiled royals. How awful that must have made him feel. "I was me, the person I wanted to be, when I was with you."

My mouth went dry. My tongue forgot how to swallow. He turned away from me after several heartbeats of silence. I willed myself to say something, anything, but my lungs had seized. My brain had become a smooth frozen lake where nothing could take purchase.

"That sounded crazier out loud than it did in my brain." He

laughed bitterly. "I know you can't understand not wanting to be who you are. You were always so confident."

"No." I interrupted him, placing my hand on his arm. "No. I. . . understand."

His arm was warm, even though the heavy fabric of the shift the healers had given him. The muscles of his forearm were tense, rippled, and hard as a rock. For a fleeting moment, I wondered if he wore as little under his shift as the nothing I wore under mine.

"I'm sorry." We echoed each other's words.

Then he flashed me his smile, his real smile so full of gratitude and longing that I felt like my stomach could rumble with physical hunger. I leaned closer, expecting his arms to wrap around me, warm me, fill a piece of that ever-hungry darkness within me.

He pulled away and straightened. A darkness deepened beneath his eyes. The crevasse grew between his eyebrows. "Not that it matters now."

My breath caught. My heart stuttered with confusion. I felt as if a horse had stopped beneath me and thrown me over its head. I had started out the conversation wanting to show Marion how angry I was, but I hadn't expected him to push me away so suddenly.

"Why?" I asked, forgetting that my voice would bounce off the rounded ceiling of the Sanatorium. "Because I know who you are now? Because I'm angry? I'm angry because you thought I would care who your father was. I loved the person you were, not your last name."

"The key word there is 'were.'" Garreth inserted himself into the conversation like he belonged. I didn't know how long he'd been standing on the edge of the arena, but he leaned against a practice dummy with an arrogance that gave me a perfect target for the anger quivering inside me. "He is definitely not the person he was, and we could have a hearty debate about the technical term of person. Human? Maybe. Monster? More accurate. Dander sniffer? Now we're getting more accurate."

I aimed an arrow at the prince's heart. This wasn't my father's bow. The healers screamed and scattered, except for Polisha who only straightened, her eyes wide. I could kill a man who'd had others whipped for his own spoiled temper tantrums. I hesitated, my thoughts catching on a missing piece like a sliver on a smoothed bow. Marion grabbed my arrow and bow, pulling them up and out of my hands, wiping his brow with the effort.

Still protecting his precious prince.

I lunged for the weapons rack and pulled out a fighting pole. I ran toward Garreth, bringing the stick down toward his shoulder. He didn't even flinch when Marion stepped between us. He blocked my attack with his real sword, cutting my pole in half. Curse Kadasha's saints and Garreth's bodyguards. Curse them all.

I threw down the half pole. "Fine. No weapons but yourself, you swine, you son of a snotle."

"And risk getting dirt on my robe?" Garreth raised his eyebrows in mock surprise. "Sounds lame. Fight her for me, Marion."

"Good to see you properly contrite after your punishment," he said, tossing my bow to the side. And your ability to insult people has not improved in the slightest." He directed these last words toward me.

He was making jokes when I was ready to carve the smile off Prince Garreth's face.

"Sorry to interrupt and to take a rain check on a very thrilling fight, but I have some business with our newest healer." Garreth motioned for Marion to move to the side. He was giving me a straight shot at him. I wasn't going to miss my chance again. But his next words stopped me.

"Did you show her?" Garreth asked Marion.

He shook his head. "Not yet."

"Show me what?" I asked.

Garreth gave a nonchalant wave of his hand like a damsel dropping her handkerchief before a joust. Marion lifted the bow that had been dangling from his fingertips since I had first seen him. It wasn't a practice bow like I had assumed. The bow had a thick stock made of osage wood with a smooth finish. Not my father's craftsmanship but finely made.

Marion put an arrow on the nock and pulled the string back as if he held a toy bow. He showed no sign of effort. He pulled past the point where the bow was ready to release, where the tension would have been the greatest, but he didn't stop. It was like he couldn't feel the pull of the bow. The wood creaked, the string groaned, and the bow snapped, breaking in an instant. He stumbled back, surprise and then disappointment flashing across his features. The broken end of the bow hung in one hand, the string dangling over his other arm.

"See?" Garreth said, putting his arm over my shoulders. I tried to put my elbow into his nose, but he moved back too quickly. "You had a crush on a normal kid who probably wasn't even as strong as you. But now, Marion is a beast of legend. He could break your skull trying to kiss you."

Marion turned away, a flush creeping up his neck. He opened his mouth like he wanted to say something but then closed it. He glanced at me, the pain in his eyes as raw as if he'd been skinned alive. Then he dropped the bow and pushed past, leaving me to stare after him with the Prince of Tuleves gloating beside me.

"What did you do to him?" I asked, whirling on the prince.

He put both hands in the air. "You mean, what did *you* do to him?"

He was right. I had given him undiluted thembus sap. I had turned Marion into a beast.

"Are you going to turn me in?" I asked. Garreth had more than enough knowledge about me to have me beheaded without this new development.

"Actually," he said, replacing his arm over my shoulder like we were long lost war companions. "I have a proposal."

CHAPTER 37

THE DRESS and the invitation arrived less than four glasses later. Neither were from the person I was expecting. Four glasses might as well have been four days the way time crept by as I stared at the blank wall of my room. The mattress was thin. It took too much effort to lie still. I had made myself dizzy spinning to face the other wall so often.

There was a buzzing in the back of my mind, something pressing, something important that I couldn't bring into focus. A fog would roll in and I couldn't remember who'd I'd been thinking about. There was the tournament. I knew I needed to win the tournament and save my father. I needed to return to Dawn once Father was with me and ask her to join us. But there was one more, someone. . .

"Healer." A soldier stood in the doorway. He leaned away from me, eyebrows raised. I hadn't heard him open the door. My fingers were curled into my hair, wild strands shooting out as I tried to massage comprehension into my mind. I must have looked unhinged.

"What?" I asked.

"The Lady has sent you a personal invitation." The soldier reached out with an envelope pinched at the very tip of his fingers. I grabbed the envelope and tried to shut the door. "And a gift for the occasion."

I stopped, holding the door a few inches from the soldier's nose. He pushed a box sideways through the crack and then turned and left. A gift and invitation from The Lady. The words sparked a memory of someone else who had been invited to see The Lady. Someone important.

I threw the box onto the bed. It opened to reveal a dress made from black fabric with tucks and ruffles and small reflective jewels that were cool to the touch as I ran my fingers along the neckline. I had never worn something so fine, not even as the daughter of a landowner. Even then I had preferred hunting leathers to women's fashion.

"An invitation from the prince arrived for you." The head healer whose face had hovered above mine when I'd first woken up in the Sanatorium walked in without knocking. She held the envelope out to me in a similar fashion, finger pinched on the end as if the envelope were full of disease instead of paper. Her lip curled with the familiar downturn of disgust that I was so used to from the villagers, although the glance between me and the black gown on the bed betrayed a hint of jealousy. "It seems your reputation has garnered attention. Your newness will wear off soon enough. You'll be expected to report for duties tomorrow morning and you will see that you are neither a royal nor a novelty. Until then, clean yourself up and represent us well."

She dropped the envelope right before my fingers closed around it. She left, closing the door behind her as if offering me some false sense of privacy. The darkened terrace windows on the tower still peered over my wall.

I crouched in the corner of the room behind the door to be out of view of the tower windows. I traced Dawn's name written in calligraphy across the back of the envelope in a deep purple ink. I had to pretend to be her until I had my father safely out of the castle walls or they would go after her again. I had to be ready to help her escape.

Taking a deep breath, I slipped my finger under the edge of the thinnest parchment I had ever seen. The paper bit into the skin of my finger like a knife, drawing blood. I sucked the blood from the cut. Then I pulled out Garreth's invitation.

You are formally invited to attend dinner with his highness, Prince Garreth of Tuleves, Octava evening.

It was my ticket to freedom. It was my bribe and my payment. He told me he would explain his proposal after dinner, but the deal felt like a trap. He knew I wasn't Dawn, but the daughter of a convicted tax evader and the Hooded Robber. He held all the cards. What could he possibly need from me?

I pulled out the other envelope and opened that one more carefully. It had no day of the week on it. It simply said, *The Lady requests your presence*. Two invitations. Two chances to leave the Sanatorium.

I needed a plan. I needed Jaim. . .

The thought slipped from my mind. The door slammed open into my head, knocking me on my backside.

"Sorry!" Polisha said, rushing in and putting her hand on my forehead. I felt her spark. I pushed her hand off me.

"I'm fine," I said, standing up. "Don't try to heal me anymore."

Her shoulders sagged. "I know I shouldn't, but I want to help. I know I can help more than they let me."

I had to turn my face away from her so she wouldn't see how much I understood that feeling.

"What were you doing on the floor?" she asked, already recovering from the disappointment. The girl was like soft moss that sprung back as quickly after having pressure put upon it. I wanted her childlike innocence to last forever, but this place would squish her flat all too soon.

"I was hiding," I said. I didn't see a reason to keep the fact to myself. "Those black windows make my hair stand on end. I hate feeling like someone is watching me all the time."

Polisha looked up. She was so much smaller than me that I wondered how much of the tower she could see over the wall. She wrinkled her nose and stuck out her tongue, making a face that made me laugh.

"What are you doing?" I asked.

"Checking to see if they're watching." She looked at the windows above us expectantly.

"I don't think that's going to get a reaction," I said, "but it made me feel better."

"I feel better, too." Her smile was like the fresh rays of the morning sun. The air was easier to breathe with her lightness in the room.

"I was sent to take you to the showers," she said, her eyes widening at the sight of the dress. "Wow! It that what you get to wear? You're going to look like royalty. I always imagine what it would be like to walk around with my nose in the air, wearing a different dress every day, looking down on people who can't take a bath at least three times a day." She held up the edges of her healer's robe like a fancy dress and pranced in a small circle around me, looking down her nose at me even though she had to tilt her head all the way back to do it.

"You would make a fantastic royal," I said. "You've got the nose and the walk. Now all you need is. . ."

The walls of my room shuddered. The plaster cracked, raining chunks of rock onto my bed. Polisha let out a yelp and ducked behind me.

My heart dropped. Not because I believed the earth was shifting, but because I knew who shared the room next to mine. And I'd never seen him lose his temper. Never seen him punch a wall. Shouts came from the hallway. Marion's strained voice apologized.

Polisha grabbed the dress, carefully picking pieces of plaster off the fabric. "Come on. I have to be back on furnace duty in half a glass. And you really do need to clean up. No offense."

She pulled me down the hall, but I kept looking back at the half-dozen healers who had congregated outside Marion's room. I yearned to go back, to comfort him, to tell him how badly I'd messed up. I didn't know what I could do to fix this. To fix him. And though he'd already told me it didn't matter, and that he'd given up on me, I wondered if there was a way to keep him from giving up on himself.

CHAPTER 38

THE LONG BLACK gown fit as if I had been measured by tailors. Polisha guided me to a full-length mirror. I sat on a bench so she could fasten the back all the way to the top and brush my hair. I didn't recognize myself. I thought for a moment I was sitting in front of a picture of Mother. We had often been told we looked alike, but the last year had melted the chubby cheeks of youth and carved out my cheekbones. I sat tall, trying to look as regal as she had as she rode her horse at the beginning of a hunt.

Next to Polisha, I was a giantess with large shoulders, warrior's legs, a woman's chest, one that barely filled the bodice. Binding my chest had helped with the hunt and my aim with the bow. I couldn't remember the last time I had pushed my shoulders back to feel like a woman. I had not cut my hair in the year since Mother's death, keeping it tied back both for robbing and for healing. The dark hair spiraled around my face in natural curls I had almost forgotten.

I was just in another costume, ready to play another role. In this dress, I was Dawn, renowned healer of Jaklin, invited to dinner with the Prince of Tuleves. I could play the part. I'd been more than one person for so long, it seemed far easier to pretend to be someone else than to wonder who I might actually be.

Polisha led me around a corner to some kind of waiting area with steps leading up and out.

"Quickly," she said. "The Lady doesn't like to wait."

She pushed me up the stairs and then ran back into the Sanatorium. I wanted to take her with me, to let her see another place with an open sky and no one watching except for the stars twinkling overhead.

Two soldiers stood at the top of the stairs, blocking the double doors. My heart faltered and my mind shouted for me to run. I took a deep breath. Not this time. I couldn't place the reason, but that internal drive to run had less pull. There was something inside me that was stronger now. I had a plan and two invitations. I had no reason to run.

I would use one invitation for two visits, then I would have a second one to use at my disposal.

I pulled out Garreth's invitation and showed it to the soldier on the right. He checked the paper, nodded once, then he and the other soldier pushed the doors open.

There was a large room to the right with a dozen comfortable sofas and three running fountains that added to the relaxing atmosphere. It seemed as if injured people were lulled to sleep while they waited for a chance to be healed at the Sanatorium.

The gurgling waterfalls reminded me of home, calling me to brush my fingers along the small rippling pools. There was no one else in the waiting room, a stark contrast to the line of people waiting outside Dawn's hut. So many in need of healing and only one healer. Here, there were so many healers and apparently no one in need of healing.

A woman in a plain dress made of a fine blue fabric the color of the sky approached. "I will take you to the dining hall to await the prince."

"Actually." I touched her arm. The woman drew back. I had breached some unspoken rules of protocol. A servant was insulted by my touch. Maybe a healer was lower on the class system that I thought. I drew back. "The Lady is expecting me before dinner. Could you take me to her first?"

"The Lady?" The woman dropped her head like the name required a bow. "No one sees her without an invitation."

"I have an invitation," I said. "Both from the prince and The Lady."

The woman did nothing to hide her inspection of me. I took in her gaze without flinching, showing only confidence.

"I was told The Lady doesn't like to be kept waiting." I spoke slowly like explaining an obvious truth to a child. "I thought it best to see her before dinner rather than after, don't you think?"

Asking her opinion seemed to break through whatever wall of resistance she'd been holding against me.

"It would be wise," said the woman. "Follow me."

I kept track of each turn, each hall and door. We passed through a great entrance hall with doors as thick as a Faengsel tree. Gold filigree layered the molding along the walls and ceiling, patterned lace draped along the windows, and the walls sported tapestries with images of the history of Kadasha, the building of the Sanctuaries, the sharing of the gift. Kadasha herself was never portrayed, only her hand was visible through the clouds or hovering larger than life on the edge of the tapestry. Always directing. Always giving.

We ascended four sets of stairs and crossed another wing of the castle. I was grateful for my sense of direction gained through years of hunting. The castle was a greater maze than the dungeons.

The woman stopped and pointed down a corridor, standing at attention like one of the soldiers. "I will wait for you here."

"Thank you. . . what was your name?"

She started, her shoulders jumping toward her ears. She looked me up and down, this time like a piece that didn't quite fit. "Elnora."

"Thank you, Elnora," I said. "I will try to not keep you waiting long."

I walked down the corridor. There were no doors, no windows, no off-branching hallways. The only interruptions in the corridor were small alcoves with bronze statues. I averted my eyes after the first few statues. The faces were not ones of strength and confidence as I would expect. They were statues of humans in different stages of agony, contorted as if in pain.

If my sense of direction was right, this corridor shouldn't exist. I would be walking out over the waterfall and cliffs of the plateau that Tuleves was built on. I placed my hand on the wall for balance and a wave of dizziness swept over me as I tried to get my bearings.

Voices reached me and because I was so used to being a thief, I slipped into the nearest alcove. Situated behind the statue, I realized what a stupid move it was. I was exactly where I was supposed to be. There was no reason to hide, but now with people in the corridor, there was no way to come out from behind the statue with any shred of dignity.

The statue of a woman stared back at me; her head turned grotesquely in the wrong direction to her body. I shivered.

"How did this happen?" Grand Councilor Levante strode down the hall, his voice all too familiar. Two pairs of shoes, one shining until reflective, the others, soldier boots, scraped and crusted in mud, were the only thing visible as I peeked around the statue.

"Stop." The Lady's command made both boots halt in their place only two alcoves past where I hid.

Curse the saints. Why had I hidden? There was no way to come out now without looking guilty.

"Why do you come to me without an invitation? Without an announcement?" The Lady asked.

"My sisters and I have a report." I recognized the voice as Captain Tevya. The captain we had stolen the blood jewels from. The fine fabric of my dress suddenly felt hot and heavy, too tight in all the wrong places.

"Have you delivered them already?" The Lady said, sounding pleased. "Kadasha must have received her gift with pleasure then to let you go so quickly."

"We did not reach Helefount, My Lady," Captain Tevya said, her words dropping to the floor like stones. "The Hooded Robber. . . tricked us and stole the jewels. We beg your forgiveness."

The tsk of a clicking tongue was the only sound. "This is most disturbing news. You swore an oath, did you not?" The words were emotionless, as cold as the surface of a pond after I'd taken all the heat and made it icy smooth.

"Forgive us, My Lady," Captain Tevya said. "We came to accept the fulfillment of our oath."

My mouth dropped open and I looked at the tortured statue's face to see if she had heard what I had. Captain Tevya had returned to forfeit her life. Willingly. She hadn't tried to run. The statue looked as shocked as I felt.

"You and your sisters will report to the Sanatorium."

"My Lady?" Captain Tevya sounded confused. Maybe The Lady meant to heal them instead of beheading them.

An image of a body, hanging from chains, his back crisscrossed with fresh scarring wounds flashed in my mind. I had to bite my tongue to keep from yelling out. The dizziness returned and I gripped the bronze statue to keep from tipping.

"Go."

The muddy boots passed, moving quickly, back the way we had come in.

"This was not what you foresaw." The Grand Councilor had stayed. The longer I hid behind the statue, the worse I was making if for myself.

"The gifting does not work like that," The Lady said. "Time has a way of bending perception."

"How does that help us now?" The Grand Councilor kept his voice even, but the pressure changed, my ears popping the way they had back in the ditch with Marion. "The jewels were a payment for the king to be returned before the coronation ceremony. Are you suggesting we let Prince Garreth become king?"

My mind whirled. The jewels had been a ransom for the King of Tuleves, for Garreth's father? King Tyndall was alive after all these years. And I had stolen the jewels. A great weight settled in the pit of my stomach, nausea rising until I tasted bile. I had stolen the blood jewels, the ransom for the life of the missing king. Iranus had been right. I didn't just destroy lives around me, I was sucking in all light, all hope.

"Be calm," The Lady said. "Kadasha will reveal her will to me. She will not send her armies to destroy this people as long as you continue to do as I say. I am your protector, your interpreter of the immortal's demands. Do not lose faith in that."

"What will Kadasha do about the blood jewels?"

"She will be angry," The Lady said. "She will demand a sacrifice to be sure it wasn't an intentional slight. To prove you are still loyal."

I couldn't see the Grand Councilor's face, but the silence that followed made the air thick enough to stop an arrow.

"Grand Councilor!" Someone called from the end of the corridor where Elnora waited. "You must come immediately."

"It can wait," he said. "You know better to interrupt me when I am with The Lady."

"Grand Councilor." The voice was smaller, wavering, but determined. "Something's happened. It's. . . your son."

My body stiffened. Something had happened to Marion. The Lady's next words froze my heart.

"Kadasha has already chosen your sacrifice."

The Grand Councilor's shoes squeaked against the floor as he turned and walked with a controlled gate past where I hid. It took every ounce of control I had not to jump out from behind the statue and run after him. My soul reflected the agony etched in the statue's twisted features.

I held my breath until the soft padding of feet retreated in the other direction. A door shut. I waited another moment, listening for any footstep or breath in the hallway. All was silent. I slipped from behind the statue, checking up and down the now deserted corridor.

At the crossroads again, my mind torn in two different directions. I wanted to run to Marion, see what had happened. But The Lady waited. And from her interactions with Captain Tevya, disappointing her could be a death sentence.

CHAPTER 39

MARION WAS AS BROKEN as the bow that had dangled from his fingers. And I had left him. I should have at least checked on him before escaping the Sanatorium.

I turned to follow in the direction the Grand Councilor had gone when I heard the squeak of a turning doorknob behind me. I whirled. *Never let an enemy see your back.* Mother would have never let herself be pinned between two impossible choices. She always knew which direction to face.

The Lady opened the door. I took a few halting steps toward her. Hopefully it appeared like I had been walking steadily down the hall. Even with the cloth covering her eyes, I didn't doubt she could somehow see me.

"Who's there?" The Lady spoke the words the way Mother had when we missed a step in our training. It was a correction. An invitation to introduce myself.

"Dawn," I said. "The new healer. I received your invitation and came as soon as I was presentable."

"I have been expecting you. Come. Don't be frightened." She extended her arm toward me. Her hand hung from the wrist like a clubbed fish. I took large steps to close the gap between us. I was anxious to end the meeting as quickly as possible. To find out what had happened to Marion before dinner, I would have to use the second invitation. The way the Grand Councilor had responded, I wasn't sure a visit to Marion could wait until after dinner. I was supposed to save him, not destroy him from the inside.

I touched The Lady's cold fingers and bent to kiss them. My lips stopped before they brushed against her knuckles.

"Is everything all right?"

I had stayed bent over The Lady's hand for far too long, even though it was only a moment. I straightened, surprised when her cloth covering was even with my eyes. I was used to being taller than most people around me, especially women. But The Lady matched me in height, despite her thin frame.

"Yes," I said, bowing my head and dropping my gaze in a gesture of humility. It reminded me of being a healer's assistant in a village that barely tolerated me, of the moment when Father was escorted away between two soldiers. The rage boiled in the back of my mind. "Sorry. This is my first time in Tuleves. I'm afraid I'm a little awkward."

We entered a formal sitting room, empty of furnishings. The three stone steps down had no decorations or pattern, but their perfection was a sign of far grander effort than any of the mosaic flooring on the main level. There were no cracks or blemishes in the stone of each step, as smooth as polished marble and dirt-free as Orblee's medicinal table where she prepared herbs.

The Lady waved at me to shut the door. It was heavy oak, solid enough to withstand a battering ram. The handle was a simple knob, gold flakes coming off to expose iron underneath.

With the door closed, the room was consumed by complete darkness, no window or lit candle. I could not even make out the shadow outline of The Lady.

"Please," said The Lady, calm and inviting. "Come closer."

"I can't see anything," I said, taking a tentative step forward, waving my hands in front of me in case there were obstructions.

"Of course," she said. "I seldom have visitors here, and when I do, they bring their own light."

"No one told me to bring a lantern. I'm sorry."

"It was by design. All things are by Kadasha's design."

I had spent enough nights in the forest to be able to move in the darkness, but this was a complete darkness I had never experienced.

"Why do you stay in the dark?" I asked.

"I am an Oracle, sworn to serve Kadasha. I have true vision and can see all that Kadasha allows me to see. My eyes were taken to increase the gifting I have been given. What need do I have of light? It only shows false images of a temporary present."

"How is that possible? The Oracles were killed, slaughtered. Using the gifting of time is forbidden."

Sadness enveloped The Lady's words. "I was not at the temple that day. I lost so many sisters and brothers. Such a waste of life. Of energy."

Snakes wiggled their way into my belly. Her sorrow sounded misplaced, though I could not find the error in her words.

"How did you come to be here?" I asked.

A small wisp of air passed my head. I jumped, imagining The Lady standing next to me, whispering her next words in my ear. When I waved my hand next to my head, nothing was there.

"I've lived here for years, long before the desolation of my people," she said. There was a clank of hardened wood shifting off to my right. I turned toward it but still couldn't see anything. "But that's in the past. We have much to discuss about your future. I've heard a great deal about you. The healer who can save a child born too early. The healer who can cure the Ethereal Plague. Dozens enter your home and all leave better for it. That takes more than most healers have to give."

I swallowed. I was talking to an Oracle. They could discern the future. Surely, she would recognize a lie. But if I revealed I was not the healer, she would try to find out who I really was.

"The tales have been exaggerated," I said, bowing my head like I was speaking to royalty although I still saw nothing. I avoided a direct lie and mixed in some truth. "The stories of me fall closer to the line of legend than reality. Those who come to me benefit from the knowledge my mother passed on and the excellent herbs in the forest." Maybe that was a little too far, but the image of my mother as she showed me life-sustaining plants and the way to hunt enough food to keep ten families alive made the words deep and tender.

"Don't be modest," The Lady said, excitement emphasizing her words. Another shifting of fabric. She was approaching me.

My eyes adjusted enough to make out bare shadows and I thought I caught the movement of a dress as she paced in front of me. I felt like prey huddled in front of the predator as it examined its next meal.

"Perhaps, if you show me what you can do, we can work together. You are more than a healer, am I right? Tell me you are the one I've been searching for these long years."

"I am a simple healer." True words again. I was a healer with no gifting. Simple indeed. "What need would you have of me when you have the entire Sanatorium at your disposal?"

"You of all people know the pain of loneliness, the hunger for true companionship," she said. I leaned forward, her words so soft that I could barely make them out.

The rising panic in my throat did not stop my heart from aching at her description. I knew the yearning for friendship. For the love of a mother I had lost. The touch of a father who had been taken from me.

"Yes," I said. "I know."

There was a spark in the darkness and a flame on the tip of a stick ignited an inch or two from my face. Where I had been blinded by darkness, I was now blinded by the light, a small flame that consumed my vision.

The matchstick pulled back and the light began to bounce off the object behind it. The Lady's face came into view, her cloth removed. And where the light should have revealed eyes, there were only two blackened holes, scarred over pits in an otherwise flawless face.

Her skin was smooth and beautiful, with a complexion of youth. Lips that were full and naturally colored, a perfect nose beneath her missing eyes.

"They blinded you?" I asked. "Was that the cost of working for the King?"

"It was done when I was very young, but I can see without them," she said, her face floating in my vision like an embodied head, her face too close and the light too weak to reveal more. "They were taken by King Tyndall's father. When King Tyndall came to power, he regretted blinding me, especially when he realized I might be the only path to salvation."

The light went out.

I stepped back.

There was a rush of wind, a sound I knew too well. I ducked and felt the breeze against my ear as something fast passed just over my head.

"Good." The Lady sounded triumphant. "Together we can be so much more. We can serve Kadasha in fulfilling her final vision for this land."

"You're talking about fulfilling a prophecy. That never works out. They're always too vague."

Something hit me in the shoulder. I fumbled to catch it before it fell to the floor. I ran my fingers up and down the shaft. Long smooth wood, rounded to allow an even grip, balanced to perfection. It was a fighting staff. The Lady was inviting me to fight her in the dark.

"All Oracle prophecies come to pass. You should know that better than anyone."

A blow to my stomach was followed by a hit to my head. I went down on one knee, curling into the pain. In the dark, I smiled. Anger filled me from the inside out and a blind woman had just given me permission to hit her.

"It is easy to say a prophecy was fulfilled when there are so few details. Or was it something that was going to happen anyway."

My strength was with the bow, but I had spent hours with Dawn and Mother, training to fight. By the time she was twelve, even Mother couldn't beat Dawn, but I never quit trying. It was Dawn who taught me instinctive reactions, split second moves, fighting faster than thought, because she always did.

I closed my eyes and pulled my breathing deep inside me. I used silent breaths that allowed me to hear the slightest sound around me. The rustle of The Lady's skirt. I stood and whirled, smacking stick against stick. The weight shifted and I imagined her moving to the right. I swung the staff up and missed. Her staff hit me square in the back, but I was already moving.

"You have so little faith in the gifting of time. I am surprised to hear it."

She spoke to me, but I had almost forgotten who I was. I was supposed to be Dawn, a powerful healer. Not a giftless criminal. Dawn would have faith in the gifting of time. Most people did. It was what gave the Oracles the power to control the people.

My staff caught in her skirts as she moved away. I tried to take her feet out from under her, but she was gone. The whistle of the staff through the air gave me the next warning and I lifted my staff to block her just in time. I only had time to make defensive moves, blocking her, shifting out of the way, blocking again. Missing. A hard hit on my right arm. I nearly lost the staff. I had flashbacks of Dawn, moving before I could even think, reacting to my attack before I had even thought to make it.

The Lady's staff hit me below the knee. I fell, rolling to stay ahead of her swings. Her hits were getting harder and more accurate. I became winded and slowed. I stepped away from her until my back hit the wall.

The Lady's staff hit beside my ear, shattering the plaster wall, pieces peppering my face and skin.

"No," she said with frustration. "How can you not be the one? I was so sure." A sigh. "Such a pity." I imagined her pulling the rod up, preparing to hit my skull with the same force she had hit the wall. I would not survive it.

I tackled The Lady, not the move of a warrior, but of a desperate thief. I lunged forward, wrapping my arms around her so that she could not move away. We hit the ground together. I tried to use my weight to pin her to the ground, but she moved swiftly and effectively, using a short jab to my throat with enough force to cut off my air. She flipped me over, putting the staff over my head and pulling it hard against my throat. I grabbed for the staff, her hands, anything for relief. There was no air to breathe as I fought to keep the staff from pressing harder. I pushed out, fighting for control.

With The Lady's skin against my cheek, pulling the pressure against my windpipe, I could not draw air.

The door burst open, letting in a light that seemed brighter than noon day. I pulled away from The Lady and sat up on my knees, coughing.

Garreth stood framed in the door, his silhouette powerful against the saving light.

Light and anger washed over The Lady's face like a splash of water as my vision dimmed. She waited an instant and then released me. She stood gracefully, leaving her fighting staff on the floor. The muscles in her face relaxed, the anger dripping off like melted wax. She reached into a pocket and pulled out a piece of cloth made of pure white silk. She wrapped it around her head, covering the empty sockets of her eyes.

"Your Highness," she said, bowing low as Garreth strode in the room wearing a clean high-collared white shirt, a red waistcoat with gold tassels, and well-fitted black riding pants. He cleaned up well.

His back was straight, his stride as confident as ever. I wondered how I looked, huddled against the wall, ready to curl up into a ball and ask Kadasha to help me disappear. His presence made me pull my shoulders back and stand despite still fighting for breath. My fancy dress had a tear in one sleeve and a splash of blood on the bodice. I pressed my fingers under my nose to stop the bleeding. How ironic that my prey should be standing in front of me, in control and in charge, while I felt like a mouse in a trap.

"I'm here to escort my guest to dinner."

I approached Garreth, faking as much confidence as I could muster. Instead of offering me his arm and guiding me straight out the door, which was what I wanted him to do, he walked to the side of the room, where for the first time I noticed the furniture pushed together to clear the center of the room for a fighting ring. Garreth pulled out a long, flat cushioned chair and lounged on it, boots on one arm of the furniture, hands behind his head resting on the other. His boots were spotless, probably never worn before, but I had the feeling he wouldn't have taken any extra care even if his boots had been covered in mud.

"I wondered if I would find you here," he said, winking at me without the slightest amount of stealth.

The Lady walked with a stiff gracefulness and sat on the end of another plain wooden chair. She posed with her back straight, her fists in her lap, her head tilted like she could watch him with her ears. It was not unlike the posture of a cornered animal, watching for a point of weakness.

"You weren't wrong," The Lady said. "What led you to her?"

Garreth glanced up at the ceiling as if the conversation was a bit of a bore. "Well, I've known this healer for all of three days and ninety percent of the time she's in the most dangerous place possible. It's like she can't resist a bit of fun. It makes us very compatible."

A smile touched my lips. His humor sucked out all the fear and oppression I had felt. The Lady suddenly seemed powerless next to the flippant young prince.

She let out a tinkling laugh. "You consider me dangerous? I'd be flattered if I thought you were the slightest bit serious. You've known me your whole life. I serve Kadasha, the same as I always have."

Garreth sat up, placing his feet on the floor and making a study of his fingernails. "Let me ask you a question. Did you know?"

"I know a lot of things," she said, a touch of annoyance slipping through her façade. "I'm the King's Oracle."

"Did you know what would happen to Marion?" he asked. "When you gave me the tip about Faengsel Forest?"

The Lady leaned back, a small start of surprise on her lips. I wasn't sure if it more of her act or if she really did not see everything. "I do not see as much as I could if I had my eyes, you know that. I see only what Kadasha allows me to see. Did you find what you seek?"

Garreth stood up and stretched. "Ask Kadasha. See if she decides to tell you."

I tried not to flinch. I had never heard someone speak so disrespectfully about the immortal goddess. The Lady's lips tightened.

He had a way of making enemies faster than I did.

CHAPTER 40

"HOW HUNGRY ARE YOU?" Garreth asked.

What a strange question to ask after saving me from The Lady. I didn't have the energy to try and figure him out. My mind was whirling with all that she had said and done. A living Oracle serving the ruler of Tuleves. A fight to see who I was. The disappointment that I couldn't block her strokes. What did it mean?

"Good," he said, even though I hadn't answered. "You may not have much time to eat."

"What are you talking about?" I asked, desperately needing something to make sense. "You invited me to dinner."

"It was a proposal."

"You want to marry me," I said, keeping my voice flat and humorless.

Garreth stopped walking and turned to look at me. He nodded slowly. "That might be an option."

"What are you talking about?"

"Listen." He faced me and placed his hands on both of my arms, like Dawn had done with Yoself when she had wanted him to understand. "We don't have a lot of time. I will be crowned King of Tuleves in three days and I'm not ready. I have to find something first."

"You were looking for something in Faengsel Forest." Marion had been right. My stomach dropped at the thought of Marion. I didn't know what had happened that had turned the Grand Councilor's attention.

Garreth glanced around us. He had somehow ditched the soldiers that protected him and had led me into another wing of the castle, one I hadn't travelled though on the way to see The Lady. This corridor had both windows and light sconces on the wall. Plants decorated the alcoves creating the feeling of being outdoors.

"If I don't find an item that will give me the ability to be a great king, I'll be killed on my coronation day. I've spent the last seven years trying to prevent my own coronation until I'm ready. But I'm not ready. I haven't found it. Not yet."

"The Lady told you that you would find an item in Faengsel Forest that would make you a great king?" I tried to tuck the ripped fabric of my dress into the sleeve to cover the tear.

"Not exactly. I didn't tell her what I needed to find, but I did ask where I could find what I sought. You know, I made it sound very proper."

"How do you know you're going to be killed, did The Lady give you that prophecy as well?" I gave up on my sleeve and looked Garreth in the eyes. If he was lying to me, I wanted to know why.

He dropped his gaze, but it wasn't in embarrassment. I recognized a reflection of the sorrow I carried around in my soul.

"No. The original prophecy wasn't from The Lady."

A couple of pieces clicked into place. His mother dying alone. His father going on a crusade to regain Kadasha's favor. "Your mother. The queen could touch the gifting of time?"

"No one knew. She would have never been allowed to remain a royal or marry my father. She kept it secret. But when she got sick, she decided to tell my father the truth. He didn't react the way she hoped."

"I'm so sorry."

He rubbed one hand down his face. When he pulled his hand away, his mouth was twisted in his familiar carefree smirk. His cheek muscles pulled tight. His lips quirked. I had just watched him put on a mask as solid as the Hooded Robber's face covering.

"If I declare us engaged, they'll have to put off the coronation and I will have bought myself a little more time to avoid my assassination. My only other idea is to commit murder, but even then, they might still crown me. The declaration of a betrothal to a healer, that will make the council struggle with indigestion. They won't crown me until they know I will marry a royal."

"And if I say no?" A fake engagement to the Prince of Tuleves was a wrinkle in my plan and I already had far too many wrinkles. My plan was a wadded-up piece of laundry left in a corner to sour.

"You'll say yes," he said simply. "You need my help as much as I need yours. If they discover you're not a healer in the Sanatorium, you'll be hung as a spy."

"Are you threatening me?"

"It's more like I'm leveraging your wants and needs to achieve my goal of not dying. Plus, I need one more favor."

"A favor on top of agreeing to marry you?" I'd gone cold on the inside. My knees felt weak. I didn't know what I was getting into, but he was right. He knew enough about me to leverage my loyalty. I needed him on my side.

"I need you." He waved up and down like a Havish Priest blessing the dead with incense. "I mean, I need the Hooded Robber. If you help me tonight, I'll get you out of the castle tomorrow morning."

A deal with the spoiled Prince of Tuleves wasn't a good idea even though I was beginning to see his façade of the rebellious prince was as much a cover as was the mask of the Hooded Robber.

"You're not as stupid as you want people to believe."

"Thank you." He looked pleased. "Now, let's go offend some important people so we can skip the main course." His smile was contagious.

He offered his arm. I accepted, acting my part in order to survive. He led me down a flight of stairs and brought me through two double doors into a dining room larger than Kadasha's sanctuary in Prontwick. An entire village could feast in this room without touching elbows.

The rectangular table was long enough to stretch the entire length of the room with dozens of council members and royalty already seated. Servants bustled between seats, setting plates filled with food.

When we entered, a silence slowly spread across the room as we were noticed.

Garreth arrived late to a dinner he was planning to leave early.

He led me to the head of the table. We sat in the two vacant chairs across from the Grand Councilor and The Lady. She had managed to arrive before us but gave no indication of having nearly killed me moments earlier.

"Prince Garreth," she said with a slight bow of her head. The cloth covered her empty sockets again. She had no marks from our fight, not even a hair out of place. I clutched the fine fabric of my skirts to keep from leaping across the table and finishing our fight while I could see her. The Lady turned her face to me as if she could hear my thoughts. "Healer." It could have been a greeting had it not been for the tone of distain.

Garreth unfolded his napkin and placed it in his lap. A few heads turned. I wondered if this were the first time he had followed proper table manners in public. I unfolded my own napkin and tucked into the low neckline of my dress. If he wanted to have a fiancée that wasn't fit to rule with him, I could also play the part.

He noticed. He glanced between the napkin and my face at least four times. A smile of approval lifted his cheeks and brightened his eyes. He lifted his fork, and without waiting for a second breath, tapped his fork against his glass. I ripped a roll apart and stuffed it into my mouth. I had a feeling I wasn't going to have a lot of time to eat. "I want to make my first decree."

"What do you mean?" asked a well-dressed woman to my right. Her age was covered well beneath powders. She held herself straight, though she was a head shorter than me.

Grand Councilor Levante made no movement. His hands rested on the table below his perfectly placed silverware. The thick soup remained untouched in his bowl, but he stared into it like it was a fathomless sea.

"It's three days until my coronation. I'm about to be king. I might as well start thinking of my subjects."

The woman huffed. "This council was created for that very purpose. Our subjects are our number one concern."

"And snotles smell sweet." I hadn't meant to say it out loud, but the anger inside me had boiled over like a kettle over a hot fire. Garreth cocked his head at me, his mouth open. The Grand Councilor looked up from his soup and The Lady spit some soup back into her spoon.

"Excuse me?" The woman glanced between me and Garreth, obviously considering the consequences of contradicting a guest of the prince.

I couldn't stop the anger from spilling out. "How can you say you care about the people when you sit here with your silk tablecloths and meat soup while the people try to survive on a few grains of baked habala seed and boiled bones." I picked up the bowl of soup in front of me. "This would be a feast for a single family. You demand everything and give nothing."

"That is not true," the Grand Councilor said. "We do what must be done. Things may be harder for a time. Many will have to sacrifice, but those who survive will come out stronger, survivors ready to face any challenge. And we will be a stronger nation for it. We must be stronger. We cannot save the weak, those who cannot pull their share, or the country will fall."

"How can your people be strong if they are starving? How can they fight if they have no resources? They can barely care for themselves, let alone each other. If you create a society that abandons a brother for their own survival, what is the point of living? We will all have hearts of stone."

Silk napkins paused halfway to mouths. Fine forks frozen between the teeth of the royals testified of the surprise that sparked around the room, lighting their guilt as clear as the seven diamond chandeliers overhead.

Grand Councilor Levante picked up his fork and squeezed it until his knuckles turned white. As he stood, the candle flames across the table leaned and flickered. A shadow appeared around him. "I have sacrificed everything to protect this people."

The Lady placed a hand on the Grand Councilor's arm. The shadow disappeared. Garreth didn't seem to notice.

"Well said." The prince rose from his seat, clapping his hands together. "But politics can get boring. I want to announce that I've chosen a queen to stand beside me when I am crowned king. Dawn the

Healer." He motioned for me to stand, but I was frozen to my seat. I knew he needed to stop the coronation in a few days, but I didn't know he meant to announce our engagement so quickly. "She'll make a perfect bride to the new King of the Land. You've already been blessed to hear her wisdom and manners. I can only imagine the improvements she'll make to the kingdom."

There was a moment of shocked silence where a single fork dropped to the floor with a clink. Then chaos erupted. Men stood, chairs toppled to the floor, women waved napkins in front of their faces like they were going to faint. I stuffed the second half of the roll into my mouth. Garreth picked up his bowl and drank the soup without the use of a spoon.

He set the bowl down. He leaned so he was balancing on the back two legs of his chair. I could tip him backward with a little tap of my toe. It would show him what kind of wife I would be. I lifted my foot and took a sip of my drink to hide the motion. I had almost reached his chair ready to push it when the Grand Councilor stood.

He clapped his hands twice. Silence engulfed the room and all attention turned to the man at the head of the table. Chairs were returned to the table as everyone found their seat. The Grand Councilor waited. He turned his attention to Garreth. I expected a public rebuke, a denial of his right to marry me, a lecture on the importance of choosing a royal for a bride. That was always what happened in the stories mother told me to get me to go to sleep as a child.

"Your Highness." The Grand Councilor lowered his head toward Garreth. "I regret to share such bad tidings on the heels of your news. But I need to inform you, Marion has been charged with treason. There was nothing I could do."

The front legs of Garreth's chair hit the ground at the same time I stood. "What do you mean treason? What happened? How is this possible?" I couldn't contain my reaction. I'd been expecting a lecture not a revelation about Marion.

"When the healers woke Marion up for dinner he was confused, angry. He demanded to see you, Your Highness." The Grand Councilor directed his words at Garreth even though I was the one with the questions. The Lady lifted her spoon to her mouth as if dinner was continuing as normal.

"No one came to get me." Garreth kept both hands flat on the table.

"The healers denied him as was my command. He was in no state to see you. He was a danger, and you are to be protected at all costs. We were right to do so. He insisted he needed to be by your side and tried to force his way out of the room."

I understood that feeling. I'd felt trapped down there without the thembus curse heating up my insides.

"He accidentally killed two soldiers." The Grand Councilor's face twisted with sorrow. "He only pushed them away, but he crushed in the chest of the first one and slammed the other into the wall so hard his skull. . . he didn't make it." As he continued Garreth's fingers curled into his palms to make fists.

I covered my mouth. "Why are they charging him with treason? He didn't attack the prince."

The Grand Councilor didn't acknowledge me. His eyes remained on Garreth. Waiting. It was Garreth who answered, talking into his empty soup bowl. ""He's a member of the royal army. To kill your fellow soldiers, to betray your oath, is charged as treason."

"Meaning?"

"They will hang him after my coronation."

"That's ridiculous. It was an accident. He didn't mean to kill anyone. It wasn't his fault." I couldn't stop myself. I moved toward the Grand Councilor with my hands out to grab his robes to plead for mercy.

Someone stepped between me and the Grand Councilor. It took me a moment to realize it was Garreth. He held me by both arms and turned me around like we were caught in some kind of twisted dance. His arm wrapped around me as he pulled me toward the door.

"We'll be right back. Give us a moment to get some air."

I refrained from kicking and screaming. Some deep part of me recognized that this was the wisest move, but I couldn't help yelling out one more time. "You can't do this. He's your son."

CHAPTER 41

GARRETH HAD a hold of my arm, but his gaze was unfocused, his eyebrows drawn. He cursed under his breath as he dragged me down another series of corridors and flights of stairs. I had lost my sense of direction and had no idea where we were. I followed blindly, tears blurring my vision, but refusing to fall.

Marion would die because of what I had done. There was no way to win, no way to be better than I was no matter who I pretended to be.

We entered a library somewhere in the lower section of the castle that wrapped around the cliff at the edge of the plateau. Books covered three walls of the room, and a window from floor to ceiling took up the fourth wall. A waterfall fell from the top of the window, disappearing out of sight below me. The river of Tuleves stretched out like a windy road out onto the plains.

He finally let go of my arm and paced between the window and the door, spinning on his heel and rubbing both hands over his face. I had never seen the prince flustered. Now he appeared completely at a loss.

"Garreth," I said, ready to slap him if he didn't snap out of it.

He looked up as if realizing I was there with him. He blinked and tried to put on his old, carefree, careless face. He did care, deep down in a way I hadn't understood. "Good job in there. You got us out of dinner faster than even I could have."

"We're talking about Marion. They're going to kill your friend."

"I know. I know." He rubbed his face. He pushed his hair back and kept his hands on his head, eyes closed. "It's like they are always one step ahead of me. No matter how hard I try, Lavante and The Lady are determined to crown me whether I'm ready or not."

"How does sending Marion to the gallows have anything to do with you being king?" I paced around him like a wild cat around something new. This was a side of Garreth I hadn't seen before. He wasn't flippant and disrespectful. He wasn't pouting or offended. He wasn't cracking jokes or passing out insults.

This version was something else. His stance reminded me of someone, a planner, a strategist. The feeling of something missing surged up so hard I had to sit in one of the plush reading chairs.

"They can use him against me. Bargain his life to renounce our engagement and willingly accept my coronation."

My mouth dropped. It was a move in a strategy game. The Grand Councilor was using the life of his own son as leverage to get his way. "They could. Would you do that? Would you become king to save Marion?"

He dropped his arms to his side and let his head fall back so he was looking at the highest point of the glass where the waterfall first came into view. "It's not that simple. I die if I accept the crown."

"It's a prophecy. You don't know how it will play out or even if this is the moment it refers to. The Lady said you'd find what you needed in Faengsel Forest. And what did you find there? Nothing. This whole thing started because you shot your friend with an arrow."

His head jerked around. I had his full attention. "What did you say?"

The thundering of the falls outside the glass windows created a hypnotic drum against the glass. The room felt too hot and too cold at the same time. The lanterns on the walls flickered. Light danced across Garreth's features and made him hard to read.

I almost stuttered at his sudden change in focus. "I said that this all started when you shot your friend."

"No. The question. You asked me a question."

"I asked what you found in Faengsel Forest."

"And what did I find?"

I threw my hands in the air in frustration. "We are going in circles. Nothing. The whole point is that you found nothing."

I smile spread across his face as he shook his head back and forth. "That's wrong. I did find something. I found the Hooded Robber. Maybe, what I've need all this time, is a thief."

My mouth went dry. I couldn't argue with that logic even when it came from a prophecy. "What would you need a thief for?"

"I need you to help me break into The Lady's quarters." It was his turn to pace. He made it to the nearest bookshelf and then came back toward me with heightened energy.

"She's an Oracle," I said, too numb to even feel shocked at his audacity. "She'll know."

"Her gifting is very selective. And you don't believe in prophecies anyway, right?" He moved around my chair and then over to the windows. He ran a finger down the pain of glass, tracing a drip of water.

"This is a little different than giving a vague reference about the future. I'll be in her rooms." I stood even though I felt dizzy. The room tipped, but I stayed on my feet.

"What could you possibly need from The Lady's chambers? I was just in there and there was nothing worth stealing. I mean, there were a lot of priceless things, but nothing worth dying for."

He came back to me and gripped my hands together. He held them between his chest and mine. His sincere excitement balanced the room and cleared my mind. "She said that what I needed was right under my nose. I just didn't know what to look for. I was sitting in her chambers at that moment. It's the only place I haven't searched. It must be there. If we find it, I can agree to Levante's demands. I can attend my own coronation without dying. We could save Marion."

"If we find the item that will help you be a great king." I said the words slowly. My doubt doused some of the fire behind his eyes, but not all of it.

He hesitated. "Yes. It has to be there."

I took a deep breath. His nearness made my heartbeat faster and my head feel light. I was promised to marry him, and it had been announced to the entire council. For a moment, I imagined what life would be like with a headstrong, intelligent, rebellious, thoughtful king. Then I thought of Marion. I pulled my fingers free of his grip and stepped back.

"It's a good thing I ate that roll. It doesn't sound like we're going to make it back for dinner."

He nodded, relief clear on his face. He ran his hand through his hair. "You know, as king, I might actually have some influence. I could pardon your father. I could make you a royal. Have you ever considered a spot on the council?"

"You're joking."

"Usually. Follow me."

The thought that some unidentified item was powerful enough to solve all my problems filled my stomach with a fluttery sensation I hadn't felt in a long time. Hope.

Instead of leaving the library to go back into the corridor, he showed me a mostly hidden panel at the back of the room. "Some of the advantages of always looking for forbidden places is finding a lot of shortcuts. This is a shortcut to The Lady's chambers. We'll have about half a glass before she finishes dinner and returns to her rooms."

He pushed on the panel and walked through. I followed him into a gap that was even tighter than the space between Dawn's hut and the wall of the Oracles. We squeezed through the interior of the castle in the dark until he opened another panel and we spilled out into the alcove behind the very statue I had hid behind earlier in the day. I almost envied the consistency of her twisted and tortured existence.

"Come on." He led me down the corridor to the entrance of The Lady's quarters. "This is where you come in. The breaking and entering. And then you'll be on lookout. All skills of the Hooded Robber, right?"

I couldn't help rolling my eyes as I stepped up to the door. There was no handle on this side, no visible lock. The door was wrapped in iron strips, but I could see no mechanism to open it. I placed my hand on the door and pushed.

It didn't budge.

"I wouldn't have needed the Hooded Robber if that worked," he said.

I closed my eyes and listened, thinking of The Lady, the Oracle that lived in darkness yet saw far beyond herself. The door had a spark, a kind of heat, but not from a flame. There was something with the strength of the living, but not alive, holding the door closed. Curious, I pulled the spark into me and felt the door shudder. I pulled more until the grain of the wood started to frost over.

The door swung open.

"Okay. Maybe I should have pulled instead of pushed." There was a light of excitement in his eyes as he stepped past me into the room, squeezing my shoulder with a light pressure.

We entered the room The Lady and I had fought in a few hours before, but there was no sign of our struggle. The furniture had been returned to their positions around the room, creating a visiting area with couches, a divan, and a beautiful rug with soft colors in a block pattern. There was a dais behind the sitting area with paper, pastels, painting supplies, and a desk. To the side was another door, cracked open to reveal her sleeping quarters. Garreth headed there first.

"What are we looking for?"

"I'm sure I'll know when I see it." He shot me an aggravating smile and disappeared into the bedroom. I checked the empty corridor, then turned back to the room, examining the area through my memory of the fight.

On the far wall were shelves with odd mini statues of animals, jars of unidentifiable substances, and dozens of hourglasses from the size of my nose to one as large as a head. All the hourglasses had sand running through as if they had all just been turned.

I checked the hall again and then moved to the dais. It was messy with documents piled haphazardly. It reminded me of Father's office. He was a fine bowmaker, but rather disorganized with paperwork. Mother had often complained about the state of his office, but he always said he had a system. He knew the purpose and contents of each pile.

The Lady appeared to be an artist despite her lack of sight. Large papers hung around the small area depicting horrific battle scenes, death and carnage. Hundreds of tiny faces all with intricate detail of suffering and pain. Mountains folding into valleys and rivers rising out of their banks. I recognized the landscapes in many of them. The meandering path of the Tuleves River, the Cracked Plains, Shirewood Forest. It seemed no part of Tuleves escaped the destruction in The Lady's mind.

I turned and knocked a paper from The Lady's desk. It was a note scribbled in hasty handwriting.

The blood jewels were found beneath the floorboards of the healer's hut. I've sent them to you with all the haste possible. I will form a squadron to escort the jewels to Helefount at first light. I will not rest until they are in the hands of the immortal Kadasha. I will not fail to ransom the king and bring him home.

The blood jewels were here. I felt around the shelves and looked under the desk. I saw no sign of the four bags, but the note had a tear in the center, like it had been attached to a cord and ripped off. The Lady could have the blood jewels on her person at this very moment. Was it possible the blood jewels were what Garreth needed? My heart stopped at the thought. I had the blood jewels in Faengsel Forrest. Maybe I'd had what he needed all along.

And I'd lost them. I shouldn't have left them in Dawn's hut. I put her in even more danger. If Dawn had run like she'd promised, she wouldn't have been there when they took the jewels. She should be safe, but I hated the thought of soldiers tossing the bed aside, pulling up floorboards, spilling her bottles and spices onto the ground.

Voices echoed down the corridor.

I whispered to Garreth. "Dinner is over. We're out of time."

CHAPTER 42

I JUMPED off the raised floor and ran to the door, closing them to just a crack a peeking through. The Lady turned the corner and walked gracefully down the corridor with. . . a face I knew, but whose name I could not recall. My mind slipped and slid over a memory that had the feeling of home. I didn't understand why I couldn't hold onto it.

Garreth grabbed my arm and pulled me from the door, pushing it shut softly. "You may be a good thief, but you're a terrible lookout. We can't get out that way. Lock the door and hide."

Lock the door? I couldn't lock the door. I could only take, not give and I wasn't even sure what this door needed to lock so tightly. I put my hand against the door and felt the spark reviving on its own, like Marion had after I stopped draining him. All I had to do was stop draining the spark. There was no time to wonder what kind of life spark could be held within a door.

We hid in the bedchamber, under the bed.

The Lady and the other person entered the sitting room. The other person sat directly in my line of sight through the cracked bedroom door. If he had looked my way, he would have seen me. I clenched my fists and stared at the familiar face. Something about it. Something about him. I wrestled with my mind the way I did when I was learning a new language. I knew the word; the memory was in there somewhere.

"You claim you have knowledge that would be valuable enough for me to pardon you," The Lady said. "You cannot possibly know the damage your little raid caused your nation."

Little raid? A memory of a death pier. A man with his hand out toward reluctant captains. This man. I did know him. We had robbed together once to take the blood jewels. Why could I not remember the very person who helped me steal the blood jewels?

Stealing the blood jewels had delayed the release of the king, but The Lady had the jewels now. She must need something else from the other thief.

"As I've said before, My Lady," the man said with his smooth, calming voice, "it was an ill-timed prank, a joke on the superstitions of the Havish." He dropped his eyes and spoke with convincing quiet humility. "I regret the damage I have done and have willingly accepted my punishments to prove my loyalty to you."

Loyalty. Those words made me want to throw up.

"Yet you refuse to give us any information about the Hooded Robber?"

My partner in crime shook his head. He was special to me. Why couldn't I remember anything more about him. "If I knew anything, My Lady, I would tell you, but I know nothing. The fact that he was there that night was a coincidence of the worst kind. If I ever find him, I will bring him in myself for all the pain he's caused me."

My heart stuttered in my chest. This man was still protecting me, lying to The Lady's face to keep my secret. As I confused as I was, I felt awe at his bravery.

"Pity," she said. "Then you are of no use to me."

"Wait." He reached out to stop The Lady who was now standing. "I've done everything you've asked and more. All I want is to be released so that I can participate in the Tournament of the People."

"You have no information valuable enough to earn your release. You will be sent with the next indentured servant train to Helefount the evening after the coronation. I hope you have better luck in Helefount than you found in Tuleves."

"You're wrong," he said. The chill in the atmosphere reached all the way under the bed. It was words The Lady might never have heard before. "I have information far more valuable than the Hooded Robber or even the location of the blood jewels."

"What could possibly be more valuable than that?" The Lady asked.

His jaw set, all humility erased, replaced by a confident seriousness that I had rarely seen in anyone but Garreth. I knew this man. Why couldn't I remember?

"I can tell you where to find the Oracle who gave the prophecy at her birth."

There was a long silence.

"From the mouth of a babe. You know the location of the last true Oracle? How could you know this?"

A knock on the door interrupted them.

"My Lady, the Grand Councilor requests your presence in his quarters."

"If this information proves correct, you may participate. Come with me." The Lady's voice was cool, but there was an underlying tension I hadn't heard before. She turned to the guard. "He probably wants to beg for his son's life, but his words will land on deaf ears. Kadasha will demand a sacrifice after his folly. She may demand it tonight. I will come immediately. Tell him I'm bringing a guest."

The soldier's shoes clicked together as he bowed. The edge of The Lady's dress swished, and her hand waved through my small field of vision. She motioned for the other thief to exit the room and followed behind, shutting the door.

"The Grand Councilor had excellent timing, for once," said Garreth. Despite the lightness of his tone, his jaw muscle pulsed.

"Did you find what you were looking for?" I knew before he answered.

There was a catch in his voice. "There's nothing. It's not here."

"Can we see him? Can we go to Marion?"

His gaze swept over The Lady's room one last time. He hadn't found what he'd come for, but the thought of Marion hanging from a rope must have been as unthinkable to him as it was to me. We escaped out of The Lady's chambers and back into the hidden passage. But when we arrived at the entrance to the dungeons through the Sanatorium, a soldier blocked our way.

"No visitors until after the Tournament of the People, by order of The Lady."

"You can't stop me," Garreth said. "You know that."

"Only you. The healer needs to retire."

I was about to argue, but Garreth leaned into whisper in my ear. "We don't need to put anyone else's life at risk tonight. This soldier would be killed if someone saw him let you through. I will see you in the morning at breakfast. Future wife."

"Are we still going through with that plan?" I asked.

"It's the only one we have so far. I'll figure out how to make it work." He gave me a final glance and then pushed past the soldier.

I went inside my tiny room to see if I could get some sleep. My eyes were heavy and my mind a maelstrom of unanswered questions.

Something crunched under my head. I reached under the small pillow and pulled out a piece of parchment. It was a note with my name, my real name, sprawled across the front. *Arianna.*

I opened the letter.

Ari,

They know you're not a healer. I don't know how, but there is plan to take you tonight. Run. Get out of the Sanatorium. If anyone can escape you can.

Every moment I had with you was a treasure. Seeing you again was like waking up in the realm beyond where eternal happiness abounds. You've saved my life twice these last few days. I can only return that favor by warning you of what is to come. Don't let them catch you. I wish that I had been worthy of you, but I am not. I have killed men, fellow soldiers, friends. I am guilty. I cannot plead any other way. Treason within the ranks. That's what they are charging me with. That is what I've done.

I would die willingly in two days, but I have a duty to protect the prince. I don't know how I will do that now, not with this fire in my very bones and a furnace in my mind. Not with a death sentence on my head. I will figure something out. It is my purpose.

First, I must make sure you are safe. I did nothing one year ago, but I did what I could this time. I distracted them and laid a false trail. I had the youngest healer leave this note for you. I could only give you a small head start. Take this chance and run. If I fail to protect the prince, at least I can die with the peace of knowing you're safe.

Love for ever more,
Marion

The letter smelled of drying ink and leather. I imagined him writing those words, writing my name. I wore a mask to become the Hooded Robber. I had to lie to become Dawn, the village healer. I had followed the expectations of Prontwick to become the healer's assistant. But for Marion, I had always been and always would be Arianna. I didn't know when it would be safe to bear that name, to show that face. It didn't matter now. I had to come up with another plan. The Sanatorium was no longer a safe prison.

CHAPTER 43

IT WASN'T AS if I had anything to pack, but I hesitated, not knowing what to do. I stretched and lay across the bed. If the eyes in the window were watching, I didn't want to tip them off that I knew of their plan.

I lay quietly, my mind racing. If I could slip past the guard and get into the dungeons, I could hide there until the Tournament of the People. But there were more guards in the dungeons than in the Sanatorium and I doubted there were very good hiding places. I could use Garreth's invitation and try to slip out the front, act like I was completely oblivious and hope they wouldn't spring their trap until I was free. That was too risky. The guard at the entrance to the Sanatorium was probably the first to know of my falsehood. I needed another way out.

The lights lowered, signaling the end of the day. I ripped the note into a thousand pieces, knowing my heart was breaking into the same number of shards. I didn't want Marion in any more trouble than treason if I was caught. The noise from the hallways quieted. It was now or never. I slipped out of my room and walked confidently into the refreshment room the healers used to relieve themselves. I dropped the pieces of the note into the bowl and pulled the string that sent the waste out to the river.

If I ran, I would be abandoning my father and Marion and now, the Prince of Tuleves, who was counting on me for a posh breakfast to make the council uncomfortable.

If I stayed, I wouldn't be able to help any of them. I would die.

A small noise behind me made me whirl. Polisha stood there, rubbing one toe against the ground.

"What is it?" I asked.

"They're coming for you," she whispered. She handed me a set of fresh healer's robes. "They know you're not the healer from Jaklin, that you were just the assistant. They're here to arrest you. I promised the hot one, I would help."

"You mean the son of the Grand Councilor." She shrugged. I threw the healer's robes over my head. "Thank you. I could use a friend right now, but I can't promise you'll be safe. I don't want to see you get hurt."

"I can always say you forced me. Or that I didn't know better. No one here thinks I am smart enough to clean a chamber pot, let alone plan an escape." She pulled me across the hall to the base of the windowed tower to avoid being seen. The main doors to the Sanatorium opened and I heard the firm march of soldier feet down the stairs.

"Is there another way out?" I asked.

She shook her head as she squeezed my hand. Despite what she said, I knew she was risking a lot to help me. "The only other way out is if you're dead and dumped into the river. I guess we could sneak you out that way, but it would take hours for the crematorium to cool down."

"Show me."

She hesitated. "I'll show you, but the sounds of punishment are terrible."

She shivered and then led me around the base of the tower to the door where I'd gone down with Garreth to watch his punishment. I didn't remember the sounds. I didn't remember Garreth being whipped at all. Odd.

She used a key from her belt, and we slipped in as quietly as we could. Before we made it to the end of the cold, white hall, a terrible scream ripped through the air. It was slightly muffled, but the animalistic nature off the scream made it sound as if it could rip out the throat.

"Who's being punished?" I asked, my heart breaking at the pure suffering in the sound.

"The captain." Polisha squeezed my hand tighter. I had to lean closer to hear since her face was buried in my healer's robes. "This is the second time this week. They don't let anyone else hear the screaming, but I hear all of it. I can feel all of it."

I squeezed her tighter, my own heart constricting, the truth of her words hitting me like a punch to the gut.

"What captain?" I asked. I prayed to Kadasha they weren't punishing Marion already. He wasn't a captain yet.

"The one from the caravan," she said. "I'm not supposed to listen when I bring them supplies, but I can't help it. She had something very valuable, something that was supposed to save us, but she lost it and now they're hurting her. I don't understand. I lose things sometimes. What if they do that to me?"

I knelt to look her in the face. "Don't worry. They won't hurt you like that. And you won't have to stay here much longer."

"You're nice," she said, using my robe to wipe her eyes, then giving me an endearing smile. "I don't think you understand things very well, but I like you."

"You don't believe I can save you?" I asked.

She looked very solemn. Her large, brown eyes almost swallowed me. "My mother was a countess and she couldn't save me." She pulled a folded piece of parchment from her pocket and held it out for me. "Will you take this picture to her? I drew it for her."

I took the paper from her hand and unfolded it. It was a simple chalk drawing of a stick figure holding a smaller stick figure.

"That's her holding me when I was a baby," she said. "I think she'll still remember me."

"Of course she will." I carefully refolded the paper and tucked it into the front of my robes.

Another round of screaming hit me as the door opened, a rasping, desperate sound. Polisha covered her ears, tears streaming down her face.

She led me to a doorway with a semicircle of healers around it, as if they were watching for sport. I could not look at any of their faces without revealing mine, so I approached a small gap in the circle of bodies and leaned my head to see through the door. Polisha slipped behind another corner.

The captain's face, twisted in pain, was barely recognizable. The woman was being tortured because I had stolen the blood jewels from her. Another person's whose pain was my fault.

The Grand Councilor and The Lady stood to the side facing the captain, their backs to me. The captain's hands were bound with leather and raised above her head. Her shirt had been ripped away, the shreds of fabric providing no modesty for the woman's exposed torso. A healer had her hand on the captain's shoulder and she slowly relaxed, her breathing evening out. The healer stepped back, leaning against the wall for support. The semicircle of healers moved to the side to let the spent healer stumble past.

The healers were not here for entertainment. They were waiting for their turn to give their life energy to torture this woman. This was no punishment. This was torture. They were using the gifting of life, the healers of the Sanatorium, for torture.

"You were tasked with the safe delivery of the package," Grand Councilor Levante said. "You made an oath with your three sisters that if you failed, your lives would be forfeited." There was a strained desperation in his voice.

The captain tried to nod, but her head simply fell forward.

"Where are the items now?" he asked. "Do you have any idea where they could be now?"

She gave a low moan. "The priest took them. He took them and then lost them. We searched for two days." The Grand Councilor stopped her from saying any more with a slap. A trickle of blood ran down Captain Tevya's chin from a cut in her cheek.

"Forgive me," she said. "I will find the items and ensure it is delivered. It is my sacred oath."

"You have proven your oaths as worthless as the life you have forfeited," he said. "Your carelessness and incompetence have lost the very hope of our kingdom. With your failure, we have lost an alliance with the immortals. We will soon see the repercussions. For that, you are sentenced to die without honors and without friends. No one will know of your fate and your bones will be scattered to the four winds."

A soldier pushed through the group of healers. "Grand Councilor, the healer, the false one, is gone."

Grand Councilor Levante turned. The healers moved out of his way, pushing me back with them. "Find her, search the Sanatorium and then find Prince Garreth. She was with him last."

I kept to the edges of the hallway, moving like I belonged with the other healers who suddenly had somewhere else to go. I couldn't help peeking out the corner of the hood of the healer's robe. The Lady had the blood jewels, didn't she? Had I misunderstood the note? Perhaps the blood jewels hadn't arrived yet.

"Let her bleed," The Lady said, giving directions to the last soldier in the room and leaving without aid, her blindfold and sightless eyes no hindrance to her.

The healers began to disperse. I did not know which direction I should go. I turned away as the remaining soldier approached Captain Tevya with a sharp, curved carving knife. The screams began again.

The blood in my veins chilled. The air squeezed from my lungs.

It took all my concentration to keep walking the other direction as the soldiers escorted The Lady and the Grand Councilor down the hall and up into the Sanatorium.

Someone pulled on my robe. I whirled, ready to fight. I looked down to see Polisha.

"The crematorium is this way," she said. She had dried tear streaks down her cheeks. Her hands were shaking where she held my borrowed healer's robes. Both of us glanced at the room. The screams had been replaced by grunts and sobs.

"In a moment," I said. "First, I want to save the captain."

"Are you the hero from the stories, the one who wears the hood." Her wide eyes seemed to fill her face. "I am your most enthusiastic admirer."

"Who told you that? You should not believe everything you hear."

Her face was too open. Her smile revealing that she believed everything she had heard. And that I was the one she believed in.

"It's dangerous to know who I am. They could kill you if they found out you knew. I can't protect everyone."

Her face was solemn but determined. "I know. But you will save far more people than will die for you."

I didn't know why she said that, but I was determined no one else would die because of me.

CHAPTER 44

I RETURNED TO THE ROOM, trying to match the unhurried movements of the other healers. When I reached the door and stepped inside, the soldier paused, lifting his knife from where he held it below the captain's nose.

"What do you want?" he asked. "We have no more need for a healer." A wicked grin split his face, revealing a man who reveled in causing pain.

"I'm here for you." I grabbed his wrist with the knife in case he tried to push it at me before I could steal his spark. But confusion made him hesitate and I was able to slow his heart with a sharp pull.

The soldier collapsed.

The room contained a skinny wall cabinet, a table where the cutting tools were spread out, and two buckets placed strategically under the captain to catch her blood. The floor was surprisingly clean. I tried to ignore the buckets, both which had several inches of red liquid in them. The sharp smell of cleaning chemicals mixed with the tang of human blood.

There was a click behind me. I whirled, ready to fight, only to see Polisha pulling in a long, wheeled cart and shutting the door. "Do you think we can get her out through the crematorium, too? We don't have time to let it cool."

"I can get her out, but you need to stop helping me. Tell me the way and then leave."

"You can't stop me." She paused as she looked at the soldier on the floor. "Well, you could, but you'd have to knock me out. Like that guy." She smiled, one that reminded me of the scarlet from Faengsel Forest. "It feels so good to do something for myself. They always tell me what to do, when to do it, how to do it, and that I'm still doing it wrong. But right now, I get to choose. I understand now why you fight. Doing something good but risky makes me feel strong." Her eyes reflected what she was saying, a light dancing in them, a look on her face that defied everything about the situation.

I took her shoulders. "You see what they do to people. It may seem fun and exciting now, but there are consequences that you can never erase." Mother stabbed through the gut. Father wasting away in a prison. Marion with a noose around his neck.

The light in her eyes didn't die. Instead, it hardened from a flickering flame to a sparkling diamond. "I would rather live a full life for a week than half a life for years." This small girl had more wisdom than all the council members I had met at dinner.

"Help me, then," I said.

There were hundreds of cuts already across the captain's back, some shallow, some wide enough to expose ripped muscle. A few reached all the way to the bone. When I touched Captain Tevya where the straps cut into her wrists, the energy from her heart was weak, barely pulsing through her body. I wasn't sure we could move her in the state she was in.

I hated to ask this young girl for one more thing, but it was the only option. "Can you heal her?"

Polisha rolled up her sleeves, exposing her hands and waving them like she was warming up to lead a band of musicians. "Of course. I'm one of the youngest apprentices in Sanatorium history. You don't get this far without some talent. Can you hold me? I've never done this much healing before. It might make me a little tired."

I moved to where I could catch her if she fell. She placed the tips of her fingers against the ribs on either side of the captain. She didn't flinch at the sight of the cuts or the blood that dripped down around her fingers.

Her spark channeled into Captain Tevya. I held my breath, afraid that I might accidentally absorb the precious energy. I did not have to physically breathe to take spark, but I hoped the act would remind me to keep from sucking in other ways.

A shallow gash near where she touched the captain healed, the skin drawing together, stitching closed. Her spark waned, the buzzing transferring out of her small body. I felt as if I was watching something sacred. I told myself I should close my eyes in honor of Polisha's talent, but I could not get myself to stop watching the captain's back heal.

A few minutes later, she slumped against me, her fingers slipping from the captain's side. I had to wrap my arms around her to keep her upright. Her head tipped against my shoulder and her face lifted to mine.

"That's all I can do," she said, her eyes filling with tears. "I'm sorry."

"It was more than enough." It was true. The deepest of the captain's cuts had become red welts while others had formed new scars. All the wounds had stopped bleeding and the captain's heart was beating strong in her chest.

I helped Polisha sit on the floor against the wall. I used the soldier's carving knife to cut the straps that held Captain Tevya. I pushed the captain's weight to the side so that she flopped mostly onto the cart, and then I lifted her feet the rest of the way. The captain was waking, her mouth opening as if preparing for a scream out of habit.

Quickly covering her mouth, I whispered in her ear. "Hush now. No more pain. We're taking you somewhere safe. Will you stay quiet?"

The captain's shoulders shook, tears streaming from her eyes as she nodded. I took my hand from her mouth.

"Why?" she whispered, though her gaze was not on me. She stared past me with a glazed look. "My life was forfeit; I would have taken my own life to honor my pledge. Why did they do it like this?"

I had no answer for the woman. I searched the cabinet in the room and found a long, white piece of linen for bedding and covered the captain. She took a deep, shuddering breath and lay still, the shape of the body clear beneath the sheet. Polisha crawled over and climbed onto the lower shelf of the cart. The sheet was long enough to hide her as well.

"To get to the crematorium, go to the end of the hall and turn left. It's the last door to the right."

There was no time for questions. I positioned the soldier I had incapacitated against the cabinet so that it looked like he was resting, then I opened the door and pushed the cart out of the room, making it to the crematorium without interruption.

The door to the crematorium was heavy, taking all my strength to open it. Pulling in the cart with two bodies on it while holding open the door was a bit of a challenge. I bumped the cart into the wall and door several times before I was able to line it up and get it through.

The temperature inside the crematorium was hotter than a midsummer day in the middle of a sand-covered desert. The room was three sizes bigger than Orblee's hut. Half the space was filled with a black oven with a door large enough for a human body. There was nothing else in the room. No windows. No tables or chairs. Plain walls just far enough away from the furnace to keep from catching fire. A coal scuttle was in the corner with a shovel sticking out of it. I imagined Polisha down here, shoveling coal as a punishment.

I pulled the sheet off the captain. She sat up slowly. Polisha climbed out from under the cart and handed another set of robes to Captain Tevya. The captain pulled on the robe, but her movements remained lethargic, like someone who had lost purpose. She was a strong woman, tall as Marion with muscular arms.

"Do you recognize me?" I asked.

The captain looked at me for the first time, my face exposed, but she just shook her head. For a moment I thought about revealing my identity, but then she would know that the torture had been my fault.

"What are the blood jewels?" I asked. "Why are they so important?"

The captain started, her head pulling back, her eyes clearing. "It does not matter now. They are gone, and without them, we will all be destroyed."

CHAPTER 45

THERE WERE two parts to my escape plan. First, I would have to absorb enough heat to cool the crematorium without hurting the captain. Second, we had to climb through a giant heated drawer filled with human ashes to be able to push through to the other side.

"Come with us."

Polisha grabbed my hand. "I will be okay. No one will look twice at the small girl who shovels coal. Once you get in, push your feet against the wall and the drawer will slide out into the lower crypt. Once a week, the priests pull the drawer out and give last rites to the remains before dumping the ashes into the river."

"What about the families of the deceased?" I asked, looking dubiously into the door of the furnace.

"They say goodbye to the body in the Sanatorium." She could barely stand. She was as pale as a snow fox, and I could swear she had some wrinkles around her eyes.

"Promise me you'll go straight to the kitchens and get some food."

"I can do that. The cook likes me. I healed her cat without telling anyone." I wrapped my arms around the small girl. She would never know how much she was risking or how grateful I was.

"I cannot go that way," the captain said. "I will be turned to ash myself."

The furnace was ready for the next body to be cremated. It wasn't as hot as when someone was being burned, but hot enough to kill someone trying to climb through.

"Not if you're with her." Polisha pointed at me. Even in her exhaustion, she managed a proud smile.

"What can you do?" asked the captain. Her strength was waning. She also needed food and rest. Despite the wounds being healed, she had lost a lot of blood. She wavered even as she planted her feet in front of me. "I have the gifting of heat, but I could only make it hotter. I am not fireproof. That is not part of the gifting, as useful as that would be."

The sound of yelling echoed down the hall. The soldier had been found and someone wasn't happy. We were out of time.

"I can absorb heat. I can suck in spark and make it dim."

"I've never heard of such a gifting."

"It's not a gift. It is a curse. I can only take and never be filled." I had never said those words out loud. The woman didn't react the way I expected. She didn't shy away or look down at me in disgust. She leaned back, wrapped the healer's robes around herself, and studied me.

"An absorber? Only in our oldest legends." Her lips pursed and she looked to the ceiling instead and I could almost see her putting two and two together. If she figured it out, she said nothing. Instead, she nodded sharply and then moved out of the way for me to go first.

"We will have to go together," I said. "I can only affect a small area."

She hesitated, then came closer to me.

"Are you prepared to commit treason?" I asked.

"They have already killed my sisters." Captain Tevya's voice was steel. Her tears had dried. "In the same way. They forced us to watch but did not question us or explain why. They collected our blood, but they did not have to do it that way. They did not have to kill my sisters so slowly. I serve the Grand Councilor no longer."

For a moment, I felt more than the captain's energy, I also felt her pain. Or it was my own pain of watching my father dragged away and my house burned that I felt reflected in the captain?

Footsteps sounded outside. Someone pounded on the doors. Polisha waved at us to go. I sucked in, taking the heat from around us. Ice crystals formed on the healer's robe and the ends of my hair. Together we climbed into the furnace. Polisha shut the door. Even with me sucking in, the heat was so intense that the ice began to form droplets around us. Metal screeched and the platform below us gave way. The captain and I fell into a pile of ash hot enough to burn my skin. I sucked in more, pulling the heat away from both of our bodies. There was so much ash in the air I couldn't breathe in and certainly did not want to inhale the remains of other people who had come this way before.

I pressed my feet against the wall the way Polisha had instructed and pushed. We only moved a fraction of an inch. There was no air to breathe. Sweat formed on my forehead as I tried to pull in even more heat. The pain in my chest flared, but I couldn't relax. I pulled harder.

The captain placed her bare feet beside mine and together we pushed. The drawer slid twice as far. We scooted down and pushed again. This time, the sound of rushing water slipped in through a gap above our heads.

It wasn't large enough yet. We scooted down some more, the heat cutting through my efforts to protect us from the hot coals directly beneath the drawer. The captain squeezed my hand and together we pushed one more time with all our might.

With a groaning of metal on metal, the drawer slid away from the wall of the furnace and then tipped backward.

The captain and I tumbled blindly through ash, landing on a hard surface. I jumped up, brushing off glowing embers. The captain moved more slowly. She had a burn mark on her cheek and a blackened spot on her head. The smelled of burned hair stirred through the air with the ash. I helped her to her feet, shaking the healer's robe free of the remains of death.

"Are you all right?" I asked. My concentration had broken when the drawer of ash tipped. I had stopped absorbing heat.

"I am alive," Captain Tevya said. "Thanks to you, though all that I lived for is gone." She glanced up at stony ceiling where an opening for the furnace drawer had been carved into the original stone of the mountain. She seemed to be looking beyond the rock barrier and into the heart of Tuleves. She had lost her sisters and the trust of the kingdom she had served. I didn't know how she felt, but I too had lost everything once.

Tears streaked through the ash on the captain's face. I placed a hand on her arm, and she nodded. She turned away and examined the small cave we had entered. The ceiling arched above us only a few feet above my head. A rushing stream cut through the center of the cave floor. There was a handcart pushed up against the wall to the right of the furnace and a door to the left, with an area of smooth stone floor barely large enough to turn the handcart around. The water rushed by us in a roar, making my ears ring and suppressing any other sound. There was an outcropping of stone on the far side of the river, but I saw no way to reach it.

The opening grew smaller as the cave approached the exit where the water rushed out. There was enough space between the water and the cave ceiling that I could make out blue sky, but nothing beyond or below.

I turned and saw the captain attempting to lift the drawer and slide it back in place. The metal was hot and her skin sizzled as she touched it. She hissed and dropped the drawer.

"We must cover our tracks," she said. "I may not want to live anymore, but I do not want to die their way. There is no honor in what they did."

"Here," I said, gently pushing her to the side. "Let me." I sucked in, giving my hands a layer protection on my palms. Before I lifted it, voices echoed through the furnace. They had already opened the door. The yells were loud enough to be heard above the roar of the water.

"They must have gone this way," yelled a voice.

My heart froze. Had they discovered Polisha? Did they know she had helped us? I dropped the drawer, shooting ash into the air again. The air was moist enough that the ash clung to us like a thin layer of mud. I rushed to the door in the wall, but it was locked. If they knew we were down here, it was the first direction they would come.

The captain leaned against the wall, her face drained, her chest heaving with exhaustion. Polisha could heal, but she could not return the captain's blood. I had to get her to a safe place. She was in no condition to fight. And if this door led back up to the castle we would be outnumbered fifty to one.

"Can you swim?" I asked.

Her eyes landed on the water rushing by her and she shook her head.

I tried the door again. I could freeze the handle and break it. When I laid my hand on the door, a pounding came from the other side. They had already sent soldiers this way to intercept us. We were out of options and time.

The water was the only way out. It was the way the ashes were washed away each week when the furnace was cleaned. It was the way we would escape the walls of the castle.

I grabbed a rope dangling over the side of the handcart and tied it around my waist and then the captain's. The door burst open behind us. I kicked the handcart into the river, and it split apart as it hit the sides of the cave opening.

"Don't drown," I said, and we both jumped into the rushing water.

Chapter 46

One small decision, like a loosened pebble on a mountain side, can start an avalanche of consequences. The cold and force of the water hit me like I had stepped in the way of a falling mountain. Instinct took over and my body fought for air and relief, but my mind was surprisingly detached as my body fell over the edge of the waterfall. I wasn't aware of when I hit the bottom. Only that I was being tossed about like a rag doll. One step had placed me on this path. One step that would end with me tied to an enemy being beaten by a force of nature I had previously relied on as a source of life.

Just when I thought that my lungs could take no more and my bones had been pummeled to mush, the river released me from the dizzying undercurrents, and I broke the surface. I gasped for breath, coughing out water. I felt a tug on my waist and heard the choking and splashing of the captain somewhere nearby.

For a moment, I could take in nothing but sweet air, my eyes and ears full of water. Mother's voice tried to speak through my desperation. *Know about everything around you before anything around you knows about you.*

I let my head sink below the water for another moment and this time, surfaced slowly. I did not recognize my surroundings. The river itself spread out far in either direction, calm and placid like a toddler who had suddenly given up on a temper tantrum. On either side of the river were flat fields, cultivated farmland from the looks of the even rows. Behind me I could see where the water had poured out of the stonework of Tuleves City, but we were far away already, the water falling from the wall no more than a ribbon of silk. The white rapids of the river ended just behind us and had pushed us from the city at a quick, although painful rate.

Polisha had said there was "sort of" a way out of the cremation room. I did not know if she had been referring to the door or the water. When I saw her again, I would have to teach her to be more specific. My stomach clenched at the thought of what might be happening to her.

I had saved the captain, an enemy, and abandoned a friend. Father and Marion were still in the dungeons. Polisha might have been taken by the soldiers. Was I really such a coward that I would abandon them all?

The rope around my waist tugged again and I looked around for the captain. Her head had slipped beneath the surface. I could not see her. I pulled the rope toward me, following it as I dove beneath the water. I found the captain and pulled her back to the surface with my last ounce of strength.

Fortunately, the remains of the handcart floated ahead of us. I pulled the captain's head back as I turned and used one arm to backstroke toward the wood. The captain needed rest and warmth, but I didn't feel safe swimming to the shore this close to Tuleves City. The soldiers would be behind us soon with their dogs and their horses.

The bottom of the cart had held together and provided a nice raft sized piece. I attempted to heave her onto the wood but I could not touch the bottom so I had no leverage. The bottom of the cart flipped as I put weight on it and nearly knocked us both in the heads. The captain helped catch the wood before it pushed us under. I didn't see what had woken her up or how she had continued fighting after all she had been through. Her deep strength testified of how she had earned the position of captain.

We let the wood right itself and then I moved to the opposite side of the raft. The captain counted to three and we pushed up onto the flat surface, rolling toward the middle at the same time.

We both rolled onto our backs and let the sun dry us out.

The captain coughed, throwing up water as she curled up. I moved to balance the raft and keep clear. She no longer resembled the large woman who had chased me through Sherwood at sword point. She had been stripped naked and left with nothing.

"I'm sorry," I said. For stealing the blood jewels and the lives of her sisters. For giving Marion the very healing paste that would mark him as a traitor. I had robbed to balance invisible scales, I had imagined myself a hero of sorts, but I never imagined I'd tip the scales so far in the wrong direction.

"You have nothing to apologize for." Captain Tevya adjusted the healer's cloak around herself like she could use it for warmth even though it was soaking wet. "You saved my life."

I shook my head. I had kept secrets from my family, my best friend, from the boy I loved, but I could not muster the strength to lie to this stranger.

"You're wrong. It was my fault," I said. "All of it. I stole the blood jewels. I am the Hooded Robber. I killed your sisters. I killed them all."

She slid toward me as we lay on the floating remains of an ash carrying handcart. She put a firm hand on my shoulder, a comfort, an anchor to the world. She did not contradict me or argue with me. "What a power you yield to have stirred up the ruling powers, causing them to swarm like a disturbed ant hill."

I expected anger, accusation, sorrow, but her voice only held awe.

I shifted my own healer's robes. They had twisted around my neck, and the string was tight around my middle. I loosened the cord and pulled the robes down. I rubbed my chest. The initial pain of cooling the crematorium had faded, but a dull throb remained. As I rubbed my thumb across the skin over my heart, Captain Tevya grabbed my hand. She pulled it away and exposed the center of my chest. She stared at the small tattoo. I pulled the flaps of my robes closed. I had glanced at the small vine. It had only grown a little, one small leave for each time I'd felt the sharp pain. Each time I had pulled spark into me with all my energy.

She had no words. She only leaned back on the wood of our makeshift wrap and began humming. The sound was hesitant at first, like it was something she had dug up from a long-lost memory. Each note grew in strength the tune became clearer.

It wasn't a song I knew. It was a song from the Havish, from her childhood before she'd been sent to train as a youth. The river pulled us farther from the city with a rocking motion that matched her song. Then her hum turned into words.

Brides will dance with blinded eyes
Babies suck for with a thirst for life
The seven immortals control the turning of time
The gifting a result of their endless loop.
Kadasha, Sadeem, Ashanti allows us time, speed, and wisdom.
Helloran grants strength and Lucera controls heat.
Galente knows life and inspires healing and recovery.
Sound is the last and the weakest, some would believe, from Forantis
They give of themselves and take more than they need
Until all that they've given is broken.
Left in a hopeless eternal storm.
The folding of the frozen land cannot be
Stopped by strength or stone or spark or light.
One with darkness deep within has the strength
The world will need to break the fold.
Sing praise in the absorbers name or death
And darkness and mortality will reign.

"That's a sad song." Her haunting words brought to mind the tapestries in The Lady's chambers. "What does it mean? I thought all the giftings came from Kadasha."

"I never stopped to ask the meaning." She paused. "I believed it to be a song to put children to sleep. It always worked for me. Kadasha is only one of the seven immortals. Why would all giftings come from her?"

I hadn't ever stopped to ask that question. I didn't have an answer for it. "It's a little dark to put kids to sleep."

"The Havish do not shield their children from the realities of the world. We are taught young to be stronger than the harsh world around us. It helps us be the soldiers we are meant to be."

"It is a wonder you have any hope at all." I tugged my robe tighter.

My head pounded as the sun rose above the fields, reflecting off the water. Thirst settled deep in the back of my throat despite being surrounded by water. "It sounds more like the absorber is the one who froze the world in the first place. Whenever I try to help anyone, I make things worse. I'm sure if I tried to save the world, I would end up folding it in half."

"That is an interesting theory. Many think the same of the prophecy of the Oracles. If we are to believe the Oracles, then we are the one who cause their visions of the future to come to pass."

"Is that what you believe?"

She was quiet for a long moment. I thought her exhaustion had caught up with her. I didn't blame her. Sleep weighed heavy on my own eyelids.

She spoke her voice quiet. "I helped to slaughter the Oracles. I helped to use their blood to make the blood jewels. We didn't kill them as cruelly as my sisters were, but we drained them of their blood, the ones that weren't killed in the fight. Hundreds of them. It took days. And I watched them weep, waiting for their turn inside their own temple. As I took the last one, a woman older than the seas, her eyes burned gold. She told me that there was still hope for me, that this path would change me, create me. She said the prophecy had been set in motion, but it didn't mean it had to be fulfilled."

My path had not changed me or created me. It had destroyed me. I was no longer even sure who I was.

"What did you do?" I asked.

"I called her blasphemer and cut her head off before she could say more."

"Why?"

"Kadasha had commanded it." She pulled a sliver of wood from destroyed handcart and squeezed it in her fist. "The Oracles had rejected Kadasha's direction and were inspiring the people to turn against her. The Oracles were using their gifts to persuade people to fight against Kadasha's influence. The immortal would have come to destroy us all."

"No," I said. "That can't possibly be true. The Oracles spoke for Kadasha."

"Not since the prophecy from the mouth of a babe." I'd heard that expression before in The Lady's chambers. She was looking for the babe who had given the prophecy. But it hadn't been me.

I pushed up on one elbow so I could look at the captain, see the lies in her face. Instead, I saw only sorrow etched into the lines on her forehead and around her eyes, a regret so deep it pulled at the corners of her mouth and left her chin trembling.

Before I could work out the truth of a prophecy that resulted in the slaughter of the Oracles, a dark cloud on the horizon caught my eye. If a storm was coming, we needed to find shelter. The rain would help cover our tracks from the dogs.

But it wasn't a cloud, not a normal storm. It shifted quickly, rising into the air to form a contained stripe up into the blue sky. The smell hit me a moment later, a slight scent carried on the wind.

Smoke. Something was burning.

CHAPTER 47

I JUMPED TO MY FEET. Our makeshift raft rocked. I reached for the empty place on my back where my quiver and bow usually hung. My bow, smashed by the Grand Councilor. Gone. It was a missing part of me, an amputated limb. The last piece of my father I would never get back.

"What is it?" Captain Tevya clung to the edges of the raft. Her knuckles were white against the wet boards. "Where are we?"

I scanned the banks, unsure of how far we had traveled or how swiftly the current had taken us. We were beyond the farmlands and there were no signs of habitation, no recognizable landmarks other than the approaching hills, low on the horizon. They were not tall enough to be the Boulder Mountains. We had not traveled as far as Renathoth.

I watched the smoke for a few more minutes. My mouth went so dry I could not swallow. It couldn't be. But in a break between the hills, I caught sight of the tall, imposing walls of the Ruins of the Oracles, although from this distance it looked like a gray smear on the horizon. The smoke came from beyond the walls. There was nothing left to burn inside of the city, but on the other side was the village.

"I have to go." I dropped to my knees and paddled with both hands. The raft rocked and spun in a useless circle.

Captain Tevya shaded her eyes, examining the smoke. "It has the scent of destruction. There will be nothing you can do. You will be caught."

"Not if I'm careful," I said. "I have to check on something, on someone." What if Dawn hadn't run? I had asked her to promise, but had she even said the words? If they were burning the village because I had escaped, that meant the villagers' lives were on my head. I couldn't imagine that they'd got ahead of me, but if they had sent a regiment to the village before Marion warned me, there was a chance.

"I will stay with you." She knelt calmly despite the spinning and rocking I was causing and put her hands into the water like a rudder. "It's better than wandering without a purpose." The raft straightened out and together we were able to row to the edge of the river.

We pushed into the reeds, the stiff grasses scratching my arms. I climbed onto firm ground, took the captain's hand, and pulled her toward me. I turned, adrenaline pulsing through me. The rising smoke rolling up into the innocent blue was not a small fire; it was not a single building. The entire village must be burning to create so much smoke.

Before I could take a step, the captain collapsed.

I knelt beside her. "You have had no food or rest since you were drained of blood. You cannot make this journey on foot."

"Go," she said. "I will follow as soon as I recover my strength." She gripped my hand, thumbs intertwined, the way Dawn and I would hold each other when we made one of our silly pacts of silence so we wouldn't get caught for our mischief.

"What is your name?" she asked.

"Arianna," I said. I had not spoken my name out loud in a long time. It felt so good, as if the person I wanted to be was still in there, beneath the frozen shell I had created, beyond the robber, and the fake healer. I was me. I had a name. "Arianna Robbins."

"Go," she whispered, her body relaxing. She was really going to fall asleep right here in the reeds and rushes of the river.

It wasn't a bad hiding place, and the dogs would find no smells to guide them here. And when the sun set, Iranus would be following my scent, not hers.

"May the seasons turn in your favor," I said.

Despite my desperate need to be moving toward the village, I took a few extra minutes to find three nests and collected the rush's eggs. I set them in front of Captain Tevya where she would see them when she woke.

I turned and began a ground-eating lope, one that I had perfected as I had traveled the distances between the trade routes as quickly and effectively as possible. Still, the village was seven or eight leagues. No matter how fast I ran, I was afraid there would be nothing left of the village to salvage.

The ground moved away beneath my feet, changing from river reeds to prairie grass, to the rocky barren floor of the Nicolaak Valley. The rising morning sun haunted me as the ground sloped up and I had to shift my direction to work my way around the walls of the ruins of the Oracles. Part of me was tempted to run my hand along the stone to see if I could find another hidden entrance, but I did not dare take the time.

The smell of smoke in the air increased to the point I had to cough to clear my lungs. Flakes of burned straw and ash drifted from the sky like gray snowflakes calmly making their way to earth. The slow decent of the flakes was maddening. I felt as if I was in a slow-moving dream, unable to get where I needed to go in time.

The air was thick with smoke as I came around the wall. I slowed and walked, waving my hand in front of me. Shadows slowly emerged as the ruins of buildings, people wandering like wraiths slowly through the streets, directionless and lost. No one noticed me as they focused on their losses. I reached the well at the center of town only to find it blocked, a "Contaminated" sign hanging from the pulley for the bucket.

The town was gone. Not a single structure remained. Dusty children sat in huddled groups; a woman swept the cobblestones with meaningless strokes. Cries rose up around me, some were the official cry of mourners, others were the gut-wrenching howls of pure loss.

I approached the sweeping woman. "What happened here?"

"It was the punishment of Kadasha," the woman said. "We supported the healer. We protected the robber. And for turning our backs on the traditions of Kadasha, she sent her army to destroy us."

"The Armies of Kadasha?" I tried not to let skepticism into my voice. The Armies of Kadasha was a legend; a story told to children to inspire them to do their chores. The story claimed that Kadasha held an army of women, raised by warriors on the top of Mount Ariantum. "They came a half-glass after dinner, right as the sun was going down."

"What of the healer? Had she already gone? Did she get away before the armies came?"

The woman's eyes were washed out, nearly white. She did not look at me, but up the hill that led to the healer's hut. "She would not leave. She stood before the warriors that came, not her whole army, but twelve of her servants just the same. Could one small girl, a simple healer, really threaten all that the goddess stood for? They didn't have to take her, even if it was true."

"If what was true?" I wanted to grab the woman and shake some sense into her words, but I waited as she spoke painfully slow.

"That she. . . that she was the last Oracle. The took the healer, said she was the last, and left the rest of us to rot."

She continued sweeping. I stumbled up the hill, back toward the walls, toward Dawn's hut. Disbelief and sorrow warred within me with such energy that I couldn't walk in a straight line. I stumbled over fallen walls and burning patches of roof. The village had been built of simple materials. Flammable. It probably only took two heat gifters to start the flames that destroyed an entire village.

The roof of Dawn's hut was gone, collapsed inward. Only one wall remained, leaning against the wall of the Oracle ruins. The stove she used to boil water was exposed, rubble piled up to the door, one shelf clung stubbornly to the wall, blackened by the smoke and fire.

The notice on the wall surrounding the Oracle Temple, written in swirling letters, was charcoal black except for places where speckles of liquid escaped. Those spots had the dark red hue of dried blood. A rotten smell came from two buckets on the ground, the brushes still in the drying liquid. It was blood. Someone's blood was used to write a message as large as Dawn's hut.

Guilty of sedition and blasphemy against the All-High Kadasha. This Oracle and those associated with Oracles, are enemies of the country of Tuleves.

The soldiers had written this, written this curse in the blood of the people who Dawn had served and healed, spending her strength on them.

I backed away from the wall and stumbled over the bucket, spilling the blood and gore onto the street. It flowed downward, staining the cobbles, filling the cracks and pooling against the crumbled stone from Dawn's hut.

Truth as obvious as the writing on the wall hit me with the force of Marion smashing the soldier's chest. My breath was knocked out of me as I accepted the truth the woman spoke as she swept ash from her broken porch step. Dawn was an Oracle, the last Oracle. And if I understood Captain Tevya's story correctly, Dawn was the baby who had given the prophecy. The Lady expected me to be able to fight her because she thought I was the healer. She thought I was Dawn.

Was it possible? It explained so much. Iranus's relentless hunt. The Grand Councilor's invitation to the Sanatorium of all powerful healers. She'd always had the gifting of time. I could see it now, all my memories of her coming together to make a complete whole. I had closed my eyes to the possibility, but it was true.

The soldiers had come to destroy the village before I was exposed. This destruction had happened a day ago. That was before I'd been discovered. No. They didn't know she was an Oracle. I had told no one else where she was, no one except. . .

A memory flared, a boy hanging from chains. A secret whispered in his ear. The face I had seen with The Lady in her chambers. There was still a hole, a name I couldn't remember, but I had spoken the words of betrayal. I had told the familiar face that I'd found Dawn. And then he had told The Lady. The information he had used to buy his ticket in the Tournament of the People.

Heat flared in me. This was wrong. Everything was wrong. The destruction of this village was done in the name of Kadasha. The creation of the blood jewels was done in the name of Kadasha. The taxing of the people, the arrest of my father, all by those who claimed to serve her. But was it the goddess herself that had demanded these things or the selfish men who used her name for power? Were giftings given to us to serve others or to serve the will of the goddess? I had never asked that question before.

I pushed back onto my feet, leaning forward until I could run my hand along the door frame, black soot covering my palm and fingers. I gripped the burned wood, a sliver cutting into my skin. Dawn had been the example of everything I believed in, of giving of oneself, of helping others. And now she was gone.

A shadow stepped from between Dawn's hut and the city wall. Relief flooded through me. They hadn't caught her! She'd found shelter and hid while the soldiers burned her house. I turned, knowing already that I was wrong. Dawn wouldn't have hidden while people were being slaughtered in her name. She would never have run the way I did. She would have been out here fighting for the people she loved.

Cold dread seeped from my heart as the familiar face stared at me with hooded eyes, crossbow raised and aimed at my chest.

"I've been waiting for you," said Iranus. The tracker had found me.

Chapter 48

I woke up in a grove, my hands pulled painfully tight around the trunk of an aged tree, the rough and bumpy bark digging into my arms and back. The last thing I remembered was jumping toward Iranus, hands outstretched like I could strangle him with my bare hands. There had been no widening of his eyes, no shock of any kind. He'd pulled the trigger and only a small dart had come out, hitting me with a sharp prick of pain.

Why wasn't I in the hands of the soldiers or back in the dungeons of Tuleves? Iranus could have collected on my thousand dinarah reward, but I could hear no noise from a soldier's camp, no smell of fire or horses. There was nothing but the silence of the forest, the rustling of leaves, and a drip of water landing on a leaf.

My mouth was dry and rough as a desert lizard. I tested my bonds. I yanked on the ropes and nearly pulled my wrists out of their sockets. Iranus had left me no wiggle room. My back screamed in pain at my movements, and a headache grew behind my eyes. Had he left me here to die slowly? To torture me? I could see no advantage for Iranus. He had a reputation of cruelty, but only when the price was right. He always delivered his prey alive.

I forced my muscles to relax despite my rising panic. I could freeze the ropes and break them. But then I needed a plan. Dawn had been taken by the servants of Kadasha, but if they knew she was the last Oracle, they would take her to the Sanatorium until her sentencing. A prison that had probably tightened down every avenue of escape after I found a way out.

I needed to get back to Tuleves for the Tournament of People. My plan had been to win, but if I had any change of saving anyone, I needed to get them out while the crowds were thick and the eyes of the council were focused on the big event. The Tournament of the People may have been a trap for the Hooded Robber, but it was going to be a distraction for me. Even if I got back to the castle, I wouldn't be able to save them all. I would only have a short time to get in, find my friends and family, and get out without getting anyone else killed.

My head dropped, my chin falling to my chest, the tears coming unbidden. It all felt so hopeless. I could not fight an entire castle, the Grand Councilor and The Lady. Especially if The Lady saw me coming through those sightless eyes.

The last time I had cried was the moment Iranus drove his dagger into my mother's stomach.

The tears dried under the flame of anger that rose in me. This man that had taken everything from me couldn't have gone far, and if I succeeded at nothing else before I died, I would get my revenge.

I lifted my head and rested it against the tree behind me. I closed my eyes and took a deep breath, sucking in. The temperature dropped, air crystalized, but the rope did not freeze.

I tried again.

The rope remained warm.

I opened my eyes. Frost formed on my lashes, clung to the bark on the trees, and crusted the small plants at my feet. My curse was still with me, but the rope had not changed.

Confused, I turned my head from side to side but could see nothing beyond the copse of trees. I listened again. The crackle of frost began to melt, the soft breath of air. . . no, it wasn't air. It was breath. Someone was breathing softly.

Iranus came around the tree with a crunch of footsteps. He wore the same clothes with dark fur lining that made him almost invisible among the shadows of the forest. He touched a flaming torch to the end of the rope, warming it. I could sense it now. The rope was not just made of braided cords of twine, but there was a flexible metal core that spread the heat from his fire and kept the rope from freezing.

"Did you betray her?" His voice was the same. Scratchy with disuse, but the bite of anger, the underlying threat seemed to be missing. It left me confused.

"Do you mean The Lady?" My chest stung from my efforts with the rope, and I imagined the creeping vines growing from my heart. "I have no loyalty to The Lady. You cannot betray someone you have no loyalty to."

"Did you betray the healer? Did you reveal her location to The Lady?" My mind tried to process the question and the motivation behind it. Iranus had no reason to question me about Dawn. She'd already been taken. Already been exposed as the Oracle, the one who had given a prophecy the day or her birth. I tried to spit at Iranus, but my mouth was too dry. I struggled against the rope. The twine bit into my wrists and burned my skin. The pain was nothing compared to the truth that ate at my soul.

"I didn't mean to." I swallowed. My tongue stuck in my throat for a moment. I worked up just enough saliva to swallow one more time, allowing me to speak. "I tried to take her place. I told her to run away and find a safe place to hide. But in the end, I brought Marion to her, I gave you the sign that I'd taken the prince. I led everyone right to her door. I betrayed her without even knowing who she really was."

"Do you believe that?" Iranus's eyes glowed like embers, intense, burning right into my soul. "You are a thief and a liar. You don't have the strength to protect her any more than I do. Stop fighting. You must yield." His fingers tightened around the rope. He shoved it deeper into the flames on the torch. He showed no signs of pain as his skin touched the fire.

"I don't understand," I said, confusion turning into anger. "Why does it matter to you? You have no religion, no god, no mercy, no love. You sell people out for the highest price." I pulled harder, sucking all the strength around me into the empty place the death of my mother had left. The pain in my heart was as sharp and strong as the moment my mother was stabbed in front of my eyes. "I may have betrayed Dawn, but you have betrayed all that is good. You killed my mother in cold blood, and you sit there and judge me for failing to save my friend. I am not the helpless girl who watched you kill her that night. I will not stand by helpless while my friend is sentenced to death. I do not yield."

The air froze to stillness around me. I sucked in not only heat, but everything I could touch, light, energy, even the air around me. The day darkened around us like a cloud covered the sun. Iranus's torch extinguished with a hiss and the rope grew cold, solid, and fragile. With a scream, I jerked against my bonds.

The rope shattered. Metal shards exploded outward. A single spike impaled itself in Iranus, throwing him backward onto the ground white with frost.

I rose to my feet, breathing hard, ignoring the spikes of pain as circulation returned to my hands and feet. I placed a hand on my chest like I could extinguish that pain with a little pressure.

I had no weapon. My bow was broken. My knives lost. I approached Iranus as he gripped the metal protruding from below his collarbone.

He looked up at me, a softening in his eyes that made my step falter.

"Jasmine." He dared use my mother's name. "You look so much like her." He shook his head. "I never meant to kill your mother. It was an accident. Like leading the soldiers to Dawn. Neither of us meant to hurt those we loved."

"Liar," I whispered. His words cut into me like a knife across the throat. I felt condemned. I was not like him. I reached forward and put pressure on the spike in his shoulder. I wanted to twist it slowly. I wanted him to feel pain the way I did. I wanted to hurt him the way he had hurt me.

He barely grunted as I jerked the frozen metal rod from his shoulder, ready to ram it home in a more damaging location. He made no move to stop me.

The rod hovered over his chest, his words echoing in my mind. *Do you believe that?* What did I believe? I believed that Dawn was beautiful and good. That she chose to help people rather than hide. That she was my friend, and I wanted to protect her. Even if the Oracles had betrayed

Kadasha, Dawn had been too young. She was innocent and I would protect her. First, I had to find her.

"What happened to Dawn?" I asked. "Where is she?"

Iranus made no move to get up but studied me the way my mother taught me to study the forest for signs of truth. "Why do you want to find her?"

"I led you to her," I said. "All of this is my fault and I need to make it right."

"Will you help her? Protect her with your life?" Iranus's question was sincere.

"What are you talking about?" I asked.

He pushed to sit up, moving closer to my raised metal rod. Blood spurted from the wound in his shoulder, running down his arm and pooling where his hand supported his body. The warm red liquid melted the frost on the ground. The blood pulsed up out of the small hole in rhythm with his heartbeat. Every hunter recognized the sign of a punctured artery. It was a kill shot.

"I wanted you to find Dawn so that I could protect her," Iranus said. "I have been seeking her all year, racing to find her before The Lady did. I remained in The Lady's service so I would know if she was getting close. And even though I was right there, she has beaten me. I do not know how."

I did. It was my own tongue that had betrayed my friend. "Someone did betray her, but it wasn't me. I intend to get her out before she is killed."

Iranus shook his head. He made no move to staunch the wound in his shoulder. I remained ready to strike again if he twitched a muscle. His face betrayed a deep sorrow, one that reflected inside me.

"Why did you want to find her if not to turn her in?" I asked. "Why bring me here instead of turning me in for the reward?"

"I had to make sure you were her friend first, that you were not the one who betrayed her. Her mother prophesied that a sibling would betray her. I needed to make sure it wasn't you." Iranus looked up, his gaze losing focus for a moment. Another prophecy that created choices without understanding the circumstances. Dawn had no siblings. I was the closest things she had. I had that racking pain of loss, of something missing, but I pushed it away. "I loved her mother, Oracle Liandra." He closed his eyes, a look of yearning covering his face as a single tear squeezed out and froze on his lashes. "We were so excited when we had a daughter. We never imagined she would speak on her first day of life nor that her words would change the course of history."

The revelation fell on me with the weight of a grinding stone. "Your daughter?" I sucked in a breath, seeing the moment that Iranus rose from the field, tripping my mother and sending a dagger into her belly. "But she lived with us. My mother cared for her and loved her."

Iranus did not open his eyes. His brows pushed down, like he could increase the darkness he was hiding in. He had lost so much blood. I had hit an artery. He only had a short time before he would bleed out, but I had questions. He had answers. I had no cloth to staunch the wound, but I could slow the flow. I touched his shoulder and sucked in heat, not his life spark. I pulled in enough to freeze the blood in his shoulder. The flow slowed. It was a difficult balance to keep the blood cold enough while letting his body have enough heat to stay awake. I needed him to talk to me. "Why did you kill my mother when she cared for your child?"

"When the Oracles were slaughtered, your mother took my daughter in. I was in no place to raise a daughter. Your mother was an Arjodite and had witnessed the massacre of the Oracles. She fought in that final battle and only survived when her Oracle, my wife, covered your mother's body with her own. Both were believed dead. Your mother failed in protecting the Oracles, but she owed a life debt. She took Dawn in and gave everything to raise her and protect her. I didn't mean to kill her. I was trying to stop her from running into a burning house. I had followed the soldiers to your property, but was too late to stop them from burning it down.

"She wouldn't have stopped. She would have run right into the flames to save you, but it was too late. Too late to save anyone. The house was consumed by heat and smoke. All I could do was try and stop your mother as she ran by me, but she fought me, trying to get to you. We fell. Her dagger was out like she could fight the fire with a steel blade." His head shook slowly. "I only meant to stop her from running into the house, but instead, she fell as she struggled, her knife pointed inward to keep from cutting me. I could not save her."

Tears blurred the man in front of me. The tracker I had feared and hated regretted the consequences of his actions as much as I regretted mine.

Iranus grabbed my wrist. I still held the rod of metal. His grip was strong but not threatening. I dropped the rod. It fell to the ground with a clink. His own body carried heat to the wound that I tried to keep frozen. Blood continued to seep through my web of frost.

I lowered myself to one knee, warm wetness seeping through the thin skiff I still wore. The blood was pooling too fast.

"Promise me you will protect her?" Iranus didn't loosen his grip. He lifted his head and sent a wave of heat to his shoulder. More blood escaped. The ice could not hold back the heat of his own heart. His neck flexed from the effort. His veins bulged as if trying to break the vine tattoo that wrapped around his throat. The vine pattern that matched the one growing from my own heart.

"I don't owe you any promises." I couldn't find the venom in me to stay angry. Mother was gone. The Oracles she had protected were gone. "But I would give my own life if it meant I could save Dawn."

He relaxed. His head falling back to the ground. He looked into the sky. "You may be the only one who can save us."

His blood would not stop. Not with his heat warring against my cold. I thought about pulling his spark to slow the bleeding, but I had two questions.

"What happened to my mother's body? Did you leave her in the field?"

He shook his head. His throat bobbed with a difficult swallow. "I dragged her away from the soldiers' eyes, but both of us knew the wound was fatal. I swore I would protect the Oracle and do everything I could to prevent the folding of the world. She had one last request."

"What was it?"

"She took my bow and held it in her bloodied hands. I handed her an arrow. 'Bury me where the arrow falls.' Those were her last words. Then she shot the arrow into the woods near your home and closed her eyes. I found where the arrow fell and gave her a small, silent, burial. Her body was not touched by soldiers nor wild animals. It was the least I could do for her."

A tear slid down my face, but I refused to wipe it away. I pulled more heat into me and then I pulled on his spark. It was different. I couldn't take it the way I had Marion's. I sensed in Iranus the same emptiness that I held inside of me.

"We are the same, aren't we?" I asked the second question, even as I knew he was dying. I could not save him. He'd already lost too much blood. "What do the vines mean? Why do they grow?"

"I have searched long and hard for the answer, but the ancient texts are forbidden and taken from the ruins. All I know is that there are three chosen vessels. Always three who balance the gifting. While all others give, we can only take. The vine connects us to Kadasha. It is some kind of measurement of what we have taken for her."

"What happens when the vines touch?" His vines were only a few leaves away from touching the original stock that rose out of his shirt collar. A full noose reached around his neck.

"I guess I will never see, but the old stories say we will no longer be able to think for ourselves. We will be Kadasha's servants. Avoid absorbing so much. Your capacity is greater than mine. I don't track people by their smell, but by the small amount of spark I absorb from them. I can sense it across great distances. But I only absorb a small amount and still the vine has almost claimed me. Perhaps this is a mercy that I will never be fully enslaved to the immortal who ordered the slaughter of my wife."

He turned his head, looking up at me, his eyes wide with fear. Every man feared death when it rides down from the eternities to collect them. But Iranus's fear was not for himself.

"We all make mistakes, terrible ones we can't erase." He placed his hand over mine as I tried to pull more heat from his blood. He pushed my hand away. He only had moments left. The blood pooled around us, melting the white frost in a widening circle, soaking our clothes. "All I wanted to do was protect her, to save her from her own damned prophecy. But they beat me to her. Now The Lady's got her. You are the only one who can help her."

His head fell back, but his eyes stayed locked on me. "Please."

"I promise."

He did not breathe in again as his spark faded. I took in one deep shuddering gasp and stumbled back, pressing against the very tree I had been trapped against only moments before. Now I felt pinned against the trunk, not by ropes, but by a raging darkness inside me.

I had killed the man I thought had taken my mother from me, but instead he had turned out to be the father of Dawn, a friend of my mother, a protector of the last Oracle. I dropped my head, tears dripping down my face. A canyon of sorrow had been carved out inside of me by a never-ending river of tears, eating me from the inside out.

Sinking down to the ground, I tried to pull myself together, but I had never felt so alone.

Who was I? A fake. A robber with a mask. A lost little girl. A clumsy fool. Iranus had made me promise and I wanted nothing more than to do as he asked, but what could I do against the Crown? What could I do to save my friends? I wasn't the hero people believed the Hooded Robber to be. I wasn't Dawn the healer. I wasn't Orblee's gift-less assistant.

I didn't know who I was or how I could keep my impossible promise.

Chapter 49

ALL THE FROST I had created melted before I could dam the flow of tears. The forest warmed even as the sun settled closer to the horizon. I took deep breaths as a few final tears fell down my face.

Father was the one who taught us it was good to cry. He encouraged us to show emotion, to describe how we were feeling. Mother was his most difficult pupil when it came to that subject. She was a hunter. Now I knew she was a warrior. Expressing emotions was a weakness, not a strength. I realized now that I was grateful for both perspectives, although, I would be sure to tell Father that crying did not make me feel better. My head hurt from the tears. I felt hollowed and emptied out. My eyes felt like I'd rubbed them against a prickle bush. My nose ran like I had spring fever.

My dried up well of tears meant it was time to move. Iranus had shared things with me in his last moments that I never would have learned on my own. Absorbing was a curse from Kadasha and the use of it would strangle my freedom. He hadn't told me how to stop it, but he had shown me I wasn't alone. There were others that absorbed spark the same way I did. Three. Now that Iranus was dead, I wondered if another baby was being born right now with the curse. My heart ached for them.

My heart ached for the man who I'd killed. His body lay across the small clearing. His blood slowly soaked into the ground. He'd buried my mother's body. I didn't have the strength to move him the distance an arrow flies. I didn't have time to dig a grave, but I could not walk away. I could not leave him without honoring his life.

I pressed one finger against Iranus's forehead and pulled the remaining heat from his body. I hesitated for a moment as the sharp pain flared in my chest. I had used the emptiness inside me to pull in the heat and spark around me many times, but almost every time had been fueled by fear or desperation.

This time, I pulled spark into me because it was all I had to give.

I felt for the heat in the air, pulling with a delicate touch, with an intention I had never tried before. With the same care I once used when drawing frozen pictures on the top of the pond at home, I began freezing the layers of air around his body. Water from the air solidified, turning into a thin sheet of ice. Then another one, and another. Each sheet of ice was thinner than lace fabric, but together, each one adding a layer of protection, they became a frozen shield, spread out across his body. A small hill of ice formed, almost clear except for the swirling patterns I carefully placed. When all the layers were complete, I stepped back, the symbol of the Oracles crystallized in white above the fallen tracker.

It was like nothing I had done before. Even as I looked at it, I knew no ice pick could dig through it and, even in the hottest summer, it would take years to melt. It was the most I could do.

My strongest wish had been to gain a gifting, even if it meant traveling to Helefount to beg at Kadasha's feet. That wasn't what I wanted anymore. My urge to tip the scales of justice, to find a balance, was still there simmering inside me. And in order to do that, I wanted the people I loved beside me.

I turned my back on Iranus the Tracker. Dawn's father. My mother's killer. He had as many identities as I did. When I stepped from the small grove, I realized two things. One, I was right outside the small village that shared a wall with the ruins of the Oracles. Iranus had not taken me far to try and find out if I was Dawn's friend or her enemy. If only I'd listened. I might have gained an ally. The second thing I noticed was it wasn't as late in the day as I'd assumed. The thick trees had blocked the sun. It was barely past midday. My world had been turned upside down in the space of half a glass.

I stumbled up an incline to the overgrown cobblestone road. Once the ground evened out, I sped up into a loping stride. I didn't know where I was headed until I'd passed the well and climbed my way up the steep street to Dawn's hut. I stood in the exact spot Iranus had found me. I had come to save Dawn, but she wasn't here. She'd been taken. And I'd made a promise to help her.

A scuffing sound behind me made me whirl. A small movement caught my eye as shadow disappeared behind the side of the hut.

"Come out." I had no blade or bow, but I placed my hand on my hip in defiance. "I have faced down Scarletts of legend, Iranus the Tracker, and even stared death in the face. I am not afraid."

I waited for soldiers or hunters or maybe a citizen who was desperate for the reward on my head. Whatever death they had designed for me, I would fight until there was no hope left. As long as I had breath in my lungs, I would never stop trying to save my father, to help Marion, and to rescue Dawn.

A small hand reached around the corner, palm out. The face peaked out. I recognized the small boy Dawn had worked with only a few mornings ago in her hut. "Did you really face down a Scarlett?"

"Who are you and why are you hiding?" I hadn't expected a child.

He stepped fully out from behind the hut and brushed at his tunic with his good hand. His other remained curled against his chest. His efforts did nothing to wipe away the soot or hide the tears in his garment. "I'm Yoself. The healer told me the prince would need me before the end. I've been waiting. I knew you'd come back."

"I don't think she meant . . ." I stopped. I had taken those words as comfort from a healer. Words of inspiration for a small boy with a difficult road ahead of him. I knew now that Dawn was an Oracle. Yoself had taken her statement as prophecy. "I don't think she was talking about right now. It probably meant when you're older and the prince is the king. He will need faithful subjects. There are many ways to interpret what she meant."

"Maybe." His simple acceptance of my doubt put me off balance.

"It would be amazing if I can help him now. You're his friend. You're the best chance I've got of finding him."

"Where's your mother?" I didn't want the responsibility of another life on my head. Whatever prophecy this kid believed he could fulfill, I wasn't about to be a part of his false belief.

Yoself looked away. "They buried her with the others who were killed by the servants of Kadasha. She stepped in to help the healer and they killed her for it, but she would want me to keep trying. She always taught me to never give up. Maybe if I help the prince, I can make sure my mother's life wasn't given in vain. I am not old and I am not whole, but mother told me I had a big heart and a wise soul. She did not doubt me. I also have a gifting. That might be helpful. Mother said the gifting made me like the Scarletts of Legend. I could hide patiently in the shadows and then pounce faster than the blink of an eye."

"Yoself the Scarlett. It fits you." I swallowed the familiar hunger both for the mother I had lost and the gifting I'd never have. "I cannot promise you protection. I do not know the way ahead."

His face brightened. He straightened one shoulder and wiggled his fingers on his curled hand. "You'll take me with you? You won't send me away?"

I choked on the answer for a minute. I had to decide what to do next.

"You'll take me with you to enter the Tournament of the People?"

"Why would I enter the Tournament?" I asked.

"Because you're the Hooded Robber. You'll win it easy. Everyone knows how the Hooded Robber shot a coin from between the fingers of a tax collector."

"They would never offer me the prize. The Grand Councilor would never hold up his promise if I were to win."

He rolled his eyes and kicked some ash down through the cracks in the floorboards that had survived the fire. "Of course not. It's a trap. That's the whole point. You're the Hooded Robber and they lure you in with promises and then you shoot like no one has ever shot before and escape the trap." He threw one hand in the air excitedly. His other hand tried to follow, but his muscles seized. The arm tucked back in against his body.

"I can't enter the tournament."

His eyes went wide. They shone like the full moon on a starless night. "You have to. Haven't you heard? They found the healer who was helping give the stolen taxes back to the people. A healer from Prontwick. If the Hooded Robber doesn't come save her, she'll hang."

Orblee. Somehow, Orblee had been discovered and arrested. Another person I could not turn my back on. Another reason to walk right into a trap.

This boy wanted to meet the prince. That meant heading back into the heart of Tuleves. But even as I swallowed again, I realized the decision had already been made. My heart had fought the urge to run for so long, the idea of giving in, giving up, twisted my soul the wrong way. I would not give up this fight. Not yet.

"What is your gifting?" I asked. I stepped over the threshold into the open ruins of Dawns hut. Only one wall still stood and barely. Even that wall leaned on the ruins of the Oracles for support.

"I have the gifting of speed." A wind rushed past me. My hair flew around my face and my healer's robes wrapped around my legs. It took a moment to realize that it was Yoself. He had run around me with such velocity that he'd taken the air with him.

"That is some gifting." I placed my hand on his shoulder and sensed his spark. Strong like Polisha's.

"I can be fast, but sometimes it works better to grant other's my gifting. My mother would sometimes ask if I could share with her. It was difficult for me to scrub dishes, which she still made me do it sometimes. But if I granted her the gifting of speed, she could clean the house in a few moments, and we'd have time to play a game before bed. I moved even more slowly the next day, but it was always worth the extra time with her. She worked so hard."

I nodded, impressed. At the same time, my brain was working on our problem. Orblee set up as a sacrifice. Father in the prisons. Marion suffering from his spark. Dawn taken to the Sanatorium.

I needed to get back to Tuleves in time for the Tournament of the People. I needed to get there before Garreth was crowned king. Or assassinated. I didn't have a lot of resources or allies. But I did have Captain Tevya when she recovered. I had a small boy with the gifting of speed.

And as I picked up the remnants of a broom from the corner and began to sweep, I also had the beginning of a plan. If only I still had my father's bow.

CHAPTER 50

I HELPED around the village for a while, but eventually I came back to Dawn's hut to finish sweeping. My broom caught on a shard of wood as I tried to clear out around the stove. Dawn didn't have a lot of belongings, but I wanted to make sure I didn't leave anything behind that had survived. I'd collected a small pile of medicine jars that were soot covered, but still sealed.

I reached under the stove to see what had caught my broom. It wasn't a piece of wood. I could barely reach the tip of it with my fingers. It was a long metal piece that disappeared into the wall. I tugged on it, but it didn't come lose. The soldiers who had found the blood jewels under the floorboards hadn't searched behind the wood stove. The stove was as heavy as a ships anchor and was hot to the touch. That didn't bother me. I pulled my hand back out and reached around for a different angle. The decoration on the metal piece was intentional and intricate. I wanted to see what it was. I tugged on it. Then I tried pushing down.

The wall shifted. No. A panel in the wall slid open. It had been invisible. I had noticed to crack or joint, but when the panel opened, I saw some hidden objects in the one place the fire hadn't touched.

The light from the setting sun hit an ivory handle covering an arch of deep walnut, the kind of wood that Father had to order from the north for his bows and let sit for several years before he would use it. I reached for the handle, my hand shaking.

Sitting in a hidden compartment in the last standing wall of Dawn's burned hut was one of finest bows I had ever seen. I pulled it from its hiding place and stood to measure the height. I recognized his work, the care of the perfectly sanded handle rise, smooth as silk fabric from the prince's own closet, the evenly curved tips and the finely woven string. Only Father could have made this bow.

My fingers slid into the ivory grip. A perfect fit. As if my father had used my own hand as a mold. It was impossible. Even if he had used my hand before his arrest, it wouldn't have been the right size. My lungs froze, unable to draw air. I was afraid to test it out, yet unable to stop myself. I placed my two fingers on the string and pulled back, touching the string to my chin, my other arm straight out in front of me. I let out a gasp of pleasure. It was perfect. Exactly my draw length. Enough tension to send an arrow soaring hundreds of feet.

I carried the string back into place and lowered the bow to my side. How could this be? My father could not have made a bow in debtor's prison. We had talked only for a moment. I had seen that his strength was gone.

The hut of an Oracle. Realization hit me and my eyes flew open. Three walls burned down. The only one that remained was the one with the secret compartment. This felt different than a prophecy. This was a very specific action designed around exact time. Oracles gave hints about the future. Oracles gave advice to avoid a certain destiny. But this? To see a future in such perfect clarity that you could direct a craftsman to make the right size bow. This was incredible.

I looked down at the bow. Dawn was not only a descendant of the Oracles, the daughter of one of the priestesses; she was an acting visionary, testing the strength of time against the laws of Kadasha.

"What is that?" Yoself asked. He was even more dirty than when I'd found him.

"This is a gift." With the bow, I could be the Hooded Robber again. I could cover my face and be the hero people needed.

"There's more inside." He pulled out a large shape covered in canvas.

I tugged at the fabric. It fell away and landed on the floor with a puff of ashes.

A quiver, made of beautifully finished leather, full of arrows with deep green fletching, made by my father. Intricate patterns were burned across the entire quiver. Together, the color and the patterns were a symbol of the Arjodites.

Mother had been an Arjodite, a true warrior who had pretended to give up her duty while still protecting the last of their race. As Yoself handed me the bow, I felt as if my father was handing me the truth. I was an Arjodite. I had an Oracle to protect.

Tears blurred my vision, but I refused to let the moisture fall. I blinked hard, like a child stamping her foot. I would cry no more today. I didn't know what I would have done had Mother and Father trusted me with Dawn's secret. All I knew was what I needed to do now.

Yoself pulled out two more packaged stuffed in the final corner of the leaning wall. One was a black cloak with a mask. The second was a tunic and shirt. The outfit of the Hooded Robber, but with a cloak embroidered with intricate designs.

My bow and my mask. Prepared from me from before the soldiers came for my father. I didn't know if I was worthy of such a gift. I didn't know if I could accomplish what they expected of me.

The last rays of the sun disappeared, leaving the cool evening air and the dim light of evening. I pulled the strap of the quiver over my head, not surprised when it fit like the arms of my father wrapping around me. I lifted my bow from the floor, carefully cleaned it of soot, and placed it over my shoulder.

There was no door frame to step through so we both jumped down onto the cobblestones. I looked up to see a familiar figure.

Captain Tevya strolled up the street. She was tall and imposing, even in the healer's robes. She held her head high. Her hair was cropped short and that highlighted the sharp features of her face. Villagers shied away from her, but she did not slow her pace until she reached me. She had found clothes to replace her healer's robes. They were men's clothes that were easy to move in and gave her the appearance of a farmer instead of a soldier. She couldn't hide the way she carried herself, though.

She examined the destruction and devastation on either side of her.

"I came as soon as I could." She held a hand at her waist like she expected her sword hilt to still be there.

"We've helped where we can. It is good to see you recovered. Where will you go from here?" I had found a rag that survived the fire and was using it to clean the words written in blood from the wall of the ruins. It was nearly sunset. I'd helped where I could. Where coals still shouldered, I would pull heat so the villagers could go through the ashes for lost belongings. I helped move fallen stone and rafters that blocked passageways. It wasn't enough. I only had a little time, but I did what I could.

Yoself had worked beside me, but I told him to preserve his gifting. We needed him moving at full speed until the time was right.

Captain Tevya gave me a look that stripped away any pretenses. "You intend to go back." It wasn't a question.

I nodded. I expected an argument. A rebuke. A warning.

Instead, she took a breath. "I will go with you. If I come this close to dying again, I want it to be for a cause I believe in, not one I was hired to fight for."

"I appreciate that you're willing to go with me, but I need you on another path. We will meet up again."

I explained my plan to her.

We had a full day tomorrow and then the tournament was scheduled for the next day. One day. There was a lot to do.

CHAPTER 51

THE PLAN WAS FAR from fool proof. There were a lot of ways things could go wrong. I couldn't put my finger on why, but somehow that felt familiar. It almost felt right. An impossible plan. Trusting to fate. It felt right and wrong at the same time, like something, or someone was missing.

We started in the unnamed village. People who had come to hide next to the ruins of the Oracles and had been found in the end. Captain Tevya stood in front of them and announced what we had rehearsed.

"The Hooded Robber travels to Tuleves to join the Tournament of the People. As you've heard, this is a trap, but the Hooded Robber would never leave those closest to them to be sacrificed. The Hooded Robber calls on you, asks the citizens of Tuleves to stand up and join the Tournament, not as yourselves, but dressed as the Hooded Robber. The more people who are willing to come to the tournament and claim to be the hero of the people, the harder it will be for the Grand Councilor to spring his trap. Let us turn the tables. Let us tip the scale of power. We the people can stand up and use power in numbers to trick the Grand Councilor at his own game. Take your darkest cloaks. Tear your thickest fabric for masks. Travel to Tuleves on the morrow and sign up for the tournament as the Hooded

Robber. The risk is high. But every person who is willing will be one extra link in the chain. Let us join together and help the Hooded Robber who has stood alone for this last year. No more. Let us stand up and be by our hero's side."

She had a dramatic flair. Even without the gifting of sound, her voice carried. She may have used her gifting of heat to warm the village. I felt waves of energy coming off her. I also felt the heat in the sting of tears behind my eyes. My mask had given me safety. I had hidden behind it to have the ability to do good in small ways. And now I was using that influence to ask others to put themselves in danger. To risk being arrested when they claimed to be the Hooded Robber. I did not know how many would be willing to heed the call. I would not blame a single person for running. The choice was in the hands of the people.

After the villagers dispersed to their makeshift tents set out around the outskirts of the village, I stood by the spoiled well with Captain Tevya and Yoself the Scarlett. A disgraced soldier. A young boy with a disfigured arm. And a wanted criminal. We were the three who would tip the scales. I could only hope we would not end up tipping them so far that they would end up spilling blood.

"I can reach three more villages tonight and five tomorrow, but that won't be soon enough to have the travelers reach Tuleves for the Tournament." Captain Tevya drank the last drops of water we had boiled on Dawn's stove. Even the boiled water was dark with grime and ash. "I have run long distances before."

"That's where I come in." Yoself used his curled hand to rub his nose. It looked like he was hiding a smile. He was about to show off for the captain. "I have the gifting of speed that will help you travel ten times faster. Or if we have a horse, I can grant the gifting of speed to the horse."

Captain Tevya's answer was quick and sharp. "There are no horses left in the village. I will go on foot. I have never been gifted speed."

"Are you nervous?" I couldn't help teasing her.

"I have no experience and you are depending on me," she said. "I want to do my part."

Yoself reached out and took her hand. The austere captain seemed to soften. "It doesn't hurt. You'll feel like you're moving at a normal speed, but everything else will seem like its moving really slow. You can cover great distances without time passing."

"How long will it last?" She asked.

"The longest my mom used it for was twelve hours. I will give you as much spark as I can. I think you can go until lunch tomorrow."

The small chirping bugs of the Cracked Plains began their song. The breeze carried the cries and mourning chants of the villagers and the sounds settled on the destroyed huts along with the dust and ashes. The smell of death hovered about my nose. I griped the edge of the stone well.

"What if it's too much?" I asked. "They've been through so much already and now I'm asking them to risk their lives. It's all they have left."

It was Captain Tevya's turn to reach out and lay her hand over mine. Yoself offered his curled fist with a small movement. I let one hand abandon the support the well was giving me and wrapped my fingers around Yoself's. We formed a circle. Each of us getting strength from the other.

"In my experience," she said, "the moment when people find themselves with nothing left to give, they discover a strength buried deep inside. I will carry your message. It will be up to the people to respond."

We stayed in that position a moment longer. Then she nodded and knelt in front of Yoself. He placed a finger on her forehead and closed his eyes. I stepped back. I didn't want to risk taking even a twinkling of either of their giftings.

I didn't see Captain Tevya leave. She was there and then she was gone with no evidence she'd been there except a swirling of ash she'd disturbed in her departure.

Yoself lowered his arm with the speed of dripping sap. He would be moving slowly for a while, but I had promised to take him with me. I scooped the boy up in my arms and carried him into the night.

We stopped and slept when the moon dipped below the horizon. It wasn't even half-way through the night. The extra weight of the boy made travel exhausting and I hadn't had a good night's sleep in almost seven days.

I placed the hooded cloak on the ground. We slept beneath the stars.

I listened to the exaggerated breaths of Yoself as he fell asleep. He couldn't even breathe quickly. Then I let myself rest.

In the morning, I carried Yoself on my back. It took him a long time to relieve himself behind a tree. It felt like an eternity to wrap his arms around my neck. I was patient, impressed with his dedication. I had always taken for granted the ability to move with speed.

We were on our way before the sun rose. It was a full day of slow travel. We followed the curve of the river and fought the elements, avoiding the roads. We stopped several times for food. I brought Yoself bird eggs and berries to help him regain his spark. I made fires to boil water. Then we would go through the painful process of having him climb onto my back again. We talked a little, but the difficulty of waiting for Yoself to be able to finish a complete sentence made most of the journey quiet and contemplative.

It was evening when the great plateau of Tuleves came into view. The river sparkled as it made its way around the plateau to where the waterfall fell from the side of the castle. The road led the other direction to the steep path that led up to the gates of Tuleves city.

My heart stopped at what I saw. The meadow at the base of the plateau was filled with tents, not the uniform tents of soldiers, but the tents of travelers. They varied is size and material. Circles of tents identified groups traveling together, but there were plenty of individual tents and even simple mats laid out for people to sleep on. It seemed as if the entire country of Tuleves had traveled to Tuleves City for the tournament. I wondered how many people Captain Tevya had been able to reach in a single day.

I wondered how many would respond.

It grew dark and we slept again in sheltered area far from the road and shielded from any soldiers looking down from the protective walls of Tuleves. We slept at the top of a rise so that in the morning we would have a view in every direction. Yoself moved at normal speeds again. He ate his egg as quickly as I did. "Do you think I will be able to watch the tournament?"

I shook my head. "We will not be going in the front gates like the others. The Grand Councilor expects I will simply show up and compete in the tournament, but I will find another way."

"It would have been fun to see you shoot." Yoself touched the bow. It leaned against a tree. I'd removed the string for travel. The wood gleamed. Even I was tempted to run my finger down the ridge of the bow. "Do you think you could teach me someday?"

We both looked at his hand curled against his body. He turned away in embarrassment. I clicked my tongue. "Don't give up hope so easy. Dawn saw your strength, but I see your cleverness. If we can figure out a way for you to draw back the string, I can teach you to aim."

His head lifted and a smile crossed his face.

A horn sounded through the valley with enough strength to rattle the branches of trees and disturb tent flaps throughout the valley. Yoself's shoulders came up toward his ears.

The gates of the city were opening for the Tournament of the People. The meadow of tents turned into a disturbed ant hill. What I saw stirred a piece of my heart I had not known existed. The people teaming around the meadow and climbing from their tents wore black cloaks and masks. Nearly every group of people had at least one or two Hooded Robbers among them. At least a hundred. Maybe more.

The burn of tears made me blink.

Yoself let out a sign beside me. "They came for you. They heeded the captain's call."

The villagers and citizens slowly formed a procession. Lines of people headed for the gates of Tuleves. I couldn't see the soldiers guarding the gate from this far away, but I imagined their nervous shuffling. The lower ranks calling for their captains for direction. If they decided to arrest every person dressed as a hooded robber, the guards would need backup. Every soldier on duty might be called to the front gates. That was one piece of the plan.

"I wish I could see what was happening inside." Just because I had a plan, didn't meant mean I understood every piece. I didn't know where the gallows were placed or the arena for the tournament would be located.

"I could share my gifting with you," Yoself said. "You could run through the city and be back before the Hooded Robbers reach the gate."

I shook my head. "I don't want to take too much of your spark."

Polisha had tried to heal me, and I'd absorbed too much of her spark. But someone had used their spark on me. I just couldn't remember when. There was an empty space in me that left me cold and breathless. "But maybe you could be my eyes. I will make my way to the base of the waterfall. Meet me there. Tell me where they have Orblee and where they are doing the Tournament. Can you do that after all you've done?"

He nodded with enthusiasm. "I've recovered my spark. And if I am quick, I will only be slow for a short time. No one will see me."

I hadn't realized how much I had enjoyed the boy's company until he was gone. I moved along the edge of the river. I climbed over the rocks near the bottom of the falls. The water churned where the falls collided with the pool at the bottom. I imaged Captain Tevya's and me falling from the top of the plateau. I had survived this once, but I could not fall this time.

Once I froze the water, a fall would be a death sentence. I couldn't freeze a moving torrent. All of the spark in the world wasn't enough for that. But I could freeze

I focused on the drops around me. The water that had bounced from the surface after a violent collision with the bottom of the falls. I sucked in and froze one droplet at a time. The effort was small at first. I hesitated. I didn't know how much spark I could suck in without making the vines grow. Without getting one leaf closer to being strangled under Kadasha's control.

A noise behind me made me whirl around. Yoself relaxed on a boulder like he'd been there the whole time.

"Did you see anything?" I asked. "How many people are scheduled at the gallows?"

His nod was as slow as a wagon stuck in the mud. He had four fingers held out like he'd already anticipated my question. Four. Four people scheduled to hang today. I only knew that they'd captured Orblee. I didn't know the other three who were going to face the noose.

"You'll have to try and tell me more while we climb. See if you can get your faced washed in the river while I freeze us a path to the top."

I didn't have the patience to watch him clean up, but I had something else to focus on. This wasn't time to be conservative with my growing tattoo. There might be a day where Kadasha had her own noose around my neck, but that wasn't today. And I had people counting on me.

I sucked in again. This time, I didn't hold back. I opened myself to all the energy around me. I sensed the energy in a drop of water, in a speck of air. The falling water resisted freezing. The kinetic energy resisted the absence of heat. It was the mist in the air that I focused on. I started with the drops closest to the rock surface of the plateau cliff. I used the same method I had used on Iranus' tomb. I made sure the water froze in tight crystals that clung to the rock. Moving outward, I created icicles in swirling shapes with jagged edges.

It was beautiful. A swirling pattern of ice the dangled from the rocky outcropping and slowly covered the side of the plunging water. My breath was visible in front of my face. A ladder of frozen waterfall formed in front of me. I had escaped the Sanatorium through the cremation room. I would break back into the Sanatorium the same way. Dawn was my first promise. I would find her while the soldiers were distracted with the fake Hooded Robbers.

I kept the spark pulled into me, knowing I would have to freeze more as I climbed. Yoself had finished cleaning his face. I wrapped my cloak around him to protect him from the cold. I used ropes to secure him to my back with my bow.

Then I began to climb.

CHAPTER 52

My chest seared with pain like a branding iron was being held against my skin. My arms shook from effort. My fingers were red and blistered from the cold. Only a few more handholds. I could see the dark, gaping cavern where the river poured from beneath the castle. Three more rungs of my frozen ladder.

Two.

One.

I pulled myself over the ledge and dragged myself across the platform where the handcart had been stored. I lay gasping for breath. I pressed my hand against my chest to ease the pain.

The sound of cracking ice and splintering glass echoed through the chamber. My frozen ladder collapsed into the churning river below.

Yoself squirmed from the ropes that had kept him secured to me through the journey up the waterfall. The climb had taken long enough that he seemed recovered. He leaned out over the edge of the water to watch the last frozen icicles pierce the river below.

"Give me a moment to catch my breath." I was too tired to even sit up. I flopped over on my back and stared at the water dripping from the top of the cave.

Yoself came over and tugged on my hand. "We have to hurry. The soldiers have blocked the gates. They are trying to pull out the Hooded Robbers one at a time and question them. Many of them have already been whipped, but the people are getting impatient. They are surging on the gates and the soldiers have drawn their swords."

"What of the condemned? Did you find them?" Even forming the words took all my strength. I had to dig deep the way Captain Tevya had said. *When everything has been taken, people find a well of strength deep within.*

"There are four people standing at the gallows with their eyes blindfolded and the nooses dangling in front of their faces. It was awful."

"They've already placed the prisoners on the platform? How far is the platform from the tournament fields?"

"That's the worst part. They are on the fields. Down at the side of the arena. There are stands for a thousand people. The hanging is meant to be a spectacle."

I closed my eyes. The hard rock dug into my sore muscles and the back of my head. I had to get up. "At least we won't have to go far to find them. Are you sure there were four?"

"Yes." He wiped some frozen drops of water from his forehead. His cheeks were bright red from the cold. "One was an old woman, hunched with age."

I rolled back over and pushed myself onto my hands and knees.

"One was a prisoner. He was skinny, malnutritioned, with a scruff of a beard. Sunken cheeks. His knees were shaking even as he stood with the others."

Could it be? There were plenty of prisoners in the dungeons, but the description sounded like my father. The Grand Councilor had found me outside his cell.

"The third was a man who had arms the size of tree trunks and back muscles that were visible through his shirt. Barely an adult. But he couldn't stand. He was curled up on the platform, curled into himself."

Marion. I had left him to deal with the heat of the spark on his own.

"And the fourth?" I couldn't imagine this getting any worse.

"A young girl in healer robes. Hardly taller than the muscled man groaning on the ground. I saw her try to reach out to him and help, but she jerked back like the touched had burned her."

No. I had wondered what had happened to Polisha. Now I knew. She was about to be hanged for helping me.

I found the strength to climb to my feet with this last piece of news. I strung my bow, pulling the string to the perfect tightness. I readied an arrow.

Despite the pain in my chest, I pulled the heat from the door handle, freezing the metal. I used a large rock from the platform and smashed the handle. The door swung open.

We climbed the circular stairs. It was dark with only a few torches, but I recognized the shape of the tower in the center of the Sanatorium. We came to a door and pushed our way through. The light blinded me for a moment, and I blinked to adjust my vision.

"It's about time you joined us," The Lady said.

Every hunter knows if you have one shot, make it count. This time, I did not hesitate.

I let the arrow fly straight at The Lady's empty eye socket.

She caught the shaft of the arrow, her hand reacting faster than my eye could track. She held the arrow for a moment, the tip touching the bandage stretched over her face. If I had thought to suck the energy from the arrow, she might be freezing right now, but pulling strength from the stones around me now would do no good.

I shoved Yoself to the side and he disappeared around the tower. I hoped he could find a safe place to hide. I had not expected to be caught in the trap so easily. So early in my plan.

Hope drained from me. My core was as cold and tumultuous as the depths of a winter blizzard. I had followed the fox down the hole and was now staring at a well-sprung trap.

Dawn was tied to a chair in the middle of the Sanatorium with the Grand Councilor on her right and The Lady on her left. Four soldiers lined the hall behind them, shoulder to shoulder like a brick wall. Fleeing down the stairs the way I had come was the only option, but if I took it now, I would be leaving Dawn to the mercy of The Lady.

Every fiber of my being screamed to turn and run, to save myself. I could almost feel the flames climbing around me, the flames that had consumed my house, flames that had stolen my mother and my best friend as I ran and hid.

Not today. Never again. Dawn was right in front of me. Her head was up, her eyes on me. There was a gag in her mouth. A trickle of blood made its way down her face from a cut on her forehead. There was a bruise on her left cheek. All the coldness inside me melted away under the burning rays of anger that filled my soul.

"Why don't you sit down so we can talk," said the Grand Councilor. He motioned toward a chair that sat against the wall directly in front of them.

I let out a harsh bark of laughter. "I'll sit down when the both of you are ashes on the wind."

"I can see how the prince might have found you charming," he said without inflection. "You have so much in common, including a stubborn streak that could resist the pull of a thousand rye ox. You have no understanding of the forces you are dealing with. They are bigger than you can possibly imagine. Your feeble efforts are no more than the whining of a gnat in their ear."

"There will always be powers in this world greater than myself. But I'm not worried about that right now. I am here to stop you and no one else. Whatever other forces you're talking about right now, don't matter. I will take Dawn with me and leave you to rule your kingdom."

"This has never been my kingdom. I have fought to protect us from the displeasure of Kadasha since the king left. These people have no idea what I'm holding at bay."

"Then why hurt us? Why capture healers and hold them in a Sanatorium? Why tax the people into the ground until they can't even feed their own family?"

I let one hand wander to the top of my bow. The arrows brushed against my ear. A heartbeat. I only need a heartbeat to pull another arrow and this time it would be aimed at the Grand Councilor's heart.

CHAPTER 53

"KADASHA HAS TURNED her displeasure on Tuleves." The Grand
Councilor fingered a long staff he carried with the head of a Scarlett
carved into the handle. "As an immortal she has armies at her disposal. She
can control the gifting she's granted us. I may have hurt our people, but
I've done so to protect them from a greater danger. She calls for payment
both of men and coin to keep from descending on us and destroying us. I
thought I had finally found a way to satisfy her, but you've taken that
hope. You've stolen the blood jewels and put the entire country at risk."

Dawn had worked her gag out of her mouth. "Kadasha must not
have the blood jewels. Her attempt to use the energy of the Oracles will
ignite the folding of the world."

Anger and concern roiled in me. The blood jewels were not what I
had thought. They were not a ransom for the king. They were not a way
to get Garreth's father back. They were a bribe for protection from
Kadasha's wrath. A bribe that had taken fifteen years to create and send
to Helefount. I had stopped them from arriving for a short time, but in
the end, The Lady had found the blood jewels. If the note in her office
was right, they were on their way to Helefount as we spoke.

The Lady swung her hand around and caught Dawn in the jaw with the back of her hand. "Silence. We are in Kadasha's domain. She watches us from the towers. Be careful what you speak."

I cried out with rage and lunged forward. Two soldiers lifted their swords and placed them against the back of Dawn's neck. My breath came in heaving gasps, anger and frustration nearly blinding me. I stepped back and shoved the soldiers off me. I put my hands up as if in defeat.

I wasn't a smooth talker. I was a hunter with a bow in my fingers and my prey in my sights. All I had to do was move faster than the soldiers. I counted four heartbeats as each person in the room watched what I was going to do.

In the fifth heartbeat, four arrows flew from my bow, two into the necks of the soldiers who had their swords against Dawn, one into the eye of the soldier behind the Grand Councilor and one into the shoulder of the soldier behind the Lady. She didn't bother to catch that one, but her head turned as if her eyes followed the direction of the arrow.

The soldier with the shoulder wound stumbled against the Grand Councilor, knocking him off balance.

That was all I needed. I ran forward and slid on my knees toward Dawn. The Lady opened her mouth, but I didn't hear a scream. I heard only my heartbeat in my head, the squeak of my leathers against the tiled floor, and the thudding pressure coming from Grand Councilor Levante as he threw the soldier to the side.

In the infinitesimal instant that I had, I reached for Dawn's bound hands, freezing the rope and pulling it in the same motion so that it shattered like a dropped wine glass. Dawn moved so that her hands were free of the ropes before the shards could pierce her skin. I was no longer alone.

Yoself appeared beside Dawn. He dropped a fighting pole from the training ring into her hands. She caught it as she stood to face The Lady. Yoself shot me a quick smile and sped away again. He would need to find a safe place to recover for a few minutes.

Dawn fought The Lady with the speed of a viper. I had never seen her fight so well. I had always thought it was a game, never realizing that her ability during training to avoid all our punches and kicks was because she could see them coming.

She swung in a full fisted punch. The Lady dodged to the side, bending at the waist, throwing her head back. She turned and kicked out a leg, aiming for Dawn's stomach. Dawn backed up a step. The Lady's foot brushed the cloth of Dawn's skirt. Back and forth the two women went, unable to land a punch with pole or fist when the other moved out of the way an instant before it came.

It was a deadly dance of snakes, but I couldn't sit and watch, as beautiful as it was. The Grand Councilor's hand came down on my shoulder before I could turn toward him. I had left myself defenseless to save Dawn. I wondered why he would use his hand instead of a sword. He could have cut off my head with a swish of steel.

Instead, his fingers dug into me as he pulled me to my feet. I may not have had the close-quarter fighting skills that Dawn had, but I had my own means of defense. I pulled, feeling for his spark, but something was wrong. There was nothing to pull.

"No." The word echoed in my head with the strength of a wildcat's scream, but they barely made it through my lips as a whisper.

The Grand Councilor, with strength beyond anything I had ever felt, slammed me against the wall. "Why do you continue to be a thorn in our side? We were meant to work together. All the signs in the heavens pointed to you. Give me the blood jewels. Tell me where they are and we can still save the kingdom."

I struggled, prying his fingers off my shoulder, kicking out at his nether regions. I connected with nothing. The pressure below my collarbone increased, black spots exploding behind my eyes from the pain. He looked at me without anger or hate. Instead, his eyebrows were drawn down in confusion. He studied me as if I were a puzzle he was unable to solve.

"What are you talking about?" I asked. Maybe I could try and talk my way out the way Jaimeson did. "The Lady already recovered the blood jewels. They are on their way to Helefount right now. She knows I am not the one you seek."

His grip tightened, but his eyes flicked to the fight as Dawn and the Lady slammed into the side of the tower. "You lie."

"You are sending enough power to Kadasha to enslave all of Tuleves. Why would I help you make slaves of your own people?" I spat at him, anger overwhelming the pain. If I could not make him pass out, I could still freeze him.

I tried to pull the heat from around us, but I still had contact with his skin. His empty soul pulled me in, a sucking sensation I couldn't resist. It was like falling into the emptiness inside of me, but it was a deep pit of darkness inside of the Grand Councilor. I jerked on his silk tunic and pulled the collar down. There at base of his neck where his jugular met his collarbone was the creeping vine tattoo. He was the third absorber. My heart dropped. My stomach flipped over. I had never fought someone like myself. He was a servant of Kadasha even before the vines encircled his neck.

Instead of giving up, I pulled harder. The sharp pain in my heart pinched my chest, but I didn't stop. There had to be some life spark in him, something I could drain. The pressure in my chest went from a pinching to a throbbing. I started gasping for breath.

"You're fighting against the wrong enemy," the Grand Councilor said. He stared at me and for a moment, I saw Marion in his eyes, pieces of his son that he had passed on, but then the images of the burning of Dawn's village appeared, the starving farmers and their families, the trains of sorrow along the road to Helefount. Father. Mother. Iranus the Tracker. They had all fought against this man. I would not let their sacrifices be in vain.

"You're the enemy," I said, taking one final deep breath. "You are a monster." The crescendo of pain felt like a knife being twisted into my bone, but I pulled harder. It was like pulling an entire castle up a hill with a thin rope. Nothing moved. Nothing gave under my efforts.

"You are just like me." The Grand Councilor's voice echoed in the black void I was sinking into. I couldn't see him or anything around me anymore, only a starry blackness. The pain of his fingers digging into my shoulder seemed to be the only thing tethering me to the world.

I looked up into the ever-watching windows of the Sanatorium tower, their darkness as deep as the blackest night.

Realization hit me. It wasn't that I was trying to suck power from an empty source, it was that I was surrounded by it. Like trying to fill a bucket at the bottom of a lake, I was surrounded by power, drowning in it. The pressure built around me as the darkness began to take form. The shadow of a woman, darker than the black that surrounded her. I could make out arms and legs, a shapely torso, and long flowing hair that shifted around her as if she were also underwater. She moved with the strength of my mother, with the intention and purpose of my father. Then the head turned, hair flowing out like whips, and two pinpricks of light where the eyes should have been turned directly on me, searing me like a branding rod, cutting straight to the pain in my heart.

I was staring into the heart of Kadasha, an all-consuming force that craved the power of spark the way a wolf craved meat, and I was feeding her.

I stopped trying to take the energy and let my whole body relax. I stopped pulling. Instead of pulling, I shoved out the ice and emptiness and darkness inside me and gave it all to her.

I thought a heard a scream, coming from deep underwater. I could breathe again, but the Grand Councilor now had me by the throat.

A crashing sound split through my skull, scattering the darkness and the images like I was surfacing from a deep dive. Breath returned to my lungs as I hit the floor with enough force that it felt like I had fallen from the ceiling.

Yoself had shoved a large cart over the top of the Grand Councilor who was struggling to get to his feet.

"Enough," The Lady commanded. Dawn had somehow gotten ahold of a sword from one of the downed soldier's swords. She had it pressed against The Lady's neck. The Sanatorium went still. Even the Grand Councilor stayed down on one knee, waiting to see what would happen. "You would not kill the last of your kind. You are the last Oracle of legend. You are the babe who predicted the Oracles would betray Kadasha. You've seen the folding of the world."

"And I've seen that you will help bring it about." Dawn lowered the sword. "But I cannot kill another Oracle."

The Grand Councilor rose from the ground. He pulled on the head of the Scarlett on his staff and a sword appeared from the staff. He moved with impossible speed, almost disappearing and I realized he had a grip on Yoself's arm. He stole Yoself's spark and pushed Dawn to the side.

It was his own sword that slipped into The Lady's ribs right below her heart. Her mouth fell open in surprise. Perhaps it was the first time she hadn't seen an attack coming. Perhaps it was the first time she hadn't been able to react to something she hadn't expected.

She crumpled to the ground.

He turned to Dawn. "You are the last Oracle." He turned to me. "And you are the Arjodite warrior meant to protect her."

"You killed her." It was obvious, but I couldn't help saying the words. Shock left me shaking.

"She has been a spy for Kadasha for long enough." He released Yoself. The small boy sunk to the floor in slow-motion. He couldn't even collapse quickly. "If what you say is true, and the blood jewels are already on their way to Helefount, then we must continue with the plan. We must appease Kadasha, or we will all be destroyed."

I felt exhausted from my head to my toes. "What does that mean?"

A soldier ran into the Sanatorium. "I know you asked not to be disturbed, but the people are beginning to riot. My soldiers are struggling to keep them from charging the gates. We haven't found the real Hooded Robber and more continue to come."

The Grand Councilor looked straight at me. "Let them in. Let everyone in. We will appease the people with a Tournament. And then we will keep them in line by showing them what happens when you cross the crown."

The soldier bowed and ran back out of the room.

"There will still be a tournament." The Grand Councilor picked my bow from the ground where I had dropped it. He handed it to me. "The people came to witness the Hooded Robber try to save his friends. We will not disappoint them."

"You know I'm the Hooded Robber?"

"I saw your skills with a bow when you killed my men. Who else would be able to break into the Sanatorium? While hundreds have risked themselves to protect your identity, you've exposed yourself."

"You're still going to let me win the Tournament of the People?"

"Oh no." The Grand Councilor walked to the door. "You will not win. I never intended to let you win, but I knew you would come. The people need to see their hero defeated. And who better to defeat the Hooded Robber, than the son of an Arjodite.

My thoughts caught in the cogs of logic at they stuttered and stopped. The son of an Arjodite.

Before I could respond, the Grand Councilor opened a door and let in a man. Tall. Young. Familiar. The spark that I hadn't realized had been gifted to me disappeared.

My memory rushed back in as I faced my brother.

Jaimeson stood next to the Grand Councilor, the bow Father had made for him strapped to his back.

CHAPTER 54

"I TRUST you can find your own way down to the field. Neither of you will want to miss this moment." The Grand Councilor turned to leave.

"And what if we don't. What if we choose to walk away and not participate in the Tournament of the People?"

"Then I win." He didn't even honor the question with a full stop. His words seemed to linger after he'd left the room. "Those you love will die for your rebellion and the people lose their hero. You may not understand the difficult decisions that have to be made when protecting a nation from a vindictive immortal, but what I do is necessary for our survival as a nation."

I waited to see if he would come back or if he would send soldiers to escort us, but the doorway remained clear. The decision was mine. Dawn and Jaimeson both seemed content to let me speak first. I had some questions as I scanned the destruction of the deserted Sanatorium.

"You owe me an explanation." My arrows of accusation aimed toward Jaimeson first.

"I thought we had an understanding." He gave me a weak smile. "You run until you're safe and I get to stop worrying about you. It was the only way I could protect you."

"By making me forget about you?" I recovered one of my arrows from a fallen soldier. My anger fueled me as I jerked it free.

Dawn handed me my other three arrows. She had not escaped the battle with The Lady unscathed. A cut in her arm left a trail of blood down her sleeve. She had bruise under her left eye and one of her ears was swollen.

"I knew you'd never run if you knew I was here." His smile was sad, but it sent a thrill of pride through me. "No matter how much reasoning I used."

Yoself came around the tower. His speed was back to normal, but he looked exhausted. The boy needed some rest.

"Do you have a plan?" I asked. He always had a plan. This was my brother, Jaimeson.

"I wanted to win the Tournament of the People to become a Nobel. A way to make a difference. Now, I plan to beat the Hooded Robber. I have to."

"And then you'll pardon me?" I saw his plan as clearly as a wild cat's eyes reflecting firelight on a dark night. "All of this. Getting captured and whipped. Telling The Lady about Dawn. All of this was to be able to pardon the Hooded Robber?"

"I'm your older brother. It's my job. And Father made me take an oath to protect you."

Yoself stood transfixed by my brother. Jaimeson had the gifting of reason. He wore an archer's uniform with Kadasha's colors. He was impressive, but he was my brother. I knew him inside and out.

"But what about the people? They've been taxed to the very limits. They came here to feel hope and the Grand Councilor is determined to crush it. What makes you think the Grand Councilor would even keep his promise to pardon me?"

"I have to have faith in something." Jaimeson sounded more desperate than I'd ever heard him. "But if he does not, I will make a distraction for you to get away."

"What about Father? Where does this leave him?" My head hurt like it was pressed in a clamp. It was all too much. I turned to Dawn. "You're an Oracle. You must have seen a way to save him. You know what's going to happen."

"I thought you didn't believe in prophecies." It was a statement without guile or accusation.

"Things are different now." I felt as if the floor was dropping out from beneath me. Jaimeson was going to try and beat me at the Tournament of the People based on an empty promise from the Grand Councilor. Dawn was staring at me with expectations I had no ability to fulfill. "My bow. You saw the need for this before my father was taken. That's not a prophecy. That's a vision."

"There is little difference. Even an Oracle can't always know if what they see is a warning of possibility of a view of an unescapable reality. But like Jaimeson. I have to have faith. I've seen the folding of the world, but I cannot know for sure if the things I've put into motion will be enough to stop it. After all I did to try and stop it from happening, the blood jewels are already in the hands of Kadasha."

"So, it isn't fail-proof. The prophecies and visions."

"The blood of a thousand Oracles wouldn't be crying from the ruins if it was fail-proof. But I believe there is a power even greater than the immortals, an energy that wants life to exist, to continue. It is to that end I will give all my gifting. A prophecy from someone with the gifting of time is simply a small candle flame in the distance to help guide us through the dark."

I cleaned my arrows in a water bucket near the tower. The eyes in the windows above me had gone dark like Kadasha's presence had been expelled with the death of The Lady. For the first time, I let the prophecies of the Oracles float to the surface of my memory. Not ancient prophecies, but ones given recently.

Orblee: *You will protect an Oracle just like your mother did before the massacre. But your story will not end as your mother's did.*

Dawn: *It is time to show your face.*

Dawn: *The blood jewels will give Kadasha the strength to ignite the folding of the world.*

And one more. The queen who died with only her nine-year-old son by her side. *You will die if you are crowned before you are ready.*

"I also have been given a prophecy." Yoself's voice was small but confident. "The prince will need me before the end."

I had walked into this room believing two things: my ability to make a difference came from wearing a mask and prophecies were impossible to interpret, a trick from those with the gifting of time to inspire action that would lead to the fulfilling a prophecy that never would have happened without that person's choice.

I loaded my arrows into the quiver and strapped it onto my back. I lifted my bow. I was wrong about my first belief. A mask would no longer give me the influence I wanted. My own face, my own identity, was the most powerful tool I had.

The second thing, that prophecies were fulfilled by choice. I was about to test that theory and hope that I was right. I was about to choose to fulfill those prophecies today, whether that was the original intent of the prophecies or not.

"We can't just walk into Helefount and demand the blood jewels," I said.

Dawn lifted her head. An energy returning to her that had gone out of her since the fight. "We?"

"Yoself, do you think you can you your gifting of speed one more time today?" I touched him on the head. He nodded under my touch. His hair tousled under my hand with the movement.

Then I walked past my brother, hitting his shoulder with mine. "You would need a thief and a plan to best an immortal. But first, Jaimeson, I'm about to enter the Tournament of the People. As your sister. As the daughter of the Robbins' estate."

"You want me to let you win?" Jaimeson asked. I sensed the competition. Him accepting the challenge.

"No. I want you to try to win. You know I've always been a better shot than you."

"In your dreams."

"Then let's see you try. But whatever happens, when the time comes. I need you to betray me. I need you to expose me as the Hooded Robber."

CHAPTER 55

WE STOOD in line to sign up. Dawn had taken a bow from the training arena. It wouldn't get her past the first round, but that was part of the plan. I signed my name with a flourish. Arianna Robbins. Over half of the people around me wore the robes and mask in imitation of the Hooded Robber. The soldiers kept their eyes on them and off of me and Jaimeson. These were good people. They deserved better than the hand life had dealt them. I didn't know if I had the power to change that for them.

Even knowing what I was going to see, my knees went weak. I had to grip Jaimeson's shirt as we stepped into the high walled arena. There were benches built into the sloped viewing area on either side. It was as if the viewing area was as tall as the plateau itself. The field in the center was larger than four arrow shots across. Still, I could see the figures on the far side, standing beneath each of their own nooses.

Orblee.

My father.

Marion.

Polisha.

I knew these people hadn't been chosen at Random. Orblee had been chosen to manipulate the Hooded Robber. A known accomplish.

My father had been chosen to manipulate Jaimeson. Polisha was there because of me. I had used her to escape the Sanatorium, and the Grand Councilor had put her up there to make sure the girl who had impersonated a healer would fall in line. But how had Councilor Levante known about Marion? Our relationship had been secret before. And he couldn't know that I Arianna Robbins was the one who would be participating in the Tournament.

Why would he use his own son as a message to the people? What good would it do when he already had a way to control each of his enemies with the people they loved on the line?

On a raised platform in the center of the stands, Grand Councilor Levante stepped out from behind the curtains. The movement caught the eyes of the crowd and soon the field was hushed into silence. My finger twitched to pull an arrow and let it fly straight for his heart. What he had done to my family, to the captain, to the nation of Tuleves was justification enough. But even if I succeeded in shooting that far, I would never make it out, never be able to save a single person. I gritted my teeth as his voice echoed across the field, strengthened with a gifting from one of his attendants who kept his hand on the Grand Councilor's arm.

"Welcome to the Tournament of the People!" His voice grated on my nerves. He sounded so confident, so sure that this tournament would subdue the people. He had to pause while the swell of cheers worked its way through the crowd and then ebbed away. "Many brave men and women are here to fight for a new beginning. Today, many of you seek to become lords and ladies. My best of wishes to all of those who seek greater things." His voice softened in tone, but not in volume. Everyone could still hear, but it was the voice of someone ashamed. "Some of you are here to cheer on a hero. A hero that many of you dressed as today. Let this pronouncement stand. Your efforts to shield your hero today have been in vain. The Hooded Robber will fail you. But it is not too late for the rest of you to be forgiven. My people, today is a day for second chances, for renewal, for hope for all of us."

Anger shot through me with such force I had to clench my teeth from yelling out. He invoked the commoners like a king, a ruler that loved them. His voice carried sincerity that I knew could not exist in a man who did the things he did to his own citizens.

"Sounds great." Another voice matched the volume of the Grand Councilor from the opposite side of the crowd. Soldiers, prisoners, contestants, and observers created the sound of a rushing wind as they all turned as one to see who would dare interrupt him. I did not have to look to know who could sound so carefree and condescending at the same time. "We'll have a tournament, a hanging, and then a coronation. It will be the party of the century."

The people grumbled. Prince Garreth had not won the hearts of the people with his exploits against the council. Despite the resistance against the Grand Councilor, few believed the prince would be a better king.

"Tulevians," he said, addressing the group gathered as if they were one people. Heads moved back and forth, each person studying those around them as if with new eyes. "As Lord Levante has declared, today is a day of second chances, of a future full of promises. There are rumors that I will reject my birthright or refuse my coronation." The jokester was gone. The arrogant boy seemed to expand before my eyes, standing above us like a man.

Like a king.

"I, most of all, need a new start, a chance to try again," he said. "I have failed you as a prince, forgotten what my responsibilities were, what it meant to be truly royal. Today, like many of you, I am hoping to turn over a new leaf, to forget past wrongs, and begin the journey toward a better tomorrow. I want to make this promise. As your king, I will listen to the voice of the people. I will give the power to the citizen. It will no longer require noble heritage to have a vote on the council. I will invite those who keep food on our tables and health in our homes. Those who make the weapons for the country will vote on how we use them. What do you say? Can you forgive my childish past and look to a future with me at your head?"

He was asking for the approval of the people. I could see two strategies. Perhaps he won over the people, the assassin would not come from the crowd. If the council had planned to kill him before the coronation, perhaps the wrath of the people would make them reconsider.

He had come to the coronation to save Marion, but he had not given up on trying to save himself as well. I guess he had not changed that much. He still loved to ruffle feathers, pet wildcats the wrong way. There was a pause, a silence that settled on a thousand onlookers at once. He could try to undermine the Grand Councilor, but if he didn't have the support of his people, all his efforts would be pointless, damning for him as a future king.

A single whistle broke out, carried over the heads of the crowd. I couldn't see who had done it, but it broke the spell. Hesitant claps. Then an uproarious cheer. The sound was deafening. Contestants around me shouldered their bows to add their approval and pat each other on the back. Tuleves had hungered for their king for the last decade, withering under the rule of the Grand Councilor. They were more than ready for their young prince to rise to the challenge.

He had come to the coronation, despite his fear of being killed. Despite not finding the item he so desperately had searched for. I realized now that Marion was not standing on the gallows for me. Marion was there to force the prince to show up to save the life of his friend. From the look on the Grand Councilor's face, this wasn't the speech he'd prepared for Garreth. A prophecy he'd tried to follow and failed. I'd seen how fearful he was of his mother's prediction. He fully expected to give his life in his effort to save Marion.

When the noise finally began to wind down, the voice of the Grand Councilor rang out again. "You have won the hearts of your citizens," he said. "Let this truly be a day of new beginnings. A fresh start. We will clean the prisons for our new King. All those who are not pardoned today will be marched to Helefount as indentured servants." He made a large bow, waving his hand in a salute toward Garreth even as the crowed grumbled and booed. The long sleeve of his cloak waved like a flag signaling the start of the tournament. "Let's see who comes of this a hero, and who lives to see the end of the day."

Then he straightened. "Let the tournament begin!"

I held my breath. I didn't know if it was only me, but that had felt like a direct threat on the prince's life.

"Are you ready, little sister?" Jaimeson stood beside me. "I don't think I've ever been more excited to show you how this is really done."

CHAPTER 56

I CHOSE the third target from the end, glancing up and down the line for Jaimeson. I didn't see him. The crowd settled down as a heat-gifted woman danced out of the field, waving lit torches in fast circles and then blowing the flames up into the air, the towers of fire reaching above even the prince's pavilion. Garreth placed his hands on the railing, leaning over as if examining the field below.

My vision was swimming with unshed tears as I thought of the lives that depended on this plan. A soldier motioned it was my turn to shoot. Each contestant shot three arrows when the blue flag waved. When the red flag replaced the blue, runners ran for the arrows and recorded the score.

The red flag waved as the runners returned across the field carrying arrows with fletching of every color. Some were recovered from the targets, but many had fallen short. This was a large field, over two hundred spans across. Many would use their gifting to strengthen the push of the bowstring, but it gave them less accuracy.

I approached the line, dozens of other men and women matching my movements up and down the tournament field. I took several deep breaths, letting the noise die away, blinking back the sorrow and shoving it deep down. Until I proved I was worthy of making it, I would not think about the decision. I couldn't save a single life unless I won the tournament.

The red flag disappeared, and the blue flag lifted in its place. I pulled the string to my chin, held my breath, and released. The power surprised me, the bow far stronger than my old one. I aimed too high, and the arrow barely punctured the top of the target. A thrill ran through me. This was something I could do. Something I was good at. The bow seemed to thrum with my own energy.

My next shot hit dead center.

My third cut through the fletching of the second.

Not perfect, but enough to move on.

Everyone who scored less than twenty points was escorted from the field. My twenty-one points put me at the back of the advancing archers. I wouldn't only have to do better the second round. This time I would need to be perfect.

A man swore as he broke his bow, throwing it to the ground. He was large and wore fine clothes, likely a landowner who had hoped to move up to a lord. I had no pity for him. Dawn also verbally expressed her disappointment. She walked up to one of the field officials and began arguing. Two soldiers took her by the arms and moved her to the side of the field where the lower class watched the tournament. Only a few feet away from the gallows.

For the second round, the targets were moved to the long side of the field, twice the distance as before. Fourteen of us started. Only five scored above twenty. Three were landowners who could increase the strength of their bows, the drain on their spark already showing on their faces. Jaimeson and I were the other two, both trained by a master archer, a mother who taught us to hunt. We both knew how to adjust our shots to the wind and the distance.

As my bow struck the center of the target three more times, I felt the energy of the crowd. Whispers and pointing. Each time I lined up for my turn, the announcer would say my name. Arianna Robbins.

Jaimeson shot his fourth and last shot, landing exactly between two of my arrows.

The crowd rose to their feet.

"Do you think it's him, momma? Has he come to save the prisoners?" The voice was high and clear. It carried across the field to me. Jaimeson and I exchanged a glance. No other arches who had dressed as the Hooded Robber had made it through the second round.

The third round favored both Jaimeson and I over the strength gifted. The targets were now flying clay pigeons. One man missed all five. The other two managed to hit a few. I hit the first four as did Jaimeson.

We stood side by side, my brother and I, as the world watched us, the Grand Councilor and the Prince of Tuleves. Jaimeson looked at me and smiled. For a moment, the field melted away and there were just the two of us, brother and sister, playing at a game as familiar as breathing.

"I'm impressed," he said. His words were casual, yet they struck a chord in me that made my eyes sting with traitorous tears. His admiration, his acceptance was all I had ever wanted, even after we lost Father and Mother. "If there was any other way. . . Arianna, I'm sorry. I can't let you win."

"You haven't won yet." I raised my bow.

The hiss of the releasing pigeon made me turn my head. Jaimeson and I shot three more. He clipped the edge of his last pigeon, but it did not break.

The crowd groaned in disappointment.

Without my mask, without hiding who I was, with this last shot, I would give hope to a kingdom. When the final clay pigeon flew across the field, I took aim and hit exactly where Jaimeson had.

We were tied.

The Grand Councilor stood. "You have all done well. But as many of you expected and have known. This was always meant to find the thief in the woods. The one you claim is your hero. He has come to rescue his friends, but there is no escaping the arena. There will be one final round to prove who the Hooded Robber really is."

Several guards took Jaimeson and I by the arm and marched us to the middle of the field. From here, the only targets were the four people standing under their nooses.

"The final round will prove who your hero truly is. Each of the final archers must choose one of the condemned to shoot. It will be a mercy. Who will the Hooded Robber save from the painful death of a hanging?

Will it be the child who should never have to dangle from a rope? Will it be the woman who helped with the distribution of the stolen taxes? Who will the final archers show mercy on?"

Marion was forced to his feet. Polisha was lifted onto a stool. The ropes were lowered and placed around each of their necks. The crowd was riveted as well as the soldiers. I saw Dawn move silently to the side. The soldiers weren't watching her.

Jaimeson stood close. "What if I miss? You are the better archer."

My father looked at us across the field. His eyes were full of love, of acceptance.

"It's an impossible shot. Whatever happens, this was never your fault. I trust you. I always have."

I had a choice. I had a plan. I stepped forward.

"You have until my arrow falls." The Grand Councilor pulled out his own bow. He held it out over the crowd below him. He aimed toward the middle of the field. "When my arrow hits the grass, the trap doors will open, and they will all hang. Choose who you grant mercy."

Jaimeson stepped up next to me and raised his bow along with his voice. He didn't have the gifting of sound, but I felt the pulse of his gifting of reason. His words would be felt through the entire stadium. "Arianna Robbins is the Hooded Robber. She will lose the tournament to me."

I heard the twang of the Grand Councilor's bow string and I almost hesitated. I almost aimed for the rope above my father's head. I could save him. He knew I could. But he'd asked me to make a different choice. To save the one who would make the most difference.

At the same time as the arrow thudded into the ground behind me. I turned. Aimed into the stand. And shot Prince Garreth in the heart.

Dawn moved with the speed of an Oracle and sliced through Polisha's rope, catching the girl before she dropped. I was able to get a second arrow on my string and through the rope that tightened with Orblee's weight. She hung in the air for an instant and then crumpled to the ground.

Jaimeson's arrow sliced through Father's rope but didn't snap it. Marion dangled, feet kicking. Then he broke the binding on his hands and pulled the rope from his own neck. Both Jaimeson and I had an arrow nocked and aimed for Father when another arrow took him through the stomach.

The arrow of the Grand Councilor. We'd been too slow.

I ran forward. Maybe Orblee could heal him. Maybe we weren't too late. But Jaimeson stuck to the plan. He always did.

He tackled me to the ground and used his gifting of reason to make it impossible to move. He froze my muscles as effectively as he'd stolen my memory.

"I have the Hooded Robber. I've captured the Hooded Robber."

Soldiers surrounded us. I saw the chaos beneath the gallows. Polisha and Dawn were swarmed. My father hung as Orblee tried to reach for him but was pulled back by more of the Grand Councilor's men.

It was Marion's actions I hadn't considered. He fought. The enraged spark in him was a flaming fire as he tossed men from him. They flew into the air and landed in the crowd. His face was red, and his muscles bulged. His neck pulsed. His face was twisted in pain.

And I couldn't move. The plan was for Jaimeson to hold me down, to expose me so he could be pardoned. But I couldn't leave Marion that way. I wanted to yell at Jaimeson to stop, to let me go, but his gifting of reason even robbed me of the power to speak.

A tear leaked out of my eye. I couldn't even blink to clear my vision. Marion. I couldn't leave him like this. Either he would kill more of his fellow soldiers and hate himself for it or he might succumb to the energy inside him and die. Either way, I would risk this final part of the plan for him. For Marion.

I pulled in. The world got colder. Ice formed on my eyelashes. Then I pulled on Jaimeson's spark. He was strong. He always had been. He tried to resist, tried to convince me to give up and lay still. But I couldn't.

I pulled harder and Jaimeson slumped to the ground. I took the soldiers spark as they reached for me and each one crumpled to the earth. I ran to Marion's side. I ducked a swing. I flinched as the jaw of a soldier behind me crushed from impact. I wrapped my arms around Marion and pulled. I sucked the spark that was brighter than the burning sun into me.

The pain seared in my chest. This was more effort than freezing a waterfall. He was an unquenchable furnace.

I didn't realize he had stopped fighting for a moment. But finally, I looked up at him. He had tears in his eyes and concern between his eyebrows, but his pain was gone for the moment.

Then seven soldiers swarmed us. Something hit me on the back of my head, and the world went black.

CHAPTER 57

"Is she dead?" That was Polisha's voice. Her matter-of-fact voice made me smile, even in the dark painful void where I floated.

"She's laughing," said a child's voice I didn't recognize. "Only the Hooded Robber would laugh after destroying an entire city wall."

"All in a day's work for the Hooded Robber." Marion. Hearing his voice pulled me to the surface.

I blinked to clear the darkness, but the world stayed very dim. I was in a cell, small and crowded. A smell made my nose wrinkle. As much as I had planned this, I had hoped for at least a clean prison. I guess that had been a little too much to hope for.

My back felt like I had been thrown from a horse, aches and pains from my tail bone to my neck. A large lump was tender to the touch on the back of my head. "What happened?"

"You saved us," said Polisha. "But then we all got thrown into prison. Just like the Grand Councilor promised. We're scheduled to march to Helefount tomorrow as indentured servants."

"All of us?" That hadn't been part of the plan. Dawn and I were supposed to get sent to Helefount. Not everyone else.

Yoself stepped into the dim light next to Polisha. "You didn't think we'd let you go without us, did you? You promised me I could come."

"You were supposed to save the prince. That was as far as I was going to take you."

He smiled and pulled the arrow from behind his back that he'd been hiding. "I made it just in time. I caught the arrow and shoved the prince to the ground. I am stronger than he is. Everyone around us thought he was hit. I granted him the gifting of speed to get out of there before anyone could examine him."

Large hands pulled me to my feet. Marion nodded to me and then let go, stepping back even though there was hardly any room. Dawn leaned against the bars of the cage behind him. Everyone else was in shadow.

"Did we get everybody?" I asked.

Marion dropped his head. "Orblee was surrounded by the crowd. There was a full-on riot, and they got her out. Enough people fought back to get out of the city that the Grand Councilor used his soldiers to make sure they didn't come back in. Your father didn't make it."

I swallowed the lump in my throat and blinked back the tears. I'd failed to save my father. After all of that. Even with an Oracle, I couldn't save him.

I counted the people around me. Marion. Dawn. Yoself. Polisha. And Garreth, napping on a pile of straw in the corner like he didn't have a care in the world. He must have felt my gaze because he cracked one eye. "I think I deserve a rest after you tried to assassinate me. I'm sure you could have thought of other ways to get a one-way ticket to Helefount."

"I already had a ticket to Helefount. You were just icing on the cake."

He sat up. "Thank you. I'll have more time to search not that everyone thinks I'm dead. If my mother was right, you saved me from a real assassination attempt."

"Or perhaps I was the one your mother saw." Prophesies were so hard to interpret. But it was nice to have a little peek into the future when coming up with a plan.

Dawn spoke from her corner of the cell. "The risen corpse of the Prince of Tuleves will cause a stir that will rock a nation."

"Was that a prophecy?" Marion asked. "Is that literal. Like is Garreth actually going to come back as a corpse or will everyone just think he's a corpse because we faked his death to save his life?"

I laughed. "Prophecies are hard to predict, but that one will be fun whether we make it happen or it happens on its own."

"I still don't think you quite understand the gifting of time," Dawn said as she shook her head.

The door to the cell opened and a seventh person was shoved into the cell. His nose was bloodied and one eye swollen shut, but I knew that face anywhere. I would trust him with my life. "I thought you were going to stay and convince the council of the error of their ways?"

Jaimeson shrugged. "Isn't this a group of merry men. You all look like you're ready for a death march. Which I wasn't going to let you take without me, just so you know. I made a promise."

Yoself yawned and sat next to Marion. He curled up against him like Marion was a warm fireplace. Hesitantly, Marion patted the boy on the shoulder.

"This isn't a journey any of you should take lightly. We are going into the city of the immortals. We may make a very powerful enemy. And the hardest part might be trying to survive the journey to get there."

"You mean we won't get three course meals?" Garreth took a deep breath. "I'll take it upon myself to complain the most."

Polisha giggled. "You're going to complain about the food?"

"I guess if there isn't any food, I won't have anything to complain about."

Jaimeson sat down next to me as Garreth sat up and looked at every person in the cell. "There are seven of us and seven immortals. I think we've got a fighting chance. Besides, I have a big motivation to survive and come back. Right now, I'm engaged to be married to the Hooded Robber. Wouldn't that make the wedding of the century."

Dawn picked up straw and threw in at him. Jaimeson threatened to use his gifting of reason to give the prince some wisdom.

"What do you think happened to Captain Tevya?" Yoself asked. "She probably doesn't even know if the plan worked."

Dawn smiled. "I think she was watching. I would bet our journey to Helefount will have an ally on the outside."

The Oracle had spoken. I didn't know if we would win or lose. If this was the right group of people to attempt a robbery from the seven immortals. But whatever happened, I was glad not to be alone.

The End

ACKNOWLEDGMENTS

This is my seventh full novel. To thank every person by name who has helped me during my writing journey would fill a million pages. What a beautiful life! What a world full of beautiful people! I am so thankful to be able to share another story created from the recesses of my brain. It is wonderful to see how those weird little ideas that cross my mind at a stop light or pop up in the middle of writing a work email come to life.

First, I want to thank my family, my husband, Philip, who works harder than most people could possibly imagine, my kids, Evan, Jacob, and Katelynn. They know my writer's quirks and unique personality traits and they still love me.

I want to thank my amazing writing group, The Hot Mess Writing Group: Heidi, Valerie, Patrice, Jessica, and Jordan. They've read every manuscript over the years with me and so many of their ideas are floating around in the final version. It is with their critiques my manuscripts really begin to sparkle.

I am grateful for my amazing editor, Julia Allen, with Better Than Spell Check. She scrubbed this manuscript and then hinted at ways to make it better. I made it better because of her, but she didn't get a chance to rescrub. Any errors in this version is from the edits of the author and not any oversights from Julia. She is amazing.

The designer of the map at the front of the book is from BMR Williams. He was a great listener that took a napkin drawing to a country sized map.

I will never be able to express the gratitude I owe to my mom. I have seven quilts with my book covers carved into our snuggle time. She has spent countless hours reading and sewing and supporting me beyond anything I deserve. My dad took the time away from his outdoor adventures to read my books and I recognize the effort. I have wonderful parents.

Thank you to the writing communities of Writing and Illustrating for Young Readers and Storymakers. Carol Lynch Williams is one of my greatest mentors and these two conferences have been my cocoon of growth as I learned how to be a book butterfly.

About the Author

Tracy Daley wrote her first book in fifth grade and will forever be grateful for amazing teachers who encourage and empower their students. She spent ten years working in the publishing industry and has developed her love of storytelling through reviewing, acquiring, and reading every great book she could get her hands on. She owns her own publishing company, Night Nook Publishing, where she publishes her own stories and is working to support other writers in the future. She loves skiing, eating, and traveling with her family.

ALSO BY TRACY DALEY

The Descendants of Angels Series

Loss of the Unguarded

Fall of the Guardian

Rise of the Captive

Demon Confessions of Sansa Plath A Short Story

Trapped in the Last Angel's Tomb A Short Story

YA Contemporary

The Wrong Side of the Setting Sun

Cut Scenes and Impossible Things

MG Historical

If the Fire Comes

Sign up for Night Nook Publishing Newsletter for updates on new books from Tracy Daley.